"I spoke with Emme this morning. She said there's been no sign of anything that would give them a clue as to what happened to Ian."

"But knowing Robert, he'll keep on looking until . . ." She paused, overcome by emotion.

Mallory squeezed the woman's shoulder. "They'll keep looking until they find him, one way or another. Now that Robert has reason to suspect the baby might still be alive, he isn't going to give up until he finds him."

"He isn't a baby anymore. He's two and a half already." Trula wiped away tears. "He's a toddler. He's probably walking and talking, maybe even going to preschool somewhere. He's grown so much, learned so much, since we saw him. It's killing Robert, you know, to have missed all Ian's firsts."

"Hopefully, once they find Ian, having him back will make up for everything he's missed."

"Assuming they can find him." Trula began to peel the peaches, her knife working furiously. "Someone has that boy and knows he isn't theirs. People see that child every day, and don't know that he's not who they think he is."

"Assuming he's still alive," Mallory reminded her.

mariah STEWART

ACTS OF MERCY

A MERCY STREET NOVEL

BB

BALLANTINE BOOKS • NEW YORK

A Ballantine Books Mass Market Original

Copyright © 2009 by Marti Robb

Published in the United States by Ballantine Books, an imprint of The Random House Publishing Group, a division of Random House, Inc., New York.

BALLANTINE and colophon are trademarks of Random House, Inc.

ISBN 978-0-345-52069-2

Printed in the United States of America

www.ballantinebooks.com

9 8 7 6 5 4 3 2 1

ACKNOWLEDGMENTS

As always, the wonderful team at Ballantine Books deserves huge thanks for their endless support—Kate Collins, Linda Marrow, Libby McGuire, Scott Shannon, Kim Hovey, Theresa Zoro, Sarina Evan (with congratulations—such a beautiful bride!), Kelli Fillingim, Nancy Delia, Crystal Velasquez—and apologies to anyone I may have forgotten!

Once again, several charities have benefited from donations made by the generous souls who won raffles or silent auctions entitling them to lend their name to a character in this book:

Carole Woolum (who requested that her character be "bad but not horrible"), whose donation benefited California's Citrus College;

Chris Coutinho's donation to the Woodlawn School in North Carolina bought him a "good guy" role;

Don Holland wished for himself and his wife, Laurie Heiss, to be villains (and Don, I took you at your word!)—and so they are, by virtue of their donation to Union Hospital, Elkton, MD.

I hope you all are happy with the characters that bear your name.

I must also thank Trula Comfort for once again lending her name to the recurring character who lends so much color and, well, *character* to this book.

Mary Corcoran for letting me use her name once again in this book which is known in some circles as "Mary III."

And thanks, as always, to my family for putting up with me.

ACTS OF MERCY

ONE

Her high heels clicking across the hardwood floors, Mallory Russo walked through the quiet foyer of the handsome Tudor mansion that served as home to business mogul Robert Magellan, as well as being her place of business. Uncharacteristically silent, the house seemed to reflect the sad spirits of all who'd come under its roof today. Earlier that morning, Mallory and her coworkers had gathered here before filing into the limousines that would take them to Our Lady of Angels Church a few miles away in Conroy, Pennsylvania, where Father Kevin Burch, Robert's cousin, conducted the memorial service for Robert's late wife, Beth.

Mallory removed the wide-brimmed black hat she'd bought for the occasion and walked the length of the hall to the wing of the house where the Mercy Street Foundation offices were located. She snapped on the overhead fan as she entered the room and went straight to her desk. She tossed the hat on a nearby chair and tried to remember if she'd ever owned such a thing before. Under the desk, her feet kicked off the heels she seldom wore and her cramped toes wiggled in the hopes of bringing back the circulation.

She wasn't sure when the others would be back but she hoped to get some work in between now and the time those who'd been invited back for a luncheon began to arrive. No one had seemed in much of a hurry to leave the cemetery after the service, gathered around chatting as they'd been, but she'd been ready to leave even before the priest had begun to speak. There was something unsettling about holding a funeral for a woman who'd been dead but not buried for well over a year, so when Charlie Wanamaker, her fiancé and a detective with the local police force, had whispered in her ear that he'd be taking off, she asked him to drop her off on his way to the police station.

One would expect that, as a former detective herself, Mallory would be beyond the point where death had the power to spook her, but there was something about this death that rattled her right to her soul. Beth Magellan and her infant son had been missing for many months, but the car they'd been in had only recently been found in a deep ravine in the mountains of western Pennsylvania. Beth's remains still were strapped into the driver's seat when the car was discovered, but there'd been no trace of the baby other than his car seat. That someone had come upon a dead or dying woman and had walked away without calling for help was beyond Mallory's comprehension, but the knowledge that this same person had most likely been the one who'd walked away with the woman's child was haunting her. Had Beth been alive, even conscious, when Ian had been taken? Had her last breath been spent calling for her son? Had Beth been aware that she was dying? The horror of it sent a chill up Mallory's spine. Robert was a good man, and she'd grown very fond of him. He didn't deserve to suffer like this. She suspected that the only thing that kept him going now was the knowledge that Ian most likely was still alive. Somewhere.

It was this last part that added an extra layer of sadness to the morning's service: where was *somewhere*?

Robert Magellan had founded—and funded—the Mercy Street Foundation to provide private investigative services to those for whom law enforcement agencies were making little or no progress finding missing loved ones. Robert knew the pain of not knowing what had happened to the two people he loved above all others—his wife and his son—but circumstances had blessed him with the means to hire professionals to search for them. That they had failed hadn't diminished the fact that he could afford to take those steps.

Not that any of the PI's Robert hired had had any success, Mallory reminded herself. It had been Susanna Jones, a member of Robert's own staff, who'd eventually found Beth's missing car. But the point was that he could afford to hire an army of investigators. Most people were not that fortunate. The Foundation was intended to do for them what they could not do for themselves: get the best investigators on the case.

While still in its infancy, the Foundation had taken only two cases, but both of those had met with success. There'd been an overwhelming response to their solicitation of applicants for their services, as well as their call for experienced law enforcement personnel to add to their staff. Mallory was charged with the task of sorting through all the applications and pulling out those cases that might best benefit from their services. She was also responsible for reviewing hundreds and hundreds of resumes to find those individuals she thought might best meet the Foundations needs.

On her desk, she had both their next case and, she hoped, their next hire.

The letter from Lynne Walker had captured her imagination even before she'd read through the news articles that accompanied it. Lynne's husband had been murdered under very odd circumstances, and the cop in Mallory couldn't help but be enticed by the challenge. Even now, she couldn't stop herself from reading through the file again: the body of Ross Walker, a construction supervisor, had been found behind the soup kitchen where he and Lynne volunteered one night every week. The torso had been stabbed repeatedly and left posed, seated against the fence with a very large hamburger from a fast food restaurant stuffed into his mouth.

The police investigation had been at a standstill almost since the very beginning. Whoever had murdered Ross Walker had been careful to leave no trace of himself, and interviews with the folks who'd been in and out of the kitchen had proved fruitless. No one had seen or heard anything.

Yet someone had gone to a lot of trouble to kill Ross Walker and leave his body in plain sight. The man's widow had submitted it to the Foundation for consideration. After more than a year, she wanted to move on, wanted her children to be able to start a new life. But not knowing who had killed her husband and why was keeping them all stuck in that moment when the doorbell rang and her seven-year-old son had opened it to find two police officers standing on their front porch.

Yes, this case would do nicely. Mallory hoped the others on the selection committee would agree.

Mallory turned her attention to the second folder on her desk and opened it. Over the past several weeks, she'd reviewed hundreds of resumes from law enforcement officers from every agency and just about every state. She'd been separating them into two piles: *interview* and *toss*. At the top of the interview pile sat the resume of Samuel J. DelVecchio, who had spent the past sixteen years with the FBI, most recently as a profiler.

A resume like that moved Sam DelVecchio to the very top of Mallory's most-wanted list.

For one thing, she reasoned, a former FBI agent would have a lot of contacts within the Bureau, contacts that could prove invaluable, not only for this case, but for future cases as well. For another, he'd worked just about every kind of crime imaginable, and would bring a wealth of experience to the Foundation. Kidnappings, sex crimes, white slavery, serial killers—Samuel DelVecchio had seen them all.

Mallory went back to Ross Walker's folder and pulled out a newspaper article that included part of an interview the local chief of police had given three months after the murder. That the body had been posed carefully suggested that the killer was sending a message, he was quoted as saying, but what that message was and who was supposed to receive it, well, no one had figured that out. Mallory figured an FBI profiler might be able to do exactly that.

Yes, Samuel DelVecchio looked like he just might be the right guy.

Sam DelVecchio stopped at the gate that blocked entry onto the grounds owned by Robert Magellan and waited for the guard to wave him through. The gate swung aside and Sam drove his rental car along the drive that wound past an island of newly planted trees. When Magellan's Tudor mansion came into view, Sam hit the brake. Although he'd seen pictures of the house on the Internet, he hadn't been prepared for how impressive it was.

"Nice." He whistled appreciatively. "Very, very nice."

He parked on the right side of the drive, as he'd been instructed, and got out of the car, pausing to put on his suit jacket and straighten his tie. It had been a long time since he'd been on a job interview, and he wanted to make a good impression. What, under the circumstances, could be more appropriate than basic FBI black? He walked to the door and rang the bell. Almost as an afterthought, he removed his dark glasses—perhaps a little too MIB?—and tucked them into his jacket pocket as the wide front door opened.

A woman of indeterminable age stood at the threshold.

"Samuel DelVecchio?" she asked.

"Yes."

"Come on in. You're early. But promptness is a virtue not everyone appreciates. Can I take your jacket for you? Must be warm out there." The woman barely seemed to take a breath before adding, "Late summer around here can be really toasty. Not to mention humid. You want to go right on up those stairs, second door to the left. Conference room. Mallory should be in there. If she isn't, give a shout and I'll find her for you."

She held out a hand for his jacket, and for a moment, he was tempted to hand it over. But he was meeting with one of the nation's most successful businessmen, and he wasn't sure the casual look was the way to go.

"I'm fine," he told the woman—the housekeeper, he assumed.

"Suit yourself." She smiled and waved and set off toward the back of the house, and Sam headed up the steps as he'd been directed.

At the second door on the left, he knocked lightly. When there was no answer, he pushed it aside slightly and took a step inside. A woman stood looking out the back window.

"Excuse me," Sam said, and she turned around as if startled.

"I'm sorry," he told her. "I'm Sam DelVecchio. I was told to come up here and . . ."

The woman laughed and waved away his apology.

"I'm the one who should apologize. I was daydreaming. Sorry. Please, have a seat." She walked toward him, her hand out in greeting. "I'm Mallory Russo. We spoke on the phone."

He shook her hand, then sat in the chair she'd pointed to.

"I have your resume here . . ." She sorted through a

pile of papers in a fat folder at the head of the table. "Just give me a second . . . here we are."

"Excuse me, but I thought Mr. Magellan—" Sam began, and Mallory waved him off.

"I conduct the interviews. I am responsible for the hiring," she said without taking her eyes from the resume she was scanning. "If I think you're the right fit, I'll discuss it with our committee for their input. But the final decision is mine."

She raised her head and met his eyes. "Do you have a problem with that?"

"No, of course not. I just assumed that Mr. Magellan would be—"

"So." She brushed his explanation aside. "May I ask why you left the FBI after sixteen years?"

He'd expected the question, but hadn't expected it to be the first one. "Well, truthfully, I just had enough."

Might as well just toss it out there.

Mallory raised an eyebrow.

"If you've read my resume, you know I've worked with the Behavioral Analysis Unit for the past several years," he said in answer to her unspoken question.

"That was what made your resume stand out from the others. I thought that someone with profiling experience would be an asset to the Foundation." She paused, then asked, "You do understand what the Mercy Street Foundation was established to do, don't you?"

"It's my understanding that your purpose is to help find people who have gone missing. Cases that the local law enforcement agency had to put aside for one reason or another. People who have been lost, and never found."

"Well, we haven't ruled out cases where we know death has occurred but the case was never solved. Those families need closure, too. Robert likes to think of us as a facilitator or catalyst for finding the truth, but our focus so far has been on missing persons. Some of those people will be found alive—our first case involved two missing teenagers who we did in fact find and return to their families. Our last case did not result in a happy ending. We did find the young woman we were looking for, but unfortunately, we were too late by months to save her. The case I'd like to handle next involves a homicide. The bottom line is that we're searching for answers. What happened to this person? Dead or alive, what caused them to go missing? If we know from the outset the person was a victim of a violent crime, our job is to find out who and why, if law enforcement hasn't been able to do so."

"I think your website describes your work as private investigation with a twist," he said.

"The twist being that if we decide to take on a case, it's because there's something about it that interests or speaks to us, and therefore our services are free." She sat back in her chair, her arms crossed against her chest. "Do you see where a profiler's skills might come in handy to an organization like ours?"

"Well, yes, but—"

"Did you think the cases we take on would be easier than the cases you worked for the Bureau?"

"I thought they were mostly missing persons cases." He shifted a bit uneasily in his seat.

"You mean, 'Someone is missing—here, track them down'?"

He nodded. "Pretty much, yes."

"And that appealed to you?"

"To some extent," Sam admitted sheepishly.

She closed the folder. "Mr. DelVecchio, I think you'd be better off working for another private investigative firm, if that's what you're looking for."

"Miss Russo, maybe we should start this interview again from the beginning. I've obviously gotten off on the wrong foot."

"I've already told you that your experience as a profiler made your resume stand out, so that cat's already out of the bag. Why don't we cut to the chase and you just tell me flat out why you left the Bureau and why you're reluctant to sell yourself on your profiling skills."

Sam nodded.

"For the past six years, I've been on call to several of the Bureau's top investigative units. That meant every time a child was found raped and murdered, every time a body was found and there appeared to be a pattern to the attack, every time serial crimes were identified, I was one of several people who could be called in to study the crime and try to interpret the behavior in a manner that would help our agents get a handle on the killer." He hesitated momentarily while he debated with himself how much of his personal story to add, then decided to omit it. If he came on board with the Foundation, it would come up sooner or later. Right now, for the purpose of this interview, he decided he was more comfortable leaving it out.

He leaned forward, not liking what he was about to say, but knowing he'd say it anyway. "Miss Russo, the things I've seen over the past few years are the stuff of nightmares. When I say I've had enough, I mean I've had enough of children who have been tortured and degraded and had any sense of humanity stolen from them. I've had enough of young women who have been sold or slaughtered, of bodies that had been hacked beyond recognition as anything human. I've had enough of destroyed lives."

Mallory held up a hand to stop him from continuing. "I was a cop for nine years," she said softly. "I've seen my share. I understand."

Sam hesitated, rethinking his decision to not bring up Carly. He suspected that Mallory, as a former cop, would understand. But before he could speak, Mallory went on.

"Your references are impeccable. The recommendations couldn't be better. Your superior at the Bureau has made it clear that he'd take you back in a heartbeat. Very unusual for the FBI, I'd say."

Sam nodded. His old boss was one in a million. If circumstances had been different, he'd have been happy to stay, and if he was ever inclined to go back, John Mancini would be the first person he'd call.

"What I need to know is, if we have a case that involves the type of victim you just mentioned, where we'd need those skills of yours—a child who has been abducted, a young woman who's been tortured, maybe a particularly gruesome murder—are you going to be willing to do the job?"

Remembering Carly, the words came before he could think about what he was saying. "Not if I'm going to be sitting around waiting for a case like that to come in, no."

She studied him for a long moment, then opened another file and turned it around.

"No wait necessary, Mr. DelVecchio." She slid the file across the table to him. "Take a minute to read this over—the newspaper articles as well as the letter on top—then look me in the eye and tell me you wouldn't be more than happy to be the one who finds this son of a bitch."

TWO

By three thirty in the afternoon, Sam had seen just about all there was of Conroy, Pennsylvania. He'd driven back to the city from Robert's plush suburban grounds, past vast fields of tall corn, and orchards where peaches were being picked and apples still ripened. The farms he passed, with their centuries-old farmhouses and red-roofed barns, reminded him of his Nebraska roots and the three-story clapboard home of his youth. He tried to remember just how long it had been since he'd gone back and couldn't, which in itself told him that it had been way too long. He'd meant to go after he returned from what his mother and brother Tom referred to as "Sam's wanderings" this past year, but from his hotel room near the Newark International Airport where he'd stayed after a mind-numbing flight from Turkey the week before, he'd seen an interview with Robert Magellan on CNN and was intrigued by the mogul's new venture. Who'd have guessed a businessman of his stature would have such an altruistic streak that he'd personally bankroll a foundation set up specifically to help other people search for their missing loved ones?

Laid low by what he'd dubbed travel plague, Sam spent two days more than he'd intended in Newark, his time shared almost equally between sleeping and channel surfing before returning to his old apartment in Virginia. He spent most of one afternoon on his laptop, researching Magellan and his Mercy Street Foundation, and found himself wondering what it would be like to start over with a private investigative firm instead of a law enforcement agency. When he quit the Bureau to take some badly needed time off, he'd given little thought to what he'd do when he came back. Hell, he'd given little enough thought to *when* he'd come back. He'd only known that his life was killing him, and he had to walk away from it. He still wasn't sure what had prompted him to submit an application to the Foundation, and hadn't bothered to examine his motives for driving to Pennsylvania for the interview with Mallory Russo.

As he approached the city, the country road widened. In the distance he could see the smokestacks of factories that had once fueled Conroy's economy. From his Internet wanderings, he'd learned that the factories had closed, one by one, back in the seventies and eighties, until the city's unemployed outnumbered those who still brought home a paycheck every week. He drove over a metal two-lane bridge that crossed a stream feeding into the Schuylkill River about a half mile west, and on impulse, took the street that ran past the deserted factories. Empty water towers stood on spindly legs and flocks of pigeons roosted along shingled roofs. Cyclone fences wound their way around the now-silent buildings, and other than a stray dog that dragged part of a chain behind him, there wasn't a living soul to be seen. The heat rose off the crumbling sidewalks and the streets had potholes large enough to hide a Hummer. All in all, it had been a depressing tour of the city he might find himself living in. He felt at loose ends and at odds with himself over why he was here in the first place.

The road bent sharply to the right, and Sam followed it, relieved to be heading back toward town. A sign for a diner a few blocks up reminded him why his stomach was grumbling. He'd had breakfast at a chain restaurant right off the New Jersey Turnpike around seven that morning, nothing since, and even his bottle of water was empty.

It was almost four in the afternoon when he parked in the steaming parking lot and walked through the glass door into the welcome cool of the diner.

"You by yourself?" The waitress sat on one of the red-leather-covered stools at the counter and turned completely around to look him over. She was in her late fifties, with hair a shade too strawberry to be considered a true strawberry blond, and eyeglasses trimmed with rhinestones hanging from a beaded cord around her neck. She wore a blue and white striped dress that zipped up the front and a name tag with NANCY written in red script.

"Yes," he replied.

"Booth near the windows okay?"

"As long as it's out of the sun."

"Yeah, it's blazing today, all right." She led him to a booth on the shady side of the narrow building. "Nearly blistered my hands on my steering wheel.

Swear to God." She handed him a menu. "What can I get you to drink?"

"Water's fine. Lots of ice." Sam slid across the cool vinyl seat and took off his sunglasses. He placed them on the table and opened the menu.

"You missed the lunch specials," the waitress told him when she returned with his drink, "and you're too early for the dinner specials."

"Can I just get a burger and fries?" he asked.

"Sure. Be right back with that." She took the folded menu from his hands and walked into the kitchen through double swinging doors.

Sam stared out the window at the traffic, just beginning to pick up as the end of the work day drew closer. Two police cruisers passed with lights flashing but their sirens silent. A group of five or six young girls, laughing and pushing each other playfully, their hair wet, walked by in short summer cover-ups, each carrying a large tote bag.

"Is there a public pool nearby?" Sam asked when the waitress returned with flatware and a napkin.

After placing them before him, she leaned one knee on the bench opposite his seat and asked, "You're new in Conroy?"

Sam nodded. "My first time here, yes."

"You just passing through?"

"I haven't decided yet," he told her.

"The pool is about four blocks up. Nothing fancy, but it's wet and the young families enjoy it. Used to be more for the folks who had a little money, but these days, people with any serious money have their own pools, someplace other than Conroy, so the city pool has had to open its membership to anyone who can afford the fee. Anything you want to know about Conroy, you can ask me. I've lived here all my life. Isn't anything that happened around here that I haven't heard about."

Sam suspected as much. "You've heard about the Mercy Street Foundation?"

"Oh, yeah." She gestured with one hand as if to say, *Of course, who hasn't.* "Robert—that's Robert Magellan, the one who started it up—he comes in every once in a while with his cousin, Father Burch. He's the Catholic priest over there at Our Lady of Angels. Nice guys, both of 'em. Both good tippers, too. Shame about Robert's wife." The waitress shook her head slowly from side to side.

Sam had read everything he could find on Robert Magellan. It occurred to him that though he'd spent several hours with Mallory Russo that morning, the tragic disappearance of Robert Magellan's wife and child had never come up.

"She disappeared a few years ago, right?" Sam knew, but wanted a local's take on it.

"You been on Mars or something?" She crossed her arms over her chest and frowned.

"Close enough."

"The wife and their baby had been missing since right before Valentine's Day, 2007. They just found her car not long ago. Just buried her last week. Beth was still strapped in her seat behind the wheel, but the baby was gone." She lowered her voice as she delivered this last part.

"Gone?"

"Gone, as in someone must have found the car down in that ravine and took that baby and left poor Beth there all this time." She shook her head disapprovingly. "You ever heard such a thing? Take a woman's baby and leave her lying there dead?"

The tinny ring of a bell from the kitchen called the waitress to the pick-up window. She returned with Sam's meal and placed it before him.

"No leads on what happened to the baby?" Sam asked. That had been left open in every article he'd read.

"None. He was just gone."

"Any chance he could have gotten himself out of his car seat and got the door open and wandered off?"

"Not unless he was Baby Superman." The door opened and she turned to see who was coming in. A party of four, obviously regulars, waved to Nancy as they seated themselves. She stood and walked to the counter for their menus. "Ian Magellan was only three months old when he went missing."

He should have remembered that much, Sam thought as he took a bite from his burger and digested the information. Clearly Magellan's own tragedy had been the motivating factor in establishing the Foundation, and Sam wondered if he'd hired an investigator to work only on finding his missing son. He took another bite without tasting and chewed slowly. He knew what it was like to lose the person you most loved in the world. He and Magellan had that much in common.

How had Magellan survived losing both his wife

and his son? That he had, and now spent a considerable chunk of change helping other people find their missing loved ones told Sam something about the man's character.

"You need another water?" the waitress asked as she approached the table.

"Just the check."

"You finished with that?" She pointed to his half-eaten burger.

Sam nodded. "I wasn't as hungry as I thought I was."

"Coffee? We have some nice Boston cream pie. Just came in from the baker this morning."

"No, thanks. Just the check."

"You staying in Conroy for a while?" She placed his check on the table.

"Maybe for a few days."

"You stop in tomorrow morning and have breakfast with us"—she smiled as she turned to walk away—"your coffee's on me."

"I'll do that. Thanks." He picked up his sunglasses and stood. He counted out enough bills to cover his lunch and a tip, and left it next to his plate. The diner was beginning to fill up, with most of the booths by the windows already occupied.

Sam stepped out into the heat of the late summer afternoon and immediately wished he hadn't. By the time he got to his car and turned on the air conditioning, he was sweating. He wondered what was wrong with him, even considering a move to a place where the temperature in August rose to one hundred degrees with nearly one hundred percent humidity. Why would he, who hated the heat so, choose to live in such a place, when for the first time in his life, he had total control over where he would live, had no one to answer to but himself?

And why would he want to put himself in a position where he'd be dealing with the same demons he'd just spent seven months trying to exorcise? He'd used up a good portion of his savings in his attempts to put his past behind him. What in the name of God was he doing contemplating the possibility of walking back into that same fire again? He couldn't even claim fatigue; he'd just returned from the longest vacation he'd ever had. So what had possessed him to apply to the Mercy Street Foundation in the first place?

Well, he did need a job, he rationalized, now that he was back in the States.

And, he reminded himself, he hadn't expected his profiling skills—which were considerable, even he had to admit that—to be an issue. Mallory Russo had been correct in suspecting that Sam had thought the job would be easier, less stressful, than what he'd been used to in the Bureau. She'd disabused him of that quickly enough, even went so far as to wave a particularly tantalizing case under his nose to tempt him.

The air came on with a hot blast. He leaned back against the seat and waited for it to cool him. He left the parking lot and drove aimlessly past a row of boarded-up storefronts in a neighborhood where young and not-so-young hookers stood on the sidewalk and eyed every car that passed, including his. Jumpy young men in sleeveless T-shirts gathered on the corner, gesturing and posturing, maybe for the hookers, maybe for each other. Sam had watched the same scenes play out in a dozen other cities on hot summer afternoons. The seamy side of Conroy was nothing new.

On his way back to the motel where he'd spent the night, he stopped at a drugstore and picked up two newspapers—one local, one national—and a news magazine. He'd been out of touch for months, and it was time for him to catch up. On his way to the cashier, he grabbed a copy of a sports magazine with a picture of the quarterback of his favorite NFL team on the cover.

It was still early, so he took the long way to the motel, choosing streets that wound through the town, past brick row houses close to the factories and larger, more stately homes overlooking the river, away from what must have been some serious emissions from those smokestacks back in the day. A side street brought him past Our Lady of Angels, and he recalled that Nancy had mentioned that Robert Magellan's cousin was a priest there. Several blocks away he passed another church, this one smaller, older, in need of some paint and some general maintenance. Beyond the church, white stones of varying sizes rose up from the ground. Without thinking, Sam parked the car and got out. He walked around the building, noticing that the front door was padlocked, and walked through the quiet churchyard.

A dense row of evergreens grew tall along one side and he followed the shade until he reached what he suspected was one of the oldest sections of the graveyard. The headstones were shorter, sprouting from the ground like mushrooms. The names on most of them were eroded by time and weather, but on some the names of the deceased were clear enough to read. *Mary Jenkins, good wife of John, lies buried here,* read one. Another said simply, *Ann Hamilton,* the dates illegible. He walked aimlessly through the untidy rows, careful not to step on anyone's grave, and wondered if Carly was given the same respectful courtesy by visitors to the cemetery in Illinois where seven generations of her family had been laid to rest.

He crested the top of a small rise and found himself almost face-to-face with a couple who appeared to be in their seventies. They were busily tending a grave bearing a simple white marker that was taller than the ones in the older part of the cemetery.

"Afternoon." The man nodded to Sam.

"Afternoon," Sam returned the greeting.

"Hello," the man's wife said and smiled. Sam smiled back, feeling awkward as hell. He sensed he'd interrupted something very private, and wanted to extract himself as quickly as possible from the situation. He walked around the headstone that was the object of their attention to make a casual retreat.

"Hot as a son of a gun today, isn't it?" the man noted.

"Sure is." Sam paused. Against his will, he found himself reading the stone:

HERE LIES AN ANGEL
Evelyn Joy Erickson
Born October 12, 1959
Taken from her loving parents
on May 30, 1976 at Age Seventeen

"Your daughter?" he heard himself ask without thinking.

They nodded in unison.

"I'm sorry," Sam said.

"Thank you, son." The man wiped sweat from his brow with the back of one hand.

"She loved roses," the mother told him. "We planted a small bush here for her, but the groundskeepers didn't like it." She smiled wryly. "It got a bit out of hand, started growing where it shouldn't, even though I tried to keep it trimmed. So every week I bring her some fresh ones." The woman stood. "Evie would have liked that."

"You've been bringing her flowers every week since . . ."

"Since the day we laid her to rest." The man nodded. "Spring of '76. She left for school one morning and never made it." His face drooped and Sam started to open his mouth to tell him it was okay, he didn't have to share the story, but he couldn't get the words out fast enough. "They found her almost a week later, in a drainage ditch. She'd been—"

"I'm so sorry," Sam interrupted to spare the man from speaking aloud his private torment. "Did they ever find whoever . . ."

"No." The woman's face hardened. "No, they never did. A night doesn't pass that I don't pray that he has a tortured passing from this life, and that the devil is waiting for him on the other side."

"Francie." Her husband reached out to her.

"I know it isn't the Christian thing, John." She

met Sam's eyes. "But there are some things . . . some acts . . ."

"I understand completely," Sam told her. *This is why* rang in his ears.

"She was our only child," the woman told him simply. "We miss her every day."

"I'm sorry." Sam tried to think of something else to say, but nothing that came to mind seemed appropriate.

"You've lost someone, too," she told him as he turned to walk away.

Sam nodded. "My wife."

"I'll pray for her," the woman said. "And for you."

"Thank you."

The lump in his throat grew bigger, so he nodded once more to the couple and went through the rows of marked graves directly to the car. As he walked away, he tried to drown out that voice inside him that insisted, *This is why. Because of people like the Ericksons, who have been tending the grave of their only child for more than thirty years and who have never had closure; people like Lynne Walker, who needs to help her children understand why their father had been brutally murdered, left propped up by a Dumpster like a broken doll, his chest slashed to ribbons and an oversized hamburger stuffed in his mouth.*

Sam started the engine and took a deep breath of cool air, and understood why he'd sent in an application to the Foundation, and why he'd take the job if it was offered to him—because good people suffered at the hands of the evil every day, and if he walked away, there would be one less person to stand between the innocent and those who would do them harm.

Sam drove back to the motel, and waited for Mallory's call.

THREE

So what did you think of him?" Trula wiped down a counter where she'd rolled out dough for a peach pie. "Sam? That was his name, right?"

"I think he'd be perfect." Mallory swiped one of the peaches and took a bite before Trula could stop her. "I'd love to have someone on the staff with his credentials, someone who has a deep understanding of criminal behavior. Someone who has some real insights into what makes these people tick."

"By 'these people,' you mean the bad guys." Trula searched a cabinet, noisily moving pans from one place to another. She found what she was looking for—a glass pie plate—and closed the cabinet door.

"Yeah. Sam has a lot of experience there. He was in some special FBI unit that handled the most challenging cases. The letter from his superior was glowing."

"So what's the problem?"

"I get the feeling he isn't sure that he wants the job." Mallory grabbed a paper towel to wipe the peach juice from her chin. "Great peaches, Trula. Where'd you get them?"

"The farmers' market in Toby Falls." She went

about the business of pie making without missing a beat. "So why would he apply for a job he doesn't want?"

"I don't know. Maybe it seemed like a good idea at the time."

"Did he say he didn't want it?"

"Noooo, but . . ."

"Then if you think he's the right person for the job, if you think he'd be an asset . . ."

"I definitely think he'd be an asset."

". . . then offer him the job and see what he says."

"I wanted to talk to everyone about him first," Mallory told her.

"In that case, I hope you're not looking to bring him on board any time soon. Robert, Susanna, and Emme are still in West Kingston working with those search parties they organized to look for Ian, and they won't be back until Friday. Kevin took some of the seniors from Our Lady of Angels to the cathedral in Philadelphia today. He won't be back till late this afternoon, but he does have his cell with him." Trula shook her head. "If I get my hands on whoever it was who took that baby, it's going to take an act of God Almighty himself to keep me from throttling the life from him. Or her."

"I spoke with Emme this morning. She said there's been no sign of anything that would give them a clue as to what happened to Ian."

"But knowing Robert, he'll keep on looking until . . ." She paused, overcome by emotion.

Mallory squeezed the woman's shoulder. "They'll keep looking until they find him, one way or another. Now that Robert has reason to suspect the baby might still be alive, he isn't going to give up until he finds him."

"He isn't a baby anymore. He's two and a half already." Trula wiped away tears. "He's a toddler. He's probably walking and talking, maybe even going to preschool somewhere. He's grown so much, learned so much, since we saw him. It's killing Robert, you know, to have missed all Ian's firsts."

"Hopefully, once they find Ian, having him back will make up for everything he's missed."

"Assuming they can find him." Trula began to peel the peaches, her knife working furiously. "Someone has that boy and knows he isn't theirs. People see that child every day, and don't know that he's not who they think he is."

"Assuming he's still alive," Mallory reminded her.

"He's still alive," Trula said. "He's alive and someone is raising him as if he's theirs." She slammed an angry fist on the counter. "What kind of person does something like that?"

"I don't know, Trula." Mallory sighed. "All those years I was a cop, I saw things . . . things that most people can't even imagine. And every time, I'd wonder that same thing: *what kind of person can do this and live with themselves?*"

"I don't suppose there's ever been an answer."

Mallory shook her head no. "Sometimes you meet people who are so good, inside and out, that you feel lucky to have had them cross your path." Like you, Trula, she could have added, but Trula being Trula and prickly at times, Mallory decided against it. "Then there are others who are so filled with hate and anger and evil, that you wonder how they could even be human." She leaned on the counter. "There aren't always answers. There isn't always a reason."

Trula sighed and turned around to face Mallory. "What are the chances?" she asked. "Is it even possible to hope that Robert will be able to find him?"

Mallory chose her words carefully, though not quite as carefully as she had when Robert had asked the same questions.

"It is possible. It's a matter of finding the right lead."

"Of which there have been none."

"So far. But we'll see how it plays out. Sometimes it's a matter of simply asking the right questions of the right people."

"Robert will never stop looking until he finds Ian."

"He shouldn't stop looking. I wouldn't, if Ian were mine." She glanced at the clock. "In the meantime, we have a business to run here. I'm going to call Robert and the others and we'll see what the consensus is."

"Robert's going to tell you to do what you think is best. Kevin will tell you to follow your instincts, and Susanna is going to ask you what Robert said. Emme will be happy to have another investigator to share the workload." Trula smiled. "Sam seemed like a nice enough fellow. I say go for it. So when Robert asks you if I had anything to say, you can tell him."

"I'll call Robert first."

"Good move." Trula went back to preparing the filling for her pie.

"By the way, what are you going to do with that pie?" Mallory asked. "Who knows when Robert and Susanna will be back. And if I remember correctly, you don't like peach pie." She leaned on the counter. "So who's the pie for, hmmmm?"

"It might go home with you for a certain detective who's had to work around the clock for the past two weeks." Trula watched from the corner of her eye as Mallory stealthily pocketed another peach. "Then again, maybe it's for Father Kevin."

Grinning and assured of one great dessert to share with Charlie when he got home that night—if he got home that night—Mallory went back to her office, the second peach and another paper towel in her pocket.

Trula had been spot-on in her predictions: Robert had, in fact, told Mallory to do what she thought was best.

"Hire him if you think he's the right guy," he'd said, obviously distracted by the ongoing search for his son, which at the moment consisted of a sort of dragnet through the area of woods where the car had been found. "You're in charge of staffing. I trust your judgment one hundred percent. Besides, I'm not thinking a whole lot about the business right now, so if you like him, bring him on. We still have that six-week probationary period, right? If he doesn't work out, he's gone when the time's up."

Her next call was to Emme, who'd been delighted at the possibility of another investigator coming on board.

Susanna was also distracted by the ongoing search for Ian, and as expected, had deferred to Robert. Kevin had been characteristically diplomatic: "Listen to your gut," he'd said.

*   *   *

Mallory made the call to Sam DelVecchio, and was surprised at his immediate—and positive—response.

"When do I start?" he asked.

She realized that she'd been so uncertain he'd even take the job that she hadn't given a starting date much thought.

"When would you like to start?"

"I'll need to tie up a few loose ends," he said. "Is two weeks too long?"

"Not for me, but it might be for Lynne Walker."

"Good point." He paused, then said, "I'm going to have to go back to Virginia, take care of a few things, and then I'm going to have to find a place to live there."

"I think I mentioned at the interview that you'll be on probation for six weeks or until your first case is resolved, whichever comes first."

"So what you're saying is, don't be in a hurry to put an ad in the paper to sublet my apartment."

"That's pretty much it."

"I'll still need to find some temporary lodgings there."

"Emme Caldwell—she was our first hire—stayed at a nice enough motel when she first started. I'd be happy to make a reservation for you at the same place. It's not too far from the house and it has a restaurant and pool."

"That would be great, thanks." He paused. "I'm assuming I'll be meeting Mr. Magellan sometime during the six-week period?"

"Possibly. He's a little busy right now. But don't address him as Mr. Magellan. He much prefers to be called Robert."

They discussed the Walker case and Sam said he could be up and running by Monday morning, which suited everyone just fine.

Mallory hung up and immediately placed a call to Lynne Walker.

"This is Mallory Russo from the Mercy Street Foundation," she began when the call was picked up. "I'd like to speak with Lynne Walker."

"This is Lynne." There was a pause. "Who did you say . . . ?"

"Mallory Russo, from the Mercy Street Foundation. We've reviewed the application you sent in regarding your late husband. We'd like to take on the case, if you're still interested in us doing so."

"Is this a joke?" Lynne Walker's voice was trembling. "Because if this is supposed to be funny . . ."

"It's not a joke, Mrs. Walker. We'd like to look into your husband's murder."

"Oh, my God. You're serious. I never thought you'd really choose us." She began to cry. "I can't believe you're really going to do this."

"We have an investigator ready to start work on this, next week. He'll be contacting you on Monday or Tuesday to set up a meeting."

"I can't believe this," she said again. "I can't believe there's a chance we might finally find out what happened to Ross."

"There are no guarantees, Mrs. Walker. Please understand that. We will do our best, but we can't promise that we'll find anything the police haven't already found."

"Which is basically nothing," she said bitterly. "They aren't any closer now than they were the day

Ross died. I call down there to the police department and every month it's the same. 'I'm sorry, Mrs. Walker, but there have been no new developments.'"

"I understand your frustration, but I'm sure the police have done the best they can with the personnel they have."

"I read about those other cases you people solved. Those kids there in Pennsylvania, and that college girl down in Maryland. You people get results."

"It's much easier when all your efforts and resources are concentrated on one case. The police generally don't have that luxury."

"I don't think they cared one way or another."

"It might seem that way sometimes, but having been a police officer myself, I can tell you that every case is important, and nothing rankles like the case you could not solve."

"You said someone would be calling me next week."

"Most likely late afternoon Monday or sometime on Tuesday." Mallory hesitated. She probably shouldn't box Sam in but it was too late now. "The investigator will be Sam DelVecchio."

"Tell Mr. DelVecchio I'll be waiting to hear from him. I'll wait here until he calls. I don't want to miss him."

"I'm sure he'll leave a message if you're not there, so if there are things you—"

"You don't understand," Lynne Walker said, cutting her off. "I have waited months to make some sense of what happened to Ross. I want to move past the horror of what happened, I want to move away from this town and this house and this life. I want my children to stop being afraid that the person who killed their father is going to come back to kill me, or to kill them. We need answers, Miss Russo. Until we have them, we're just stuck right here, right where we were on the day Ross was murdered."

"We'll do our best. I can't promise more than that."

"That's all I can ask," the woman replied. "Thank you—and thank Mr. Magellan for what he's doing. I saw on the news where they found his wife but not his baby boy. I'm praying for him."

"I'll let him know that," Mallory assured her as she hung up from the call. "We're all praying for him, too."

FOUR

Sam slowly turned the coffee mug Trula had handed him so that he could read whatever was written on it, but didn't want to appear obvious.

IN EVERY REAL MAN IS A CHILD WHO WANTS TO PLAY. NIETZSCHE

Well, yeah. Who doesn't know that?

"We have orange-pecan muffins this morning," Trula was saying. "Help yourself. I'm assuming you already had a decent breakfast?"

"Oh, sure." He nodded, then met her questioning eyes from across the room, and felt compelled to tell the truth. "Well, actually, I had a donut I picked up when I got my coffee at that convenience place across the street from the motel."

She appeared to look him over, as if to assess him somehow. "Sit down and I'll make you some eggs."

"Oh, no. Don't bother. You don't have to . . ." He protested, but there was that stare again. Trula pointed to the kitchen table, a farmhouse-style affair of planked oak with a banquette that wrapped around two sides to form an *L*.

Sam sat. He was still sitting when Mallory came through the back door.

"We're having eggs this morning," Trula told her without turning around.

"What kind?" Mallory placed her handbag on the table and smiled at Sam.

"Brown organic ones." Trula's sarcasm was unveiled.

"I know that." Mallory rolled her eyes and turned to Sam. She stage-whispered, "That's all Trula buys. There should be a sign over the front door: Abandon hope of ever eating junk food again, all ye who enter here."

"Very funny," Trula muttered.

"Junk food is not food." A small dark-skinned girl of perhaps four or five appeared in the kitchen doorway. "It will make you fat and give you headaches and make your teeth soft."

"You tell them, Chloe." Trula smiled broadly as the girl skipped into the kitchen. "Child is smarter than most of the adults I know."

"Chloe, this is Sam," Mallory said. "He's going to work with us starting today."

"Hello, Sam." The child approached the table solemnly, as if she, too, were sizing him up.

"Hello, Chloe," he returned the greeting, and wondered who she belonged to.

"Do you eat junk food?" She climbed onto a chair opposite him and studied him with large brown eyes.

"Sometimes." He nodded and tried to look contrite.

"Trula won't let you have bad food here. She only makes good things to eat and makes everyone eat it, even if it's something you don't like," Chloe confided and Mallory choked back a laugh.

"What did I make you eat that you didn't like?" Trula turned to ask.

"Chard," Chloe answered without hesitation, "and Brussels sprouts."

"Chloe is Emme Caldwell's daughter," Mallory explained. "When Emme has to go out of town, Trula keeps her company."

"Chloe keeps *me* company," Trula corrected. "She's my sous chef and number one baking apprentice."

Chloe nodded and thanked Trula for the glass of milk the woman placed before her. She took a sip, then told Sam, "Me and my mommy are going to live in the house out back 'cause we can't find one we like. Trula's having people clean it while Mommy's away. She went with Robert and Susanna to help look for Robert's missing baby. Someone stoled him."

Trula looked over Chloe's head to Sam to explain. "There's a carriage house on the grounds that has been unoccupied for who knows how long—at least since Robert's owned the property—but it's still in pretty good shape. We decided to spruce it up a bit so that Emme and Chloe could live closer to Emme's work, and so that when Emme isn't here, Chloe can stay with me. I'm hoping that it will be in move-in condition by the time they get back from this trip. That motel stay was too long for a child."

"And I couldn't have my kitty there," Chloe added.

"Where is Foxy this morning?" Mallory asked.

"I let her out earlier," Trula replied. "Chloe, do you want to go see if you can find Foxy while I finish making breakfast?"

"Uh-huh." Chloe jumped off the chair and sprinted out the back door.

Trula closed the door behind her, then turned to Sam and said, "You'll hear this soon enough, I suppose, so I might as well tell you right up front. Emme adopted Chloe as a newborn from a woman who was in prison for selling narcotics and who was killed there shortly after Chloe was born. Chloe's father is— there's no nice way to put this—a Mexican drug lord. A few months ago, he decided he wanted her—she's his only child—so he put out a reward for whoever brought her to him in Mexico."

"That's pretty scary. Who's the father?" Sam asked.

"His name is Anthony Navarro," Mallory told him.

"Navarro is her father?" Sam frowned. As a former FBI agent, he knew the name well. "He's real bad news."

"So we hear. Emme was hoping Chloe would be safe here, but a few weeks ago, someone gave Navarro a tip that they were here in Conroy. He sent someone to look for her. Only the quick thinking of a member of Father Kevin's parish saved Chloe from possibly being whisked away to sunny Mexico. We think the threat has been deterred for now, but who knows?" Mallory shrugged.

"We're hoping that he's looking elsewhere," Trula added. "But none of us are willing to take any chances."

"Navarro is definitely not one to mess with," Sam told them.

Trula's chin set solidly with reserve and she began to crack eggs into a bowl with a bit more vehemence than Sam suspected might be necessary. "No one is taking that child from her mother."

"What Trula means is that no one is taking that child from *Trula*," Mallory added. "She and Chloe are like best buds now. I pity the fool who tries to abduct that girl now. Hence the move onto the grounds here."

Trula sniffed. "It was Robert's idea."

"After you planted it," Mallory noted.

"Emme works long hours. Someone needs to watch Chloe when she comes home from school," Trula countered.

"She could have hired a babysitter," Mallory pointed out.

Trula fixed her with a glare, and Mallory smiled as if she'd been expecting the reaction.

"We all agreed that Chloe has to be protected," Mallory told Sam. "And we all agreed there's no safer place for her than here. She goes to all-day preschool at Our Lady of Angels so Kevin keeps an eye on her there, and Robert has beefed up security here at the house as well."

"Which he needed to do anyway," Trula said. "This big house and all these acres of grounds—for a while all he had was a puny little alarm system. Now, I'm not one to be paranoid, but when you're Robert Magellan, you need to take some precautions. I'm glad he finally hired some guards and had the fencing and the alarms upgraded like I've been telling him to do for the past two years. I hate to think badly of my fellow man, but ever since Beth and Ian disappeared, and we didn't know if they'd been abducted . . ." She shivered.

"How's the search going?" Sam asked.

"It's going," Mallory replied. "No news. I'm thinking it's going to take some creative thinking on their part to find that boy."

"It was creative thinking on Susanna's part that found the car in the first place," Trula reminded her. "If Robert didn't need her to run his life, he could hire her to work on cases. She'd make a crack detective."

Sam watched Mallory open a cupboard and sort through a shelf of mugs until she found one that apparently pleased her. She filled it with coffee and returned to the table where she sat and added cream and sweetener. He craned his neck to read the writing on the mug. ELVIS HAS LEFT THE BUILDING.

What, he wondered, was up with all the mugs?

"You met Susanna Jones last week as you were leaving. She's been Robert's personal assistant since before he even had his own company. Since the police put the case on the back burner, Susanna spent nearly every weekend traveling the route Robert's wife would have taken to get back home from her sister's in Western Pennsylvania. She took every side road, every mountain road, every hill and valley between here and Pittsburgh, until she found the place where Beth's car had gone off the road and down the side of a mountain into a ravine where it couldn't be seen from the road." Mallory shook her head. "That's determination."

"I read about it online. I was amazed at her persistence," Sam said.

"We all were. If anyone can find that baby, it's going to be Susanna." Trula nodded. "She and

Robert and Emme together, they're going to find that boy."

"Let's hope so." Mallory turned back to Sam. "And speaking of finding someone . . ."

She reached into her briefcase and pulled out a file.

"This is all we have on the Ross Walker case." She handed him the folder. "I spoke with Lynne Walker on Thursday. She's expecting to hear from you today or tomorrow. I thought you'd want to start with her."

"Thanks." Sam put the file on the table next to him.

"Aren't you going to look at it?"

"Sure. But right now, I'm going to eat the eggs Trula is putting onto one of those plates, and I'm going to drink my coffee. Then I'll go to whatever place you've set aside for me to use as an office, and I'll read everything you've given me."

"Don't you want to talk about it?"

"Not especially. Not right now, anyway," he said honestly. Might as well put that out there, right up front.

"I get it." Mallory shrugged. "I should probably be insulted, but I get it."

"Get what?" Trula set a plate in front of them both.

"Sam likes to work alone."

"It's nothing personal," he told her. "It's the only way I've ever worked."

"Haven't you ever had a partner?"

"Not recently."

"But when you were called in to work as a profiler, surely you had to play nicely with the others."

"Mostly I studied whatever information there was

and talked to the people in the field, but I rarely worked a case with anyone else." He thought about that for a moment. "At least, not until I'd had time to digest the information and talk to a few people, get a feel for it. But even at that, I was really just giving my opinion and my thoughts."

"Well, once you've had time to do a little digesting of Ross Walker's case, I'd appreciate your thoughts on it." Mallory took a piece of toast from the plate that Trula had placed between them on the table and began to butter it. "Actually, I'd more than just appreciate it. I'm going to require it."

"So I should think of you as sort of the special agent in charge of the Mercy Street Foundation." Sam nodded, glad to have the hierarchy spelled out. For some reason, he had assumed he'd be reporting directly to Magellan. Clearly he'd been wrong. It was good to get that straightened out on the first day.

"Something like that." Mallory smiled and turned her attention to the scrambled eggs and bacon Trula was serving. "Nice analogy. I like it."

Sam glanced at the sparkly round diamond on her ring finger and silently wished a lot of luck to the guy who'd placed it there. Mallory must have caught the look, because she grinned and wiggled her finger to catch the light with the stone.

"Pretty, isn't it? My guy done good, don't you think?"

"Very nice, yes." Sam nodded, and Mallory laughed.

"You'll meet Charlie soon enough," she told him. "He's a detective in Conroy, and there are times when we need him to get a little info for us. Of course, now, with your contacts in the FBI, I'm thinking we might be able to let Charlie off the hook a little."

"There are some people I can call on if we need to." Sam nodded, already planning to check to make sure the details of Ross Walker's murder had been entered into the Bureau's computer system. "I'm assuming we have copies of all the reports from the investigating police department?"

"All the ones that were sent in by the widow. But I wouldn't assume anything. I'm sure the Lincoln police have a lot more. Maybe they'll even share it with you."

"I'll give them a call. I went to college in Lincoln. Haven't been back in a while."

"That's right. I do recall reading that on your resume. Cornhusker, eh?"

"Absolutely. Nebraska born and raised." He took a bite of Trula's excellent eggs and wondered if she served breakfast to the staff when Robert was around.

He watched the older woman as she puttered, and wondered at her age—seventy-something, maybe?—and what her position here was. Robert's housekeeper? The cook? Neither would explain why Mallory seemed to defer to her or why she appeared to have so much influence over Robert.

Interesting household.

"Well, I have some calls to make." Mallory stood and gathered up her plate and her mug and her flatware and carried all to the sink where she rinsed all but the mug and opened the dishwasher. "By the way, Sam, you're in the office two down from mine. Your laptop is on your desk along with everything I think you'll need to get started. If there's anything else you need, just let me know."

"Thanks, Mallory." He was pretty sure he remembered which office was hers.

"I'm in the process of unloading so leave everything on the counter," Trula told Mallory.

"Okay." Mallory did as she was told, filled her cup from the coffeemaker on the counter. "Thanks, Trula. Perfect, as always." She waved to Sam as she passed out of the kitchen.

Trula turned to Sam and said, "I'm going outside to find Chloe. I'm going to have to get her to school soon. You can do as Mallory did and clear your own place whenever you finish."

"I'll do that, thanks. And thanks for breakfast."

"You're welcome. We usually have lunch around one for whoever is around." She left the house by the back door, leaving Sam alone in the kitchen.

He poured himself another cup of coffee after rinsing his plate and tucked the file Mallory had given him under his arm. He looked out the back window and saw Trula sitting on the ground next to Chloe, making a chain of clover flowers. So much for getting the child to school on time. He smiled at the unlikely pairing, and went off in search of his office.

Two hours later, he'd read the file through and made several pages of notes. He'd had the benefit of having seen the file contents briefly when he'd met with Mallory for his interview, but now found himself poring over every page, looking for the bits and pieces of real information scattered throughout the wordy documents. When he felt he'd extracted as much as he was going to get from the official reports, he pulled out the contact sheet and lifted the receiver to dial Lynne Walker's number. He caught the address of the Walker home—4172 Clinton Street—and for a moment, wasn't sure he'd read correctly. Hadn't his first apartment in Lincoln been on Clinton Street? He tried to remember what the building had looked like but couldn't bring it to mind. He shrugged. Maybe it had been Calhoun Street, or the name of some other president. Buchanan, maybe. Whatever.

He took his time dialing, remembering some very good times at the University of Nebraska. There'd been that hot little blonde at the Phi Mu house. Cheryl something. At the last reunion he'd attended, he'd heard she'd gone into TV reporting. He wondered what she was doing now . . .

"Hello?" a woman's voice answered the phone.

"Is this Mrs. Walker?" Sam asked, his college memories swiftly put aside.

"This is Lynne Walker, yes."

"Mrs. Walker, this is Sam DelVecchio. I'm with the—"

"Mercy Street Foundation," she said with obvious relief. "Miss Russo said you'd be calling today or tomorrow. Thank you for being on the early end of the range. I've been on pins and needles all day."

"Sorry to have made you wait." He paused for a moment. "I've finished reviewing the materials you sent. Have there been any follow-up calls from the police, or any other articles in the newspapers there in Lincoln since you submitted your application?"

"No calls, no articles that I've seen lately. I called Detective Coutinho to let him know that I was contacting the Foundation, but I had to leave a message for him. I'm sure there's plenty in his file that he didn't let me see."

"I'll give him a call and let him know we're on the case at your request, see if I can schedule a time to sit down with him."

"He's been very kind through all this. I'm sure he'll be happy to work with you. Will you stop in here while you're in Lincoln?"

"I'd like to do that. I'd like to know more about your husband."

"He was a really nice man, Agent DelVecchio."

"I'm not an agent, Mrs. Walker." He thought it over for a moment, realized he wasn't sure what his title was. Detective? Just plain Mister? Sam?

"Thanks. I'll wait to hear from you."

He hung up, still wondering if, as a private detective, he should call himself detective. He chided himself for getting hung up on something so inconsequential and searched his notes for Christopher Coutinho's phone number at the Lincoln PD.

The call was answered on the second ring.

"Coutinho."

"Detective, this is Sam DelVecchio. I'm with the Mercy Street Foundation."

"Who?"

Sam started over.

"Mercy Street," the detective muttered. "That thing on TV?"

"You might have seen something on television, but—"

"Big money guy fronting some private agency?"

"That's the general idea, yes. We've been asked to

look into a case that I understand you handled last year. Ross Walker."

"Walker, yeah." Coutinho paused. "What's your involvement?"

"His widow applied to the Foundation, asked us to take a look."

"You mean, see if you can solve the case for us." The detective's voice developed a sudden edge. "Thanks a lot. We sure appreciate it. Since, you know, we're basically incompetent."

Sam sighed. He'd expected it.

"Look, here's the thing," Sam said. "It's not a reflection on you. But we both know that when a case goes cold, when the evidence isn't there and there are no leads and no suspects, it takes a hell of a lot of digging to find even one thread to tug on. If you had nothing else to do, no other cases to deal with, you'd probably find that thread, if in fact there's a thread to be found. But you don't have the luxury of handling one case at a time for however long it takes. I do."

Sam let that sink in before adding, "Mrs. Walker came to us, Detective. We didn't go looking for this case."

Coutinho fell silent for a few moments, then said, "I appreciate you not rubbing it in that we weren't able to solve the case. It's been on my mind since the minute I walked onto that crime scene."

"Let's get something out of the way right up front. I'm not looking at this case as one you 'weren't able to solve,'" Sam said. "I know that if we are going to make any headway at all with this, it will only be because of the work you did when you caught the call, so let's look at this as a sort of collaboration."

"Do you have any idea of just how patronizing that sounded?"

"Yeah, well, it is what it is. I'm sure you guys did a bang-up investigation."

"You know this how?"

"You got a do-gooder found behind a soup kitchen with a burger stuffed in his mouth, his chest slashed up, someone is going to want some answers. Everyone's going to be on their best behavior because the case is going to have a profile. The heat would be on you on a case like this."

"You got that much right."

"So let's stop the bullshit, and talk about the case."

Coutinho's manner changed and he became all business.

"A call came in around eleven on a Tuesday night. Woman said her husband was missing, that they'd put a few hours in at the mission down on Fourth Street, Pilgrim's Place. Said she and her husband were volunteers who cooked and served dinner there every Tuesday night, that they usually finished up around ten thirty, but that night, she realized sometime around nine forty-five that it had been a while since she'd seen him. At first, she figured he'd stepped outside to talk to someone and lost track of time—she said he's a talker—or maybe he was in the men's room. So they start cleaning up and she asks the others if anyone knew where he was, and no one did. No one could recall the last time they'd seen him. So she's getting worried and she calls his cell phone, but there's no answer. So she waits a few minutes more, then calls again. Still no answer. Finally the kitchen cleanup is done, the others are getting ready to leave, and he still hasn't turned up. They search the house, inside and out, and even go out to the street to see if he's out there chatting, but he was nowhere to be found."

"Could I see the statements you took from the people who were there that night?"

"Yeah. There's not much substance. I mean, they serve a couple hundred people there every week, so during mealtime, it's pretty hectic. No one has time to look around to see who's doing what. They're understaffed and the kitchen is laid out in a sort of L-shape, so you can't see who's working there with you. Ross Walker could have walked out the back door at any time and no one would have known, but sure, you can take a look."

"Who responded to the initial call?"

"Couple of cruisers. They finally convinced Mrs. Walker to go on home, that maybe her husband ran into an old friend or for whatever reason needed to be alone. Both officers said their first thought was that he might have sneaked out to hook up with a girl-friend and things got carried away, but they weren't about to say that to the wife. She went home around midnight, but called back in around three, and then again at six. By this time, she was hysterical, said she knew something terrible had happened to him. Another car went back to the mission and the officers searched the place from stem to stern without finding a thing. But after the breakfast shift, one of the volunteers took a bag of trash out to the Dumpster, and found Walker slumped behind it on the ground, between the Dumpster and the fence."

"I'd like to see the crime-scene photos if possible."

"I can email some of them to you."

"Hold on for just a minute." Sam put the phone down and went into the hall, counted doors until he found the one he believed to be Mallory's. He stuck his head in and said, "I need an email address."

She recited the address they'd set up for him without looking up from the file she was reading. "Sorry. I meant to give you that earlier. I'm assuming you found your laptop on your desk?"

"I did. Thanks." He hurried back to his office and repeated the address for Coutinho as he opened the laptop and booted up.

A minute later the email appeared, the photos attached. He opened the document and studied each one carefully.

"Sam?" Coutinho said after several minutes had passed in silence.

"Yeah. I'm here."

"Sorry, I don't know what else to call you."

"Sam is fine," he said somewhat absently, the photos of Ross Walker drawing all his attention.

He went through them, one by one. "No suspects?" he asked when he reached the last one.

"We had a few of the usuals. The lowlifes that you bring in from time to time then have to let back out on the streets, but you know it's only a matter of time before they're back in for something big? You know the ones I'm talking about?"

"All too well. None of them panned out?"

"They were all someplace else doing other things with other people."

Sam ran through the photos again, the detective waiting patiently on the line for him to finish.

"I thought it was real odd that the cause of death is listed as strangulation when you have all that carnage," Coutinho said. "The ME said the guy had been strangled before any of the slashing took place."

"All the blood at the scene, the vic was killed right there. So what are you thinking? That the killer was waiting out back for Walker to come out?" Sam frowned, trying to see it in his mind.

"Basically, yeah, that's pretty much the way I see it. There's only one light out back there, over the door. So Walker steps out into the dimly lit area, walks back to the Dumpster, and he's brought down, strangled manually—there were no ligature marks on the neck, did you notice that? Then the killer drags him behind the Dumpster, stabs him, stuffs the burger in his mouth, and takes off."

"He's gotta be covered with blood," Sam murmured.

"Yeah, you'd think, but there were no drops of blood leading from the alley."

"So maybe he brought a bag or something with a change of clothes in it."

"That's what I figured. At least, he'd have had another shirt to change into." Coutinho paused. "But what we couldn't figure out is why all the drama with the knife if he was going to strangle the guy."

"He was blowing off steam. He wanted the guy dead quickly and quietly, so he takes him out immediately. Then he gets to take his time, do what makes him happy, make his statement."

"You think this was his way of making a statement?" the detective asked flatly.

"Yeah. I do."

"What's he saying?"

"When I figure that out, you'll be the first to know."

"We figure this was real personal, that the killer knew Walker, had some beef with him, knew his routine, knew where he'd be at that time on that night. He's all prepared, right down to the change of clothes 'cause he knew it was going to be messy."

"That would have taken a lot of planning, which would take it out of the realm of a random killing. The body was left where it would be found quickly, but not too quickly, so the killer has time to slip away. It could suggest a crime of retaliation, or revenge, but what do you suppose is up with the burger?"

"Maybe the hamburger has something to do with the fact that Walker was there at the mission serving food?"

"Hard to tie that to a possible revenge motive though. And revenge leads to the question, what did Ross Walker do to deserve this kind of retribution?"

"The wife says he has no enemies. The other volunteers and his coworkers all said the same thing. Everyone we talked to had only good things to say about him. Nicest guy in the world, wouldn't hurt a fly. Loved by one and all."

"All but one, apparently." Sam thought it over, then added, "Assuming that you're right, that this is personal, that it's revenge for something."

"What else could it be?"

"Not sure. Revenge is the obvious. But I've been around too long to believe that everything is always the way it seems."

"What else could it be? The attack after the guy

was already dead makes it appear personal to me," Coutinho said, somewhat defensively. "The killer went there prepared to kill Walker, and he did just that. Why would you think there's another explanation?"

"Something just doesn't feel right to me. If this is payback, why the burger?"

"I don't know, maybe burgers were on the menu that night. We can check on that. But like I just said, the guy was already dead," the detective said pointedly and with no lack of exasperation. "He wasn't eating that burger."

"That's my point." Sam thought it through. "The burger is part of the message."

"So you're saying the stab wounds aren't important?"

"Oh, they're important, all right. Everything about this murder tells us something important. The over-the-top number of stab wounds tells us the killer was angry, either at Walker or someone else. But the posing of the body, the food stuffed in the mouth . . . that's a part of the story, too. We just need to piece it all together."

"You have a lot of experience with this sort of thing?"

"Some."

"What did you do before you were a PI? Were you on the job someplace?"

"I was with the FBI."

There was another pause, then Coutinho asked, "Special agent?"

"Yeah." Sam debated, then added, "BAU."

"That's that behavior analysis stuff, right?"

"Yes."

"You one of those profilers, like we see on TV all the time?"

"Nothing like what you see on TV," Sam told him. "Nothing at all like what's on TV."

"But you do that, right, analyze behavior and see if you can figure out who the killer is from that?"

"That's the short version. It's more than that. You look at the crime scene, try to interpret the killer's behavior before and after the crime, try to read the evidence he leaves you."

"So you think you can figure out what motivated this guy?"

"It's tough to do that with one victim, Detective, you know that. And there's the conflict for us, right? On the one hand, you're hoping that this guy has done what he set out to do—exact revenge, settle a score, whatever—and that he won't repeat. On the other hand, with a series of victims, you see a pattern, you develop a sense of what the killer is after, what he wants."

"His statement, like you said before."

"Exactly," Sam agreed. "So while it's tougher to get a handle on the killer where you have so little evidence, you really hope that it was one and done for him. Right now, all we know is that we're most likely looking for a man because it would have taken a lot of strength to overpower Ross Walker, who, from the reports, was a big man."

"A little over six feet, about two hundred pounds," Coutinho confirmed.

"So we're looking for someone with size and strength of his own. Someone organized enough to have researched where and when to find his victim and brought with him everything that he needed, took everything away with him when he left."

"You coming out here any time soon, Sam?"

"I'd like to get out there as soon as possible. Ideally by tomorrow or Wednesday." Sam wondered how the Foundation handled travel arrangements.

"Give me a call and let me know when you're coming. I'll have a copy of the file and all the statements we took ready for you."

"Great. Thanks. I'll be back in touch." Sam hung up, and headed off to Mallory's office once again to find out how he should go about getting approval for a flight to Lincoln, Nebraska, and wondering what he'd find once he got there.

FIVE

Sam's travel arrangements had been amazingly smooth and easy. Robert had a plane that he'd authorized to be used for the Mercy Street investigators, and Mallory took care of everything. At seven AM on Wednesday morning, Sam arrived at the local airstrip where the plane was housed. He parked his car in the lot and walked around the hangar and out onto the tarmac where he looked around. There were three planes that looked as if they were getting ready to go somewhere.

He walked to the closest one and asked the mechanic who was just coming down the steps if he knew which plane belonged to Robert Magellan. He was pointed to the first one in line—a trim Cessna Citation. At the top of the steps, Sam poked his head inside and called, "Hello?"

A trim woman in her midfifties came out of the cockpit.

"Can I help you?" She leaned against the doorframe and tucked a strand of auburn hair behind one ear.

"I was looking for the pilot," Sam told her.

"You've found her."

"Oh." Sam realized that his facial expression must be registering his surprise, and he tried to cover it up. "Great. Nice to meet you. I'm—"

"Sam DelVecchio. Yes, Mallory told me to expect you. I'm just about ready to take off. You can take a seat and get comfortable." She gestured to the passenger section.

He dropped his briefcase on one of the chairs. "I didn't catch your name."

"Delilah McCabe." She smiled but didn't offer her hand. "We're scheduled to take off at seven thirty and I make it a point to always leave on time. So if you'll excuse me . . ."

"Oh, sure. Right. Go ahead and do whatever—"

"Just need to check with the mechanic."

She disappeared through the doorway and Sam glanced around the interior of the small plane. With seating for seven passengers, the aisle was narrow, and he had to hunch his six-foot, three-inch frame in order to move to the front of the plane. He took the seat closest to the cockpit and laid his jacket across the seat next to him. He was wishing he'd brought along something to read other than his file notes when Delilah reentered the plane.

"All set?" she asked.

"Any time you are," Sam replied.

"I'd invite you to come up front and sit with me," she told him as she walked to the front of the plane, "but I don't like to talk to anyone when I'm flying. I find it distracting."

"Right. We don't need a distracted pilot."

She laughed and went into the cockpit, and prepared for takeoff.

The flight took much less time than he'd anticipated. By two in the afternoon, Sam was seated in the office of Detective Christopher Coutinho, going over statements given by the witnesses interviewed by the Lincoln police.

"Like I said," Coutinho told him after he'd gone through nine of the fifteen statements, "no one saw anything."

"I guess it would help me to understand that better if I could see the crime scene," Sam said. "Can you give me directions from here? I'll stop there on my way over to see Lynne Walker."

"I'll drive you. It'll be easier for you to get around. I don't expect your rental car came with GPS?"

"Actually, it did. And I went to college in Lincoln, though it's been a while since I've been here. But I'll take you up on the company." Years in the Bureau had taught Sam to take advantage of any hospitality offered by the locals. Besides, he knew the more time he spent with the lead investigator on the case, the more he'd learn.

"Good. We can get started then, unless there's something else you need to see in the file?"

"I would like to see the rest of the photos of the crime scene."

"Oh. Sure. I didn't email them all because there are too many." The detective sorted through the file until he found a large, thick, brown envelope. "These aren't pretty, but I guess pretty isn't really an option when it comes to cases like this."

Coutinho slid the photos from the envelope and turned them around so that they faced Sam, who studied each one, from the pictures of the kitchen and the back doorway, to the last close-ups of the dark line that ran across the victim's throat and the burger that was half in, half out of his mouth.

"The burger was from a chain, as you can see from the paper it's still wrapped in," Coutinho pointed out. "Of course, we checked with every location in the city, but there were over a hundred of these things sold that night between the hours of six and nine thirty PM, which is when the ME thinks the murder occurred."

Sam studied the photos one by one. "And since we're dealing with an international chain, there's no point in trying to analyze the contents, because all the food is premade before it gets to the restaurant. Gotta love that prefab fast food."

"No fingerprints, by the way. There was some trace collected—some skin cells from under the victim's fingernails and some hair from the front of his shirt. The results from the lab didn't match up with the DNA we have from everyone he worked with that night, and there was no hit in the database."

"You got people to volunteer DNA samples?"

"Yes. There was no problem getting them to swab. Usually you have to beg, but this time they all stepped up to the plate. Said they wanted to eliminate the time we'd waste trying to make one of them fit as a suspect."

"And no one refused?" Sam asked.

"Not a one."

Sam stared at a photo of Ross Walker. "As we discussed on the phone, this was well planned, well thought out. It took time to set this up. It's hard to imagine someone from the mission following Walker outside, strangling him, stabbing him, changing his clothes, and then walking back into the kitchen again without anyone noticing the blood on his arms and face." He looked up at Coutinho. "The killer would have had a tough time getting rid of all the blood while he was at the scene, but if he left by the back alley, as he most likely did, it would have been dark enough that anyone seeing him from a distance wouldn't have seen any blood he still had on him."

"We've spoken with Walker's neighbors, with his coworkers, his family. From every account, he was a real family man. Rock of the community, devoted to his wife. Volunteered at the mission's soup kitchen as soon as it opened, coached Little League soccer and softball. Like I said, no one knows anyone who'd want to hurt him." Coutinho stood and folded the file. "We've talked to our CIs on the street, we've talked to everyone we could think of who has their ear to the ground out there. No one's heard anything about Walker. There aren't even any rumors."

"How dependable are your informants?"

"About as dependable as everyone else's," admitted the detective. "But it's unusual for no one to have heard anything. You can usually count on someone hearing at least one rumor, even if it doesn't pan out. This time, nothing, which tells me that the killer wasn't one of the usual suspects."

"Have you seen anything like this MO before?"

Coutinho shook his head. "Never."

"Did a report go in to VICAP?" Sam asked.

"Yeah, but it got in a little late."

"How come?"

"Someone thought someone else was entering the data, while someone else thought the other guy had done it." Coutinho shrugged. "It happens."

"I'd be real surprised if this guy hasn't killed before," Sam said, almost as if thinking aloud. "He was really organized, really sure of himself. First-timers are usually nervous, they screw up somewhere. I don't see any screwups here. I see someone who knew exactly what he wanted to do, and did it without leaving anything behind that would lead you to him. I think the burger in the mouth is important. It's something he didn't need to do in order to commit the crime. I think he's done this at least a time or two before."

"So you're saying this was the work of a serial killer?" Coutinho frowned.

"Not in the classic sense." Sam explained, "Very often serial murders have a sexual undertone. I don't see that here. There was no assault, and no evidence of any sexual activity on or near the body, right? No semen found?"

"Right. Nothing like that."

"So you don't have that motivation, you don't have that element of fantasy you so often see in serial crimes. But you do have other elements—again, the hamburger, for example—that makes you think there's something more here than a simple murder." Sam reflected on his words for a moment. "Not that murder is ever simple."

"So you think there are other victims somewhere with hamburgers shoved in their mouths?"

"Maybe. But I guess if there were similar cases in the system, you'd have heard from the FBI by now."

"Oh. We did."

"You did?" Sam's eyebrows rose. "When? Who called?"

"About a month ago, I guess. I don't know the name of the agent. Wanted to look over the file."

"You have the agent's card?"

"No. I wasn't here to take the call. My dad died and I was in St. Louis for about a week, helping my mom tie up some loose ends."

"I'm sorry about your father." Sam waited what he considered a respectful amount of time before asking, "Who did the agent talk to, do you know?"

"One of the other detectives. Reid, I think."

"Is he in?"

"Not till tonight."

"Would you ask him to call me with the name of the agent?" Sam was curious. Sooner or later, he'd have to deal with whoever the agent was. He hoped it was someone he knew well and trusted.

"Sure. If you're ready, let's take that ride."

The ride through Lincoln was a step back in time for Sam, who figured out he'd attended two reunions, both of them within the first ten years of graduating. After a while, it just hadn't seemed so important, when there was so much going on in his life. Starting his career, meeting and falling in love with Carly. Marrying her. Losing her . . .

"How 'bout we stop by Pilgrim's Place first?" Coutinho asked. "It's not far from here. Couple blocks down."

"Sure."

Three minutes later, Coutinho pulled his unmarked car up in front of the building from which several hundred hungry people were fed every week. Pilgrim's Place sat in the middle of a row of two-story wooden storefronts, its name painted in red on the glass windows with plain white drapes hanging behind them. The store to the left was unoccupied, and the one to the right had a sign that read SORRY, WE ARE CLOSED.

"The alley runs behind all the buildings?" Sam got out of the car and looked around.

"Yes. But we weren't able to find anyone who was in the alley that night. There's not a whole lot going on down here at night, and by the time Mrs. Walker realized her husband was missing, any place that had been open had already closed up."

Sam followed the detective through the front door. Inside, long tables covered with sheets of white paper lined the room. A man in late middle age came out of the kitchen. He was tall and thin with sparse white hair atop a broad forehead and a bland round face.

He stopped halfway across the room, a smile spreading slowly. "Hey, Detective Coutinho. How are you?"

"Good, good, Bob. How's everything?"

"We're okay." The man's face clouded. "You here to give us some news about Ross?"

Coutinho shook his head. "Sorry. There's been

nothing new." He gestured in Sam's direction and said, "Bob, this is Sam. He's a private detective who's working for Mrs. Walker. Sam, this is Bob Taylor. He runs Pilgrim's Place."

"You think you can find the guy who did Ross when the police couldn't?" Bob asked somewhat skeptically.

"I'm only going to be working on this one case," Sam explained. "Detective Coutinho doesn't have that luxury. So no promises, but I'm going to give it a go."

"Anything we can do to help. Ross was a good man." Bob's head nodded up and down. "A damned good man. Didn't miss a Tuesday night in over three years."

"Ross volunteered here for the past three years?" Sam tried for a conversational tone.

"He was one of the first to sign up. Wondered why a guy like him—good family, lived in one of those nice areas outside of town, had a real good job—why he would leave that nice house and that pretty family to drive down here."

"You ever ask him?"

"Said he'd been really lucky in his life, that any one of these guys, that could be him. Never wanted to take his good fortune for granted." Bob nodded again. "Like I said, he was a good man."

Sam glanced around the room. "This is where you feed everyone?"

"Yeah. Anyone who comes in, we'll feed. No one is ever turned away from Pilgrim's Place."

"You have a pretty regular crowd?"

"Oh, yeah. Times have been tough here for the past few years for some folks. We do have some who have been coming steadily, practically since we opened. Others have been able to move on."

"So you know most of the people who come in?" Sam asked.

"Most of them, sure. Sometimes we get someone who's just passing through, but for the most part, we recognize or know the names of just about everyone who shows up."

"How many each day?"

"Maybe forty for breakfast—we got families bringing their kids in every morning—then about the same for lunch. The older kids are in school but the adults who show up for lunch often aren't here earlier in the morning. Dinner time, we can feed sixty to eighty on any given night. Sometimes last winter, we'd run close to one hundred on the weekends."

"Do you have anyone on the door, checking IDs, for example?"

"We do have someone at the door, but no one checks IDs. What would be the point in that?" Bob frowned, the idea clearly foreign to him.

Sam didn't bother to explain. "What does the person on the door do?"

"Just makes sure there's seating for everyone. If we're filled, he'll chat up the next person in line for a while until there's an opening. We don't turn anyone away, Sam."

"So your doorman would know if someone had come in the night Ross Walker was killed who hadn't been there before? Anyone who stood out, maybe a stranger?"

"We already talked about that, me and Arnie. He works the door. He said there wasn't nobody he didn't recognize. As a matter of fact, we were down in numbers that night. Anyone odd would have stood out." Bob turned to Coutinho, who stood by quietly. "You talked to Arnie yourself. He tell you anything different?"

"No." The detective shook his head. "I spoke at length with him about who was here and who came in when, when they left. It's all in the report, Sam. There's a copy in the file I gave you."

"Appreciate it." Sam turned back to Bob. "Mind if I take a look at the kitchen?"

"Right this way."

Bob led them through an open doorway into the back room, where two large stainless steel stoves stood side by side. Two refrigerators and one upright freezer took up most of the space on the opposite wall, and down the center of the room was a stainless steel counter. The room was, as Coutinho had told Sam, L-shaped, with oversized double sinks in the short leg of the L.

"What was Walker's job?" Sam asked.

"Everyone's job changes from night to night. The volunteers arrive, they look at the menu, see what has to be done, they'll just start to work. You come in first, you start the thing that takes the longest, see?"

"What did Walker work on that night?"

"He and Lynne were a little late that night, only maybe by ten minutes, but most of the entrée and dessert work had already been taken up by someone else. Ross started on the salad, washed up some veggies. I think we had squash that night. Someone brought in a basket of yellow and green from their garden. In the summer and late fall, we get a lot of donations from private gardens," Bob explained. "Lynne didn't cook that night. She served."

"Anyone working back here with him?"

"No. He worked pretty fast on his own."

"So no one noticed exactly when he went missing?" Sam continued.

"Everyone was doing their own thing. The best we can figure out, when he finished with the salad prep, he put it out on the counter here for the servers to take, and then he must have taken the bag of scraps out to the Dumpster."

"He always take out the trash?"

"No," Bob told Sam. "Everyone cleans up after themselves. If you have scraps or garbage, you take it out yourself. At the end of the night, everyone helps out with the general cleanup."

"The bag of scraps was found in the Dumpster," Coutinho added, "so we know he made it that far. We're thinking the killer was hidden behind it, waiting."

A flicker of a frown crossed Sam's face as he gestured to the back door. "I'm assuming this is the way?"

"Yeah. He would have gone out here . . ." Sam and the detective followed Bob through the door. "There's the Dumpster out there by the fence."

"That's where it was that night?"

"That's not the same Dumpster, but it's always in the same place, yeah."

"And the light there over the back door is the only light there is out here at night?"

"Yeah. It's only about seventy-five watts, I think." Bob pointed to the brass socket with the bare bulb.

"And nothing at all back there, by the Dumpster?"

"Nothing. It's really pretty dark out here at night. I mean, you can see the Dumpster, and make out where to toss stuff, but if someone was back there hiding, you wouldn't see them."

A worn dirt path ran through the yard of straggly grass dotted with dandelions and chickweed and led straight to the Dumpster, and Sam followed it. He turned to the detective and said, "Show me where you found Walker."

Coutinho walked around the back of the Dumpster and pointed to a section of fence. "He was here. Back against the fence, legs straight out in front of him. You saw the photos, so you know how he was posed."

Sam bit the inside of his cheek and scratched the back of his neck, looked back toward the house, then back at the Dumpster again.

"We might be wrong about something," he told the detective.

"What's that?"

"I'm not sure the killer came here looking for Walker. How could he have known that Walker would be coming out to the Dumpster that night, or that he'd be alone?"

"I thought we agreed that the nature of the attack, the preparedness of the killer, all indicated that this was personal, a revenge killing."

"Oh, it's personal," Sam told him. "Personal to the killer, but not to the victim. We know that he came totally prepared to kill that night, but he wouldn't have known who would be coming out here. I think what mattered was that he was able to kill that night in the manner he'd prepared for. I don't believe it mattered to him who his victim was."

"You think he would have killed whoever came out back?" Bob frowned.

Sam nodded. "Yes, I do."

"But why? You think this guy has an ax to grind with someone here?" Bob was clearly shaken and confused. "We do good things. We feed hungry people. That's all we do here. Why would someone want to hurt someone—anyone—here?"

"I can't answer that yet," Sam said.

"Yet?" Coutinho raised an eyebrow. "You think you will find the answer?"

"If I look in the right place, chances are I will."

"You sounded pretty sure of yourself back there," the detective said after they'd said their good-byes and were back in the car.

"It's all a matter of interpreting the evidence, of paying attention to what the killer is saying." Sam rolled down his window and rested his right arm. "And no, right now, I don't know what he's saying. Right now, I don't hear him at all."

"Well, you be sure to let me know when you do." Coutinho turned the key in the ignition. "What time is your appointment with Lynne Walker?"

Sam glanced at his watch. "In about ten minutes."

"You're going to be a little late."

They rode in silence for several minutes. Finally, "You have any ideas on why Pilgrim's Place?"

"No. It could be there's a connection to the killer. Like maybe he ate there on a regular basis at one time. Maybe someone there pissed him off." Sam sighed. "Or maybe this guy just got up that morning and said, 'I think I'll kill someone today' and went off looking for a place where he could find a victim."

Sam caught the sharp glance the detective gave him, so he added, "And no, I'm not being a smart-ass. I don't know why he did what he did because I don't know him."

There was another period of silence, during which Coutinho pulled up in front of a pale yellow bungalow and turned off the engine.

"Maybe I'll try looking at this from a different angle," he told Sam. "We've been looking for a connection between the killer and the victim. Maybe the connection is to the facility. Maybe we'll take another look at the regulars and the former regulars. Arnie can probably help me out there."

Sam nodded. "Sometimes you just have to step back and look at things from a different viewpoint. The bottom line is to find out what happened."

Sam got out of the car before the detective could respond. The front door of the house opened, and a woman in her midforties stood on the top step. As the two men approached, the woman extended her hand first to Coutinho.

"Chris, it's good to see you again."

To Sam, she said, "Detective DelVecchio. I'm happy to meet you."

Sam took her hand and noticed that it trembled. He figured it had to be hard for her to be still dealing with the details of her husband's death, all the questions and no answers. He hoped to make this as quick and painless as possible, but looking in her eyes, he realized that painless was a long shot. Quick was probably doable.

"The kids are all with their grandparents this week," she explained as she showed them into the living room. "When they're all here and they're loud and fighting, you wish for just a little bit of peace. Then they all leave at the same time, and the silence rips you apart."

She gestured for them to take seats on the sofa as she sat on a dark blue wing chair that looked as if it had survived several of those fights she'd mentioned.

"How many children do you have?" Sam asked, even though he knew there were four Walker offspring.

"Three boys and a girl. The youngest is eight. Ryan." She turned to the detective and added, "He was the one who answered the door the day you came to . . ."

"I remember."

"May I offer you anything . . ." she said. "Coffee?"

"Nothing, no thank you," Sam replied. "I just wanted to stop in to meet you while I'm here in Lincoln."

"Will you be going to Pilgrim's Place?"

"We just came from there," he told her.

"Ross and I used to look forward to our Tuesday nights there. Now I can't even drive into that part of town without getting an anxiety attack." Lynne Walker shook her head from side to side. "I don't understand it. I will never understand it. My husband was a good man. A great father, a wonderful husband. How someone could hate him enough to do this terrible thing . . ."

"I am very sorry for your loss, Mrs. Walker." Sam felt like a hypocrite uttering those clichéd words. After Carly's death, he'd heard that same phrase repeated over and over until he thought he'd punch the next person who uttered it, and now here he was, uttering those same words to someone else.

"Do you know what it's like to have someone you love murdered?" Lynne Walker's question took him completely offguard, and for a moment, he wasn't sure he'd heard her correctly, until she repeated it. That she was looking directly at Sam made it clear she was addressing him.

"Ahhh, actually, yes. Yes, I do, Mrs. Walker." He felt his skin flush red, and his throat began to close. He cleared it, then nodded slowly.

"May I ask . . . ?" She appeared as flustered at his response as he'd felt at the question. It was obvious she'd anticipated a "No."

"My wife." Sam could feel Chris Coutinho's eyes on him but couldn't bring himself to turn to look at the detective. Talking about himself had always made Sam feel vulnerable. Talking about Carly made him want to walk away.

"I'm so sorry." Lynne Walker reached out to him and squeezed his arm. "Do you have children?"

"No."

"How long has it been?"

Days. Hours. A lifetime. How do you measure the time between the last time you said good-bye and now?

"Three years." *Three years, two months and four days.*

"Ross has been gone almost half as long," she murmured. "Did they ever find your wife's killer?"

"Yes." He sat more stiffly than he'd like, but didn't seem able to relax. In the past, Sam had been spared direct dealings with the grieving families. He had rarely had to deal with the heartache, and was finding he wasn't very comfortable with this aspect of his new job. He had yet to become comfortable with his own heartache. "He's in prison appealing his death sentence."

"Then you understand completely," she said softly. "What it's like . . ."

"I do, yes." Sam tried to cut her off, afraid she'd keep talking about it. He didn't want to talk about his own loss. Right now, he wasn't sure he even wanted to talk about hers, but he had a job to do.

"I think it's even harder on the children. They really have no conception of good and evil, of life and death." She paused, as if reflecting. "I suppose that's no longer true. They understand now how quickly things can change."

"It's a tough lesson for anyone to learn," Sam told her.

"Indeed it is." Lynne Walker cleared her throat. "If I could think of anything that could help you, believe me, I'd do it. I lay awake at night, trying to think back on anyone who Ross might have had words with, or anyone who might have a reason to dislike him, but I swear, I can't think of a soul. He wasn't confrontational and he disliked conflict. Went out of his way to compromise and to avoid hurting anyone else's feelings. So I can't think of anyone."

Her eyes began to fill. "I've thought back to every single person I remember seeing at the mission, going as far back as the first week we were there. I can't think of one single instance where there was any kind of adversarial conversation that involved my husband, or one time when he had something negative to say about anyone." She looked at Sam and shrugged. "People liked Ross. They gravitated to him. I can't think of one single reason why someone would want to kill him."

"Sometimes there is no reason," Sam said softly.

Ross Walker's widow excused herself and left the room, returning with a tissue she used to blot under her eyes.

"I'm so sorry that you made the trip all the way out here and I haven't been able to tell you anything at all."

"Mrs. Walker, I didn't come here to question you," Sam told her. "I came to meet you. As a Mercy Street client, I just wanted you to know that we're going to do whatever we can. There are no guarantees . . ."

"Oh, I know that." She waved a hand impatiently. "I don't expect a miracle. But I saw Robert Magellan on TV and he was talking about how he was putting together this crack team of investigators and how it wouldn't cost anything if they picked your case, and I figured, what do I have to lose? I appreciate that someone there thought our case was worth looking into." She turned to Coutinho. "Chris, I know how hard you worked on this case. You've become almost like a member of the family. I need to know that you understand that my submitting Ross's case to Mercy Street didn't mean that I thought you didn't do your job."

"I understand completely, Mrs. Walker," the detective replied. "I'm really fine with your decision. I'd love to see the case solved, you know that. If Sam can do that, I'll be the first on the phone to congratulate him."

"Actually, Detective Coutinho hasn't completely abandoned the case," Sam interjected. "He is working with us to track down a few potential witnesses."

Lynne Walker smiled broadly. "Thank you, both of you. For the first time since this nightmare began, I feel hopeful that his killer might be found."

When Sam opened his mouth to remind her not to get her hopes up, she turned to him and said, "I know. I know it may never happen. But I feel that with all the attention being paid to his case, our odds are just that much better now."

On the way back to Coutinho's office where Sam would pick up his car, the detective asked, "Was that true? What you said back there about your wife?"

"Yeah."

"Damn, I'm sorry, man."

"Thanks." Sam stared out the window. After several miles had passed in silence, he said, "The guy who murdered Carly did it to prove to me that he could. No other reason. Just to prove that he could take her from me."

"Some old boyfriend or something?"

Sam shook his head. "A serial killer I was helping to track. He'd killed seven women, all the same way. I was in West Virginia at the funeral for number six when he came into my home in the middle of the night. By the time I got home, she'd been dead for over twenty-four hours."

"Jesus, that's rough." The detective shook his head as if shaking off a curse. "You said they caught the guy."

"Don Holland. He swears he didn't do it." Sam snorted. "He kills seven other women in exactly the same manner—admits to those, by the way—but swears he did not touch my wife. His fingerprints were all over my house, and he actually admitted he was there. But he swears that Carly wasn't there and that he never touched her."

"Why would he do that?" Coutinho wondered aloud. "You'd think it wouldn't matter at that point."

"At his trial, he swore that breaking into our home was just a lark. He just wanted to tweak my nose a bit. And of course, his wife swore he was with her the night Carly was murdered."

"Do you think she was in on the killing?"

"They both said no. Holland swore he acted alone and that she had no idea he was involved in such things."

"You don't sound convinced of her innocence."

"Every year, on the anniversary of Carly's death, I get a card from her. *How does it feel to know your wife's killer has gotten away with murder for—*then she fills in the number of years. Then she signs it. *Love, Laurie Heiss.*"

"What's the point in that?"

"I guess she wants to make sure I remember the date."

Coutinho looked at Sam across the console. "Like there's a chance you're going to forget."

"Yeah. Like there's a chance."

SIX

Sam sat on the edge of the bed in his hotel room and leaned forward to untie his shoes, when his phone rang. He got up and retrieved it from the pocket of his jacket, slung over the back of a chair.

"Sam, it's Chris Coutinho. I just got off the phone with Tom Reid, the detective who met with the FBI agent who was asking about the Walker case. He found the agent's card."

"Great. Who was it?"

"Fiona Summers."

Inwardly, Sam groaned. "Thanks, Chris."

"You want the number?"

"I know how to find her, thanks."

"Keep in touch, right?"

"You got it. And thanks again for taking me around yesterday."

"Don't mention it. You can return the favor if I ever get to . . . what's the name of that town you're in?"

"Conroy, Pennsylvania. About as big as it sounds. Trust me, it won't be a long tour."

The detective chuckled and hung up, and Sam immediately dialed another number. When the call was answered, Sam said, "Will, tell me that Fiona Summers is not as big a pain in the ass as everyone says she is."

"Fiona Summers is not as big a pain in the ass as everyone says she is," Will Fletcher, one of Sam's friends who was still with the FBI, repeated solemnly. He paused, then asked, "Who says she's a pain in the ass?"

"Everyone I know who's ever worked with her."

"Sam, are you back in the fold now? You've finished racing around the globe and you're back home, with the good guys, where you belong?"

"I'm back in the States and I've had enough traveling to last me a long, long time. I'll tell you about it sometime. But I'm not back with the Bureau."

"Damn. For a moment I thought . . . but then why ask about Fiona?"

Sam explained his new job and Fiona's potential involvement with his case.

"She won't be a problem," Will assured him. "She just runs a tight ship, that's all."

"That's the nicest thing I've ever heard anyone say about her."

"She can't be that bad. Miranda's worked with her and likes her. Want me to ask her?"

"If you wouldn't mind."

"Okay, hold on. Give me a minute to find her."

Sam heard Will's footsteps echoing off into the distance, then some muffled conversation, before a light and teasing voice picked up an extension.

"Is this *the* Sam DelVecchio? The tall, dark, and, well, you know . . ."

"Ah, the ever lovely Miranda." Sam smiled. He'd

always liked and respected his former fellow agent. "How are the wedding plans coming along?"

"They're coming along. Of course, the wedding is going to be quite the extravaganza, between Will's huge family and my father and all of his many families. Imagine the clash of cultures. But of course, we'll deal with them all with our usual grace and humor."

"I'm sure you will." Sam laughed, knowing both family histories: Will was one of nine children born into a very conservative family in Maine, and Miranda's father was an aging British rock star known for his many marriages and offspring.

"So what's this Will is telling me about you jumping ship for good and going off to work for some private detective agency?"

"All true. It was time for a change," he said simply.

"Do what you have to do, buddy," she replied. "But we do miss you. The new guy isn't as good as you were. Nor is he as much fun, either." Miranda paused, then added, "At least, that's what the other ladies are saying . . ."

Sam laughed again. "Speaking of the other ladies . . ."

"Right. Fiona Summers. Will said you might have a problem with her?"

"No, I don't have a problem. At least, not yet. I'm working my first case for the Foundation, and it appears she's been making inquiries about it, picked it up from one of the databases. I'm thinking she must have something she thinks could be related, or at least something similar enough for her to have taken notice."

"So?"

"So I was just wondering how much they say about her is true, that's all. I figured I'd call you guys, because between the two of you, you've worked with just about everyone."

"Sad but true. Tell me what you've heard about Fiona."

"I heard she always thinks she's right and that she's a pain in the ass."

"Well, the part about her being right most of the time is probably true," Miranda said. "She has uncanny instincts and is not afraid of following them. And when she thinks she's right, it's pretty hard to dissuade her. But does that make her a pain in the ass? I suppose it does, if you're the type who also believes you're always right. But, wait . . . that would mean one of you would be wrong. And when it comes to Fiona, it's usually the other person who's off base. I'd say her batting average is unusually high."

"Will said you've worked with her."

"Many cases over many years. And yes, I do think she's that good, and no, I didn't think she was a pain in the ass. But then again, I don't always think I'm right."

"That helps."

"Fiona is a very self-assured woman, Sam. She knows her stuff and she takes her job very, very seriously. It's probably the most important thing in her life." She paused, as if thinking. "Actually, I believe it *is* the most important thing in her life."

"I'd heard that, too."

"Anything else?"

"That she's great to look at but has no sense of humor."

"Not true. Well, she is great to look at, but the humor thing? Definitely not true. She just doesn't joke around on the job like some of the yahoos do."

"Are you calling me a yahoo?" Sam pretended to sound wounded.

"Does the shoe fit?"

"I guess sometimes it does." Sam had to admit to his own share of gallows humor from time to time. "Thanks, Miranda. I appreciate your insights."

"So when are you going to invite us over to watch the home movies you took while you were on vacation?"

"You're welcome anytime. Of course, for at least the next six weeks, home for me is going to be in a hotel in a little town in Pennsylvania, but if you feel like making the drive, I'll provide the entertainment."

"We'll see if we can fit in a road trip," she told him. A moment later, she asked, "Sam, how are you doing?"

"I'm doing a lot better. I think getting away for a while was the right thing to do. Just like I think staying away is probably good for me, too."

"I understand." Miranda sighed. "Just know that you can always come back, if you need to. Or want to. Your friends love and miss you. We're always here for you."

"You have been, and I thank you. Both of you." Sam swallowed hard. "All of you."

"That's why we have friends, Sam. To be there when we need a little boost. And sooner or later, we all do. Now, do you want Will again, or are you good for now?"

"I'm good, Miranda. Thanks. And thank Will for me."

"I'll do that. And don't be afraid of Fiona."

"Afraid? Who said anything about being afraid . . . ?" Sam frowned, about to launch a protest, but Miranda had already hung up.

SEVEN

Photographs from three different crime scenes stood on the kitchen counter, propped up against pretty ceramic canisters with a French country theme—all empty. Flour? Fiona Summers had never baked in her life. Coffee? Best as takeout, normally on the fly. Tea? Too reminiscent of genteel ladies seated in comfy chairs before a roaring fire, chatting quietly, or at a table near a window on a snowy day enjoying a book of poems—neither a comfortable fit for Fiona. The canisters had been a housewarming gift from Fiona's well-meaning sister who obviously failed to take into consideration the living habits of the twelve-year veteran of the FBI.

Fiona leaned her elbow on the counter, her chin resting in her palm, as she studied the photos before reaching forward to place them in order of date.

Photo number one: Ross Walker, age forty-three, construction supervisor from Lincoln, Nebraska. Cause of death: manual strangulation. Numerous postmortem stab wounds to the torso made with a one-and-one-quarter-inch blade. Hamburger from a popular fast food restaurant crammed into his mouth, the wrapping partially peeled back. Date of death: February 10, 2008. Day of the week: Tuesday. Body found propped against a fence behind Pilgrim's Place, a soup kitchen/mission. Status of investigation: open.

Photo number two: Joseph Edward Maynard, age twenty-two, student at Purdue, home for the summer in Kendall, Illinois. Cause of death: manual strangulation. Numerous postmortem stab wounds to the torso made with a one-and-one-quarter-inch blade. Nothing inserted into mouth. Date of death: August 15, 2008. Day of the week: Friday. Victim found in makeshift cardboard shelter under a bridge. Status of investigation: open.

Photo number three: Calvin Adams, age sixty-two, homeless from Dutton, Nebraska. Cause of death: manual strangulation. Numerous postmortem stab wounds to the torso made with a one-and-one-quarter-inch blade. Empty water bottle upright in the victim's mouth. Date of death: February 9, 2009. Day of the week: Monday. Body found on park bench as if sleeping. Status of investigation: open.

There were unmistakable similarities, and yet the victims could not have been more different. Walker was Caucasian, in early middle age, blue collar, married with three kids, pillar of the community type. Adams was a homeless man who'd been on the streets for over fifteen years and had a severe mental disorder exacerbated by his drug usage. Maynard was a blue blood with a trust fund worth many times what Fiona could expect to earn over the course of her employment with the Bureau.

She turned on the small microphone she held in her

left hand to record her thoughts. "Victim selection appears to have been random. All in the Midwest, though. That might mean something. Killer could be from that area, now or at some time in the past. MO is identical. There's a signature but I'm not sure how to interpret it—victims one and three had something placed in their mouths, though victim two did not. The staging of victim two, on the other hand, appears totally out of sync with the victim's lifestyle. All victims were posed—I'm sure that means something but it's lost on me."

She turned off the recorder for a moment while she tried to think of what might have possibly lured Maynard under the bridge. Drugs? A girl? Unlikely. Maynard had no history of drug use and no drugs had been found in his system. As for girls, Fiona suspected that any girls Joseph Maynard may have been interested in—paid or unpaid—would not have been the type to spend time under a bridge.

"The victims would appear to have little in common other than the manner of their deaths. Oh, and the fact that two of the three—Walker and Maynard—had fought back hard enough to have gouged some skin from their attacker."

She stopped the recording again and made a note on one of the cards stacked neatly on the counter.

Run MO and DNA profiles through all databases again for possible match and/or possible recent victim.

"The murders were five to six months apart. Is there significance to the timeline?" she resumed. "The key to these killings appears to be in the props: the burger, the cardboard house that was erected around Maynard's corpse, the water bottle. Things brought in from somewhere else presumably by the killer. All three homicides took place in situ."

She clicked off the microphone. There was no doubt in her mind that there was one killer; that had been confirmed when the DNA profiles of the skin found beneath the victims' nails had matched. It vexed her to know that she'd been unable to interpret the message the killer was sending and for whom it was intended. She'd seen cases where serial killers had left a trail or message specifically for the police, or the FBI, but in all those cases, the killer had contacted the target agency and let them know he was talking to them. Not so in this case. In all three cases, there'd been no contact with anyone. Maddening.

Fiona took off her glasses and rubbed first her eyes and then her temples. She was bone tired, after having spent the last three days and two sleepless nights in Dutton gathering information on Calvin Adams, but for Fiona, fatigue was welcomed. It was her guarantee of a decent night's sleep. She was packing up her photos when the phone rang.

"This is Sam DelVecchio," a deep male voice announced. "I'm trying to get in touch with Fiona Summers."

"This is Fiona." She frowned.

"Agent Summers, I used to be with the Bureau, and now—"

"I know who you are." Didn't all the single—and some not-so-single—women at the Bureau know who Sam DelVecchio was? And didn't every one of them know his sad story and long to comfort him? "How did you get this number?"

"From Miranda Cahill." He paused. "I hope that was all right?"

"I guess it depends on why you're calling. If you're going to try to sell me something, then no, it's not all right," she said drolly.

"I'm not selling anything."

Fiona rolled her eyes. Had he really thought she'd been serious?

"I wanted to talk about a case I'm handling for the Mercy Street Foundation."

"Who?"

"My new employer."

"Right. I did hear that you had resigned. Weren't you on a trip or something? Extended vacation?"

"Yeah, but I came back and realized I needed a job." He explained to her the way the Foundation worked.

When he finished, she said, "So what's the case you're handling for them, and what does it have to do with me at"—she glanced at the clock on her oven for the time—"eleven thirty at night."

"Oh. Sorry. I didn't realize how late it had gotten. I apologize."

"Accepted." Fiona stifled a yawn. "So what's the case?"

"My case involves a homicide in Lincoln, Nebraska, over a year ago. Volunteer at a soup kitchen found behind the building—"

"Ross Walker?" She snapped to attention. "Are you talking about Ross Walker?"

"Yes."

"Explain to me how that is your case?"

"The victim's widow requested that the Foundation become involved."

"I'm afraid you're going to have to become uninvolved. This case is part of a federal investigation."

"Well, now it's also a private investigation," he told her.

"I'm sorry, Sam, but you're going to have to back off."

"I can't do that. We have a contract with Lynne Walker."

Fiona fell silent. "What exactly is the nature of your investigation?"

"Same as any investigation. We're trying to get to the bottom of Walker's death." He cleared his throat, then asked, "This case is obviously connected to others. How many others?"

"What makes you think that there are others?" she asked guardedly.

"Fiona. You just said the case is part of an FBI investigation. *Part* implies one of several making up the *whole*. So what does it hurt to have me working one part?"

"Until I have a handle on this, I don't want anyone else involved." She bit her bottom lip. "I prefer to work alone, frankly."

"Well, we have that much in common."

When she didn't respond, Sam's voice softened. "Come on, Fiona. It's no skin off your back to be nice to me. Maybe I have some information that might help you with your case."

"Do you?"

"Not yet, but I will. I'm good at what I do."

"So am I."

"So maybe we'll be even better if we share what we have. What we might have in the future."

"What exactly do you want?"

"I want to know about the other cases. How many. Where. If the victims fit a profile."

"I can tell you right now, they do not." She reached into the envelope where she'd tucked the photos of the three victims and dumped them onto the counter. The lifeless eyes of Ross Walker stared blankly back at her. "As a matter of fact, I was just looking over the three cases, trying to figure out what I'm missing. Why I can't get a handle on it."

"Three? All male?"

She hesitated. There really was no good reason to cooperate with a private detective. Then again, this PI had the reputation of being one of the best profilers the Bureau had had, and she could use his insight. Add that to the fact that if he went to John Mancini, his former and her current boss, John would probably side with Sam and tell her to talk to him anyway. Might as well cut out the middleman.

"Three," she told him. "Different ages, socioeconomics, you name it. They have nothing in common except the manner in which they died."

"Can I meet you somewhere, Fiona? Can I see your files? Can we talk about this?" Sam sounded excited in a way that she, herself, could relate to. Nothing got her going like the nuts and bolts of a case.

"Where are you?"

"I'm about seventy miles from Philadelphia."

"I need to be in Philly first thing on Monday on another matter. I was planning on driving up on Sunday. Maybe I could meet you someplace . . ."

"I can meet you in a restaurant partway between here and Philly, if you like. There's a diner out on Route 30 . . ."

"If you're thinking of looking at these photos—and you are going to want to do that, side by side—you're going to want to do that in private. These are not pictures you want John Q. Public getting a glance at over his meat loaf and mashed potatoes. Maybe I should meet you at your office."

"I'm not sure what goes on around here on Sundays. I've only been here for a week. Our offices are in Robert Magellan's house," he explained.

"You work in Robert Magellan's house? Is it fabulous? What's he like?"

"Why, Fiona, you sound like a fan."

She laughed. "I suppose I do. Sorry. It's just that he's such an enigmatic figure."

"So enigmatic that I haven't even met him yet," Sam admitted. "He's been away, working with a search group to look for his son. I guess you've heard about that."

"I have. Crazy business, finding the car with the remains of the wife, and no trace of the baby. I'm sure he's going out of his mind, trying to find his son. I'm surprised he doesn't have you working on that case for him."

"One of the investigators is with him. He has a team of local volunteers combing the woods and the ravine where the car was found. Whether the boy is dead or alive, the word around the Foundation is that he will keep looking until he finds out what happened."

"I hope he does. Anyway, about Sunday . . ."

"I'll check on the protocol for meetings on Sundays, and I'll get back to you."

"I'll wait to hear from you." She hung up the phone and tucked the photos back into their envelope. As hard as it was going to be for her to share, it would be worth it if Sam lived up to his reputation and gave her some insights into the killer she was determined to find.

She turned off the kitchen light, and yawning, climbed the stairs to the second floor, and the bed she hadn't slept in for the past two nights.

EIGHT

Susanna Jones sat on the trunk of a fallen tree and held her head in her hands. It was almost four o'clock in the afternoon and she and the other searchers had walked every inch of today's grid three ways from Sunday and hadn't found a clue to what might have happened to Ian Magellan. Once the local police had released the crime scene—the area where Beth Magellan's car and remains had been found—Robert had organized a group of local citizens who'd been eager to help look for the missing child. They'd been at it now for three days, and Susanna's head, feet, and back hurt, although perhaps not as much as her heart.

The crunch of hiking boots on the forest floor drew her attention, and she looked up to see a very solemn Robert coming into the clearing. He held a bottle of water out to her, and she took it gratefully.

"You about ready to turn in for today?" he asked.

"I am if you are."

"We still have a few more hours of daylight." He looked around. "We could make the grid for tomorrow's walk."

"All right." She tried her best not to sigh. She wanted to be upbeat for his sake, wanted to be positive, but she couldn't even begin to calculate the odds of their finding Ian after all this time. Unless, of course, he was dead, and his remains were left here someplace, though that was unthinkable. She stood and brushed off the seat of her pants. "Let's do that."

"You know, Emme and I just had a talk a few minutes ago," Robert told her as they walked back to join the group. "She still thinks we should ask the FBI to step in and treat this as a kidnapping."

"What do you think?"

"I think I want to continue looking myself." He took her by the elbow as they walked along. "No one has more at stake in this search than I do. No one is going to look as closely at every inch of ground. The FBI might send in one person to investigate, not the dozens we have out here with us now."

When she did not respond, he asked, "Do you think I'm wrong in wanting to do this my way?"

"Robert, I don't know," she said honestly. "I know the FBI has resources that we don't have."

"Like what?"

"Like maybe they know how to read the terrain better than we do."

"Suse, if you're talking about things like broken branches or footprints, those things would have been long gone anyway. It's been a long time since that car went over the edge up there. I doubt there's much to be found, if there ever was."

"Then why are we here, Rob?"

"Because there's nowhere else for me to go," he told her. "I can't think of doing anything but look for him. This is the last place where I know for certain my boy was."

She understood his anguish, and she understood what was in his heart, just as she always did.

"Tomorrow we'll go farther down the mountain," she told him. "Maybe we'll find something tomorrow."

He took her hand and squeezed it. "Thanks for not giving up on me," he said. "For understanding why I need to do this, at least for a little while longer."

"I do think we ought to send Emme back to Conroy, though. She's missing Chloe, and even though I'm sure Trula is doing a bang-up job as a nanny, I think it's time for Emme to go back."

"You're right," he agreed readily. "I'll let her know."

They walked side by side to the clearing where the volunteers who still remained were waiting to see what their next step would be.

"What's it gonna be, boss?" one of the volunteers called to Robert. "You want to keep going? Got a few more hours of daylight here."

Susanna glanced around at the expectant faces. There was no doubt in her mind that they'd stay till darkness fell if he asked them to. She tugged on Robert's hand to hold him back for a moment.

"On second thought," she told him quietly, "let's call it a day. We need to talk with Emme for a few minutes before she heads home."

"Good point." Robert nodded. To the group, he said, "We're going to wrap it up for today. I want to thank each and every one of you for giving your time and energy again today. I appreciate it more than I can say. I know you all have lives and families of your own, so your volunteering to spend some of your time to walk this mountain with me means a lot."

"You gonna be back tomorrow morning?" someone asked.

"I will, yes," Robert replied.

"Then I'll be here, too," the same volunteer told him.

"Me, too," someone else called.

"I'll be here," called another.

"Thank you. I don't want you to neglect your own families, but I appreciate any time you can give," Robert said.

"I'm bringing mine with me." A man near the back of the group cupped his hands. "Three teenagers. Gonna have 'em walk off some of that attitude."

"Good idea, Clyde. Maybe I'll bring mine, too."

There was light laughter as the crowd dispersed, with lots of *See you tomorrow*s.

Soon the clearing was deserted except for Robert and Susanna. Emme was speaking with a middle aged woman near the road. As Susanna and Robert approached, Emme looked up to meet Susanna's eyes.

"What?" Suse asked.

"This is Barbara Cooper," Emme said. "She's just back from visiting family in Florida and heard about our search for Ian."

"That's very good of you, Barbara." Robert's weariness was beginning to show. "I appreciate you coming down today to help us out."

"Oh, I wish I'd been here sooner, but I literally just got off the plane this afternoon, and when my neighbor told me about the search for your baby, I just had to come over." The woman appeared slightly out of breath. "I was just telling Ms. Caldwell about the cabin."

"Cabin?" Robert's head snapped around to stare at her. "What cabin?"

"There's a cabin about a half mile downstream from here, and—"

"Why haven't I heard about this before?" Robert's dismay was written on his face.

"Maybe because it is so far downstream no one thought it was significant," Barbara told him. "Or maybe the fact that it's located in the next county might have something to do with it."

"But you seem to think it has significance?" Susanna stepped forward.

"Well, as I was telling Ms. Caldwell here, the cabin belongs to me, but I rent it exclusively to the Sisters of St. Anthony. They're a very small order." She added wryly, "And getting smaller every year, it seems. Between sisters leaving, and sisters dying, why, the numbers—"

"The cabin is rented to a religious order?" an impatient Robert said, interrupting her.

"Yes. They used to use it for solitary contemplation— you know, when one of the sisters wanted to have some time to herself to pray and commune with the elements." She smiled and added, "The cabin has no heat, so the communing usually took place in the more moderate months."

"Please tell Robert and Susanna what you told me," Emme urged.

"Well, as I was saying, I just got back from Florida,

and when I arrived home, there was a message from one of the sisters asking if the cabin was available to be used next weekend. Well, I told her it was available, but God only knows what condition it's in. No one's been out there in almost two years. So I thought I'd go out and take a look, make sure it was tidy, clean up the dust, bring the bed linens back to freshen them, you know."

The tension in Robert's face was beginning to take on a life of its own, but it was becoming increasingly clear that Barbara Cooper would get to the point when she got there.

"So I drove out and parked up on the main road; there's no road leading down to the cabin, so I had to park about a half mile away and walk down the path. It's pretty steep, and for my old knees, it gets steeper every time. But I get down to the cabin and the first thing I notice is that the padlock is on the ground and the door is open." Barbara frowned. "So I'm standing outside thinking, what if someone is in there, you know? I tried to peek through the windows but the curtains were pulled over so I couldn't see inside. I tried to call 911, but I had no cell reception out there. So I waited for a few minutes, and realized I couldn't hear anything going on inside, so I pushed the door open slowly and peered around. Well, it was obvious no one was there, but just as obvious that someone had been. My first thought was some kids probably broke in to drink beer or make a little whoopee, you know. But as soon as I stepped inside, I knew that wasn't the case."

She ran the back of her hand across her forehead, which was shiny with sweat—a combination, Susanna assumed, of the heat, the humidity, and the experience she was relating.

"For one thing, the cabin was neat as a pin. For another"—Barbara stuck her hand in her pocket and took out something small—"I found this on the floor."

She extended her hand and held out her open palm, and Robert reached for it to take a closer look.

"It's a button," he said softly. "Suse . . . look."

Susanna peered into Barbara's palm. The button was white with what appeared to be a tiny blue boat painted on it. Susanna's heart leapt in her chest.

"It's Ian's," she whispered.

"Thank God." Robert's eyes brimmed. "He was there. Someone brought him there."

Emme leaned in to see. "It's a button, all right, and I agree it's most likely from clothing that a little boy might wear, but why are you so sure it's Ian's?"

"That's a hand-painted button," Susanna told her. "One of a kind. Well, one of the eight that were on a little blue sweater that Beth dressed him in quite often."

"Still, let's not get too excited. There must be other sweaters just like Ian's."

"Uh-uh." Susanna shook her head. "Trula knitted that sweater, and I painted the little ships on the buttons myself. It was a shower gift. No other like it. This"—she pointed to the button—"was Ian's."

"Let's call the police back," Robert said, suddenly looking less weary. "If someone brought Ian here, there was a reason. My guess? Someone found him, and took him, maybe stayed here with him until they decided what to do with him. Which means that chances are, he's alive." He turned to Susanna and hugged her. "My son is alive, Suse. My son is alive."

Susanna bit her tongue. Not knowing who had the baby, or why they'd taken him, there was in her mind no cause for celebration, but she couldn't bring herself to speak the words. Someone else could do that. Emme, or the police, or the FBI. But not her. It had been too long since she'd seen that light of hope in Robert's eyes, and she wasn't about to be the one to put it out.

"Barbara, will you take us to the cabin?" Robert grasped the woman by the arm.

Before she could respond, Susanna said, "Let's call the police first, Rob. There could very well be evidence there that could lead us to Ian. Let's not compromise anything, all right?"

He nodded and released his grip on Barbara. "Yes, you're right. We'll get the police there first."

"I think we should have the FBI called in," Emme told them. "It's pretty clear that Ian has been kidnapped, and that's the FBI's deal. Let's see if the locals agree."

The locals did agree, but weren't inclined to wait around for the Bureau to make an appearance, opting instead to contain the cabin and the path and a perimeter of approximately half a mile in every direction. The state police were called in with their crew of investigators to scour the cabin, inside and out, for every trace of evidence to be found. All of the evidence that had been removed was bagged and marked, some of it already on its way to the FBI lab at the request of the agent who was to arrive late Saturday afternoon.

"If we had our own lab," Robert said to Suse over breakfast on Saturday, "we wouldn't have to wait for anyone. We could analyze the evidence ourselves."

He was edgy, his mood subdued since the police had found several spots of blood on the cabin floor. They'd taken samples from Robert to determine if there was a match to the droplets.

"Robert, chances are that neither the police nor the FBI would be willing to turn over evidence for you to have tested," Susanna said.

"I could make my lab available to them for free. Save them from hiring out. Save them a lot of money." He fell silent. "Let's do that. Let's look for someone who can set it up and figure out what we need and hire some good techs."

"Robert, you know that there's a good chance the blood isn't Ian's. It could be from an animal, or if we're really lucky, it could turn out to be from the person who has Ian."

"Or it could be Ian's," he said. "He could have been hurt."

"It could be something very minor, like a pinprick." She fought the urge to reach across the table and smooth back the hair from his forehead. Yesterday he'd been so elated, and now that look of despair was settling in around his eyes again. She did reach out to him, touching his hand instead of his face. "Let's not borrow trouble, as Trula always says. Let's wait and see."

"I've been waiting a long time, Suse." He raised his head to look at her, and corrected himself. "*We've* been waiting a long time. You've been with me through every moment of this nightmare."

"It's what friends do," she heard herself say.

"You're the best friend I've ever had," he said. "Have I ever told you that?"

"Actually, yes, you have." She forced a smile. "Several times."

"It's true. You've always been there for me, Suse."

"And I always will be." She gave his hand a squeeze. "No matter what, I'll always be here for you . . ."

NINE

"You're acting a little antsy today," Trula observed from her place at the counter where she was trying unsuccessfully to open a jar of cherries she'd canned earlier in the season. "What is it about this Fiona person that's making you so nervous, Sam?"

"Nervous?" Sam frowned. "I'm not nervous."

"You've been tapping your fingers on the table for the past"—she paused and looked pointedly at the clock—"thirteen minutes."

"Tapping on the table is usually a sign of impatience, not nerves," he replied, reaching for the jar. "And I am impatient. She's a half hour late. It isn't as if I have nothing to do but wait for her, you know."

"No, I don't know." Trula handed the jar of cherries across the counter and he opened it with ease, the lid making a proud pop. "Hmmmph. I must be getting old," she grumbled. "Old and weak."

"Trula, I can think of a lot of words to describe you, but old and weak are not two of them."

"You heard I was making Belgian waffles for brunch today, didn't you?" She pretended to glare at him. "That's why you're sucking up to me?"

"No. I hadn't heard that." Sam handed the jar back to her. "Are you? Making Belgian waffles?"

"I promised Chloe we'd make them for her and her mom, to celebrate Emme coming home. As soon as they arrive, I'll start. You're welcome to join us. Assuming of course that your appointment hasn't arrived yet." Trula smiled. "It's hard for people to take you seriously when you go into a meeting with whipped cream on your chin and cherry juice on your shirt."

"You put whipped cream on your waffles?"

She stared at him as if he had two heads. "I said they were *Belgian* waffles, Sam. Of course, there's—"

The doorbell rang.

"That's probably Fiona." He started toward the door, then looked back over his shoulder at the waffle maker Trula was setting up on the counter.

"Go," she told him. "I'll save you something. Maybe."

Sam could see through the sidelights next to the front door that it was in fact Fiona Summers who'd rung the bell. They'd never met, but he'd seen her at several meetings. She almost always came in alone, usually just as the doors were closing, and always took a seat in the back of the room. He couldn't remember her ever speaking out or contributing to a discussion. He didn't think she'd been in his unit all that long and couldn't remember where or when he'd first seen her. She was a self-professed loner, he recalled as he opened the front door. Just as he was.

"Hey, Fiona." He stood back to permit her to enter.

"Sam." She stepped inside, all business. "Nice to finally meet you. I've heard a lot about you."

He raised one eyebrow.

"Miranda's sister, Portia," she explained as she set a bulging leather briefcase on the floor. "We ran into each other in the office yesterday, and she said that you and she went way back."

"Yeah, we worked together a couple of times." He started to shut the door behind her.

"Hold up." She reached toward the door to keep him from closing it. "I have to go back to my car for the rest of it."

"The rest of it?"

"The rest of the files." She went down the front steps and Sam followed her. When he caught up with her at the trunk of her car, she'd already popped the lid. Inside were three cardboard file boxes.

"Let me give you a hand." He reached in and stacked one on top of a second.

"Thanks." Fiona lifted the third box and when Sam had cleared the trunk, she slammed the lid down. "I debated on how much to bring along, then figured the heck with it. I'd let you sort through and see what interested you. Normally, I wouldn't do that with a PI, of course, but I talked to John, and he said to give you whatever you needed. Help you in whatever way I could."

"Thanks, Fiona."

"Thank John Mancini." She smiled. "Like I said, normally, I wouldn't do this for a PI who was working on a case of mine. But when the boss tells you to share, you share."

He wasn't sure if she resented the interference of her boss—his former boss—into her case, but the important thing was that she did bring all her files with her, which he greatly appreciated, and said so. He balanced the two file boxes on his hip and opened the front door.

Once inside, Fiona picked up her briefcase and asked, "Which way?"

"Straight up the steps, third door on your left," he told her. "We can use the conference room, gives us more space to spread out."

Ten minutes later, they were seated at the large wooden table, a stack of files in front of Fiona, two bottles of water and a couple of ballpoint pens between them. Sam twisted the top off one bottle and took a long drink. Obviously Fiona wanted to dole out the information her way, piece by piece, in the order of her choosing. Well, that was all right with him. He'd take it however he could get it. Besides, she was nice to look at: wavy dark hair pulled back in a high tail and green eyes set in a heart-shaped face, skin that was tanned just to the point of looking healthy, and a mouth that curled up just a little on one side when she smiled. She wore no makeup, but then, Sam thought, she didn't need to.

So, yeah, Fiona could drag out this meeting for as long as she wanted to. Sam had all day.

"Here's what I have on your case," Fiona was saying. "I doubt if we have anything different here."

She handed him a copy of her case recap report, which John Mancini had required of all the agents working in his unit. Sam scanned the notes. Fiona was right. There was nothing new.

At least, not until he got to about a third of the way down on the fourth page, where it was noted that the

DNA from the skin cells removed from underneath Ross Walker's fingernails matched that from the nails of one Joseph Edward Maynard.

"This Maynard case." Sam's heart began to beat a little faster. "Tell me about this one."

Fiona sorted through her files and began to slide one out from the others.

"No, talk to me about it. Don't read to me. I can read for myself later. I want to hear it the way you see it."

"Okay." She pushed the file away and sat back, an arm resting on each side of her chair, and swiveled slightly to meet his eyes head-on. "Twenty-two-year-old Joseph Edward Maynard was the son of David Maynard, of Maynard Appliances."

She paused to let that sink in.

"That's supposed to mean something?" he asked.

"Think about those commercial-grade ovens and stoves and refrigerators that are going into all the hotels and restaurants these days."

"So this kid came from money. So what?"

"So here we have this kid from a wealthy family—probably the most affluent family in Kendall, Illinois—and they find his body—"

"From where?" Sam wasn't sure he'd heard correctly.

"Town south of Chicago. Kendall. Not much there, but it's a relatively affluent area," she explained. "You've probably never heard of it. I hadn't until—"

"I know Kendall," he told her. "Carly—my wife—was from Kendall. We were married there. Her family still lives there."

"Then chances are your in-laws would know the

Maynards. They're quite active within the community."

"Carly's dad recently retired as president of the chamber of commerce as well as chairman of the board of the bank," Sam said. "If the Maynards are well-to-do the chances are damned good."

"Well, there's certainly a coincidence for you." She paused. "Maybe we can call on them later to get a little more background, if we need it."

"Tell me about this kid. What happened to him?" Sam tried to ignore the jolt he'd gotten when Kendall was mentioned. Coincidences always made him uneasy.

"His last weekend home before he was leaving for college, his senior year. Purdue. He goes out on a Friday night with a couple of his buddies to a local bar. His friends tell me he got up to go to the men's room, around one, one fifteen AM, and never came back. After a while, they go to look for him, he's not there. He's nowhere. They figure he ran into someone, started talking, maybe went out to the parking lot, and went somewhere from there."

"The guys are thinking someone, as in a girl."

"Right."

"Was he in the habit of doing that, picking up girls and leaving his buddies sitting at the bar without telling them he was going?"

She shook her head again. "They all said he'd never done that before."

"What are the chances he ran into a pro, got an offer he couldn't refuse, took off for the parking lot for a quickie, and ended up getting more than he'd bargained for?"

"That would seem to be the most logical explanation, except she'd have to be one hell of a girl to overpower him. He was almost six feet tall, close to two hundred pounds."

"So she had an accomplice."

"If it weren't for the other cases, I'd agree with you. Fast forward to the following afternoon, some kids following the creek find his body underneath a bridge on the outskirts of town. Cause of death was manual strangulation but there were numerous postmortem stab wounds to the chest." Fiona paused. "Sound familiar?"

"Go on."

"Here's the kicker. He's found underneath a structure made out of cardboard, like a shelter had been built around him. The body was lying on a blanket underneath this cardboard house." She reached for her water bottle and opened it, took a long sip, her eyes watching his face. When she'd finished drinking, she put the cap back on the bottle and said, "So say something."

"Anyone see him leave the bar?"

She shook her head no. "The men's room is right by the back door that leads to the parking lot. No one remembers seeing him, but then again, this is close to one in the morning after these kids had been drinking for several hours. Someone could have seen him, but might not remember."

Sam rubbed the back of his neck. "Anything in the guy's mouth?"

"No. But that brings us to my third case." She started to reach for the file, then stopped. "You want it off the top of my head. Right. Okay. Next up is

Calvin Adams. He's in his early sixties. Homeless man who's been battling both schizophrenia and drug addiction for years. He's found lying on a park bench, stretched out as if he's sleeping. A bottle of water," she picked up the bottle in front of her and twirled it around, then tipped it upside down, "is standing upright in his mouth and halfway down his throat, the contents frozen solid because it's winter." She set the bottle down and said, "Here's your chance to dazzle me with those mad investigative skills of yours. Tell me how the man died."

"Manual strangulation. Multiple stab wounds—postmortem stab wounds—to the chest."

"My God, you are every bit as sharp as they say you are." She shook her head in mock amazement. "You know, it's so rare that someone lives up to their reputation."

"DNA match the others?" He ignored her sarcasm.

"No DNA this time around, but since what I'm thinking is the signature—the water bottle, which to my mind corresponds to the burger found in Ross Walker's mouth—and with the MO being the same, I gotta think it's the same guy. You're free to offer up a different opinion, if you have one."

"So you've drawn a line from the two where the physical evidence is similar—Walker and Adams—to the DNA match in the Walker and Maynard cases." Sam stared into space for a moment. "So where's the guy's signature on the Maynard case? If we're assuming it's stuffing something into the mouth." He paused again. "Maybe we're not interpreting that correctly, though." He thought for another moment.

"Maybe somehow the signature in the Maynard case is the structure that was erected around him."

Fiona pushed her chair back, opened her briefcase, and reached inside.

"Here are the photos from Maynard." She opened a letter-sized brown envelope. "You've seen the photos of Walker, but we want to put them in context. You need to see all three together."

She lined the photos up across the table, repeating the names of the victims as she did so. "Walker. Maynard. Adams."

Sam stood to get a better look. He stared at each for a moment before moving to the next. After he'd studied all three, he said, "It's in the prop. The signature is in the prop. The killer is telling us something, but I don't know what it is."

He picked up the photo of Joseph Maynard. "This structure is too well thought out to have been some random means of hiding a body. He was very well organized here. I'm assuming he brought the blanket with him? Do you know?" he asked Fiona.

"No one in his family had seen it before, and since one of his buddies had driven that night, it hadn't come from the victim's car. So yes, we are assuming the killer probably brought it with him."

"The structure was carefully constructed. See here, it looks as if several large boxes were opened up and then pieced together to make the shelter." He slid the photo closer to Fiona and pointed. "This is not the work of someone tossing cardboard boxes onto a corpse to hide it. It's more than that. I just don't know what."

He placed the photo between the others and lifted

the last one to take a closer look. The photo slipped from his hands and flipped over. On the back was written: *Calvin Adams. Age 62. DOD: 2/9/09. Dutton, NE.*

Sam stared at the writing, the hairs on the back of his neck standing straight up.

"What?" Fiona asked. "What are you thinking?"

It took several moments for Sam to put his thoughts together.

"I'm thinking this is the damnedest thing." His eyes were still on the back of the photo.

"What?" she repeated, somewhat impatiently.

"I went to high school in Dutton." He sat down, the photo of Calvin Adams in his hand. "The regional high school for all the small towns around where I grew up was in Dutton."

She stared at him as if trying to follow his train of thought.

Sam stood and reached across the table for the other two photos.

"Walker was killed in Lincoln. Where I went to college. Maynard in Kendall, Illinois, where my wife grew up, where we were married. She's buried there. Adams was killed in Dutton . . ." He looked down at Fiona, who was swiveling very slowly, very quietly, from side to side. "Am I imagining something here? Am I being paranoid? Is this some cosmic coincidence?"

"You know what Mancini says about coincidences, Sam."

"Yeah. There aren't any." He tossed the pictures back onto the table. "I do not like what I'm thinking."

"Maybe it is a coincidence," she said thoughtfully. "Maybe this one time—odds being what they are—John Mancini's theory will, by percentage, be proven wrong."

They sat in silence for several long moments.

"Maybe you're right," he told her. "The chance that any of this could somehow be connected to me is practically zero. On the surface, it could be interpreted that way. I'm sure you're right. This is one of those odd times when true coincidence comes into play." He looked at her and smiled. "Sorry. It just spooked me for a moment."

"It spooked me, too." She laughed as if relieved. "For a minute, anyway."

"Okay, spooky moment has passed." Sam rearranged the photos. "Let's see if we can figure out what our killer is telling us. Hamburger stuffed in the mouth. House made of cardboard. Empty water bottle in the mouth."

"Maybe it's the locations," Fiona ventured. "Behind a soup kitchen for the poor. Under a bridge in a cardboard house. Sleeping on a park bench. Maybe they all relate somehow?"

"Excuse me." There was a tap on the door frame. "Sam DelVecchio?"

Sam looked over his shoulder. In the doorway was a man in black, wearing a clerical collar. Years of training brought Sam to his feet.

"Yes, Father?" he addressed the man.

"I'm Kevin Burch." The priest came into the room to introduce himself. "I'm Robert's cousin. Trula told me you were up here, and I just wanted to pop in to meet you. I hope I'm not intruding."

"Not at all, Father." Sam took the hand the priest offered.

"It's Kevin," the priest told him. "Everyone here calls me Kevin. Robert's kind enough to let me call this place home."

He turned to Fiona.

"Ah, Father . . . er, Kevin . . ." Sam began. "This is Special Agent Summers. She's with the FBI."

"It's Fiona." She pushed back her chair to rise and Kevin waved her off.

"Don't get up. Please. It's nice to meet you." He shook her hand as well, then looked at the table. "Looks as if I've interrupted something important here."

"We're just going over a case. The FBI has identified three victims that appear to be the work of the same killer. One of those cases happens to be the case we took on this week."

"The good Samaritan from Nebraska." Kevin moved closer to take a look. "The gentleman who was found behind the soup kitchen? A mission of some sort?"

"Yes." Sam's eyes darted to the photos, wondering if perhaps they might be too gruesome for the priest.

"Mallory called me about it." He picked up the photo of Ross Walker and studied it, but did not flinch from the carnage. "Poor soul. Do you have any leads?"

"None. We were just discussing the fact that there are two other very similar cases that—"

"What's in his mouth?" Kevin asked.

"A hamburger from a fast food restaurant," Sam told him.

Kevin studied the picture, then picked up the next one.

"What's this supposed to be, some kind of shelter . . . ?" he asked.

"Apparently. It was put around him by the killer," Fiona explained.

"And this?" Kevin next went to the picture of Calvin Adams. "The water bottle . . ."

"We don't know what it all means," Fiona said, "but we feel very strongly it's connected somehow."

The priest began to nod, as he replaced the photos in order, his expression solemn.

"If I could . . ." he began hesitantly.

"You have some thoughts, Father?" Sam asked. "Er, Kevin?"

"You're Catholic, Sam?" Kevin asked.

"Yes."

"Fiona?"

She nodded. "Me too, yes."

"You're familiar then, with the Church's corporal acts of mercy?" the priest continued.

Fiona nodded. "The call to Christians to perform acts of charity and kindness to the needy," she said. "To live as Christ would, treat our fellow man as He would."

"Well said." The priest then lifted the photos, in order, and dealt them out in front of the two investigators as if dealing from a deck of cards.

"Feed the hungry." He peeled off the photo of Ross Walker. "Shelter the homeless." Joseph Edward Maynard.

"Give drink to the thirsty." Calvin Adams.

If a pin had dropped in the room, all three would have heard it land.

"Of course, being a priest, maybe I'm just reading into the photos what I see from my own perspective," Kevin said. "Maybe it isn't that at all."

"No, that's it." Sam nodded slowly. "That's it."

"Except that Joseph Maynard was far from being homeless," Fiona pointed out. "Calvin Adams was the homeless person."

"But if the killer was selecting his victims at random, he wouldn't have known that," Sam told them. "And I'm just about one hundred percent certain that the victims were random."

He explained that the killer could not have known that Ross Walker would have been the volunteer to take trash out to the Dumpster on the night he was attacked, but the killer had come totally prepared to commit murder.

"We may never know for certain if Maynard had been picked out ahead of time or if the killer had simply been in the parking lot, waiting for someone— anyone—to step outside." He turned to Fiona. "You said that Calvin Adams was homeless and that he often slept in that park. In that case, he wouldn't have had to look too far to find a victim. Especially if Adams was already asleep."

"That's true," she said. "And since Adams was the only one of the three to have not fought back sufficiently to have gotten the killer's skin under his nails, it does make sense that he could have been asleep when he was attacked."

"So you have random victims but a specific . . . I don't know what you'd call it." Kevin frowned. "I've read a lot but don't know if you'd call the acts of mercy thing his signature or his MO."

"Signature," Sam told him. "His MO is the way in which he goes about committing his crime. The strangulation, the stabbings. But the posing, the props—they're part of whatever emotional investment he has in these crimes. That's what links him to his victims, that's his payoff, what makes these killings uniquely his. And that's what will eventually lead us to him."

"It's going to be hard to figure out though, don't you think?" Kevin was still frowning. "I mean, you have random victims in random places."

"Maybe not so random." Fiona stood and leaned against the table. "I'm still not so sure the locations are random, Sam."

"What do you mean?" Kevin asked.

"Ross Walker was killed in Lincoln, Nebraska—home of the University of Nebraska," Fiona said.

"Great football there," Kevin noted. "I've been a Cornhuskers fan for years."

"You go to school out there, Father?" Sam had never addressed a priest by his first name and had to correct himself again. "Kevin."

"No, I went to St. Joe's, in Philly. But Nebraska's teams always get TV time in the fall. They're always worth watching."

"Sam went to Nebraska," Fiona told him. "Right, Sam?"

"Right. I did. I'm Nebraska born and raised."

"You play ball there?" the priest asked, seeming to be grateful to have the conversation move from murder for a moment.

"Actually, yes, I did." Sam nodded. "I played center, backup my freshman year, started the next three."

"You must have been good."

"I had my moments."

"Well, moving along here." Fiona tapped on the photo of Calvin Adams. "Mr. Adams was killed in a park in Dutton, Nebraska." She turned to Kevin. "Sam went to high school in Dutton."

"Seriously?" The priest stared at the photo, then picked up the picture of Joseph Maynard. "Tell me you didn't go to grade school in the town where this young man died."

"No, I didn't go to grade school there," Sam said solemnly. "But my wife—my late wife—did. As a matter of fact, we were married there. Actually, she's buried there."

"Holy . . . smoke." Kevin leaned against the back of the chair and exhaled loudly.

"That's what we were discussing when you came in." Sam reached for his water bottle, the sick feeling returning to his stomach. Hearing Fiona lay it out for the priest that way made coincidence seem less and less likely.

"We were thinking it was probably a coincidence that Sam had a connection to the locations," Fiona added.

"Well, I'm not an investigator, but it seems to me that if the victims are random but the location is not, then the key would be in the location, right?" When he realized what he said, Kevin looked at Sam apologetically. "But does it really make sense that someone would deliberately pick places that had ties to you? Would someone really do that? I mean, I know on TV you see story lines like that, but in real life, do people do that?"

"I guess if they're trying to get someone's attention, they might." Fiona stated what, for her, was obvious.

"If someone's trying to get my attention," Sam said slowly, "they've got it now."

"But why would someone do that?" Kevin asked. "Why Sam? And why bring the acts of mercy into it?"

"The first question—why me?" Sam shrugged. "It could be someone who wants revenge against me for something, maybe for arresting them in the past, or maybe arresting a family member or a loved one. We can look into that through the Bureau's records. But why the posing, feed the hungry and the rest of it? That's the real question. And if we can find the answer to that, we'll have the answers to all those other questions."

"This is all speculation, Sam," Fiona reminded him. "Maybe we're reading too much into this. Maybe it is, as we discussed before, a creepy coincidence." She thought for a moment. "Let's look at this another way. You said this is your first week on this new job, right?"

Sam nodded. "Right."

"Ross Walker was killed on February 9, 2008. How would someone in February of 2008 have known that in September of 2009, you'd no longer be with the Bureau? That you'd not only be working here, but that you'd be assigned to this case?"

Sam felt a prickle at the back of his neck.

"No one could have predicted that," Kevin said.

"Right." Sam turned to the priest. "I didn't even

know that a year and a half ago. So you're probably right. It's probably just one of those creepy coincidences. I guess they really do happen."

"Sure," Fiona agreed all too readily. "I'm sure that's it. Proving that even the great John Mancini isn't invincible."

Kevin looked at her blankly.

"Our boss, John. His theory is that there's no such thing as coincidence in a homicide investigation," Fiona explained.

Kevin smiled. "I guess you can tell him that he can lay that theory to rest. Somehow this killer just managed to pick three towns in the Midwest that had a connection to Sam, but it could have been any three towns. Could have been any other three towns that had a connection to someone else, right? So there's got to be another explanation, right?"

"Right," Sam and Fiona said at the same time.

"Well, I'm glad we got that straightened out." Kevin patted Sam on the back. "Good to meet you, Sam. Welcome aboard. I'm sure we'll be seeing a lot of each other. Good luck with your case."

"Thanks, Father." She smiled as he left the room, then turned to Sam and said, "So we're in agreement, then? We're scratching the Sam connection here and we're moving ahead?"

He hesitated just a bit too long.

"What?" Fiona frowned. "I thought we just agreed—"

"You have three murders where the MO is identical. What generally happens once a recognizable pattern is identified, Fiona?"

She didn't answer right away. "Once the details are

entered into VICAP, sooner or later someone will pick up the similarities."

"And if there are three or more . . ."

"Someone will stick the serial-killer tag on them. And sooner or later, the chances are very good that the case will fall into the lap of the Bureau, where odds are—at the very least—it will be reviewed by one of the profilers."

"And since there were only two of us working for John's unit—Anne Marie McCall and I—sooner or later, the connection would be made." Sam looked at Fiona. "Annie knows I'm from Nebraska. She knows I graduated from UNL. She would have brought it to my attention."

"So if we go back to the theory that the killer is trying to get your attention, he would most likely have gotten it."

"Right. I think the only real coincidence here is that I came on board with the Mercy Street Foundation at the same time Lynne Walker applied to have her husband's murder investigated. If I'd stayed with the Bureau, the connection would have been obvious." Sam sighed. "And there's one other thing I should bring to your attention."

She tilted her head to one side, waiting.

"My birthday is February ninth."

He waited for the significance of the dates to click in. He didn't have to wait long.

"Walker was killed on the ninth in '08, Adams on the ninth in '09. Maynard, though, was killed on the fifteenth of the month, right?"

"That's right." He swallowed hard. "August fifteenth. The anniversary of my wife's murder."

"Holy shit." Fiona stared at Sam. "Why didn't you say something when Father Burch was here?"

"Because I think that bomb ought to be dropped on Mallory Russo and Robert Magellan first."

"I guess I'd better call in to the office and have someone start running a list of all the cases you handled over the years, and see if anything jumps out. It would have to be someone you pissed off really badly, Sam."

"Well, that should narrow the field down to a couple hundred people and their families and closest friends," Sam said dryly. "You can lay an awful lot of track in sixteen years . . ."

TEN

Sam's first inclination was to decline the waffles Trula had saved for him, even though he knew it would have been rude. He felt too distracted to eat. But he'd wanted to meet Emme Caldwell and he might as well do it now. So even though he wanted to close the front door behind him and keep on going when he helped Fiona carry her boxes back to her car, he went back into the house.

"So how was your meeting with the FBI agent?" Emme asked after the introductions were made. She'd just tucked Chloe's shirt into her shorts and sent her outside to play with her kitten. "Did it seem weird, since you used to be the agent meeting with non-Bureau personnel?"

"A little odd, but Fiona and I worked with a lot of the same people and have some mutual friends, so it didn't seem as strange as I suppose it could have," he said as he dug into the pile of fluffy waffles, whipped cream, and cherries that Trula prepared for him. "Dear God, Trula, this is one of the best things I ever ate."

"Well, you've been eating a lot of meals at the Conroy Diner," she replied, "so anything decent is going to taste even better."

"How do you know where I eat when I don't eat here?"

She merely smiled, then turned back to what she was doing. Emme laughed out loud.

"Trula knows just about everyone in Conroy. She stops in at the diner once a week 'for coffee.'" Emme made quotation marks with her fingers. "Which is just her way of keeping her ear to the ground."

"You have to keep up with what's happening in your community," Trula sniffed.

"There's a local paper for that," Emme reminded her. "The *Conroy Courier* comes out once a week. You could get your news from it."

"I get better info at the diner."

"Were you able to learn anything helpful from the agent?" Emme turned back to Sam.

"Possibly. She's going to have some reports copied and shipped here for me to take a look at. We'll see where it goes." Sam couldn't wait to change the subject. "So when do you suppose Mr. Magellan will be back? I'm looking forward to meeting him and working with him."

"You won't be working with him for long if you call him Mister to his face. He prefers Robert," Emme told him. "Even Chloe can't call him Mr. Magellan."

"Must be a family thing," Sam observed. "His cousin, Father Burch, stopped in upstairs this afternoon. He apparently doesn't like to be called Father."

"He likes to be called Father," Trula told him, "he just likes to be Kevin at home. And this is, for all practical purposes, his home. His family. Therefore, first names apply."

"Does he get involved in all the cases?" Sam asked.

"Only if there's an area where he can contribute," Emme said. "Why do you ask? Did he get involved in yours?"

"Actually, he had some good insights to share." Sam related the priest's interpretation of the crime scenes.

"Wow." Emme sat down across the table from Sam. "That's bizarre. The acts of mercy?"

Trula turned around and leaned against the counter, a puzzled look on her face.

"You say you have three murders?" she asked.

Sam nodded.

"But . . . weren't there *seven* acts of mercy?"

The fork that was headed toward Sam's mouth stopped in midair and hung suspended there. His appetite suddenly gone, Sam cursed softly under his breath.

Seven acts of mercy. He should have remembered that from his long-ago catechism classes after school with Sister Ignatius.

Seven acts of mercy. Three deaths.

Were there four they had yet to discover, or were there four more victims on the killer's list?

"Fiona, it's Sam." He was disappointed to have to leave voice mail. "Sam DelVecchio. Please give me a call when you get this message." He repeated his number. "It's important."

He disconnected the call and drove through the gates at the front of Robert's property. He waved at the guard in his little protective house that sat just outside the gate and drove off. It was too early for dinner—Trula's admonitions aside, the Conroy Diner actually served pretty good food—and Sam was in no mood to return to his hotel. He envied Emme's residence on the Magellan property. Before he left, she'd given him a tour of the carriage house where she and Chloe would soon be living, and he admitted to experiencing pangs of jealousy. The quarters were spacious and light, with lots of windows and beautiful views of the gardens he'd noticed Trula tending even as she supervised a crew of gardeners.

"I know what you mean," Emme had said. "We've been looking at houses for several weeks now, and this is so much nicer than any place we've seen. Easily as nice as our old house back in California, and even bigger. We're very lucky." She pointed out the living room window to where her daughter and Trula sat on a lounge near the pool. "The luckiest part is finding Trula. She's the best thing that's happened to Chloe and me, probably ever. She's the grandmother Chloe hasn't had. She's the mother . . ."

She stopped there, and Sam realized she was afraid of revealing too much of herself to a stranger. Well, Sam didn't fault her for that. He was pretty close-mouthed about most things himself. But he figured that he knew what Emme had been about to say, that Trula was the mother she'd never had, and he wondered about her story. Not that he'd ask—that would be intruding. If she ever wanted to talk about it, she would, if they became friends.

What he did want to talk about was Robert's search for his son.

"Are they any closer to finding the little boy?" he asked.

Emme shook her head. "Yes and no. They have established that Ian had been in the cabin in the woods we found out about yesterday. The FBI has been called in and in the meantime, the state police crime-scene techs have been all over it. Lots of fingerprints, lots of trace. The case is being treated like a kidnapping now. Maybe you saw that on the news?"

When Sam admitted that he hadn't had the TV on all weekend, and that he'd forgotten to pick up a newspaper that morning, Emme continued.

"It's being assumed that whoever took Ian from the car stayed with him in the cabin, and that he's alive somewhere, that someone is passing him off as their own. The FBI is preparing a computer-generated age-progression photo to show what he probably looks like now. That will be as widely circulated as possible. TV, newspapers, magazines. Robert's goal is to get that photo in front of the public at every opportunity. He figures that the publicity plus the reward he's going to offer is going to get someone's attention."

"What's he offering?" Sam was curious.

"One million dollars."

Sam whistled. "There's some incentive to keep your eyes open."

"Here's hoping. Susanna says now that Robert is pretty sure his son is alive, there will be no living with him until they find him. She said he's been relentless these past few days. Not that I blame him, of course." She paused. "Do you have any children, Sam?"

"No. My wife is deceased. We never got around to having kids before she died." Sam could have added that he and Carly had just started investigating fertility treatments when she was killed, but after the day he'd had, he didn't feel up to bringing that into the conversation.

"I'm sorry. How long has it been, Sam?"

"Three years." He hoped she wouldn't pursue it but knew that she would.

"May I ask, was she ill . . . ?"

Sam took a breath and told the story.

"Sam, that's horrible. I'm so sorry."

"Thanks," he'd told her. What else could he say?

He'd taken the long way back to his hotel, past the old factories and through the narrow streets where the workers of those boarded-up factories had once lived. Some of them probably still did, he reminded himself. He drove up the hill leading to the nicest part of Conroy, the gracious homes the factory owners had built for themselves and their families. This part of town seemed to be experiencing a rebirth, evident in the number of homes that sported fresh coats of paint and new roofs, porches with colorful potted plants on the newly repaired stairs. For some reason, it raised his spirits to know that here, at least, someone was looking to the future with some optimism. For the past several hours, Sam had felt an anxiety he'd never experienced before.

Was he somehow responsible for the deaths of those three men? Were there others?

He drove to a park on the outskirts of town and left his car in the lot. He began to walk, first to the pond, but there were children there and he merely walked around it. There was a hiking path that led into the woods and he followed it without thinking. He walked the full 10.7 miles around the park—which signs identified as the Merriweather Arboretum—but even the exertion required to walk that distance in clothes better suited to a professional meeting than a hike in ninety-three degree heat did nothing to calm him. He returned to his car and drove back to the hotel, where he changed into shorts, a tank, and his running shoes, and took off somewhat mindlessly.

Sam ran for the better part of an hour before he stopped, his breathing labored and his clothes stuck to his sweating body. He pulled a five-dollar bill from one of his socks and went into a convenience store and purchased a bottle of water, which he drank even as he paid for it. He left the change on the counter and stuck the remaining bills back into his sock. He pitched the empty plastic bottle into the trash bin just outside the door. He walked the first half mile on his way back to his room, then picked up the pace and ran the rest of the way. With every footfall he asked himself the same question. *What had he done that had cost those men their lives?*

Sam emerged from his shower to hear the phone ringing. He caught it just as voice mail was kicking in. He glanced at the number of the missed call and redialed. Fiona answered on the second ring.

"Hi," she said. "I was just leaving you a message. What's up?"

"Have you by any chance called anyone at the Bureau about running a list of my old cases?"

"Actually, yes, I called Will. He's the best I know when it comes to the computers. He can wring information out of even the most reluctant program." She paused. "Was there someone else you had in mind?"

"No, no. I was thinking Will would be the person to get on this. He is the best, I agree."

"And he never whines if you call him on a Sunday, which I just did. He said he'd get back to us as soon as he could but it might take a few days to narrow down the field."

"Narrow down the field?"

"He said it was unlikely that everyone on the list would have a reason to be gunning for you. He gave me a few examples, like wives who were just as happy to see their husbands behind bars, kids who'd shed no tears when they were removed from abusive homes, that sort of thing. Most of the actors you had involvement with are still in prison or dead, so that would eliminate a lot of potentials right there. So we'll see what he comes back to us with." Fiona added, "He said he was going to have Annie McCall look over the list to see if anyone stood out to her."

"I can do that," he protested. "Annie's busy enough these days."

"Well, the new guy does appear to be a bit of a dud, between you and me, but maybe he'll do better once he gets his feet on the ground. But I think John thinks that maybe you're too close to the . . ."

"Wait a minute. You went to John with this?"

"I had to, Sam. He's my boss. Regardless of your relationship with him, I still answer to him. If something relevant comes up on one of my cases, he needs to know about it."

Sam stewed in silence. It was annoying enough that she'd discussed this with his former boss, but even more annoying to know that she was absolutely right. His long history with John aside, he was now potentially a player in a case the Bureau was handling.

"Sam? Are you there?"

"Yeah. I'm here."

"I'm sorry. I couldn't avoid talking to him about this. Especially if there's a killer lurking in one of our files, someone out to seek revenge on one of our agents because of something said agent may or may not have done while working a case." She corrected herself. "Former agent, that is. You understand that, right?"

"Yeah. I understand."

"So did something occur to you after I left? Any flashes of brilliance that will lead us to the killer?"

"The only flash of brilliance came from Trula Comfort. She reminded me that there were seven acts of mercy." He let that sink in for a moment.

"Shit."

"That was pretty much my reaction, too."

"So what's that mean? Either there are four more we haven't caught up with yet . . ."

"Or four more to come. Either way, it isn't pretty."

"I'm going to have to go back to VICAP and see if I missed anything. Maybe there were others and I was too focused on the strangulation followed by postmortem stab wounds. Let me see what else I can come up with."

"Will you get back to me?"

"Absolutely. I promise. I'll be tied up all tomorrow morning and possibly the afternoon as well, but I'll get back to you as soon as I can."

"Thanks. I'll wait to hear from you." He was about to hang up when Fiona said, "Sam?"

"Yeah?"

"Be careful."

"I don't think I'm in any danger. This guy's going after random victims, right? If this has something to do with me, I wouldn't be random, would I?"

"Hasn't it occurred to you that maybe these random victims are substitutes for you?" she said softly. "That maybe this is a revenge thing intended to get your attention, drag you into it, so he can play with you a little before he comes after you?"

Sam thought it through.

"If that's his goal, wouldn't it have occurred to him by now that I'm not on the case? Well, I am, but not the way he may have intended. If he means to take me on, play with my head, wouldn't you think he'd have noticed that I *haven't* noticed?"

"Maybe he has, Sam. Maybe he's got something else in mind. Who the hell knows?" Fiona was beginning to sound a little annoyed. "God, sometimes I hate people, you know what I mean?"

"Yeah." Sam sighed. "I know what you mean . . ."

ELEVEN

"You're awfully quiet today." Mallory poked her head through the doorway into Sam's office. "I wasn't even sure you were here."

"I'm here." He looked up from the file notes he was making on the Joseph Maynard case. He could have admitted that he'd been deliberately quiet coming in that morning because he hadn't really wanted to engage anyone in conversation. He'd been up most of the night trying to decide how best to handle the dilemma he found himself in.

"Trula said you had a meeting with the FBI over the weekend." Mallory took a sip of coffee. Sam craned his neck to see if he could read the mug but she was too far away. "How'd that go for you?"

"Fine." He debated how much to tell her. He decided to keep it simple for now. "There are two cases—one in Nebraska, another in Illinois—where the crime scenes are very similar. The special agent handling those two—Fiona Summers is the agent— was kind enough to bring her files along so I could take a look at them and copy some reports and things that might be useful to us."

Mallory smiled. "Now, see, that's exactly what I hoped would happen, with you being a former agent. Not that I wouldn't have hired you anyway for your experience," she hastened to add, "but those contacts at the federal level are priceless. I'll bet the information you got from her will prove to be very helpful to your case."

"It's beginning to look that way." Sam sighed. He hated deception in any form. He looked at Mallory, who was so pleased to have him on her staff, and knew he couldn't keep any of this from her. She deserved to know what was going on. What the hell had he been thinking, that he'd hesitated to tell her?

He had just needed to remind himself who he was working for here.

"Actually, Mallory, there's something we need to—"

Mallory's cell phone rang and as she reached into her pocket for it, the hand holding the mug turned toward Sam.

WHEN ALL ELSE FAILS, MANIPULATE THE DATA, it read.

She glanced at the number. "Gotta take this—it's the boss. Maybe you can fill me in at lunch. Trula's doing burgers and homemade fries today."

She answered the call as she left the room and Sam tapped his pen on the side of his own mug. (GOOD MORNING! LET THE STRESS BEGIN!)

He'd placed a call to John Mancini earlier that morning and was still awaiting a callback. He knew Fiona was tied up, so he didn't expect to hear from her until later in the afternoon, and then only if she had something new to tell him. In the meantime, Sam was trying to separate his personal feelings from his professional responsibilities. Any way you sliced it, he needed to lay it all out for the others here at the Foundation. They needed to know that he could possibly be a player in the case he was supposed to be resolving for their client.

But how could he possibly look Lynne Walker in the eye and tell her that had it not been for someone with an ax to grind with *him,* her husband would still be alive?

He ran a hand through his hair and thought that if this were happening to someone else he probably wouldn't believe it.

"Hey, good news." Mallory poked her head back in. "That was Robert. He and Susanna are on their way back. They should be here in a few hours, so you'll finally get to meet your new boss." She glanced at her watch. "Gotta run. I'm supposed to be interviewing someone right now."

"Talk to you later." Sam nodded and forced a smile.

"And I'm sure looking forward to meeting Robert Magellan today," he muttered after Mallory disappeared into the hall. "So I can tell him about the wrench I'm throwing into his new case."

"Walk me through this again, Sam," Robert said after the hoopla of his return had died down and Sam had been called in to his office to meet him. "You think our client's husband may have been murdered by someone who's trying to get your attention?"

Sam had been surprised to find the man alone in the room. He'd been hoping that Mallory would be there, too, so he could get this over with once and for all.

"It's beginning to look like it." Sam's jaw clenched with the tension. This was one hell of a way to introduce yourself to your new boss. "I'd like to say that maybe I'm wrong—maybe the FBI is wrong—but I've gone over this thing backwards and forwards and I honestly can't see this any other way. Someone is playing with my head, and it's working."

"Have you discussed this with Mallory?"

"Not yet, sir. I was going to this morning but she—"

Robert groaned. "Please. Do not *sir* me. I hate to be *sirred*."

"Sorry. Habit."

"Have you mentioned this to our client? What's her name?"

"Lynne Walker."

"Right. Walker. Does she know about this?"

"No. As I said, this theory just came to light yesterday, and I wanted to discuss it with Mallory. And you, of course."

"Then that's all this is? A theory?"

"The killer has struck three times in places that have some significance to me—on dates that are significant to me—because he's trying to get my attention. Send me a message." Sam slumped in the chair.

"What places?" Robert was obviously intrigued. "What dates?"

"The town in which I went to college . . ."

"Which was?"

"Lincoln, Nebraska. UNL."

"University of Nebraska—Lincoln is a big school, isn't it? Main campus, right?"

"Yes."

"How many students, would you say?"

"Last alumni bulletin said something in the area of eighteen thousand undergrads."

"And what's the population of Lincoln?"

"About a quarter of a million, I suppose."

"But given all those people, you still think this murder has something to do with you?" Robert looked skeptical. "You're going to have to do better than that."

"The murders in Lincoln and in Dutton—I went to high school in Dutton—both occurred on February ninth. Which is also my birthday. The murder in Kendall, Illinois—where my late wife grew up, where she's buried—happened on August fifteenth. The date of her murder."

The room was silent as a tomb.

Finally, Robert said, "Your wife . . . was murdered?"

"Yes. The three-year anniversary just passed."

"I don't know what to say, Sam."

"That's okay. I guess it's all been said, but thank you. And condolences to you, too. About your wife. Your son."

"Changes your life in ways you could never imagine, doesn't it?"

"To put it mildly, yes."

The two men regarded each other for a moment, each acknowledging the other's loss until Robert broke the silence by moving past it.

"This puts a different spin on things." Robert rubbed his chin. "The dates, the places . . ." He nodded slowly. "Yeah. It's all pointing back to you, isn't it?"

"That's how it seems to me, and to the FBI as well. So if you want me to resign and go on back to—"

"Why would I want you to do that?" Robert frowned. "Our job is to solve this murder for Mrs. Walker. Who is going to be better able to do that than you?"

Sam was speechless for a moment. "It could be seen as a conflict of interests."

"A conflict of whose interests? She wants the case solved, you want the case solved. We want it solved. Now more than ever. We're willing to put all our resources behind you to that end. And the FBI is going to work with you on this, right?"

"Right."

"I don't see the conflict. As long as you're not afraid of pursuing this, I don't—"

"Why would I be afraid?"

"Because the killer is probably after you, right? Why else would he be trying to get your attention? Why wouldn't you be afraid?"

"I've had killers after me before," Sam told him.

"And that didn't scare you?" Robert's eyebrows rose.

"It made me more aware of my surroundings, made me more conscious of who and what was going on around me, but I wasn't *scared* to the point where I couldn't do my job."

"Let me ask you something. Those cases—the ones where someone was hunting you—how did they end?"

"Twice with the killer being arrested, prosecuted, and sentenced to prison. The other was shot and killed by a SWAT team."

"So in other words, each time you got your man; he didn't get you."

"In other words, yeah."

"That's the bottom line, Sam. Get the fucker." Robert sat all the way back in his chair and it tipped toward the wall. He was about to say something else when Father Burch came into the room.

Robert stood and the two men embraced.

"I heard there's reason to be optimistic," the priest said.

"We're pretty sure Ian was alive, at least while he was in the cabin." Robert's joy was written all over his face. Sam got up to leave. This was a family moment, and he thought the cousins might want to have some time alone, but Robert stopped him.

"No, no, don't feel you have to leave. Tell Kevin what you were just telling me. Wait. Let me get Mallory in on this. And Emme." He paused with his hand over the phone. "Hell, let's just all go down to the kitchen and have a meeting and tell everyone at the same time."

There was something about Robert Magellan that made Sam's head spin, he was thinking as he followed the other two men down the hall. The man was decisive. He evaluated situations and people very quickly, then made a decision and moved on, which had obviously worked well for him in business.

Sam was almost to the stairwell when his phone rang. He looked at the ID and called ahead to Robert.

"I'll meet you down there." Sam held up his ringing phone. "FBI."

He went back to his office and closed the door.

"Fiona?"

"Yes, Sam, it's me." She sounded rushed and excited. "Listen, Sam, I'm coming back out there in the morning. I'm going to have a little company. Do you think we could use your conference room?"

"I guess so. I don't know why we couldn't, but I'll clear it and let you know if there's a problem." He sat on the side of his desk. "Who's coming with you?"

"Annie McCall and possibly John."

"Why?" The word tumbled from his mouth before he could stop it.

"Because there's been another killing."

"Another . . ."

"Three Saturdays ago." She paused as if waiting for him to react. When he did not, she said, "August fifteenth, Sam."

He hadn't forgotten the date, but at that moment, he hadn't been thinking that it had been three weeks since the third anniversary of Carly's death.

"So we're gathering the guns to talk this over," she went on.

"Where this time?"

"Sanderson, Virginia."

Sam felt his knees go weak.

"We were living there when Carly was murdered," he whispered.

"I know. John told me. He wants to talk to you tomorrow, alone, so he's going to arrive around ten if that works for you."

"That works."

"Great. I'll let him know. If there's a change, give me a call. Annie will be flying in to the Philly airport and I'll pick her up around eleven, then we'll drive out there together. I'm having copies of the case in question delivered to you overnight so we'll all be getting a first look at the same time. Any questions?"

"No." Sam cleared his throat. "Not right now."

"Sam, I'm so sorry. I was hoping . . . we were all hoping . . . that the others would turn out to be a fluke somehow."

"Yeah. Me too." *No one more than me.* "So, is Will working on that list of cases?"

"He said as soon as he's done he'll email it to all of us at the same time."

"Thanks, Fiona."

"I'll see you tomorrow, Sam." She disconnected before he could say anything else.

Sam sat for a while staring out the window trying to collect his thoughts, his palms sweating and his stomach in knots. *Another death.* Each one felt so personal to him, obscene gestures only he could see.

He'd been in Barcelona on August fifteenth, one of those places he and Carly always talked about visiting but never found time to get to. His entire trip had been planned that way, taking her memory to every place they'd talked about visiting someday but hadn't gotten around to. The weeks he'd spent traveling had exhausted him. Mind, body, spirit—all had suffered through every leg of his trip. He'd spent the last two weeks with his parents at their B and B in Tuscany, trying to heal, trying to find the strength to move on. He thought he'd been making some real progress—and then this.

"Sam? Did you get tied up on the phone or something?" Emme called from the hallway. "Everyone's downstairs in the kitchen, waiting for you."

"I'll be right there," he answered.

He blew out a long hot breath, then went downstairs to join the others. There was no avoiding the meeting, since Robert was the one who'd called it. Besides, Sam told himself, he wanted to get it all out there in the open. Maybe then it wouldn't feel so much like a festering wound.

In the end, it hadn't been as bad as he'd feared. Once the initial shock had passed, and the appropriate sympathy had been offered, the core of the Mercy Street Foundation got down to work.

Mallory and Emme—both having been police officers in the past—thought maybe Sam shouldn't be involved in the case. Kevin, Susanna, Trula, and Robert—none of whom had ever worked in law enforcement—agreed that he should stay at the forefront of the investigation as long as he was comfortable doing so.

"The decision could be taken out of our hands," Sam told them. "The FBI might want us to back off."

"Can they do that?" Trula frowned. "If this is a private firm, and we have a client who has asked us for help, how can the FBI make us butt out?"

"I think they can strongly suggest it. But let's not jump to conclusions. I'm only bringing it up because my former boss—who is head of the special investigative unit I worked with—along with the agent who is handling the federal case and their top profiler will be here in the morning." Sam turned to the side of the table where Mallory and Robert both sat. "Will it be all right if we use the conference room?"

"Absolutely. Use whatever you need. I don't think I want us to go head-to-head with the FBI. There are going to be times when we will need them to cooperate with us." Robert appeared thoughtful.

"I think I might have mentioned to Fiona—Special Agent Summers—that we had a contract with Lynne Walker." Sam thought he should clear this up. "Do we?"

"No, but we should." Mallory nodded. "We definitely should. I'll draw one up right after lunch and email it to our attorney. Once he signs off on it—assuming there are no problems with it—I'll email it to Lynne Walker. She can fax it back to me."

"Do we know if she has a fax in her house?" Trula asked.

"She faxed me some information she'd forgotten to send with the file, and the number was the same as her home number," Mallory told her, "so yes, it should be simple for her. I'll tell her I just realized we'd neglected to send it before. I don't expect a problem with her."

"Great. So unless we have a problem with the FBI, we're all agreed that Sam should stay with this case." Robert scanned the faces around the table.

"I'm not agreeing one hundred percent," Emme told him, "but I'll go along with it."

"Mal?" Robert asked.

"Sure. We're already into it. Let's stick with it."

"Suse?"

"As long as Sam is willing, why not?"

"Trula, Kevin, and I have already voiced our opinions, so Sam, unless you want out, as far as the Foundation is concerned, this one is still yours."

"I don't want out," Sam told them. "I never wanted

out. But I do think Lynne Walker deserves an explanation."

"And I think you should give her one at the appropriate time." Robert nodded in agreement. "I trust you'll know when that is." He slapped a hand on the table. "So that's that. Sam stays in."

Robert turned to Mallory. "So tell me how we're going to go about finding some really great lab people. And what do we think about the lab itself? Should we buy a building somewhere, or should we build one here . . . ?"

Just like that, Sam thought, his head spinning. A little discussion, a little consensus or not, and the matter was decided by committee. Then on to the next topic, whatever that might be. Coming from the FBI, he wasn't used to a democratic approach.

He smiled. Robert Magellan's process could very well grow on him.

TWELVE

So. How are you doing?" It looked to Sam as if his former boss and longtime friend, John Mancini, was trying a little too hard to appear relaxed. John's fingers were tapping on the side of his coffee mug, and Sam knew from experience that John rarely tapped on anything unless he was agitated, impatient, or tense. Given the circumstances, Sam was going with tense.

"I'm good, John. Going away for a while was a good move."

"You get a chance to visit with your folks while you were in Italy?"

Sam nodded. "Spent the last two weeks there. What a life those two have. They're living their dream."

"Genna and I are planning a trip to Italy for October. We're going to visit some of my father's family this time—a cousin is getting married—but we're thinking a few days in a villa in Tuscany would top off the trip quite nicely."

"You should definitely go. Give my mom a call and tell her you want the second-floor suite with the balcony that overlooks the gardens."

"I'll do that. Do they miss Nebraska?"

"With its winters? What do you think?" Sam grinned. "My mom does miss her friends and her family, but the deal she and my dad made when they got married was that they'd do the Nebraska farm thing until the kids were off on their own and then they'd move to Italy and open a B and B. As far as I can see, they're both really happy with the decision."

"Gen and I saw the website. Villa DelVecchio looks beautiful. But it's a long way from the corn farm." John took a sip of coffee. "How's your brother doing with the farm, by the way?"

"He and Kitty are still plugging away, though I think she'd be happy to sell it tomorrow. It's a hard life, farming." Sam remembered his growing-up years, before he left for college. He knew exactly how hard life on a farm could be. "On the one hand, I'd hate to see it sold. Mom's family has owned that land since 1871. You can still see traces of the original sod house out near the barn. But on the other hand, like I said, it's hard work, and I can't blame anyone who doesn't want that life. Tom figures he has about ten, fifteen more years there. Hopefully one of his boys will want to take it over so it can stay in the family."

"Any chance you'd want it?"

"Me?" Sam laughed. "Uh-uh. Farming's not my thing. Never was. I couldn't wait to get to college and leave all those chores behind."

"So how are you, really?"

"I'm doing fine, John." Sam studied his old friend's face and clearly read the tension there. "Seriously. I'm fine."

"Bullshit." John raised the mug halfway to his

mouth before stopping to read it. KNOW THYSELF. SOCRATES. "I've known you too well for too long to buy that. There's a lot going on here, buddy. I don't know if I should pull you off this or not."

"John." Sam quietly put his own mug down on the tabletop. "I mean this with all respect for you, but, you know, I don't work for you anymore. You can't really pull me off this case."

"Yeah, I know." John sighed. "I was hoping I could just bluff you on this one."

Sam laughed. "Nice try. Now why don't you tell me why you're here. And skip over the part about how much you miss me and go right to the truth."

"Well, yeah, I do miss you. But that's not why I came." John averted his eyes for a moment. "I'm concerned about you."

"I'm a big boy, John. I can take care of myself. I'm not afraid to take this guy on, whoever he is."

"That's not the part I'm concerned about." John paused. "Do you own a gun?"

"Yeah, but I don't have a license to carry in Pennsylvania yet. Thanks for reminding me that I need to take care of that."

"It's going to take a while to get that through. Maybe we can do something to expedite that."

"I'd appreciate it. Thanks. But you still haven't told me why you're here."

"Look, we've been friends for many years. I know how you are," John told him. "I know how you think."

"So, what am I thinking?"

"You're thinking that this whole thing is somehow

your fault. That somehow, you're to blame for these murders."

"John . . ." Sam shifted uncomfortably in his seat, thinking that the problem with people you've known for a long time is that they always seem to know where your head is.

"I've been where you are, Sam." John's voice dropped to a near whisper. "And it almost destroyed me."

"Sheldon Woods." Sam nodded. The child rapist/ murderer who'd terrorized the East Coast for three full years had saved his best form of terror for the FBI agent who'd hunted him relentlessly. Woods had made a game of abducting a child, and then calling the agent and making him listen helplessly while he tortured the young boy. John Mancini had been that agent, and for six months after Woods's trial, he'd been MIA while he tried to heal from the emotional trauma. John had almost lost his job, as well as the woman he loved. Sam knew the story all too well.

It wasn't much of a stretch to see the parallels.

"Yeah. Sheldon Woods." John swallowed hard. "For months after we caught him, I got the shakes every time my phone rang. I was afraid to fall asleep because of the nightmares. I had a hard time talking to people, even my family, even Genna—especially Genna. I had a hard time relating to anyone. I'd lost Genna, and nearly lost my mind."

"Genna's always loved you. She understood. That's why she took you back."

"I paid the price for walking away from her for those six months, believe me." John smiled, as if he were making a joke, but they both knew better.

There'd been nothing funny about the situation. "What you need to remember here is that this isn't about you. It's about the killer."

"The killer is someone who's pissed at me for some reason, and he's taking it out on innocent people. So it very much is about me."

"That's where you're wrong. That's the same mistake I made. I carried the weight of all those dead little boys for a long, long time before I realized I didn't have to." John leaned toward Sam slightly, closer, his voice lowering, as if sharing something very personal, which he was. "I could have been anyone. It just so happened that I was the one who was assigned to his case, so I was right there in his line of sight. But it was Woods making the decision to snatch those kids, Woods making the decision to kill them. It took me a long time to really understand that I had no control over what he was doing."

"This is different. This is personal. Otherwise, why me? Why places, dates, that have a direct relation to me? I'm not even with the Bureau anymore."

"But does he know that?"

"What?" Sam cocked his head to one side.

"Maybe the killer doesn't know you aren't with the Bureau anymore." John let that sink in for a moment. "Let's assume that somehow you got on this guy's radar for some reason. For the purpose of this conversation, it doesn't matter what that reason is. As best we know right now, he started over a year ago planning ways to get your attention." John paused again. "It's got to be someone who knows you, or knows of you, someone who would know you were working as a profiler in the unit that handles serial murders. Someone who would assume that the case would either be assigned to you, or that you'd be called in to consult because of the Nebraska locations."

"That's what I'm talking about." Sam's stomach clenched again. "He knows I handled cases like this. He knows the case will get my attention, that's why he's doing it. He wants my attention."

"He's doing it because he likes it, Sam," John said softly. "You're not the reason he kills. You're just the excuse he gives himself."

Sam fell silent. Intellectually, he knew John was right, yet he could not shake the feeling that there was something more to the killings than someone looking for an excuse to kill.

"In any case, I just wanted you to know that I know what it feels like to have someone use you to cause pain to other people. I know how heavy that burden is. If you let it, the guilt will destroy you. And then he's won. He's off the hook." John looked straight at Sam. "Don't let him have that peace of mind, Sam. For God's sake, don't let the killer know that you're willing to accept responsibility for what he's done. Work with Fiona. Between the two of you, figure it out. Find him. Kill him or bring him in. But do not let him ease his conscience by letting him know how willing you are to take on his guilt."

"It's hard to convince myself that it doesn't fall on me."

"I didn't say it would be easy. But if you're going to work on this case, you're going to have to put your own feelings aside or you won't be effective."

Sam nodded slowly. He'd be saying the same things

to John if the tables were turned. Come to think of it, he *had* said those same words to John, back when Woods was doing his best to make John crack.

"Fiona said Annie was coming with her," Sam said. "Is she coming to read me, or the killer?"

"Probably both." John smiled. "But mostly the killer. I think she figures you're smart enough to figure out the rest of it yourself."

"Apparently not." Sam looked slightly chagrined. "Since you had to come all the way up here and point it out to me."

"That's what friends are for. And for the purpose of this meeting, we're friends, not colleagues. Former colleagues," he corrected himself. "By the way, did you get your annual love note from Laurie Heiss?"

"Yeah, but I didn't open it. I was out of the country on August fifteenth, and when I came back, I did pick up my mail at the post office. But I know what her card says. I'm sure there's nothing new there. I just haven't been in the mood to read it."

"When was the last time you saw Don Holland?"

"A month or so before I left on my trip."

"He's still denying that he had anything to do with Carly's murder?"

"Yes," Sam said, "and I don't know why. His fingerprints were all over my house . . ."

"Which he explained by saying he'd broken in there when neither of you were home, just to prove he could, and that he could get away with it. That always bothered me."

"What, that he admitted he was in my house a few days before the murder?" Sam snorted. "That's just another way of tweaking me."

"That's the point I'm making. He's giving you the finger."

"And he's still flipping me off by continuing to insist that he didn't kill Carly. By having his wife tell me every year that the real killer is still out there." Sam dragged a hand through his hair. "They want me to believe that someone is walking the streets free because no one is looking for him. *That's* what pisses me off."

"What if it's true, Sam?"

"What if it's . . . ?" Sam stared at John as if he hadn't heard correctly. "It's not. He's fucking with me from his prison cell and she's helping him."

Sam got up and smacked a hand on the back of the leather chair he'd been sitting in. "They're lying."

"Just stop and think for a moment."

"I've thought about nothing else for the past three years. You know the evidence. Holland's prints were in my house. He killed Carly in exactly the same way he killed all those other girls. Same MO, same signature." Sam grimaced. "Right down to cutting off her fingertips."

"Why weren't hers with the others?" John swiveled around to face Sam. "You found the souvenirs Holland took from every other victim. Nothing from Carly. Why not?"

"Maybe he didn't have time to put them with the others," Sam snapped, annoyed that John would even question this. He must know that Sam needed to believe that the man who had taken his wife from him had been caught and punished. Sam had to believe that the system had worked for him, that Carly had gotten justice. Anything less was unthinkable.

"Maybe he didn't have them."

"Are you serious?"

"John Mancini is always serious," a feminine voice floated into the room from the doorway. "He doesn't have a nonserious bone in his body."

Sam turned as Anne Marie McCall came into the room, accompanied by Fiona.

"Annie." Sam opened his arms to hug his former colleague. "It's really good to see you."

"Good to see you, too, sport." The petite blond profiler was, as always, impeccably dressed in a linen suit in spite of the ninety-degree weather.

"How's the husband? Still holding on to his cop job?" Sam asked.

"Holding on with everything he has." Anne Marie dropped her briefcase to the floor with a thud. "But not to worry. We'll bring him around sooner or later."

"I've been trying to lure Evan to the Bureau for the last few years without success," John said. "He likes being a detective, so until I can offer him something better . . ." John shrugged. "Our loss."

"Sam." Fiona smiled a greeting. She wore white Capri pants and a black T-shirt and looked very tidy. Casual, but tidy. Sam wondered if she ever looked mussed or if a hair was ever out of place on her pretty head.

"I hope we're not too early, that you two had time to finish your discussion. We were here with time to spare and were content to sit out in the car for another fifteen or twenty minutes, but the lovely woman who runs this fine home—hard to believe someone actually lives here, isn't it?—well, she saw us out there and took pity." Annie took a seat next to Sam and leaned down to open her briefcase. She took out several files and placed them on the table in front of her. "She forced us to come inside and have iced tea and the most delicious lemon cookies I ever tasted."

"Ah, you met Trula." Sam nodded knowingly. "She's a rare gem."

"And the little girl, Jill," Fiona added. "She was darling."

"You mean Chloe?" Sam asked. "Dark hair, dark skin?"

"Yes, but she said her name was Jill." Fiona laughed. "But after she went outside, Trula confided that when Chloe found a name she liked, she tried it on for a while. Trula said she does it all the time. Today she's Jill."

"She is one funny little kid," Sam agreed. "Her mom is an investigator here. Emme Caldwell. She was their first hire."

"So she told us." Annie opened a file. "Now. Business. Will Fletcher pulled up all your old cases and their dispositions." She handed Sam a copy of a three-page report. "As you can see, just about every one of these characters who's still living is still in prison. Most of them divorced, deserted by their families once their horrendous deeds became known. A number of them are dead, either by their own hand, a fellow inmate, or the state. So the field is narrowed considerably."

"Maybe there's a copycat, someone who wants to be like one of these guys." Sam scanned the list.

"You knew them, Sam. Does any name stand out as someone who'd be wanting revenge on you for something? Anyone there who threatened to 'make you pay'?"

"Annie, right now, looking at these names, it could be any one of them."

"So it could just as likely be none," she replied.

"What's that supposed to mean?" He frowned.

"You've been trained to pick out the aberrant. Remember those picture puzzles we used to get in school, where you'd have to look at several pictures and decide which one wasn't like the others? Well, profiling, as you very well know from your own experience, is often like those picture puzzles," Annie explained. "You look for the one who isn't like the others. The one who stands out." She held up the file. "None of these stood out to you."

"So?"

"So I'm thinking the guy you're after isn't one of these people."

Sam took another look at the list of names, going from page to page. It had to be one of them.

He paused over one name. "Here. Peter Longacre. Twelve years ago, I testified against him for . . ." His voice died away as he finished reading the information that followed Longacre's name. "Oh. Died in the prison infirmary seven years ago." He continued to check the list. "Well, then, here. This one. Frank Myles." Sam waved the page. "He was convicted of a double rape and homicide nine years ago. I was the one who tracked him down. You think maybe he might have stored up a little resentment since he started serving those two life sentences? No chance for parole?"

"Sam, have you seen the book, *My Life, Revisited*?

It's been on all the bestseller lists." Annie folded her arms calmly on the table.

"Sure." He blinked. "Oh, shit. Frank Myles? He's *that* Frank Myles?"

Annie nodded. "He's totally turned his life around. He's become a minister, counsels the other prisoners."

Sam started to say something and Annie cut him off. "And yes, I know he isn't entitled to any of the proceeds from the book, but he doesn't want the money. He's donated it all to a charity that provides college money for the children of victims of violent crimes."

"That could all be bullshit, and you know it," Sam said.

"It could be. I for one don't believe it is. I've met with him. I've talked with him. I think he's the real deal."

"Annie, you of all people know how good these guys are at pulling off a con."

"I do know that. But this time, I think it's for real," she insisted. "He has nothing to gain. He'll never come up for parole. There won't be any time off for good behavior, and he doesn't want any. He wants to serve his sentence—his debt, he says—but he's determined to do what little good he can do while he's in prison. So no, Sam, I don't think you have anything to worry about where Frank Myles is concerned."

Sam sighed. "Okay, so no one pops out at me. That doesn't mean that someone here"—he tapped on the folder—"isn't behind the killings."

"We'll take a good hard look at each of those people," John assured him, "but for now, I think we have to look beyond that list."

"Why don't you tell Sam what you're thinking, Annie?" Fiona suggested.

Annie took off her reading glasses and set them on the table. "The fact that the killer has deliberately selected locales that are tied to you, and that he seeks his victims randomly on dates that are anything but random tells us a great deal about him. I'm sure it's occurred to you that he's very organized. He's willing to wait for months to kill again because he needs the date and the place to be right. That tells me he's patient, that he's used to having to exercise patience. He has the will power to put off doing what he wants to do until the time and place are what they must be. So I'm thinking we need to go back in time, maybe even before you were with the FBI. Is there anyone back there who might have reason to blame you for something? More specifically, think about who might believe he has cause to blame you for something he himself might have done."

Sam shook his head. "I can't think of anyone like that, Annie."

"Take your time. It could be something very subtle. Hopefully, it will come to you in time, but probably not today, which is fine. We have other things to discuss." Annie pushed back her chair and stood. Sam knew within seconds she'd start to pace around the room, a habit of hers. She'd once said she thought better when she was moving.

"This latest murder." Sam's face went white. "Whoever this person is, he knows the details of my life. Well enough to know that Carly died on August fifteenth. Well enough to know that, even if I missed the others, killing someone on that date in that particular place is going to get my attention."

"And that's what this is all about, Sam. He's waving a red flag in your face, challenging you. *See me. Find me.*"

"Stop me?" Fiona wondered aloud. "Is that what he wants? For Sam to find him and stop him? Maybe even kill him?"

"Death by cop? Or in this case, ex-FBI? Could be." Annie stopped to ponder the possibility. "I actually like that a lot." She leaned on the back of the chair. "So, Fiona, have you given any thought to trying your hand at profiling? I heard there's an opening."

"I thought it was filled. What's his name?" Fiona frowned.

"Doesn't matter. He quit. He wasn't any good anyway," John told her.

"Anyway, to get back to our actor. Okay, he has Sam's attention. He has all our attention, though he doesn't give a flying fuck about the rest of us. It's Sam he's challenging. So we have to ask ourselves, to what end?" Annie glanced around the room. "What now?"

"Well, he's trying to draw Sam out, to engage him," Fiona began, then stopped. "You said maybe he wants to be stopped, maybe even to be killed. Maybe by Sam's hand."

Annie agreed. "So the next question is, what has he done that was so horrible that he deserves to die? I don't mean these current murders. These are all just means to an end to him. I believe there's something in his past—way back, maybe—that he feels guilty about." She turned to Sam. "John and I talked about this earlier this morning. We both know you feel personally responsible for these murders, but here's the thing, Sam: this is all about his guilt, not yours. He's projecting it onto you because he can't face what he's done—not what he's doing now, but something he might have done a long time ago."

"You're saying someone he used to know did something that's haunting him now, but he's trying to get even with Sam for it? Like, somehow he holds Sam responsible, but only because he can't admit to himself that he was the responsible party?" Fiona frowned. "Did that make any sense, Annie?"

"It made perfect sense. That's exactly how I see it. Unfortunately, we have no way of knowing how far back we have to go to look for him. We're going to have to rely on Sam to come up with a few possibilities."

"Honestly, Annie, I can't think of anyone."

"We all have people in our past who we might have injured in some way without even knowing it. It could be someone like that," John said.

"I'll give it some thought, but I've made it a point all my life to just get along, let others live their lives, not judge. Shit, I can't even remember the last time I had a real argument with anyone."

"There's someone there someplace," Annie assured him. "I only wish I could help you sniff him out."

"In the meantime, we have another murder," Fiona reminded them.

"You didn't give me any details on the phone," Sam said.

"That's what I'm going to do right now." She passed around several photos of the crime scene. "These were taken by the medical examiner's office."

Sam stared at the pictures. The man's body was dressed all in black and was propped up against a heavy chain fence.

"What's this in his hands?" he asked.

"It's a Bible," Fiona told him. "And that building in the background is the Virginia State Correctional Institute at Calumet. It's right outside of—"

"Yeah, Sanderson. I get that part. But I don't get the Bible." Sam stared at the photo.

"The victim is forty-seven-year-old Kenneth Wilke. He worked at a nearby convenience store," Fiona said pointedly, "but he's dressed like a—"

"Like a priest. Minister to the incarcerated," Sam muttered. "One of the acts of mercy is to minister to prisoners."

"Right. Wilke worked the late shift. Surveillance cameras show him leaving the store by the back door ten minutes after his shift ended. All the employees park behind the store. Wilke's car was still there the following day, but he never showed up for work. They called his home number but his girlfriend said she hadn't seen him since the day before."

"She hadn't called the store to find out if he was there?"

"She also works at night. She stocks produce at a local supermarket. She generally gets home before he does, so she hadn't noticed until the next day that he wasn't there."

"So the theory is that he was taken as he exited the building, forced into the killer's car and driven to . . ." Sam thought it through. "I'm guessing he wasn't killed where he was found."

"Right." Fiona folded her hands in front of her on

the table. "There's a field on one side of the prison. The police found an area where the high grass has been tamped down and there are tire tracks leading into the field. They believe the killer drove into the field and got as close to the most remote section of fence as he could without being seen. They found the kill site in the field near where the tire marks stop. They also found a pair of jeans and a white shirt with the name of the convenience store on the front. They figure the killer made the victim change into the black clothes, then strangled him right there. That would have been easier than killing him first, then trying to undress and dress the dead body. The postmortem stab wounds were made after the body was posed at the fence. There's no evidence the body had been dragged, so we're figuring he must have picked the victim up and carried him."

"How big was the victim?"

"Six feet, one hundred eighty pounds."

Annie let that sink in before stating the obvious. "The man we're looking for is one big, strong guy."

"One big strong guy with a big nasty grudge, if your theory is correct," Sam said.

"Big, strong, dangerous, and holding a grudge. Not a good combination," Fiona noted.

"So what's your next move?" John asked her.

"I'm going to Sanderson to see what I can find out about this latest victim." Fiona turned to Sam. "I'll give you a call and let you know what I find out."

"I'm going with you."

"Sam, you don't have to do that. I'm sure you must have some very bad memories connected with Sanderson."

"I'm coming with you," he said levelly.

"If you're sure—"

"I'm sure."

"All right," Annie said. "We have four deaths. Seven acts of mercy. Three acts left. Anyone know what they are?"

"I know them all. I looked them up." Fiona ticked them off on her fingers. "We've already seen the killer run through feed the hungry, give drink to the thirsty, shelter the homeless, and this latest, minister to prisoners. The three remaining are heal the sick, clothe the naked, and—"

"Bury the dead," Sam murmured, remembering, a chill running down his back.

Somewhere long ago, Sam had seen something that had depicted all of the acts, but where and when was locked in his memory. He had the uncomfortable feeling that somehow, that place, that time, was related to the killings. He tried to focus on it, but the image was elusive. He couldn't call it back up.

Maybe Annie was right. Maybe the killer *was* from his distant past.

Maybe with any real luck, he'd put it together before someone else had to die.

THIRTEEN

The drive back to Virginia with Annie hadn't proven to be as interesting as Fiona had hoped. She'd wanted to pick the profiler's brain on a number of topics—starting with Annie's take on Sam DelVecchio, for one—but no sooner had Fiona turned the key in the ignition than Annie had put her seat all the way back and closed her eyes.

"You don't mind if I try to get a little nap in, do you?" she'd asked. "I haven't had a full night's sleep in eight days and I am close to the stupor zone right now."

"Of course not. Go ahead and sleep while you can," Fiona had replied with as much sincerity as she could muster. She knew what it was like to go for days without enough sleep, knew exactly how it felt to just want to crash. She couldn't begrudge Annie her nap. She just wished she'd had a little time to ask a few questions, though.

Like, do you know if Sam has dated anyone since his wife's death? Or, do you think he's moved past his wife's murder enough to consider going out with someone else?

Fiona didn't want to appear ghoulish, didn't want Annie to get the wrong impression. After all, Sam's wife had been dead for three years now, and a lot of guys move past their losses in a lot less time than that. Still, she suspected perhaps nearly as many did not. Sam might well fall into the latter group.

Fiona just couldn't read Sam at all—at least, not yet, she couldn't. She'd only been in his company twice, but she was looking forward to working with him on this case. Certainly the case itself was intriguing, but Sam intrigued her just as much. Something about him drew her, and for someone as notoriously picky as Fiona Summers, that in itself said something. She wasn't quite sure what it was, but she thought it might be worth exploring. If he hadn't been dating, hadn't gotten past his wife's death, she wasn't willing to make a fool out of herself by letting him know she might be interested. She'd figured Annie McCall was her best bet in terms of finding out where Sam's head was, but Annie had nodded off almost as soon as they'd pulled through the gates of Robert Magellan's mansion.

Fiona turned the radio on low and headed south, thinking that maybe it was for the best. Maybe it wouldn't be the wisest thing to let anyone—even Annie—know that she was attracted to the former agent. She'd learned long ago not to discuss her private life with anyone. You never knew who you could really trust, and who would sell you out in a heartbeat. By the time she turned seventeen, Fiona had learned the very hard lesson of not speaking her heart to anyone. She'd kept very close counsel ever since.

It wasn't that she didn't have any friends. She had a few. Mostly, she acknowledged, within the Bureau. But wasn't it natural to become friendly with the people you spent the most time with? There were friends to go to dinner with, friends from her unit she could hang out with at the local bars on those rare times when she let her hair down and went out for a few beers at the end of the day. But, she admitted, there were no confidants, no girlfriends—or boyfriends, for that matter—with whom she'd bare her heart and soul. It had been a long time since she'd wanted one.

For a moment, her life sounded crappy even to her.

It's not that bad, she told herself. She had a job she loved—the only job she'd ever wanted—and she was damned good at it. She'd decided that the FBI was her future when she was seven years old, and had never considered any other path. She'd majored in criminal justice in college, minored in history. Upon graduation, she taught at a community college for three years to get her work experience in before applying to the FBI. She knew she'd be accepted. She was in top physical shape and she tested well, interviewed well. She'd been concerned that perhaps her personal background—her childhood—could be an obstacle, depending on who interviewed her, but that hadn't proven to be the case. The woman who interviewed her had known exactly who she was, and had appeared to be tickled that Fiona was applying to join their ranks. She'd been twenty-four years old on the day she applied, and had been delighted to find herself included in the next class to begin training at the academy.

The Bureau had been her goal for so long, she'd known exactly what she needed to do to excel at the physical challenges. She worked out daily at a gym to build strength and stamina, and long before she was eligible to apply, she started spending several hours each week at a local firing range. Before she entered the academy, she'd become quite a marksman. The very few people who knew who she really was were impressed by her determination and her dedication. Of those few people, fewer still understood why she'd chosen the FBI. To Fiona—and those who did understand—it seemed the most natural thing in the world for her to do.

Of course, there were many more who thought she'd lost her mind, and who could not understand why she'd give up what she could have had to play "cops and robbers," as someone had put it.

That that someone had been her mother still rankled.

She made the turn onto Annie's street slowly, so as not to jar the sleeping woman; better to wake her gently once the car was stopped. Fiona pulled up in front of the town house Annie shared with her husband, Evan Crosby, and turned off the engine.

"Annie." She leaned across the console. "Annie, wake up. You're home."

"Hmmm?"

"I said, you're home."

"Home?" Annie's eyes flew open. "As in . . . *my* home?"

"Yes."

"Wow." She tried to sit up but the seat was leaning

too far back. "Talk about an ungrateful passenger. You should have poked me awake so I could keep you company." She reached down and found the lever that moved the seat into a sitting position. "I'm so sorry."

"Don't be. I'm used to traveling alone. It's okay," Fiona assured her.

"At least come in and let me feed you."

"No, no. That's not necessary. I'm not very hungry, but I am a little tired."

Annie got out and opened the rear passenger door and grabbed her briefcase. "Why don't you bunk here for the night, rather than drive the rest of the way home tonight?"

"It's only another forty-five minutes. Besides, I have to meet Sam tomorrow morning. If I stay over, I'll have to get up super early to get home and change my clothes. I'm better off just going now. But I do appreciate the offer."

"As long as you're sure you're not too tired to drive."

"I'm not. I'll be fine."

"Well, if you think of anything else you want to talk about or if something else comes up on this case, give me a call."

"I will."

Annie was just about to slam her door when Fiona said, "Annie, did you know Sam's wife?"

"Carly? Sure."

"What was she like?"

Annie set her briefcase on the ground and leaned into the car. "Oh, Carly . . . let's see. Well, she had a good sense of humor. Liked to play practical jokes. Short and cute, blond and bubbly. Cheerleader type, if you know what I mean. Very perky. Impulsive. Lively."

"How long were they married before she was killed?"

"I don't know exactly, but I'd guess maybe five or six years." Annie angled her head to meet Fiona's eyes. "Is this professional or personal curiosity I'm hearing? Not judging, just asking."

Fiona could not look Annie McCall in the eye and lie. "A little of both."

Annie nodded as if she understood.

"Carly and Sam knew each other slightly in college—he was three years older, and she was in the same sorority as his sister, Andrea. After he graduated, he went into the service. She went to graduate school. They met up again at his sister's wedding."

"Did you like her?"

"I liked her okay." Annie seemed to be thinking it over. "Carly and Sam were so different. You've seen what he's like. Very smart, very focused, very serious about what he does. She never seemed to take things very seriously. Sometimes she did things that struck me as, well, as not very smart."

Fiona couldn't keep herself from asking, "Like what?"

Annie slid back onto the seat, facing Fiona. "Okay, I've never said this to anyone, not even Evan, but you know how Carly died, right?"

"A serial killer broke into their house and murdered her."

"Uh-uh." Annie shook her head. "There was no break-in, no signs that he'd gotten into the house any way but through the front door. Which had either been unlocked, or she'd opened it to him."

The two women stared at each other, Fiona not sure what Annie was implying.

"Fiona, her husband was an FBI agent who specialized in understanding the behavior of serial killers. That night, he was out of town, at the funeral of one of the victims of the killer he was tracking. She knew what's out there, she'd been hearing about it for years. So the front door is unlocked at nine o'clock at night? Or you open your door to a stranger at that hour? That doesn't strike you as reckless?"

"How do you know the killer was there at nine?"

"One of the neighbors saw a strange car park at the end of the street, and a few minutes later saw a man walking up the DelVecchio's driveway."

"They didn't call the police?"

"Why would they? There hadn't been any sign of anything being wrong. There'd been no screams for help, no call to the police."

"No description?"

"Only that he was tall and well built. The neighbor later said she'd thought it was Sam, but at the time, it had been too dark to really see him."

"Sam said Donald Holland killed her."

"Don Holland admitted to having killed a lot of women, but steadfastly denied having killed Carly DelVecchio."

"Do you believe him? That he didn't kill her?"

"John does. I think it's a possibility. One Sam will not entertain, by the way."

"Curious," Fiona mused. "You'd think he'd want to find the truth."

"He thinks he already has."

"But you think it's possible that this stranger the neighbor saw wasn't Don Holland?"

Annie nodded. "I think there's a chance that Holland is telling the truth about this. He didn't bother to lie about any of his other victims. Bragged about it, actually."

"What if it wasn't a stranger that night?" Fiona said thoughtfully. "What if it was someone she knew?"

"Well, if it wasn't Holland, I suppose that would fit."

"Maybe she did have her door locked. Maybe she didn't open it to a stranger."

"Well, that's never been considered. They dusted the house for prints and found Holland's. The MO was the same as Holland's other victims. It looked like a duck, it walked like a duck . . ."

"But maybe it wasn't a duck at all."

"Are you interested in Sam, Fiona? As something other than a colleague?"

"I was just curious about it all, you know." Fiona tried to shrug it off, then laughed at her feeble effort. "Okay, yes, I am interested in Sam."

"He's a great guy. I'd love to see him start to have a real life again."

"I guess what I really want to know is, has he been dating at all since Carly died?"

"Not that I know of, but then again, I don't know that he'd go out of his way to tell me. He was obsessed with bringing Holland to justice, obsessed with making sure her killer received the maximum sentence, which of course he would, having admitted to so many murders. Then, once the dust had settled, Sam quit the Bureau and took off on this trip to all different parts of the world. From what we could tell, he mostly roamed, like a nomad, from one place to another. What he did while he was wandering, and with whom . . . ?" Annie shrugged. "Next thing we heard, he was back in the States and had been hired by the Mercy Street Foundation, which may be a good move for him. John was happy that it brought Sam back into our orbit. We've all missed him and some of us were a bit worried. I was relieved to see him looking well and getting back to work again." Annie smiled. "Even if it isn't for us. Does that sum it all up for you?"

"Quite nicely, yes. Thank you."

"Well, good luck." Annie reached over and patted Fiona's hand. "I've been where you are. Evan caught my eye the minute I first saw him. There's never really been anyone else for me. It was as if I was waiting for him—and I knew right away that he was the one I'd been waiting for."

"Wow. Who'da thought cool, analytic, precise Anne Marie McCall . . ."

"Would be the one to fall in love at first sight?" Annie laughed and got out of the car. She slammed the door, then leaned in the window and said, "Trust me when I tell you that no one was more surprised than I was. So again, I repeat, good luck."

"Thanks." Fiona waved as she drove away from the curb, thinking that it would take more than luck for Sam to notice her.

All the way home, she thought about Annie's description of Carly. "Liked to play practical jokes. Short and cute, blond and bubbly. Cheerleader-type, if you know what I mean. Very perky. Impulsive. Lively."

Could Fiona be more different than Carly?

Short and cute? Fiona was tall and leggy and hadn't been called cute since she was ten years old.

Blond and bubbly? Fiona was dark-haired and was positive that no one had ever described her as bubbly. Simmer was more her speed.

Liked to play practical jokes, for God's sake?

Fiona had had enough played on her as a child that she cringed at that sort of humor. She knew that on the best day of her life, she'd never have been considered perky, nor was she impulsive. She was—had always been—serious and deliberate.

The cheerleader type? Hardly. Fiona hadn't had many friends in college. She'd made a habit of spending more time alone in her room or at the library than she'd really needed. She'd requested a single room her freshman year and after that lived alone off-campus, which practically eliminated her social life, which was fine with her. The fewer people she had contact with, the fewer times she'd have to answer the question, "Say, aren't you the girl who . . . ?" That too was fine. As long as people saw her only as the person she had been, she'd never be anyone else.

So, yeah, she was about as different from Carly DelVecchio as night was from day.

On the other hand, now at least she knew that she was not the sort of woman Sam was looking for, if in fact he was looking at all. Better to know now, she told herself, than run the risk of making a total fool out of herself later.

She pulled into the driveway and turned off the engine, gathered the bag of Chinese takeout she'd picked up on the way home, then took a few files from the trunk and locked the car with the remote. There was no mail to be picked up—Irene Lentini, her thoughtful next-door neighbor, brought it in for her when she was away for more than a day—and no newspapers lying on the front porch or the lawn. If she wanted a paper, it was easier and more efficient to pick one up in the morning when she stopped for coffee. Most days, she read her news online.

Next to the front door stood pots of pink petunias that cascaded over the rim in bright ribbons. Irene, who had been retired for ten years and widowed for six, planted and tended the flowers. In the winter, she hung a wreath on Fiona's front door, and in the fall, she'd planted spring bulbs. "Otherwise," she'd told Fiona, "folks will think the house is vacant. Then, next thing you know, we'll have break-ins in the neighborhood because word will get out that there's an abandoned house over on Forest Drive."

Fiona had laughed and cheerfully reimbursed Irene for whatever seasonal display was chosen to adorn the porch or the front door.

The house welcomed Fiona home with hushed silence, as always. The light on her answering machine was blinking, but she ignored it. She went straight to the kitchen and turned on the overhead light, then dumped the mail on the counter. Later, she'd pick out the bills and toss the rest into the trash. She had no time for junk mail, and rarely got a personal letter. There were few bridges to her past that she hadn't burned.

She grabbed a fork from a drawer and a bottle of water, and went out onto the back porch with the carton of chicken lo mein. She sat on the back step and ate while she watched the light fade from the sky as the sun set behind the trees. She saw the first stars of the evening begin to twinkle overhead and closed her eyes and wished that either she hadn't asked Annie about Carly DelVecchio, or that the answer had been very different.

Sam pulled up in front of the one-and-a-half-story cedar-shake bungalow and checked the address Fiona had given him. Nineteen Forest Drive. This was it. Somehow the house looked cozier than he'd expected, with the pots of flowers on the front porch and the wreath of something colorful on the front door. Fiona hadn't impressed him as being the cozy type. Which wasn't a bad thing, he reminded himself as he walked to the front door. Not everyone did cozy. He sure didn't.

He rang the bell but hadn't needed to. Through the glass pane of the oak door he could see her walking toward him. She was leggy and graceful and he wished the hall had been longer. He liked watching her walk.

"Hey, you're right on time." Fiona opened the door with a smile. "Come on in and I'll get my things."

Sam stepped inside and tried not to look around with as much curiosity as he felt, but he couldn't help himself.

"This is a great house," he told her.

"Oh, thanks," she called from the kitchen, where he could see her closing a window.

"How'd you find something like this?"

"I just told the realtor what I wanted, and waited until they found it."

"Did you have to wait long?"

"No. I got lucky. I just need to run upstairs to close a few windows. We're supposed to get some rain this afternoon."

Sam waved her off. "Take your time."

He wandered into the living room, which was comfortably furnished with a deeply cushioned sofa and two overstuffed chairs that flanked a stone fireplace. An oriental rug that looked like a real antique covered the hardwood floor and a simple oak table held a leather-bound book and a stained glass lamp which looked like a Tiffany to Sam but must have been a knockoff. He'd lived on a special agent's salary, and he'd never been able to afford a real Tiffany lamp. Or, he thought, a real Turkish carpet.

A group of photos lined the mantel, and Sam stepped closer to look. Family photos, he guessed. A picture of a younger Fiona with a little girl and a younger boy—probably her siblings—and another of a very good-looking man and woman. Her parents?

One of Fiona by herself, sitting on rocks overlooking the ocean, her hair swirling around her head in the breeze, and another that appeared to be a studio shot, the latter of a very different Fiona, this one with blond hair and makeup.

"Ready?" she said from behind him.

"Sure." He turned but didn't take a step. "Is this your family?"

"Yes."

When she didn't elaborate, he asked, pointing to the appropriate frames, "Your siblings? Parents?"

"Yes. Are you ready?" she repeated.

Feeling somewhat rebuffed but not understanding why, Sam walked to the front door and out onto the porch to wait while she locked the house.

"Do you want me to drive?" he asked.

"I'll drive. You've already driven several hours today."

"Do you know how to get to the prison?"

"Route 9 to Turner Highway."

"It's faster to go through Sanderson than around it," he told her as they got into her car.

"I don't know that way."

"You can stay on this road right into Sanderson," he said.

"All right."

"On my way down here this morning, I spoke with the assistant Warden. He said he'd meet with us out at the prison. I think he didn't understand why we wanted to drive out there."

"And you told him . . . ?"

"Like the boss always says, you have to be at the

scene yourself. Breathe the same air the killer breathed. See what he saw." He smiled. "Any boob . . ."

Fiona laughed. ". . . can look at photographs, I know. I've heard it too."

"That's John. Get out and get into it."

"Do you miss it?" She didn't have to explain what *it* was.

"I did at first. For a while, anyway. But I was traveling around so much that after a few weeks, that was my focus. The countries I traveled to. The people I met. The things that I saw."

"What countries did you visit?"

"Ireland. Spain. Portugal. France. Poland. Greece. Turkey. Kazakhstan. And on the way back, I stopped to see my parents in Italy."

"Your parents live in Italy?"

"They own a B and B there. It's one of those places where you can go and take cooking lessons for a week, drink the local wine, that sort of thing."

"Your parents are chefs?"

"Nah. They just own the place. They have a local guy do the actual teaching."

"Sounds very cool."

"It is very cool." He looked out the window. "I'm really happy for them both. They're having the time of their lives."

Fiona turned onto Sanderson's main road and Sam felt a tightening in his chest. He'd avoided this ride for a long time, but he knew that sooner or later he'd have to do this. It might be better, he'd reasoned, if someone else was driving, someone who wouldn't be tempted to pull over to the side of the road. This time, the first time, just a pass-by would be enough.

"Take a right at the light," he told her.

"The prison is that way." She pointed straight ahead. "Just about six miles down the road."

"I know," he replied.

She made the turn at the light.

"Now another right," he said after they'd gone several blocks.

Fiona stopped at the stop sign, then made the requested turn.

The street was narrow and there were cars parked here and there on either side, requiring her to slow down. The houses were small and cottagelike, with bay windows and leaded glass and flower boxes.

"Cute street," she said.

"Yes."

Finally, they were almost there. Sam leaned forward and craned his neck to look out the driver's side window.

There. There it was, the white house with the black shutters and the red door, the color having faded a bit since the last time he'd been here. The grass was patchy and unkempt, and weeds grew up through the cracks in the walk that led from the street to the front door. The Realtor's sign was still out front, but Sam suspected there'd been precious little interest in the house.

Fiona slowed.

"Sam, did you want to stop . . ."

"No. That's okay. Thanks."

Fiona accelerated and drove on.

"Thanks," he said again, and he knew from the

look on her face that *she* knew without asking that the house they'd just passed had been the house he'd shared with Carly, the house in which she'd been tortured and killed.

They rode the remaining six miles to the prison in silence.

FOURTEEN

There's the crime scene." Fiona slowed down and pointed to the bright yellow tape that marked off a long rectangle from the side of the road to well past the middle of the field.

"I guess you can park anywhere along here. We'll walk out," Sam said.

"Walk all the way out there?" She frowned.

"Why wouldn't we?"

"No reason," she mumbled.

She pulled to the side of the road and parked, then got out and looked across the field. The grass and weeds were almost knee-high. Sam was already in the field. He turned and looked back at her and stopped. "Are you coming?" he called.

"Sure." She stepped into the grass and felt it tickle the bare skin under her pants legs. She shuddered and tried to decide which was worse. Not looking, and therefore not knowing what manner of creature lurked in the tall grass, or watching every step and therefore possibly avoiding anything that might be there. And anything could be under the grass and weeds. Snakes. Mice. Ticks. Spiders. Rats.

She reminded herself that she'd read somewhere that field rats were nothing like city rats, that they were smaller and much less aggressive. She decided to follow in Sam's footsteps—literally. She walked the path he'd made into the field and prayed that he'd scared off anything that might be living there.

"Hey, you okay?"

"I'm fine," she told him, feeling more than a little foolish. She'd faced serial killers and child murderers and kidnappers, but the thought of some unseen furry or crawly thing making its way up her leg made her blood run cold. "We all have our little quirks," she muttered.

"What?" Sam turned to her as he stepped over the yellow tape.

"I said, I guess it's impossible to tell exactly where Wilke was killed. Since he was strangled here, there's probably no physical evidence. All the blood would be over near the fence, where he was stabbed." With one arm she brushed away the low-flying squadron of insects that had been flushed out of the grass.

She caught up with Sam in the middle of the section that was cordoned off. "Well, I suppose even as late as last week it would have been easier to see where the killer parked the car. This much later, there's nothing."

"I'm surprised the tape is still in place," he remarked. "I'd have thought between the press and the curiosity seekers, it would have been down by now."

"Maybe people are just being respectful. I suppose it does happen now and then."

"Or maybe they're concerned about him." Sam turned toward the prison.

"Who?" She followed his gaze to the watchtower that overlooked the field. "Oh. Him."

"I wonder why the killer wasn't too worried about being seen the night of the murder," he said. "We're standing, what, fifty feet from the outer fence, and the tower is another fifty feet from the inner fence. That's roughly one hundred feet away."

"And the guard would have been elevated, so it would have been easy for him to see a car from that distance."

"The killer would have had his headlights off, and probably would have turned off the interior lights as well. Still . . ."

Fiona nodded. "The guard should have seen something."

"Do you have a copy of his statement?"

"No, but we can get one."

"Maybe we should get our own statement."

"An even better idea. I'm sure we can get his information easily enough."

"Let's take a walk over to the fence." Sam motioned to her to follow him. "Let's see how long it takes the guard up there to come to the window to see what we're doing."

"He already knows. John called the prison and told them we'd be out here."

"All the same, you'd think he'd be curious." Sam forged ahead and sure enough, before they reached the fence, they could see the guard standing and looking down at them.

"There you go, see?" He pointed upward. "He's expecting us but he still wants to see what we're up to. So the question is—"

"How come the guard who was on duty the night of August fifteenth didn't bother to check out the movement he must have seen in the field?"

"Well, he could have been asleep, or drunk, or reading a really good book."

"Any of the above would work. The problem is getting him to admit to it."

"Sometimes you don't need an admission to know, but let's not get ahead of ourselves." Sam stopped and nodded toward the ground, where a small, white makeshift cross was planted in the dirt. He knelt and inspected the heavy wire fence immediately behind it. "This is where the killer left Kenneth Wilke's body. There are still traces of blood on the wire here."

Fiona looked back over her shoulder at the distance they'd walked from the field to the fence.

"So we're to believe that the killer carried a body from fifty feet in that field, propped it up here, then stabbed it forty or so times, and no one saw or heard anything?" She shook her head. "I'm not buying it."

"Well, then, let's scout up the guard who was on duty that night and see if he can explain how all this could have gone on under his nose without him knowing."

"I'll put in a call"—Fiona took her phone from her pocket—"and see if we can meet with him this afternoon."

"Have you eaten here before?" Fiona asked when they'd been seated at the first restaurant they came to on their way back from the prison.

Sam nodded. "A few years back, but I think it's

under new management now. Let's hope so. It wasn't very good."

"So why didn't we look for another place to eat?"

"One, because I'm starving, and two, because, like I said, new management." Sam smiled at the waitress who brought them their menus, and the waitress smiled back as she listed the lunch specials.

"I'll give you a minute," she said, her eyes still on Sam.

Fiona studied the menu and pretended she hadn't noticed. Sam did the same. Within minutes, the waitress was back.

"Have you decided?" she asked.

"I'll have the turkey club, whole wheat toast. Iced tea. Unsweetened." Fiona closed the menu and handed it over. "Are your tomatoes local?"

"Sure." The waitress turned to Sam. "And for you?"

"Hamburger. Medium rare. Fried onions, Order of fries." He slid his menu toward her. "Water's fine."

Fiona's phone rang and she answered it.

"We can see the guard at two o'clock back at the prison," she told him after she completed her call. She turned her wrist to check the time. "Which doesn't give us too much time."

"We'll eat fast."

She could feel his eyes on her, and finally asked, "What?"

"You look like someone."

"Like who?"

"I don't know. It will come to me, though. I guess if you'd lived in Nebraska at some time in your life, you'd have mentioned it by now."

She smiled.

"So where are you from?" he asked.

"Kansas, originally."

"And after that?" He tilted his head. "You said Kansas originally, which means you're from somewhere else after that."

"I grew up in California."

"One of my favorite states. Which part?"

"Around L.A."

Sam appeared to be studying her face. "You don't really strike me as an L.A. type of girl."

She merely smiled and leaned back as the waitress served their drinks.

"So," Fiona said as she added sweetener to her tea, "have you given any more thought to what Annie said, about maybe the killer being someone from your past?"

"I've thought about nothing else, but I just can't see anyone. Unless it's something really overt, you just don't think about someone holding a grudge for that long. What could be that important?" He shook his head. "You know, you could look back on your childhood, your teen years. Is there someone there who'd wish you harm or who'd want to repay an old debt? Someone so unhinged that they'd kill to get even with you? I'll bet you wouldn't even know, couldn't name them if you tried."

Bet I could. In a heartbeat . . .

Aloud, she said, "Maybe you should consider hypnosis. Maybe something will come to you that way."

"I'll think about it."

Their sandwiches came and they ate with one eye

on the clock. At one forty-five, Fiona said, "We need to go."

They made it back to the prison with three minutes to spare. By the time they went through their check-points and waited for George Cranshaw, the assistant warden, it was twenty past two.

"Lee's waiting for you in the conference room," Cranshaw told them as he led them down a short hall.

"Lee?"

"Lee Watkins, the guard you wanted to talk to." He stopped in front of a closed door. "Right in here, folks." He opened the door and stepped inside. "Lee, the people from the FBI are here."

To Fiona's eye, Lee Watkins looked to be no more than twenty years old, but she was pretty sure he had to be older than that.

"Sam DelVecchio." Sam introduced himself without bothering to correct the assistant warden. "How are you, Lee?"

"I'm okay." Watkins looked from Sam to Fiona and back. He was clearly not okay about being there.

"Did you need me to stay?" Cranshaw had one hand on the door handle, as if ready to flee.

"No, I don't think so. We'll be fine." Fiona smiled at Watkins who looked as if he was about to bolt. She patted the young guard on the shoulder as she passed behind him, glancing down at the backpack that sat at his feet. It bulged all the way around, the contents squaring the material.

She sat directly across from him, the better to maintain eye contact with him.

"Lee, how old are you?" she asked.

He glanced at Sam before answering. "I'm twenty-six."

"You're young to have such a responsible position here," she said.

"Not really." He still appeared leery.

"How long have you worked here?"

"Seven years."

"Seven? So you were nineteen when you started?"

He nodded.

"Have you been on the night shift all that time?"

"No, ma'am. I started out first on one of the medical wards, the afternoon shift. I didn't get the night shift until I went on the tower."

"Was that a promotion?" She continued to question him in a conversational tone, holding his eyes, making it difficult for him to look away without seeming evasive.

"Sort of. Well, actually, I asked for it."

"You wanted to work at night?"

"Yes, ma'am. I wanted to go to school during the day, so I could only work at night."

"Working a full-time job and going to school at the same time?" Fiona raised one eyebrow. "Very impressive, Lee. That's a rough way to get an education. I admire your determination."

"Thank you." He seemed to relax slightly.

"Where are you going?"

"Eastern Virginia College."

"What are you studying?"

"I want to be a history teacher."

"Excellent. We always need good teachers. Good luck with that." She smiled. "So, are those your books there in your backpack?" she asked.

He glanced down at his feet, then nodded.

"I guess you need to study whenever you can, right? Coffee breaks, that sort of thing?"

He nodded again, his eyes shifting to one side.

"It must be hard to keep up with all the reading." Fiona rested her elbows on the table as if chatting with a friend. "I used to tape-record the lectures so I could listen to them later. Have you tried that?" Before he could answer, she continued, "Of course, you wouldn't use a tape recorder. The technology is so much better these days, isn't it?"

"I guess," he mumbled.

"Sam, did you have any questions for Lee?" She pushed her chair back from the table.

"About the night that Kenneth Wilke was murdered out there in the field." Sam paced off to the left.

Fiona slid her phone from her pocket, pretended to look at the screen and said, "Will you excuse me for a moment? I have to return a call . . ."

Sam nodded and turned back to Watkins. "You were about to say . . . ?"

"What did you want to know?"

"I want to know what time you first noticed the car in the field," Sam told him.

"I never saw the car." Watkins shook his head. "I told the cops, I never saw the car, I never heard anything."

"How is that possible? You were sitting right there, maybe a hundred feet from where the car was parked. How could you not see or hear what was going on down there?"

Watkins shrugged. "He must have not had the lights on. I don't know."

Fiona activated the Internet connection on her phone, and opened a search engine, and typed in the name of the college Lee Watkins said he attended. When she found what she was looking for, she closed the phone and returned to the table, where Sam was still interrogating Watkins.

She listened quietly to his questioning for a few moments, then said, "Sam, you can ask him the same questions fifty different ways, but if Lee didn't hear or see anything, that isn't going to change, regardless of how many times you ask."

Sam turned to look at her for a long moment, then nodded slowly.

"You're right, Agent Summers." Sam sighed deeply. "All right, Lee. Unless you have something else to add, I suppose we're finished here."

"I don't have anything else to add." He shook his head firmly, side to side. "I don't know anything."

"Thanks for your time, then." Fiona opened the door and held it for Sam. "And good luck with school."

They checked out at the front desk and walked through the automatic doors to the visitor's parking lot.

"Okay, so what did you find out that made further questioning unnecessary?" Sam asked as they walked toward her car.

"Eastern Virginia College video-records many of their professors' lectures and makes them available to their students on the college website," she told him. "So if you miss a class, or get distracted, or come in late, or whatever, you can still catch the entire lecture online. You can watch them at any time that's convenient for you."

"So while Watkins is sitting in the tower, he's catching up on the day's class work on his iPhone."

"Sure. He had the phone in his shirt pocket. I saw it when I walked behind him. He probably has to leave the back pack in his locker, but I'll bet no one's ever questioned him about the phone. Can't you just picture him sitting in his chair, maybe with his feet on the desk, the earplugs in, listening to a lecture, maybe playing certain parts over several times to make sure he's getting it right, maybe taking notes?"

"So he isn't lying when he says he didn't hear or see anything in the field that night," Sam nodded.

"Right," Fiona agreed, "because he wasn't looking. So at least we know he wasn't lying."

As they left the parking lot, she asked, "Do you want to go back the same way we came?"

"No." Sam shook his head. "But thanks for asking."

When they arrived back at Fiona's, she asked, "It's too late to go in to the office. Want to come in for a beer?"

"You must have read my mind." Sam followed her up the front walk. "I could seriously use a beer right now."

She unlocked the front door and walked straight through to the kitchen and went right to the refrigerator. She took out two bottles and put them on the counter.

"I'm afraid I can't offer you anything to snack on with that," she told him. "I don't keep much food in the house."

He was staring at the open refrigerator. "It looks like you don't keep any food in the house. I haven't seen a cupboard that bare since I read about Old Mother Hubbard."

Fiona laughed. "I never know what time I'm going to get home. I did used to try to buy stuff to make for dinner, but it always went bad because I was too tired to cook once I got home. So I started doing takeout."

"You do takeout every night?"

She nodded. "It works for me."

"I'm impressed. Most people who do a lot of take-out are overweight. You certainly are not." He opened both their bottles and handed one back to her. "You look terrific."

"Let's go sit out back on the steps," she suggested, trying not to read anything at all into his comment.

She unlocked the back door and they went outside. There was a landing that could not be considered a porch, but the stairs were wide enough to serve as comfortable seating. They sat side by side on the top step, the distance between them not enough to keep them from bumping arms or shoulders from time to time.

"I sit out here every night," she told him. "Rain, snow, whatever. I like to watch the trees turn with the seasons." She pointed to a wooded area at the end of her long narrow back yard. "The deer come out most nights, if I time it right."

She pointed to a tall pine at the side of her garage. "There's a pair of hawks who sit up there, watching the bird feeders. I had to take mine down. They were picking off the little ones that came to eat."

She turned to him. "You must have a lot of wildlife out where you're from."

Sam nodded. "Bears, deer, elk, raccoons, prairie dogs, bobcats, mountain lions, coyotes, antelope, big-horned sheep, depending on the part of the state you're in."

"Stop." She laughed. "You had all those animals living near you?"

"Pretty much, yeah. I'm from an area close to the western part of the state. It's still pretty much the way you might picture the Old West in some places."

"You ever think of moving back there?"

"Not in this lifetime." He shook his head. "My family farmed. It isn't for me. My brother and sister are still there, wouldn't live anyplace else. They're always trying to get me to come back. They have families, though, and I understand the appeal of raising your kids in a place like Blackstone."

"Blackstone?"

"The town where I grew up." He laughed softly. "Town is a bit of a stretch. We do have a grocery store, a bank, a feed store, a café . . . that sort of thing. Not much more, though. I guess it's not as bad with the Internet—you can buy anything and have it shipped to your door, which is great for people who have no stores nearby, but we didn't have anything like that when I was growing up. If we needed to shop for almost anything, we'd have to go to Henderson Falls. That's the nearest big town. The regional junior high was there—we only had a grade school in Blackstone." Sam grinned. "And they have a library. My mom spent a lot of time there in the afternoons. She'd have to come in to pick me up from football practice every day, so she'd meet my sisters at the library every day and they'd do their homework and mom would read all the latest magazines and pick up the latest novels. She loved mysteries, romances, thrillers. She still spends a part of every afternoon reading."

He paused, as if remembering.

"And Henderson Falls has several streets with houses on them." When she laughed, he turned and explained why that was worthy of note. "Blackstone was mostly a farm community. There were a few houses in town, but not many. We only had about five different streets."

He was so close she could feel his breath on her cheek. When he turned toward her, they were almost eye to eye. She held his gaze, wondering who was going to look away first. She might still have been wondering if her phone hadn't started to ring.

"I should get that." She went inside and looked for her phone, found it at the bottom of her purse.

She listened for a long time, asked a few questions before saying, "All right. We'll be there."

Fiona turned off the phone and stood in the kitchen, wondering how she was going to tell Sam what she'd just been told. Moments later she heard the back door open and close, and she looked up to see Sam come into the room.

"What's wrong?" he asked.

Fiona cleared her throat. "There's been another killing. Same MO. There's no question it's our guy. We need to go. John's having a plane sent for us in less than an hour."

"Where this time?"

"Henderson Falls, Nebraska."

He stared at her for what seemed to be a long time, the color draining from his face.

"Who's the victim?"

"They don't have a name just yet."

He took his phone from his pocket and speed-dialed a number.

"Kitty. Hey, it's Sam. Yeah, everything's fine. Listen, can I speak to Tom . . . ?" He stared out the window, his eyes focused on something she could not see. "Do you know when he'll be back? Would you have him call me? No, no, nothing's wrong, Kitty. I just need to ask him something. Just tell him to call . . . he has the number."

He hung up the phone and turned his face to Fiona's. "My brother went into Henderson Falls to pick up a part for his tractor," he told her. "He isn't back yet."

"You don't think he's . . ." She couldn't bring herself to finish the sentence.

"If this guy's trying to get to me and thinks he's failed, what else can he do but make me come to him?"

FIFTEEN

"Agent Parrish, what else can I get for you?" Trula stood at the side of the kitchen table, her hands on her hips, and pointedly ignored the glare Robert was sending her way.

He knew she was ignoring him, knew the FBI agent had overstayed his welcome now by about two hours. Two hours the man had spent mostly talking to Susanna.

"Not another thing. You've already been way too good to me," the agent replied. "I haven't tasted cookies like that since my grandmother stopped baking and took up tennis."

"How old was she when she did that?" Trula asked as if it really mattered.

"She was into her sixties when she started taking lessons."

"God bless her," Trula smiled.

"Let's wrap this up, can we?" Robert grumbled. He'd had about enough of this good-looking guy monopolizing Susanna's time. He had a business to run, and Suse was an integral part of it. He glanced at the clock. It was now late in the afternoon, well past the time Suse usually left for home.

"Ms. Jones, I'm just so impressed that you were able to locate the exact place where Mrs. Magellan's car went off the road, after all that time, and after all those law enforcement agencies had given up." Luke Parrish's smile was one of admiration.

"There was no giving up," Susanna replied. "And call me Susanna."

"Then call me Luke." The agent turned to Robert. "You are so lucky to have such a clever investigator on your staff."

Before Robert could respond, Susanna said, "Oh, I'm not one of the investigators. I'm Robert's personal assistant."

Parrish raised an eyebrow and told Robert, "Her talent is being wasted." To Susanna, he said, "You should think about applying to the FBI. You'd be great in the field."

"I'm afraid I'm past the age of recruitment."

"You have to be kidding. You don't look a day over thirty," Parrish told her.

Robert could barely believe his eyes. Susanna was blushing.

Susanna never blushed. At least, Robert could not remember a time when she had.

"So tell me what you're going to do to find my son," Robert said to bring everyone back on point.

"As I said earlier, I'm going to spend the day tomorrow with the Sisters of St. Anthony. I'm going to need a list of all the sisters who stayed at the cabin since they started renting it, and a list of everyone the owner ever rented or loaned the cabin to. We'll start narrowing the search by contacting every one of them. We've run the fingerprints that were taken at the cabin but there were no matches, so at least we know that whoever has your son has no criminal record," he told Robert. "I'm also going to canvass all of the merchants in the area to find out if they remember if anyone was buying baby equipment and food around the time your son disappeared. It's a pretty rural area, the town's small. Most places like that remember strangers. Maybe not that far back, but we'll see what we can find. It's a starting place."

"The accident was in February," Susanna said. "The cabin isn't heated. Maybe whoever was staying there bought wood for the fireplace from one of the locals, or maybe propane for the stove."

"An excellent suggestion." Parrish turned to her. "See, what did I tell you? You've got really good instincts."

Robert cleared his throat and Trula shot him a dirty look.

"Well, I need to get going." The agent stood. "Trula, I can't thank you enough for your hospitality."

"Well, here." Trula busied herself at the counter. She handed him a small bag. "Take some of those coconut cookies with you."

"I'd be polite and refuse them if they weren't so delicious," he said. "Thank you. I'll snack on these later." He turned to Robert and extended his hand, which Robert took and shook with what he thought would be a bone-crunching grip. Parrish merely smiled and returned the crunch.

"Robert, I'll be back to you as soon as I have something for you."

"I hope it's soon."

"So do I." The agent nodded again to Trula as he started for the door.

"I'll walk out with you, Luke," Susanna told him. "I should be heading home now. Bye, Trula. Robert, I'll see you in the morning."

"Right." Robert remained standing until Parrish and Susanna left by the back door.

"Isn't his car out front?" Robert frowned.

"I'm sure he's just being polite and walking Suse to her car," Trula pointed out.

"Suse always manages to find it on her own," he grumbled.

He pretended to sort through that day's household mail, his eyes straying every few seconds to the backyard, where Susanna and Luke Parrish were in an animated conversation.

After nearly ten minutes, he said, "What do you suppose they're talking about all this time?"

"I'm sure I don't know, Rob. Why don't you go on outside and find out?" The smug tone in Trula's voice was unmistakable.

He shot her another dirty look before going back to the window. Susanna and Parrish were standing close to her car now, still talking. Damn.

All at once, he saw Chloe running down the drive. When she saw Susanna, she came to a quick stop, then skipped over and said something that made Susanna and Parrish laugh. Then the kitten she and Trula had adopted from the local shelter and named

Foxy ran into a nearby flower bed, and Chloe's attention was diverted.

Robert remained fixated at the window, his curiosity just about killing him. The agent was clearly flirting with Susanna, and if Robert wasn't mistaken, she was flirting back.

"He's flirting with her," he told Trula.

"Of course he's flirting with her. She's a very lovely woman, and he's not a blind man." She added under her breath, "Unlike some others I might mention."

"What?" Robert looked over his shoulder.

"I said, why wouldn't he be attracted to her? Suse is very pretty, she's smart, she's funny—" She paused. "Was that a harrumph I just heard? Did you harrumph?"

"No."

Robert stood back from the window as Chloe came running through the back door, the kitten in her arms.

"Trula, I think Foxy is hungry. She was trying to eat a bug." Chloe set the cat on the floor. "A very big bug. Like a grasshopper, but with long long legs and a funny little head."

"A praying mantis?" Trula asked.

Chloe shrugged. "I don't know if it was praying, but it was big."

"Chloe, did Susanna introduce you to Agent Parrish?" Robert asked.

"Uh-huh." Her dark head bobbed up and down.

"Did you happen to hear what they were talking about?"

Trula shot him a look of disapproval but she said nothing.

"Uh-huh. The man was asking Susanna where is a good place to have dinner and Susanna told him some places and how to get to them."

"So she just gave him directions . . . ?"

"Uh-uh. She started to, but he said, why don't you pick your favorite and join me."

"What did she say?" Robert leaned against the counter.

"She said, okay, you can follow me and we can—"

"She said *okay*?"

"Uh-huh." Chloe sat on the floor attempting to distract the kitten while Trula prepared its dinner.

Robert scowled and looked out the window in time to see Parrish's car pull to one side of the driveway in order to let Suse's car pass before falling in line behind her.

"Damn," Robert whispered as he watched both cars ease down the drive and disappear through the gates.

SIXTEEN

The flight to Nebraska was a tense one, with Sam on the edge of his seat, unable to get through to his brother, and not wanting to explain to his sister-in-law, Kitty, that there was a chance—at least in Sam's mind—that Tom might be in danger. What if he was wrong? That Tom had been gone for several hours in itself was no cause for concern. Tom was notorious for being chatty. A stop at the gas station to fill up his pickup could last anywhere from ten minutes to an hour, depending on who he ran into. On the way to the airport, Sam had tried Tom's cell phone several times, and had even tried calling their cousin, Greg, to see if he'd talked to Tom at some point this afternoon. Sam had not managed to get through to anyone, and he was becoming more frustrated by the hour.

Sam glanced across the narrow aisle of the small plane to the seat next to him where Fiona slept. He wanted to wake her, wanted to hear her cool reasoning on why he shouldn't jump to conclusions. One thing he really liked about her was her ability to reason and to think things out logically. He'd spent years with a woman who seemed to be lacking the common-sense gene and whose nature suffered from an over-abundance of the impractical. Carly held the world of whimsy by the tail most of the time, and at first, that had been part of her charm. She was so totally unlike anyone Sam had ever met. She was light to his dark-ness, fun and games to his studious, solemn nature. He'd been told all his life that he was entirely too se-rious. When he met Carly, he believed that a woman like her would help him to lighten up, and isn't that what everyone always insisted he do?

Marriage to Carly had sometimes seemed like a too-long day at the fair, a day filled with too many sweet sodas and too much cotton candy. There'd been many wonderful moments, many good memories, and Sam would never deny that they'd loved each other, but for the last eighteen months before she died, he'd been wondering if the lightness of her being wasn't perhaps a heavier burden than he'd ever imag-ined. It had become very difficult, after days of track-ing a killer who left mangled children in his wake, to come home to reruns of *The Simpsons* and entertain-ing her friends over the elaborate dinners she was fond of preparing. There had been times when he wished only to get into the shower and stay there until he could wash the stain away from his soul, but there would be dinner for eight that night.

He'd tried to explain to her how hard it was for him to switch from one mode to the other, but she insisted that it was better for him to socialize with fun people than to retreat to his study where he'd brood and dwell on whatever case he was handling, that all he really needed was some good times with friends to forget about the nastiness of his job. For Sam, those good times hadn't been so good, and the friends were mostly hers. He'd never once ended one of those nights without a massive headache. He'd never really fit in with her circle of friends, most of whom lived in the same carefree, fun-filled world wherein Carly dwelled. Sam knew better.

Fiona stirred in her sleep, bringing him back to the present. The cabin had grown cool during the flight and she'd wrapped her arms around her midsection as if chilled. Sam found a blanket in one of the overhead compartments, and tucked it around her lightly. She smiled in her sleep, and that alone had made him smile. Her dark hair spilled over her face, and he was tempted to push it back behind her ear. After a moment, he did just that, lifting the heavy silken strands with his fingers and draping it carefully over her shoulder. He leaned back in his own seat and closed his eyes, trying without success to relax.

The first thing Sam did once he climbed down from the plane was to try Tom's numbers again. It was now two thirty in the morning, and there was still no answer and there'd been no return call.

"They have kids in school," Sam told Fiona. "You'd think someone would be there to pick up the phone."

"There could be any number of reasons why no one's answering, Sam," she replied calmly. "Some people turn off their ringers at night. If the kids fall asleep with their iPods on, they won't hear the phone." She paused. "Does the house have central air?"

"Central air?" He frowned. "The farmhouse is almost a hundred and fifty years old. No, there's no central air."

"Then they probably have those window units, right?" When he didn't respond, she repeated, "Right?"

"Yeah, probably."

"The newer ones are pretty quiet, but the older ones . . . those suckers are loud. And if they have them, you know they're running tonight. It's pretty damned hot. So chances are they're not hearing the phone."

"I'd like to think Tom would have called back if he heard my message."

"Let's not jump to conclusions, all right? First, we need to get out of here."

"We need a car." Sam gazed around the private airstrip. "How can we get a car at two AM out in the middle of nowhere?" He frowned. "Where the hell are we, anyway?"

"Someplace called Afton's Fork." She walked around the building that served as a hangar. "As I'm sure you've already figured out, the airstrip is private. It's owned by a friend of John's who lets him use it when he needs to. Which, from what I understand, is practically never."

She continued to walk and he continued to follow. In front of the building a dark SUV was parked. Fiona opened the driver's door and reached under the seat.

"Sam, heads up." She called and tossed a set of keys in his direction. He caught them in one hand.

"You drive," she said as she walked around to the

passenger side. "You're more likely to find the way out of here than I am."

"Well, that remains to be seen," he told her as he started the engine. "I'll bet it's been twenty years since I was in Afton's Fork."

"And the last time I was here would have been . . . let me think." She fastened her seat belt. "That would have been never. You drive."

The paved road wound through endless fields. Sam drove slowly, the headlights the only illumination. They passed a large house, darkened in the dead of night, and it was then that Sam realized that this was actually someone's home. He tried to think if he'd ever known anyone in the area who had the kind of money that would enable one to have a private airstrip and a home like the one he'd just passed. He was pretty sure he never had.

He gave up and asked Fiona, "Whose place is this, do you know?"

"I have no idea. Someone John knows, that's all I was told."

He drove past several barns that looked new, past fenced-in pastures, and finally arrived at the main road.

"Which way is Blackstone?" she asked.

He thought for a moment. "East, I think. If I recall correctly, Afton's Fork is farther to the west by maybe forty miles or so." He glanced at the compass above the rearview mirror. "So that means a right turn here. We'll see where that leads us."

"At some point there should be a sign to identify the road we're on. It would help if you knew the name of the road."

"Big time." He pointed to the dash. "It looks like we have GPS, but I don't recognize the system. Would you look in the glove compartment and see if there's a manual?"

"Yes, it's here. Give me a moment." Fiona turned on the interior light and skimmed several pages before activating the system. "Where do we want to go?"

"We'll go straight to the farm. It's 731 Old Yellow Creek Road."

She entered the information.

"Well, it looks as if we're headed in the right direction, anyway." She leaned closer to the screen. "You were close. It's about fifty miles east." She pointed to the map that had appeared. "We are here."

He eased off the accelerator slightly and scanned the screen. "I know where we are. We can make it there in less than an hour."

Fiona settled back and said, "I suppose you don't need the voice activated directions."

He smiled. "I don't need the GPS now at all, thanks. You can turn it off. Unless it amuses you to watch us eat up the miles."

"I admit there are times when I am amused by my GPS." She looked over at him. "It isn't always as accurate as I'd like it to be."

"Name one other thing that amuses you," he surprised himself by asking.

"*I Love Lucy* reruns," she answered without hesitation. "I have all of the 'Best of' collections on DVD. For me, there's never been anyone with better timing or who better knew how to use her own natural gifts. How 'bout you? What makes you laugh?"

"Actually, I prefer the more sophisticated humor of the Three Stooges," he deadpanned.

"Steve Martin as King Tut," she countered.

"Soupy Sales with a pie in his face."

"Nothing like those classic comics when you need a good laugh," she agreed.

"Is Steve Martin old enough to be considered classic?"

"I'm not sure age is the determining factor."

The road was a straight line ahead of them for as far as they could see, and Fiona commented on it.

"Roads are going to bend when there's something to go around," he told her. "There's nothing out here to go around. Therefore, straight roads."

A few minutes later, Fiona asked, "So, the plan is to go right to your brother's and check up on him, then go to Henderson Falls?"

"Assuming my brother is there, and everything's okay, we'll bunk there for the rest of the night, then yes, go into Henderson in the morning."

"It's almost morning now," she reminded him. "It's going on four, and if we don't get to Blackstone until five, there won't be any 'rest of the night.'"

"I need to go there before we do anything else."

"I wasn't suggesting that we not go. I was just pointing out that—"

The car swerved suddenly to avoid hitting a small herd of deer that fled across the road and vanished like ghosts. Sam hit the brakes so as to not crash into the last in line.

When the animals disappeared into the black night and he resumed driving, he told Fiona what he'd been trying not to think about.

"There's no better way to get my attention than to target Tom."

"You think that's what's happened? That the killer has your brother?"

"I'm starting to think it might be."

Fiona took her phone from her bag and dialed the number she'd been given for the Henderson Falls PD.

"This is Special Agent Fiona Summers with the FBI. I'd like to know if there's been an ID on the victim that was . . . Yes, I'll hold . . ."

She turned her body to face Sam more directly and said, "It should be a capital offense for any governmental entity to play Muzak when they put a call on hold.

"Yes, thank you . . ." Fiona explained who she was and why she was calling. She took a small pad of paper and a pen from her bag and made some notes. "How do you spell that?"

She scribbled quickly. "What else can you tell me?"

A few more notes, and she said, "Thank you. Please leave a message for your chief that I and a colleague will be there in the morning and we'd like to meet with him. Thanks again.

"The victim's been identified as Jerry Perillo, age forty-two."

Sam was embarrassed by the flood of relief he felt when he realized that his brother had not been the victim. For someone else's family, the news would be heartbreaking.

"Where was the body found?"

"This is a really sick one." She tucked her notes into her bag. "Perillo was a cancer patient. He was found inside the parking garage at County Memorial Hospital. He'd just come from his chemo appointment."

Sam pulled to the side of the road. "County Memorial Hospital," he repeated flatly.

"That's what he told me, yes," she replied.

"My sister died in that hospital."

"I'm confused. I thought you said your sister was married and lived in Blackstone."

"That's Andrea. My younger sister, Eileen, died when she was eighteen. Right after she graduated from high school. She had a summer job in Dutton at an ice cream shop. She thought that was so cool."

"What happened to her?"

"She was on her way home from work one night and one of her tires went flat. Eileen was not the type of girl who wanted to be bothered learning how to change her own flat. She was sure that she'd always find someone else to change it for her, that someone would come along to help her. And for most of her life, that held true. She was the kind of girl the guys fell over themselves just to talk to." He smiled sadly. "But that night, no one came along, so she started walking. She was only about a hundred feet from her car when she was struck from behind. Hit and run. The vehicle that hit her never stopped. Just left her there to die in the road." Sam shook his head. "How do you do that to a kid? How do you leave someone lying in the road to die all alone?"

"Sam, I'm so sorry."

"Yeah. Well, someone eventually did come along, and they called for help, but it was too late. She was taken back to County Memorial but they couldn't bring her back around."

"How long ago was that?"

"Fifteen years ago."

Sam never thought back on that night without his throat tightening. "She was a really good kid. And the thing is, she always thought she was invincible. She always said she'd cheated death once so she was good until she reached her old age."

"What did she mean by that?"

"When she was, oh, eight or nine, I guess, a bunch of us went ice skating on one of the lakes outside of town. Me, Eileen, a couple of my buddies, and their little sisters. The big brothers—we were all about five years older than the girls—were supposed to be keeping an eye on the girls. Our parents all thought we'd be responsible enough to look out for them. Well, you know how that goes. Some other guys came along and we started playing hockey, and the game got pretty intense and we . . . well, we . . ." Even now, all these years later, the words were hard to get out.

"You forgot about your sister and she got hurt?"

"It was so much worse than that. We were really involved in the game, like I said, so when the kids started screaming, we barely even heard it. Then someone grabbed me from behind and swung me around and was yelling in my face that the girls had fallen through the ice. They'd skated onto a section where a stream feeds in, the ice was thinner there. Anyway, three of them went under the ice. We all panicked.

"The ice was too thin to hold us, so we made a chain, you know, the kind where you lay down and hold on to the legs of the person in front of you. I was first in the chain. I got to the hole in the ice and I could see them down there, all of them thrashing around. You couldn't tell who was who. I just reached in and grabbed the hair of the girl who was closest and pulled her out. It just happened to be Eileen. The guy behind me took her to the ambulance that someone had called and I reached in and grabbed the next girl. But the third girl panicked and got stuck under the ice. I went into the water but I couldn't get to her in time. I couldn't save her."

Fiona reached across the console for his hand.

"Anyway, after that, Eileen thought she was immortal." He turned to Fiona. "Can you imagine surviving something like that only to be run down ten years later by some cowardly asshole who couldn't even be bothered to call an ambulance?"

He jammed the car into gear and pulled back onto the roadway a bit faster than he should have. The tires spun and the back of the car fishtailed.

"Sorry," he muttered. He eased up a little on the accelerator, and tried to will away the image of the churning water, the colors of the girls' woolen hats just under the icy surface, the arms and legs thrashing, the frenzied gasping for air. His own desperate attempts to save that last girl. He'd discussed the incident once with Annie McCall, and she'd given him the only advice that had stayed with him over the years.

"Maybe there are some things we're not supposed to forget," Annie had told him. "Not to assure that we carry the guilt with us forever, but so that we remember that sometimes our very best effort isn't going to be good enough. It's a hard lesson but an important one, one we all have to learn. We're not always going to win. We won't always save the day. There are some things that are simply out of our hands. All we can do is to try with everything we have to make things turn out right. But if we succeed even half of the time, we should consider ourselves very fortunate."

The words hadn't eased his guilt or soothed his conscience over the child who had died, but it had made sense to him and had turned out to be true. He hadn't always been able to save the day, but he never stopped trying.

"Heal the sick," Fiona said after they'd driven a few miles, shaking him from his reverie.

"What?"

"Heal the sick," she repeated. "It's one of the remaining acts of mercy. Perillo was sick, he was at the hospital for treatment. But he's broken his pattern. It's a long way until February."

"The whole thing with the dates was to get me to make the connection. He probably knows I've noticed. He doesn't have to bother with the details anymore."

"He's really escalating."

"Well, why wait when you don't have to?" Sam turned to her. "Besides, I don't think he can. I think he's reaching that point where he can't wait to kill again."

"Only two more acts, Sam," she reminded him. "Two more victims. Then what?"

"Then it will be over, one way or another." Sam

stared straight ahead at the dark stretch of road that led him home. He knew who the last victim was supposed to be, and he'd deal with it when it came to that. He wasn't afraid of facing the killer. But he was afraid of who the next victim might be.

He pressed down on the gas and prayed that he'd get to his family in time.

SEVENTEEN

It was not quite daybreak when Sam turned off the road and onto the long hard-packed dirt lane that led to the farm that his great-great-great grandfather had laid claim to so long ago. In the eerie first light just before sunrise, the farmhouse looked like a mirage. The twin silos for which the farm was known rose through the mist toward the sky. The corn stood motionless in the wide flat fields, their pale tops like silken threads, the fat ears plumping for the coming harvest.

Sam drove slowly and quietly, the light spreading with every passing second. Up ahead the farmhouse glowed softly.

"The house is beautiful, Sam," Fiona said as they approached it.

"It was white forever, for as long as I can remember, even in all the pictures we have from a hundred years ago." He smiled. "But the last time it needed painting, Tom's wife said, 'For God's sake, Tom, every damned farmhouse for miles around is white. If we're going to pay someone to paint it, could we please paint it something pretty?'"

"The yellow is pretty. It's cheery. And, oh, look"—
she leaned forward as they drew nearer—"the front
door is blue."

"Only yellow farmhouse in the county. Only yellow
farmhouse with a door that shade of blue in the state,
or so Kitty insists. She could be wrong, but I'm not
going to be the one to tell her that."

Sam continued past the front porch to park near the
barn.

"Later, when there's more light, I'll show you where
the old sod house stood," he told her. "If you're interested, that is."

"Minored in American history," she replied. "Of
course I'm interested."

They got out of the car and Fiona stopped once to
inhale deeply.

"It smells so good here," she said.

"Smells like home." He took a deep breath, too, before walking toward the house.

"Don't you ever miss it?" She caught up to him.
"It's so beautiful here. I don't know that I'd ever want
to leave."

"I do miss it sometimes," he admitted. "Not
enough to move back full-time, but yeah, I do miss it.
Life is very different here than any place I've ever
been."

"How often do you come back?" she asked as they
reached the porch steps.

"Not often enough." A tall man stood in the open
doorway. Within seconds he'd crossed the porch to
embrace Sam. The two men held on for a long moment, then pushed back from each other. "I couldn't

believe it when Kitty said you'd called and that you were on your way home."

"So you got my message?"

"Sure, I got it."

"Why didn't you call me back?" Sam asked.

"I didn't figure I had to. I knew you were coming. You knew you were coming." Tom DelVecchio looked past Sam to Fiona, who stood on the top step. "Hey, who's this? Sam, you brought a woman home with you?"

"Ahhh, Tom, this is Fiona Summers. She's working with me on a case." Sam stepped aside to allow Fiona to step onto the porch. "Fiona, meet my brother, Tom."

"Nice to meet you," Tom said. He turned back to Sam. "I thought you said you left the FBI."

"I did."

"Then what case—"

"Let's go inside, Tom. That's what we're here to talk about . . ."

Tom's wife, Kitty, a diminutive gamine with short curly dark hair, was already up and had coffee on. The four sat around the worn round table in the kitchen and Sam spelled out what brought Fiona and him to Nebraska. When he finished, Tom sat dropjawed across the table from him.

Kitty was the first to speak. "You are seriously freaking me out, Sam."

"I have to admit to being a little freaked out myself," he replied.

"You think someone is killing all these people to get back at you for something?" Tom said incredulously.

"It looks that way." Sam nodded. "Actually, with this latest murder, I'm thinking the killer is someone from around here. Someone we know."

"Here?" Tom's eyes went wide.

"That's crazy, Sam." The coffeemaker beeped and Kitty got up from the table. "I can't think of one person who would want to harm you." Her head was shaking side to side emphatically as she grabbed mugs from a cupboard and placed them on the table. "And those other things you said this killer has done . . . uh-uh. No one around here would do something disgusting like that."

"Kitty, it's been my experience that you can never count anyone out. It seems like it's always the guy you'd least expect. The friend you trusted for years. The next-door neighbor who was always so nice, maybe mowed your lawn when you were away. Someone always says, 'I can't believe it's him. He was always so nice.' Or, 'He was such a good boy.' Believe me when I tell you that you cannot tell the good guys from the bad guys just by looking at them."

"So what do we do?" Tom still appeared bewildered.

"The first thing we do is figure out how we're going to keep you and the kids safe until this is over," Sam said softly.

"I thought you said the killer was after you." Kitty froze halfway to the table, the coffeepot in one hand and a pitcher of cream in the other.

"I think I'm his ultimate goal," Sam told her, "but he still has two more 'acts' to go. I figure he's saving the last one for me, but I can't rule out him trying to get to someone I care about for the sixth victim."

"We need to call Andrea." Kitty placed the pot on a trivet on the table and grabbed for the phone. "She and Pete need to be warned."

"Warned about what?" Tommy, her oldest son, came into the kitchen, all legs and shaggy hair, in baggy shorts and a bright green tank top. "Hey, Uncle Sam." He shook Sam's hand, then did some sort of elbow bump thing that Sam would still be trying to figure out an hour later.

Sam introduced Fiona, and Tommy acknowledged her with a nod. "FBI lady. Cool."

"Mom, are we going to have breakfast? I have football practice at seven thirty and if I wait too long to eat, I'll be spewing eggs all over the field."

"Thank you for that visual, Thomas." Kitty moved away from the phone to the refrigerator. "Of course we're having breakfast. Sam? Fiona? Bacon and eggs all right with you?"

"Better than all right." Sam nodded.

"Tell me what I can do to help," Fiona said.

"Nothing, really. Sit." Kitty pointed to Fiona's chair.

"I've been sitting for hours. At least let me set the table. Or make toast or something." Fiona added, "I can make toast."

"Okay. Thanks." Kitty pointed to a nearby cupboard. "Plates are in there."

"So what are we being warned about?" Tommy asked.

"There's been a murder in Henderson Falls." Sam chose his words carefully. He'd been hoping that his nephew would have forgotten what he'd heard when he first came into the room.

"No sh . . ." Tommy caught the look his mother shot from across the room. "No fooling? A *murder*?"

"I'm afraid so," Sam told him.

"Anyone we know, Dad?"

"I didn't catch the name," Tom said. "Sam, do you know who the victim is?"

"A man named Perillo. Jerry Perillo."

"That name familiar to you, Kitty?" Tom asked. "Jerry Perillo?"

"I think there's a kid named Perillo in school. I think he's a freshman. Jody would know," Tommy said thoughtfully.

"Jody's in high school already?" Sam frowned. "How did that happen?"

"Sam. It's been more than two years since you've been here," Kitty reminded him.

"I can't believe it's been that long." Sam shook his head.

"Wait till you see how big Gil is now. It won't be long before he'll be almost as tall as you," Tom told him.

Over the next ten minutes, the other two children—fourteen-year-old Jody and ten-year-old Gil—joined them in the kitchen. There was a lot of chatter amidst the passing of platters of eggs and bacon and toast, one spilled glass of juice and several refills of the coffeepot before Tommy stood and announced that he had to leave.

"I'm not ready," Jody complained.

"Me, either," Gil said.

"Then get ready if you want a ride with me," he told them. "Else wait for the bus."

"I can't wait for the bus," Jody whined as she dashed out of the room. "I have cheerleading and besides the bus is always late . . ."

Her voice trailed behind her as she raced up the steps.

Gil shoveled one more forkful of eggs into his mouth before following his siblings from the room.

"Tommy." Sam followed him into the front hall. "What we talked about before . . . let's keep it between us for now. I'm not sure it's out there yet."

"Okay. Sure." The boy nodded.

"In case the family . . . you know."

"Gotcha. I won't say anything to anyone. Not even Jody." Tommy grinned. "Especially Jody."

"Thanks." Sam slapped him lightly on the back before heading into the kitchen.

"Hey, Uncle Sammy," Tommy called to him. "We have an open practice this afternoon. That's where people can come and watch us practice. We're going to be good this year. Coach thinks we could even win our division."

"That's great, Tommy. Good luck."

"They moved me to wide receiver, just like you played." Tommy went uncharacteristically shy for a moment. "Maybe you could come and watch this afternoon."

"I'd love to do that. I'll try to be there, Tommy."

Sam's nephew nodded as if he had low expectations of what adults usually meant when they said they'd try to do something.

"What time?" Sam asked.

"We're generally on the field by three."

"I'll do what I can to be there. Thanks for the invitation."

"Yeah." Tommy nodded. "I hope you make it."

Sam went back into the kitchen in time to take the phone from Kitty to explain to his older sister Andrea why he was there, what was going on, and why she needed to keep her family close.

"Sam, do you think we should all go into town and stay at Andi and Pete's?" Kitty asked.

"Go stay in town?" Tom shook his head. "I have crops to tend to, Kit."

"You have children who could become the target of a serial killer," she shot back.

"They'll be safe at school," he countered.

"And you'll be safe where, Tom?" his wife asked.

Tom looked to his brother for assurance.

"That's my point, Tom," Sam told him. "Of all of you, I think you're the biggest target."

"The fields aren't going to dry up overnight," Kitty reminded him. "Let it go for a day. We'll go to Andi's, the kids will go there after school, and we'll see what happens from there."

Knowing he was defeated, Tom nodded. "Just for today, since I can see you're so rattled. But just today."

"We'll see," she told him. "We'll see . . ."

His brother and sister safely under one roof, Sam left for Henderson Falls with Fiona. Sam hadn't stopped the kids from attending school, but before they left Blackstone, he had a talk with the chief of police. They agreed a cruiser should be posted at the elementary school, and another would make regular runs past Andrea's house. Sam made a similar request of the Dutton police chief, the result of which was an officer being stationed at the high school.

Fiona asked for copies of any reports that would be forthcoming from the investigating officers, once they had time to write them up.

"I understand that there won't be anything for a few more days," she told Dean Worth, the chief in Henderson Falls. "But I would appreciate copies emailed to me." She handed him one of her cards.

"Tell me again why the FBI and the . . . what was the name of your organization again?" he asked Sam.

"The Mercy Street Foundation," Sam told him.

"Why are you all interested in this?" the chief asked, and for the second time that morning, Sam explained, starting with the murder of Ross Walker and ending with their trip to Nebraska.

"Well, sure sounds like someone has it in for you." Worth scratched his chin. "But why would someone target you? I mean, someone you brought in sometime, I could see that. But I don't remember you saying you ever arrested someone from around here."

"I never did. We're not sure what the connection is," he admitted.

"But we do feel it's someone local," Fiona told him. "It just seems as if these killings are bringing Sam closer and closer to home. This latest killing here—in the same hospital where Sam's sister died—that makes it seem more likely to us that Sam is somehow at the heart of it all."

"County Memorial Hospital is the only hospital out here for miles," the chief noted. "A lot of people

have died there over the years—including my wife
and both my parents—so I'm not real impressed by
that bit. But when you take it all together, yeah,
there's something fishy there." He turned to Sam.
"You being from around here, and all that with the
dates. Yeah, there could be something there."

"We'd like to talk to the detective who's handling
the case," Sam said.

"Well, right now that would be me," Worth told
him. "My detective is recovering from a heart attack,
so I picked this one up myself." He stood. "Let's take
a ride out to the scene and you can tell me if it looks
like those others of yours."

Sam had to park the car on the street, the entrance to
the three-story garage being roped off. They met
Chief Worth out front, then followed him inside,
walking up the ramp to the third level, where the
body of Jerry Perillo had been found.

"The poor guy was found propped up against the
driver's side of his own car," Worth told them as they
approached the spot. "There was blood everywhere—
pooled but, oddly, not spattered."

"Because he was already dead when he was stabbed,"
Fiona told him.

"Well, now, I don't know that that's been established." The chief kept on walking without breaking
stride.

"It will be. This killer has been strangling his victims, then stabbing them repeatedly in the chest. The
blood isn't spattering because the heart isn't pump-
ing."

Worth glanced back over his shoulder at her.

"Someone spent a lot of energy slicing the bejesus out of this man. Why would anyone do that to someone who's already dead?"

"He killed him to hold my attention," Sam replied. "The stabbing is just a means for him to blow off steam."

"You're telling me the guy did all that just 'cause he was pissed?"

Sam nodded. "That pretty much sums it up, yes."

The chief turned and continued on to the crime scene, muttering something about profilers and the FBI and off-the-wall theories.

Up ahead a crowd of technicians were still working the crime scene.

"State sent them in," Worth told them. "We don't have anyone who can process a scene like this one."

He walked closer, Sam and Fiona still in his wake.

"There's where the body was found." He nodded to the crime scene techs as he walked by. "We used to use chalk to outline the body. No need for that here. The blood outlined it for us."

Worth's phone began to ring and he excused himself as he stepped off to one side to answer it. Fiona stopped one of the techs to ask him about getting copies of all the photographs.

Sam stood in the garage remembering the last time he'd been there, waiting for the release of his little sister's broken body.

"That was the ME. He's finished the autopsy." Chief Worth walked toward Sam. "I'm guessing you're not going to be surprised at the cause of death."

"Manual strangulation."

"All that blood, and the guy'd been strangled first, just like you said . . ." Worth shook his head. "What kind of a crazy bastard does something like that?"

"That's what we're trying to find out," Sam replied.

"So I'm guessing this looks pretty much like the others?" The chief pointed to the stains on the concrete floor.

"Right down to the blood stains on the wall."

"Are you sure you don't mind?" Sam parked in the lot behind the high school but left the motor running, just in case this time—the third time he'd asked—Fiona decided she did in fact mind that they were taking time off to watch a high school football practice.

"Sam, I don't mind. Turn off the car and let's get over to the bleachers so we can get seats." She looked around at the full lot. "Unless the team has several hundred players, I'd say there are a lot of other people here to watch, too."

"I'm not surprised. Football is big in Nebraska." He shut off the engine.

"I thought that was Texas." She got out and stretched.

"There, too." He locked the car and held a hand out to her without thinking. She took it, and they walked down a hill to the field. As expected, the bleachers were half full on both sides of the field.

"If this many people show up for practices, how many come for the games?" she wondered aloud.

"They only have one or two what they call open practices at the beginning of the season. The rest of the time, only a few die-hard parents show up. This is sort of like an exhibition, except they're not playing another team." He tugged on her hand to follow him up the side of the bleachers. "There are seats about eight rows up. Come on."

The seats were not the best for viewing the field, especially when most of the crowd appeared to prefer standing.

"Where's your nephew?" Fiona shielded her eyes from the afternoon sun.

"I don't know." Sam scanned the field. "He should be wearing a number in the eighties."

"Why?"

"Because he's a wide receiver, and that's where their numbers are."

"Why?"

"You sound just like Andrea's three-year-old." He draped an arm over her shoulder.

"I'm just curious why numbers are assigned like that."

"So that you can look at the field and even if you don't know the players, you know what positions are on the field and you have an idea of what kind of play might be called."

Fiona shrugged. She supposed his explanation made about as much sense as anything else.

"Boy, I haven't been back here in years." Sam looked around with a sort of wonder on his face.

"Tommy said you played, too?"

"Yeah. My brother played but he broke his arm his sophomore year and he just wasn't the same after that. I was lucky—I never had any serious injuries and I was recruited to play in college." He smiled wistfully. "Man, we had some times here in this stadium. We played some football here."

"I thought that was you." A figure slipped into the empty space next to Sam.

"Hey, Drew!" Sam greeted an old friend. "I was just thinking about you. It's good to see you."

"Good to see you, too. How long's it been?"

"Too long." Sam turned to Fiona. "Fiona, this is Drew Novak. We went all through school together. Kindergarten through high school. Drew, this is Fiona Summers."

Fiona smiled and took the hand Sam's friend offered.

"What brings you back, man?" Drew asked.

"Just wanted to see the family." Sam turned his attention to the field where the team was lining up for a play. "My nephew Tommy's out there somewhere."

"He's number eighty-three," Drew told him. "My son Jake is the quarterback. They hang out together a lot."

A smile crossed Sam's face. "Eighty-three is my old number."

"I know. I told Tommy if it was available he should ask for it."

"Nice of you to remember."

"How could I ever forget?" Drew laughed. "Those were our glory days, pal."

"You had your share of glory in college, as I recall."

"It wasn't the same. High school, now that mattered." Drew glanced around the stands. "You, me, Steve, Vic, Blake—we mattered."

"I know what you mean." Sam nodded. "The five of us were together all those years."

"Steve and Blake are around somewhere." Drew

scanned the crowded stands. "I saw them both earlier but I don't know where they are now."

"They're still in the area?"

"Some of us never really left, Sam. You're the only one who did."

"Do you still see those guys? I mean, on a regular basis?" Sam asked.

"Pretty much. Some of us drifted back after college and settled down. Brought our brides with us from school or married someone from town. Me, I married Jessie Makefield. Remember her?"

"I sure do. Prettiest girl in the class two years behind us."

"Yeah, Jessie's still the same. We have three kids. Jake's the oldest." Drew patted Sam on the arm. "I heard about your wife. I'm real sorry. I should have called you but . . ."

"It's okay, Drew."

"Well, it's nice that you're seeing someone." Drew nodded in Fiona's direction. Sam could have corrected him, but didn't. He merely smiled.

"How long are you home for?"

"Just a few days."

"If you find yourself with some spare time, give me a call, okay? I'm in the book."

"I'll do that."

"I better get back down there, gotta keep an eye on my boy. He's going to ask me when he gets home how I thought his arm looked."

"It's looking damned good to me."

"I'll tell him you said so. You're still a legend around here, you know."

"Oh, Christ." Sam grimaced, and Drew laughed.

"Good to meet you, Fiona," Drew said as he went down the bleachers to the bottom row.

"A legend?" She smiled. "Sam DelVecchio, local legend?"

"It was all a long time ago."

"Not in the minds of some."

Sam turned to look around the crowd. Here and there he saw once familiar faces. Steve Molino, one of his best friends all through high school, was seated on the top row. Farther down and close to the middle sat Blake Carter, another old buddy. Down on the field stood Billy Finnegan. Finn hadn't changed much at all, Sam mused. He wondered what he was doing with himself these days.

"You said Tommy was number eighty-three?" Fiona poked him in the ribs.

"Yes."

"He's on the field now."

Sam stood with the rest of the crowd to watch, his arm around Fiona. The quarterback—Jake Novak, Drew's son. Sam shook his head. It was almost surreal to him. His nephew, Drew's son . . . probably the sons of other old friends out there, too, he thought. I'll have to ask Tommy if he has a copy of the roster.

The crowd ooohed as the lofting pass sailed into Tommy's hands and he sprinted down the field toward the end zone.

"The boy's got some speed," Sam noted.

"Is that family pride I hear in your voice?"

"Damn right. He's going to be good."

"As good as you?"

"Better."

They watched the entire practice, and when it was over, applauded the effort along with everyone else.

On the way back to the car, Sam encountered a number of people he knew from his past. Several classmates, even some old teachers, caught up with him in the parking lot.

"I don't know why I stayed away so long," he said to Fiona when they were on their way back to Andrea's. "It's so good to see everyone again."

"Well, it was good to see who's still around," she told him. "I think it will help in the long run to identify the killer."

"Are you serious? You're talking about people I've known all my life."

"One of them is a killer, Sam."

"Why does it have to be one of them? Why not someone else from around here?"

"Someone random?" She shook her head. "You know better than that. It's someone you've known, someone you've been close enough to that he'd know things about you. Like your birthday. Like the day your wife was killed."

Sam frowned. "How would someone from here know the exact date? The Bureau kept the story out of the news as a courtesy to me, and I know neither my brother nor my sister talked it up around town."

"That's a good question. Maybe we ought to think about that."

"What are you saying? You think this guy . . . this guy we're looking for killed Carly?" He looked at her as if she'd just sprouted a second head. "Are you crazy? We know who killed her, Fiona."

"I'm just saying, maybe we should consider—"

"No. It isn't possible." Sam waited in line for his chance to pull out of the parking lot, his jaw set, his eyes avoiding hers. "Christ, you sound like Mancini."

"Sam, like it or not, we've already agreed that someone from your past—my guess is someone you considered a good friend—has set this all up to bring you back here. You even agreed that it was someone—"

"That was before I came back and saw people again. You just met a couple of my best friends from growing up. Seeing them . . . I can't believe that any of them could have killed anyone. I can't think of one reason why any one of them would have cause to hate me so much."

"Sam the legend. Sam the great football player. Sam the college star. Sam who got out of town and made it big as an FBI profiler." She leaned back in the seat, her arms crossed over her chest. "Should I go on?"

"No. You're wrong. It isn't one of my friends."

"I can't believe you just said that," she said quietly. "You of all people know better."

They drove the rest of the way in silence.

EIGHTEEN

He sat on the hard metal seat, his feet on the row in front of him, his arms resting on his knees, a smile on his face.

He was so damned smart. He couldn't get over just how smart he was. All those years, everyone thought DelVecchio was the smart one. Man, if they only knew how he'd been outsmarted—his mind had been played with all these years.

If they could only know how much he'd taken from Sam . . . how many sleepless nights he'd caused him . . . how much pain.

Plenty more where that came from.

It had all been so very simple, so easy. Even now, he marveled at how easy it had all been, how clever he'd been, right from the start.

Of course, his very cleverness was both a blessing and a curse. A blessing because no one—no one— could ever guess the lengths he'd gone to over the years to break Sam DelVecchio. A curse, because, well, because the very nature of the game ensured that no one could ever know, *would* ever know, how he'd bested the best over and over. But it was okay, he assured himself, because in the end, in the very end, Sam would know all, and he'd understand that the price that was exacted was merely what was due.

Sam had ruined his life. It was only fair.

He watched Sam move through the crowd, his arm around the pretty woman with the long black hair. She might do, but he really didn't like dealing with women. It just didn't seem quite right. But then, there was the boy. Sam was obviously very fond of him. Of course, there's the brother . . .

So many targets to chose from, only one act left. Well, two, actually, but the last was going to be very special, and that was reserved for Sam.

Oh, yes. Payback was a bitch.

NINETEEN

"What do you mean, Tom left?" Sam frowned at his sister after she'd given him the news. "When did he leave?"

"Around three. He said he was going to watch Tommy's football practice and would try to meet up with you there. From there, he said he was going home." Andrea was tall and slender and in midpregnancy with her third child. "And before you start yelling, keep in mind that Tom is older than you and he's very stubborn, and he's going to do what he wants." She held a hand up in protest when Sam started to speak. "What he wanted to do was watch his son on the football field, then go back to the farm to see how his hired guys were getting along. He was bored out of his mind here today. And yes, I tried to explain to him that you were going to be annoyed but as usual, that really wasn't much of a deterrent."

"Is Kitty still here?"

"No. She went with Tom to the field. They were going to pick up Gil from school on their way back to town." She glanced at Fiona and said, "This is a sorry introduction to Sam's family. This is merely the usual DelVecchio drama."

It was apparent to Sam that Andrea was reading more into Fiona's presence than there was, but he did nothing to correct her. Instead, he kissed his sister on the cheek, patted her growing tummy, and said, "It's not your fault. Tom is who he is: one stubborn cuss. I should have known he wouldn't be able to hang around for a whole day doing nothing. It isn't in his nature."

He assured Andrea that the police car would remain on the scene for as long as they needed it, but didn't really think she'd be in any danger.

"This guy has never gone after a woman," he told her. "I think there will be two more targets, the last one probably being me. The next one . . . I'm not sure who that's going to be."

"You think it could be Tom," Andrea stated.

"I think there's a chance it could be him," Sam replied slowly. "I'm thinking the killer's going to go after someone close to me. Why else draw me back here unless to heighten the threat? I could be wrong about that, but I don't think I am. My instincts are telling me he wants to close this out soon."

His sister's face had gone completely white, and he realized how insensitive he'd been in speaking so candidly.

"On the other hand, Sam could be completely off base about all of this. And as much as I hate to be the one to break this bit of news, he really isn't infallible. His read on this could be all wrong," Fiona hastened to tell her. "Let us worry about it, okay? You have enough to deal with here. But be assured that your home and your family will be protected."

"I'm not worried about me," Andrea told her. "I'm worried about Tom. If you think the killer is going to go after someone close to you—most likely a man, you said—then who is going to be protecting Tom?"

"I will be," Sam said.

"That's great, Sam." Andrea stood with her hands on her hips, clearly not impressed. "But who's got your back?"

"I do," Fiona told her. "I've got Sam's back."

"Well," Andrea said, "let's hope that's enough."

"It will be," Sam assured her. "Fiona's got a reputation as a real marksman."

Fiona drew back one side of the big shirt she wore partially buttoned over her tank top.

"I don't leave home without it." She tapped on the small handgun in the black holster that rode her waist on the right.

"I was raised around guns. I have a lot of respect for them," Andrea told Fiona before kissing her brother good-bye. "Be careful."

He hugged her again and promised, "I will be."

Once they were back in the car, Sam's temper—stifled for the sake of his pregnant sister—erupted. "I'm going to rip him a new one."

"Let it go, Sam. From what you and Andrea both said, Tom isn't likely to change. You said it yourself: he's going to do what he wants."

"Kitty's too young to be a widow. His kids need him." His eyes shielded by his sunglasses, he pulled away from the curb with enough speed to catch the attention of the police officer who sat in a car across the street. Sam waved as he passed by.

"You need to get a grip," she told him. "Scaring the crap out of your entire family is not going to help the situation."

"My family doesn't react to anything unless they're scared shitless. They all think they're immortal."

"Like you do?"

"I've seen too much. I know I'm—"

"Oh, can it. You're running around as if you don't have a target on your back."

"He's saving me for last, Fiona. He's not going to come after me until he's finished with the sixth act."

"That may be the most likely scenario, but you don't know that for certain. And you don't know that he hasn't killed that last victim already. Maybe there was one—one other one—that we didn't find, Sam. Someone we hadn't heard about. Maybe he's on his last one already and we just don't know it."

When he didn't reply, she continued.

"I'm calling John, and I'm going to ask him to send out some backup. The farm is too big and fronts onto several different roads. Two people cannot possibly ensure that no one gets close to the house. If you want to ensure that Tom and Kitty and the kids are safe, we need more people."

"All right." He dragged a hand through his hair with impatience. Giving in had never been easy for him. "But I'm not letting Tom off the hook."

And he did not.

"What the hell is wrong with you? I told you to stay at Andrea's and you just take off without even telling me?" He started yelling the minute he walked into Tom's house.

"Since when do I take orders from you? I had things to do," Tom replied calmly. "I wanted to see my boy. I figured I'd see you at the field. I ran into Blake Carter and he told me he'd seen you in the parking lot but that you'd already left."

"Did you think to call my cell phone?" an exasperated Sam asked.

"No. I left mine at home. It never works around here half the time anyway. And I figured you'd be stopping at Andie's on your way back, so you'd know where I was."

"And if I'd gotten back to the farm and you weren't here?"

"Sam, give it a rest. I'm not hiding in my house, all right? I talked it over with Kitty, so don't think you're going to turn my wife to your side. I have a bunch of guys working with me out there in the fields, and I have my rifle and I have a handgun. I'll take them both out with me if it makes you happy. Can't say I've ever ridden a tractor with a twenty-two caliber Winchester Wildcat lying across my lap, but I suppose there's a first time for everything."

"You'll be lucky if you don't shoot your knees off."

Tom hesitated. "You think maybe the handgun's enough then?"

Fiona was still awake in her room in the back wing of the old farmhouse at almost 1:30 AM. The house had been still and silent for the past several hours, since everyone—Fiona included—had turned in for the night. There'd been bickering most of the evening—

between Tom and Sam, Tom and Tommy, Tommy and Jody, Jody and Gil—to the point where her head was spinning.

If anyone in her family had disagreed with another, they kept it to themselves. Disapproval always meant the cold shoulder, the withdrawal of whatever small amount of affection there might have been before the offending opinion had been spoken. She'd never witnessed the collision of tempers and opposing viewpoints, followed by a round of good-natured ribbing and good-night hugs as if nothing had happened.

The DelVecchios, on the other hand, seemed to all hold different opinions to one extent or another on just about every topic. At the end of the evening, Fiona couldn't recall hearing any one of them say, *Yes, you're right,* the entire night. To be sure, they had been good-natured about their bickering, and had even seemed to be enjoying it, as if arguing amongst themselves was a form of sport. She hadn't taken part, of course, in any of the discourses, being an outsider on the one hand and a person who, in her personal life, always sought the avenue of least resistance. But it had been fascinating, she had to admit, to see how the personalities played off each other, how the different relationships wove into one another. She wondered how it might have felt as a child, to have been encouraged to express herself as openly as Tommy, Jody, and Gil had been earlier. Would her life's choices have been very different if she'd been allowed to voice her thoughts? She hadn't done that until she turned eighteen, and then the results had been somewhat disastrous.

She heard a door down the hall open and close quietly, heard careful footsteps move toward the steps and fade down the back stairwell. Moments later, she heard the porch door squeak as it opened and squeal as it was closed. She got out of bed and tiptoed to the window and looked out on a star-filled night sky. She could make out a form headed toward the lounge on the back porch, and she knew it was Sam. Fiona sat on the edge of the bed and tried to talk herself out of joining him. She could think of several reasons why she shouldn't and only one why she should: she wanted to. She wanted to sit with him in the moonlight and she wanted to kiss him and see if he tasted as sweet as she thought he might.

She got up and pulled a T-shirt over the tank and sleep shorts she'd worn to bed, and crept from her room to the first floor before she could talk herself out of a trip down the steps.

The inside door of the kitchen stood open. Fiona turned the handle of the outer screen door and stepped out onto the porch.

"I thought I heard you," she said as she walked toward him. "Having trouble sleeping?"

Sam nodded and held out a hand to her. She took it and let him tug her down onto the chaise next to him. The evening air had gone cool, but his arms and body were warm and welcoming. "You too?"

"I usually have one or two sleepless nights each week," she told him. "I guess this is one of them."

"I usually don't have a problem sleeping," he said, "but tonight, I guess there's too much on my mind."

"You're worried about Tom."

"Sure. Wouldn't you be if he were your brother?"

She nodded, prompting Sam to ask, "Do you have a brother? You never talk about your family."

"I have a brother. He's a few years younger than I am. Also one sister, also younger. They both live on the Coast. I don't see them very often."

"Are they in law enforcement too?"

Fiona laughed softly. "Hardly."

"What do they do?"

"I'm not really sure. As little as possible, probably. Last I heard, my sister was trying her hand at some little theater, and my brother was trying to get a contract with a recording label in L.A."

"Sounds like a theatrical family."

She smiled wryly. Her family had thrived on theatrics.

"You really enjoyed seeing all your old friends today, didn't you?" She thought now would be a good time to change the subject.

"Oh, man, did I ever." He smiled broadly, his fingers playing with hers. "They were such great guys, every one of them. Seeing everyone again just made me realize that I need to keep in closer touch with them, need to get back here more often. It's good to keep those ties alive."

"Why haven't you?" She inched closer to him and settled in the crook of his arm. He played with her hair, lifting the long strands, then letting them fall.

"I don't know. I guess because for a long time, I was busy with work and busy with Carly when I wasn't working. Then, after she died, most of my energy went into making sure that Don Holland accepted responsibility for what he'd done to her. Of course, he never did . . ."

"Well, you can't change the past, but you can make it a point to stay in touch now that you've reconnected with your old friends."

"Yeah, I'm definitely going to do that. We had some real good times back in the day. We were really close back then, went all through school together."

"That's what you said. I find that amazing, that you'd all gone from kindergarten all the way through twelfth grade together."

"Well, all of us except Steve. His parents divorced when we were juniors in high school and he left to go live with his mother when she moved to Sioux City. He moved back after college. But it's not so amazing when you consider how small our elementary school was. If you grew up in a really small town, there might have only been two classes per grade. Some schools might only have one class. You California kids probably had bigger classes." He glanced down at her. "How many kids were in your grade-school class?"

"Well, actually, there was only me. I was mostly homeschooled." She shifted uncomfortably.

"For high school, too?"

She nodded.

"No prom? No football games? No team sports?"

"No." Talking about it made her feel bad about it all over again.

"You must have had friends from . . . I don't know, Sunday school? Summer camp? Girl Scouts?"

"I never did any of those things," she admitted. "So I've never had those long-term connections. I guess that's why it all seems so strange to me."

She took a deep breath, then said, "Something smells so wonderful. What do you suppose that is?"

"Probably the garden. My mom started it when she first moved out here, tended it all those years. Now Kitty's keeping it up."

"I'll have to check it out tomorrow, see what all she has growing down there." She pointed up at the sky. "Look, there's a shooting star. Quick! Make a wish."

She closed her eyes and wished for what she wanted. When she opened them, she saw Sam was staring at her.

"What?" she asked.

"Was that uberagent Fiona Summers, superior marksman and investigator extraordinaire, wishing on a falling star like a six-year-old on her first camping trip?" He poked her in the ribs.

"What's your point?" She sniffed with feigned indignation.

"Madam, you have a reputation to protect." He grinned at her. "Hard-assed agents do not wish on stars—shooting or otherwise."

"I guess I didn't get that memo."

"We'll let it go this time." He gazed down at her and asked, "So are you going to tell me what you wished for?"

She smiled.

Reaching up, she drew his face down to hers and kissed him full on the mouth. If Sam was surprised, he recovered quickly.

It had never been Fiona's habit to make the first move, but there was something about this man and this place that she needed to hold on to. Sam DelVecchio was the most decent man she'd ever met, and if she was ever going to let him know how she felt, it was going to have to be now. Tomorrow, things could change, she knew that all too well. Maybe there would only be tonight. If so, she needed to take advantage of that. If other days, other nights, were in the cards, she was fine with that, too. She'd welcome them. Right now, she was trying to ignore the voices in her head that were telling her that she should have waited for him to make the first move.

There'd been nothing tentative about that first kiss, nothing tentative in his response. She held his face in her hands and looked into his eyes, wanting him to know without her telling him that she was in this for wherever it would lead. She teased the inside of his mouth with her tongue and he reciprocated. She felt as if she couldn't get close enough to him, and when he moved back on the lounge to reposition her, she settled into him as if she belonged there. When his hands ran up and down the sides of her body, she raised her arms and wound them both around his neck to give him better access. She kissed him with total abandon and for the first time in her life, didn't bother to outline the potential consequences first. She got a glimpse into what her carefully constructed life had been missing, and it was exhilarating. His mouth moved down the side of her throat as his hands moved on her breasts, his touch on her bare skin sending a quick shot of heat to her very core.

"Hey, Sam, is that . . . oh." Tom stood half in and half out of the door. "Sorry. I didn't . . ."

Startled, Fiona bolted upright.

"Not a problem," Sam said with a great sigh of resignation, as he pulled her shirt down as surreptitiously as possible.

"The dogs were getting restless, coming in and out

of our room for the past half hour," Tom explained from the doorway, "so I let them out the front. Then I came into the kitchen for a glass of water and saw the back door open, and thought for a minute we had a visitor. Sorry. Didn't mean to interrupt." Tom began to disappear into the house.

"It's okay, Tom. Come sit with us." Sam pointed to the row of rocking chairs.

Tom appeared hesitant until Sam said, "I guess we're all having trouble sleeping tonight. Everyone's a little on edge."

Tom took a few steps toward them. "Yeah. Then when I saw the kitchen door open I thought maybe I let the dogs out the wrong side of the house. Stopped my heart in my chest until I realized it was you two out here."

He grabbed one of the chairs and turned it around to face Sam and Fiona. She tried unsuccessfully to act as if sitting there in Sam's arms was the most natural thing in the world, something she did every day.

Well, it had felt natural, until Tom showed up and scared the crap out of her.

"It's a beautiful night, Tom. The flowers in Kitty's garden smell great." Sam pointed overhead. "Beautiful stars. Fiona and I were just admiring the overhead view."

"Yeah, the old place has its charm." He nodded. "I think I'll grab me a cold something out of the fridge. You want anything while I'm in there? Sam? Fiona?"

"I'll take a beer if you've got one," Sam said.

"Nothing for me," Fiona replied. "Actually, I think I'll be going back up. The mosquitoes are beginning to like the taste of me a little too much."

Tom disappeared into the house.

"I like the taste of you, too," Sam said, pulling her down for one long, last kiss. Fiona slowly pushed from his embrace and stood up.

"I'll see you in the morning, Sam."

She'd gotten as far as the back door when he called her name.

"Fiona."

When she turned around, he was sitting on the edge of the lounge.

"Did you get what you wished for?" he asked.

"Not *all*, but it will do for a start." She smiled and went inside, waving to Tom in the kitchen, and shot quietly up the back steps to her room on the third floor.

It was well past dawn before Sam awoke the next day. After Fiona had gone to bed, he and Tom sat outside and talked for another hour or so, the first time in years they'd done that. Still, if he said he'd been pleased when his brother had shown up, he'd be lying. He'd been wanting to kiss Fiona practically since the first time he saw her, but it had been so long since he'd made a serious move on a woman that he was afraid he'd botch it. While he'd never cared much for aggressive women, that Fiona hadn't waited for him but had, rather, taken matters into her own hands—so to speak—had delighted him.

He sat up against the wooden headboard, thinking that she just might be the first woman he'd ever been comfortable with on every level. Carly, for all her love for him, had never really understood who he was, nor had she understood how seriously he took his oath to

seek justice, to stand for the innocent. A bit of a
Pollyanna, Carly had believed that every man had a
good heart and if given the opportunity, would always choose to do the right thing. Sam knew better.
Fiona did, too. There were things he'd never have to
explain to her, and that in itself was liberating. She
knew, as he did, that evil was a real force in the
world, that it had to be met head-on, and she was as
unafraid to put herself on the line as he was. That she
was beautiful was just a bonus. It was her heart and
her spirit, her character, that he was falling for. Apparently, she felt the same way about him. In spite of
everything that was going on around him—including
a potential threat to his own life—Sam was feeling
pretty good, possibly even optimistic.

He lay in bed until he heard the old grandfather's
clock in the front hall chime eight times, then, surprised at how late it was, jumped out of bed and
grabbed his clothes before going down the hall to the
bathroom. Once showered and shaved and dressed,
he knocked quietly on Fiona's door. When there
was no answer, he opened the door slowly, hoping to
find that she, too, had overslept. The thought of kissing her awake was hugely appealing. But when he
stepped into her room, he found the bed already
made. Disappointed, he made his way downstairs,
the tantalizing scent of pancakes and sausages leading
the way.

"Smells incredible, Kitty," he said as he came into
the kitchen. Tom and his son were already chowing
down, but no Fiona. He walked to the open back
door. "Did Fiona go out to the garden? She men-

tioned last night that she wanted to see just what all you were growing out there that smelled so good."

Kitty turned from the stove, a bowl of batter in one hand, a large wooden spoon in the other.

"She left around five," Kitty told him. "She said something came up unexpectedly and she had to go. She said she had to take the car but I told her not to worry, that you could use one of ours. Now she did say that you could rent one and the Bureau would pay for it, but I told her—"

"Did she say where she was going?" Sam frowned. Fiona left? Without even waking him to tell him she was leaving?

Kitty shook her head. "No. Just that she got a message and there was something she had to do. I thought maybe it might be something to do with your case . . . but then again, I guess she would have told you. She was in a big hurry, though. She was starting to write a note when I came down but I told her not to worry, that I'd give you the message."

He stood in the center of the room feeling as if the wind had been knocked out of him.

"Sam?" Kitty was saying. "Should I have let her write the note?"

"No, no, it's okay." He went to the table and took a seat, feeling anything but okay.

Why would she run off like that? Had something come up on the case? If so, why didn't she share whatever it was with him?

Whatever it was, why hadn't she shared it with him?

He reached into his pocket and pulled out his

phone. Excusing himself, he went outside and dialed John Mancini's number.

"John, it's Sam. Have you heard from Fiona today?"

John hesitated for just a beat too long.

Sam didn't give him time to respond. "What's come up on the case that you're not telling me?"

"Nothing's come up on the case, Sam," John replied.

"Fiona was here, in Nebraska, with me. She left at the crack of dawn. Are you telling me you haven't heard from her this morning?"

"I've heard from her, yes."

"So where is she?"

John took his time answering. "There was an emergency. She needed to be somewhere."

"John, cut the cryptic crap, will you? Where did she go?" Sam had to work at not sounding as desperate as he felt.

"She'll have to discuss that with you herself, Sam. It isn't my place to—"

"What kind of bullshit is this? Is she on some kind of secret mission or something?"

"It's a personal thing. If she wants to tell you about it, she will." John sighed. "Sam, we all have our secrets. If Fiona wants to share hers with you, she will. Right now, I suspect she's having a very hard time, so respect that, will you?"

"Sure. Thanks a lot."

"She did ask that we send some backup out there, so you can expect a few more agents to show up before the day is over."

"Well, they won't exactly be *backup*, now, will they? Since there's no agent here to back up?"

Sam disconnected the call and walked back into the kitchen, an uneasy feeling spreading through him. What had been so important that she'd leave without telling him? He'd thought they'd forged a bond, not just the night before, but over the past week. Why would she just walk out?

"Everything all right?" Tom asked.

"Everything's fine," Sam said.

"Here's your coffee." Kitty handed him a cup and pointed to the chair next to Tom. "Sit down and help yourself before it gets cold."

"So what's on the news this morning, momma?" Tom asked his wife, who'd been watching one of the early morning TV shows on a small set on the counter since dawn.

"Oh, the usual. The president is giving a speech on the economy at one this afternoon. They found remains of a small child in the Arizona desert last night—they think it might be that little girl who went missing from Cleveland last month. Your favorite baseball team lost again. The guy who used to play the cop on that TV show set in Boston—you know the one, it's been in reruns forever, we used to watch it all the time. Anyway, he's in the hospital and they don't think he's going to make it. Oh, and a private plane crashed in Nevada, right outside of Reno. They don't know if there were any survivors."

Tom looked up at Sam and said, "I don't have to watch a minute of TV to keep up with the news. I can always count on my wife to keep me up to the minute.

It's a miracle she can get breakfast on the table in the morning, she's so glued to that set."

"I like to know what's going on in my world when I start the day," Kitty said, defending her TV habit. "Besides, I like the folks on this show. They always have good guests. I like hearing points of view other than the ones held by certain members of this family."

Tom rolled his eyes, passed his brother the platter of pancakes, and with his customary sarcasm, said, "Now, little brother, tell me what your plans are for today, and how you're going to go about making Nebraska safe for DelVecchios."

TWENTY

Has Susanna gotten here yet?" Robert looked anxiously out the kitchen window.

Trula glanced at the clock on the oven.

"It's barely eight o'clock in the morning, Robert. Susanna usually isn't here until eight thirty."

"Maybe she's hung over," he said. "Do you think maybe she has a hangover?"

She frowned. "Have you ever known Susanna to drink too much?"

"First time for everything," he muttered.

"Why would you even think such a thing?"

"She went out drinking last night with that FBI guy who's supposed to be looking for my son. Not trying to make moves on my . . . employees."

Trula sighed. "Robert, they went to dinner."

"Dinner usually means wine," he reminded her. "And it was the third time this week."

"Dear lord, Robert, the woman's allowed to have a life."

He mumbled something unintelligible under his breath and Trula turned around, her hands on her hips.

"You know, Rob, if I didn't know you better, I'd think you were jealous."

"Yeah, well, you do know me better, so you know I'm not."

Trula laughed out loud. He scowled and started to say something when they heard a car in the driveway. Trula peered out the window, and chuckled.

"Well, here comes that old drunk now. Maybe I should get out the aspirin. Maybe I should be making Bloody Marys instead of orange juice this morning."

"Maybe you can forget the part about the hangover," he said as Susanna breezed in the back door.

"Who has a hangover?" she asked.

"No one." He waved off the question.

"Robert thought you might," Trula said, ignoring the dirty look he shot in her direction. "Because you were late."

"Why would you think that?" Susanna frowned as she poured her coffee. "And I wasn't late. Actually, I'm early."

He chose not to answer, pretending instead to be absorbed in the morning paper.

"So how are we this morning?" Susanna asked him.

"Fine," he replied coolly from behind the front page.

"Did you want me for some reason, Robert?"

"No, why?"

"Because you seemed concerned that I wasn't here."

"I wasn't concerned. I was just . . . curious, that's all."

A moment later, he asked, "How's Agent Parrish?"

"He's fine."

"How was dinner?'

"Great. Terrific. We went to Loki over in Toby Falls." She looked over that morning's plate of muffins and picked one that she recognized as peach and pecan, one of her favorites. "They have a new chef. You should try it sometime. The fish was excellent."

Robert's reply was a grouchy *hrrrmph*.

Susanna smiled from ear to ear, and winked conspiratorially at Trula.

"The new décor is lovely, by the way, Trula. All in chocolate brown and pale blue."

"I'll have to try it some night." Trula smiled back. Robert was still hiding behind his newspaper.

"Let me know when you'd like to go and I'll go with you," Susanna told her. "I'd love to go back. Maybe we can go on Friday."

"Maybe Agent Parrish will take you," Robert grumped.

It was all Trula could do not to laugh out loud.

Susanna let it ride. Years of working for Robert had taught her when to change the subject. She leaned against the countertop and asked, "Robert, what's the one thing you always said you most admire about me?"

"Is this a trick question?" He lowered the paper.

"No, seriously. What is it you first noticed about me?"

He looked her up and down, head to toe, not sure what he was being asked. "This is a trick question."

"Robert . . ."

"Okay. Well, I guess your organizational skills." *Good answer,* he told himself.

"Which are legendary, I don't mind saying, but no. That's not what I had in mind."

"Your sense of humor?" He tried again.

"Also fine, but no once again."

"I don't know, Suse." He looked up at her, wondering what she was getting at. "The fact that you know me better than just about anyone and yet you like me anyway?"

"Good one, but guess again."

"That you're smarter than any woman I know? That you have great legs? That you're very insightful?"

"All true, all part of the whole," she said, but still she shook her head.

"I give up." He held up both hands, palms up.

"Think back to all those meetings we used to go to together. You always said that what you most valued—what you found most useful—was the fact that I have a—"

"Photographic memory," Robert recalled. "It never failed to amaze me, how you could look at something one time and be able to remember everything, pull it all up a week later, if you had to. Just like a computer. Never saw anything like it." He shook his head. "We haven't had much cause to use that skill lately, have we?"

"Not until last night," she told him, her eyes sparkling.

"What happened last night?" He was almost afraid to ask.

"I got Agent Parrish to show me the list."

"The list?"

"The list of all the people who'd rented the cabin

over the past ten years. Including the names and addresses of all the Sisters of St. Anthony who stayed there."

"You have it?" His eyes widened. "Where is it?"

Susanna tapped herself on the side of the head.

"For God's sake, Suse, write it down." Robert all but tripped himself getting to the desk to look for a piece of paper and a pen.

"Don't need to. It's all right here."

"What if you got hit by a car? Or struck by lightning?"

From the opposite side of the room, Trula cleared her throat.

"Just kidding," he said.

"Me, too." Susanna opened her bag and took out a sheet of paper, telling him as she unfolded it, "I couldn't wait to get home last night to write it all down."

She spread the paper out on the tabletop. Robert leaned closer for a better look.

"Suse, you're a wonder. You're irreplaceable. Amazing. You realize that if I ever see Ian again, it will be because of you."

"Yes, I do realize it. It's true."

"I don't know how to thank you."

"I'll think of something." She smiled, then a second later was all business. "Okay, let's get started. Boot up that demon computer of yours. We're going to give those mad skills of yours a workout . . ."

She started out of the room ahead of him, then turned and asked, "Do you really think I have great legs?"

"World class," he assured her. "Absolutely world class . . ."

Despite interruptions from Emme and Mallory, by the time Trula took a tray of lunch up to Robert's office, the list had been narrowed down to five people who could possibly look good for the kidnapping of Ian Magellan.

"How did you figure that out so quickly?" Trula set the tray of sandwiches and fruit on the edge of Robert's desk. "You've only been working on it for"—she checked her watch—"four hours and thirty-five minutes."

"It's actually easier than it may sound," Susanna replied, since Robert was still focused on his findings. "We went through the list, first doing the obvious, a general search on—what else—Magellan Express. We were able to weed out several who were deceased, several others who were nowhere near Pennsylvania when the accident occurred."

"How could you know where any of these people were on that date?" Trula frowned. Other than her email, the occasional use of Magellan Express, and a little online shopping now and then, Trula had little use for the Internet.

"Well, here, let me show you." Robert typed in the name of one of the people from the list. He clicked a few links, then turned the monitor around to face Trula. "Here's a picture of one of the women on board a cruise ship that was docked in Cabo, Mexico, on Valentine's Day, 2007. As we know, the accident was on February eleventh of that year. The cruise set sail on February ninth, so we could eliminate her right away."

Robert held up the list. "We were able to cross off a lot of names because they were in places which could easily be confirmed. Many of the nuns are teachers who were, in fact, in their classrooms on that day."

"How could you know that?" Trula's eyes narrowed.

"I figured out ways to . . . figure it out," Robert said, averting his eyes.

"Robert, is any of this illegal?" she asked sternly.

"Well . . ." He cleared his throat, scrambling for the right answer. "There could be a gray area."

"Which means that some of it's black and white."

"Depends on how you look at it."

Trula sighed. "So show me one who could be the kidnapper."

"Sure. Here's one. Margaret Alice Davies. We haven't been able to pin down where she was back then, but we're still working on it." A few keystrokes and Robert pulled up a page of entries. "She's on the list because we weren't able to eliminate her in any other way—former nun, no trail after December of 2006. Could be something will turn up as we proceed. But right now, could she be our girl? Sure.

"She stayed at the house the previous summer, then left the convent, so she knows the area. Might have had a key copied and kept it." Robert looked up at Trula and explained, "The thing about that cabin is that no one went there on a regular basis. The owner didn't bother with it—she said most of the time she pretty much forgot about it until someone asked about renting it, which she said no one ever did in the winter. So any one of these people could be the right one."

"Like this one." Susanna waved a sheet of paper. "The former Sister Teresa Joan LeMaster. Goes by Terry, now that she's left the convent. Apparently she's been in and out of St. Anthony's for the past eight years, which tells me she's a woman with a lot of conflict. Lives in West Virginia—not too far from the convent and the cabin. Doesn't work, so she could have been at the cabin on that Sunday in February."

"I'm assuming the sisters hadn't arranged for anyone to use the cabin that weekend. I suppose that would be too easy," Trula noted.

"Way too easy. Like I said, it was winter, remember, and the owner doesn't rent it out during the cold months. No heat. So far, we haven't been able to determine where Terry LeMaster was that day."

"Well, suppose you find out all of them were close enough that day to have taken him. How are you going to narrow that down?"

"Well, for example, we can figure out which one of them has a baby that they didn't have before," Robert explained.

"How could you do that?"

"We can ask around their neighborhoods," Susanna replied.

"Or we can check to see if any of them started purchasing baby supplies back in the winter of 2007," Robert said thoughtfully.

Trula looked from Robert to Susanna and back again, then made a disapproving face. "Whatever you're doing is illegal. I knew it."

"Trula, kidnapping is illegal," he said quietly. "The

more we can narrow the search and hasten the time when the FBI finds the person who has Ian, the sooner we'll have him back."

"True. So at the very least, you should have Colin doing this sort of thing," she admonished, tossing out the name of Robert's former business partner, the one who even Robert acknowledged had mad scary computer skills. "At least nothing could be traced back to you."

"Colin." Susanna nodded. "We didn't think of Colin."

"Colin," Robert repeated. "I can have him check for purchases in February 2007 as well as this current month. Just to make certain, you know . . ." He thought aloud.

"And he can get in and out of places, look around, and never leave a trace." Susanna grinned. "No one will ever know that he was looking."

"Even assuming he finds someone who's been buying diapers for the past two years, what can you do? You're not going to ring that woman's doorbell and say, hey, we've checked your"—Trula gave him a dark look—"whatever it is you're going to check, and by the way, I think that baby belongs to me."

"No, of course not. Once Colin tells us who looks good, we go there, we make up an excuse, and we ring the doorbell. We see if the child is a male the right age, then we leave and we call Agent Parrish."

"And you tell him what, Robert? You tell him you had someone perform illegal acts and you checked things out yourself, found your child, and now— please, kind sir—come and get my son for me?" Trula stood with her hands on her hips.

"No. I'll tell him the truth." Robert glanced at Susanna, who raised an eyebrow. "Well, part of the truth. I'll tell him that we got the names of the former nuns from the sisters at St. Anthony's—"

"Which you haven't done," Trula reminded him. "How do you propose to do that?"

"We'll send Kevin to the convent to ask for the names. Everyone likes Kevin. They won't turn him down. No one ever turns him down when he asks for favors."

"What if by, oh, some miracle, the mother superior has respect for the privacy of the ladies in her order, and against all odds, defies expectations and withholds the information?" Trula would not let up.

"Then I suppose Kevin will have to resort to bribery."

"Bribery! You'd ask a priest to bribe a nun?" Trula shook her head. "Really, Robert . . . that's shameful, even for you. Besides, have you thought about what Kevin might say to the mother superior that would get her to give up the names?"

"Easy one. If it comes to that, he's going to say that several names have come to his attention from an anonymous source—"

Trula snorted.

". . . and he merely wanted to confirm with her that these ladies were in fact at one time members of the order. He'll say that Ian is his nephew—almost true, since Kevin is as close to a brother as I've ever had, as you well know—and that he's hoping to find whoever has the child before the FBI does, because, well, you know how the FBI can be. He can say anything he wants, that he wants to help this poor soul—"

"This is another one of your plans with half an ass, Robert." Trula-speak for a half-assed plan.

"One of these women could have my son. I want him back. I've waited long enough. We're this close to finding him." He turned the monitor back to face him. "If Kevin has to promise them a new convent, even a new school—do you really think I care what it will cost? I'll do whatever I have to do, but I will get my son back."

Susanna leaned over and turned the desk phone around. She dialed a number, then waited while it rang. When the call was answered, she smiled.

"Colin, hi. Susanna. Very well, thank you. Listen, I'm going to put Robert on the line. He needs your help."

TWENTY-ONE

Time to check in with the people who are paying me this time around, Sam told himself as he dialed Mallory's number.

"What's going on?" Mallory sounded concerned when she picked up.

Sam brought her up to speed.

"What a hot mess this case turned out to be," she said. "Have you been in touch with our client recently?"

"I was going to call her," Sam told her. "I'm just not sure how to tell her I'm at the heart of all this."

"Do you think you should do that at this time?"

"I don't know. I've been going back and forth on this. On the one hand, I feel I owe her the truth. On the other, I don't know how much it could muddy the water. I wouldn't blame her if she got pissed off when she found out that the investigator she has asked to look into her husband's death was actually the cause of his murder. But what if she takes it one step further and decides to call a local paper or TV station to complain or to vent? Maybe the only advantage we have right now is that there's a chance the killer still might not know that we've figured out that he's targeting me. If this goes public now, we're going to lose that, and it's a slim enough edge as it is."

"Good point. My advice would be to hold up on contacting Mrs. Walker. If she calls in for a status report, I'll take the call and let her know you're still working on it."

"Okay, thanks. Let's see how this plays out over the next couple of days."

"I read your email about the fifth murder. I'm assuming you still haven't been able to come up with any possible suspects."

"Fiona is sure it's someone from my past. Since I've been out here, I've run into a lot of my old friends. I hate to admit that I need to look at each of them as a potential killer. I just don't see that in any of them."

"Maybe you're not looking at them with a clear eye. Maybe you need to be a little more objective. Why not talk to Fiona about your relationships with each of these people—the good times and the bad— and see if anything looks out of place? Maybe something that seems innocuous to you might jump out screaming at her."

"If I knew where she was, I'd do that."

"I thought she went to Nebraska with you."

"She did. She left early this morning. She told my sister-in-law that something came up and she had to go."

"Well, maybe if you call your contact at the Bureau . . ."

"Already did that. He won't tell me. So I guess I

just have to wait until the rest of the posse shows up."

"What posse?"

"John—my old boss—is sending out a few agents as backup here today. There are only two more acts of mercy left, and I'm thinking this guy is going to go after my brother. The last act, I believe, will be saved for me."

"Why do you think he'll go after your brother?"

"At this point, he wants to hurt me, so he's going to take someone I care about. No more anonymous victims. In the past, he's only killed men, so I'm thinking he's going to target my brother, the guy who means the most to me. Then he'll come after me."

"How can you be so sure?"

"Because that's what I would do."

"What do you mean, he's gone?" Robert stared at Susanna from across the room. "Gone where?"

"I don't know, Robert. I just got a call from Luke saying that he was being temporarily reassigned to some emergency and that he'd be back on the case as soon as he could."

"Wonder what the emergency could be," Trula thought aloud. "Do you think there's going to be a terrorist attack? Maybe I should turn on the TV and see what's on the news."

"I don't know what to think," Susanna told her, "but I'm sure it must be something very important."

"It had better be damned important." Robert was

beginning to steam. "He's supposed to be looking for my son."

"I'm sure the FBI wouldn't pull an agent from a kidnapping case unless they had a damned good reason, Rob. I'm sure he'll be back as soon as he can."

"That's not really good enough." He shook his head.

"It's going to have to be, for now," Susanna countered.

"Why? We have the same list of names that he has. We've already started to narrow down the field a little. Why do we have to wait for Parrish?" Robert's stance was defiant.

"Because we have no authority to go knocking on people's doors, that's why," Suse reminded him. "He's got a federal agency behind him. We have—"

"Kevin." Robert nodded slowly. "We have Kevin. And he's backed by a higher authority than the FBI."

Robert grabbed the phone and hit speed-dial.

"Rob, what are you going to do?" she asked quietly.

He appeared not to have heard her.

"Hello, Mary?" he greeted the church's secretary when the call was picked up. "Good morning. It's Rob Magellan. Good, good, yes, we're all fine, thanks. I'm trying to track down Father Kevin. Have you seen him? Great . . . yes, I'll hold." Robert glanced over to Susanna and said, "When you only have one card, you have to play it."

"What card . . . ?"

"Kevin, hey, I need you. Now. Come to the house . . . get someone else to cover that for you. No, it can't wait, bro. Today's the day." Robert appeared to be listening for a moment. "Great. See you then. Oh, and Kevin? Wear your collar."

"Rob, I'm almost afraid to ask what you're doing," Susanna told him when he hung up the phone.

"Who knows how long Parrish is going to be tied up? Days? A week? More?" Rob's jaw tightened. "Supposing the person who has Ian is moving. Maybe she's nervous about staying in one place for too long, maybe she's renting and her lease is running out, maybe she's psychic and knows we're coming after her—I don't know." He reached for her arm. "Don't you see? We're this close. I can't sit around and wait for Parrish to finish up whatever it is they've got him doing."

"Rob . . ."

"Please," he pleaded, "don't ask me to wait. Give Colin a call and see if he's come up with anything else." He picked up the list from the counter. "And let's see if we can maybe map out an itinerary."

"An itinerary? Meaning you're planning on tracking down these people by yourself."

"Not by myself. With you. You're going to help me, aren't you? Suse? I don't think I can do this without you."

"Of course I'll help you." She sighed, resigned.

"And Kevin. I need Kevin." He paused, then grabbed the phone again and began to dial. "Delilah, get the plane fueled up and ready to go. I'm not sure exactly when. Just be on standby. Be ready."

He hung up and turned back to Susanna.

"One way or another, we're going to find him, Suse. I can feel it. We're going to find Ian." His eyes filled. "After all this time, we're going to find my son . . ."

TWENTY-TWO

Sam, who are all those people?" Tom asked as Sam came in the front door shortly after several strange cars had pulled up the driveway.

"FBI, most of them former colleagues of mine," Sam told him. "Someone at the Bureau thought the best way of keeping everyone here safe would be to call out the troops."

"How many of them are there?" Kitty looked anxious as she peered out the window.

"Enough to keep the wolves at bay, Kitty," Sam assured her. "But the thinking is that everyone needs to stay close to home over the next few days. I'm sure the kids won't mind missing a few days of school."

"Tommy's not going to like missing football practice."

"I realize that, Tom, but it can't be helped. I'm sorry," Sam said.

"You really think something's going to happen?" Tom folded his arms across his chest. "You honestly think this guy is going to be coming here?"

"I think there's a damned good chance he's going to strike real soon, yes."

"I don't need the FBI to protect my family, Sam."

"Actually, this time, you do," Sam told him bluntly. "Besides, it isn't your call to make."

"Even though this is my property?"

"Your life—and mine—could depend on them being here."

"For how long?"

"I don't think it's going to be long at all now." Sam shook his head. "He's escalated over the past few weeks. He's in high gear now. He's not going to wait much longer to make his next move. He won't be able to."

"Doesn't it work on you sometimes, Sam?" Kitty turned from the window where she'd watched another car pull up. "Getting inside the head of these people? Trying to think like they do, trying to understand why they do what they do?"

"Yeah." Sam nodded wearily. "It works on me. That's why I left the Bureau and went to work with the Foundation. I needed a change."

"Some change, Sam," Kitty scoffed. "Looks to me like you're doing the same thing, dealing with the same kind of people. You just traded one set of problems for another."

Sam had no retort, the same thought having occurred to him. He merely nodded, then went back outside to meet with the latest arrival.

There were five agents standing in the driveway, all in black T-shirts and jeans.

"Wow. Men in black. Not a suit in the crowd, but still. Men in black." Sam walked toward them. "You know, you might blend in a little better with the locals if you changed it up a little. A gray T-shirt here, a blue one there. If you're trying to pass as farmhands, you're going to have to do a little better than that."

"We wanted to make sure you knew who the good guys were," someone called to him.

"I know the faces, I know the names, the uniform is optional," Sam replied. "And I'm glad you're all here. I know it's part of the job, but—"

"This is more than a job. This is personal," another agent said. Sam was surprised to see Luke Parrish in the group.

"I thought you were on the Magellan case," he said.

"I was. Still am. I'll get back to it," Luke told him.

"I hope my boss doesn't find out you left his case to work on mine."

"I won't tell if you don't." Luke slapped him on the back. "By the way, where's Fiona? I heard she was on this job."

"She left this morning. Said something came up."

"So why don't you fill us in on the backstory here, Sam."

Sam nodded. "Come on inside, and I'll bring you all up to date."

*

He came into the house through the door that led from the garage into the kitchen. The house was quiet, as he knew it would be. His wife would be picking up the kids from their after-school activities, and she'd be stopping on the way home to pick up dinner. Of course, he could have hung around school when he finished for the day, picked up the kids himself, but he was too jumpy. It had been all he could do to get through his last class. The last thing he needed right then was a few more kids working on his nerves, even if those kids were his. Especially if they were his.

He opened a beer and took it out to the screened porch and stared into space. Things weren't going the way he'd wanted. He'd figured that out by noon, when he overheard a couple of seniors talking about how Tommy DelVecchio hadn't been at practice the day before. He'd been in school, but his dad and someone else had come to get him and he wasn't in school again today.

He hadn't needed to drive by the DelVecchio farm on the way home, hadn't needed to see those cars all lined up across the barnyard to know what was going on. Which meant Sam *had* figured it out and had called in the troops. The chances of getting to any one of them now was pretty damned slim, he had to admit. He'd just have to be patient.

As soon as he'd thought it, he grimaced. Patience was not something he had a whole lot of right now. He'd already waited longer than any mortal should be asked to wait, hadn't he? And who's to say how much longer Sam was going to stick around? He could leave that night, could be packing right at this very second. Shit, for all he knew, Sam was already gone.

He got up and began to pace. It was so hard to think sometimes when he was sitting still.

All right, he told himself. So he won't be able to get to Tom. He'd really wanted that sixth one to be Tom. That would have been the best. He'd never liked Tom, thought he was a real know-it-all, and he'd never been nice to them when they were all out at the farm with Sam. But the smartest people in life, the most successful, are the ones who can adapt, right? Survival of the fittest, and all that.

So he'd adapt. He'd think it through. He'd come up with the right one, of course he would.

He walked out into the backyard and waved to a neighbor who was out watering her flower beds. He didn't stop to chat as he might otherwise have done. He didn't want to break his concentration.

When it came to him, he smiled with satisfaction. Why he hadn't thought of it sooner . . . well, it was even better than what he'd planned.

He walked briskly back to the house, his game plan falling quickly into place, a line from his favorite Stones song—the one about getting what you need rather than what you want—running through his head.

TWENTY-THREE

"Sam, wake up. Come on, Sammy."

Sam opened his eyes to see his brother standing over him. Tom's face was sheet white, his eyes wet, his expression one of total disbelief.

"What?" Sam sat up. "What's happened?"

"Vic's on the phone. It was Drew he went after." Tears rolled down Tom's face. "He got Drew."

"Who got—" Sam's heart stopped in his body as the meaning of his brother's words became clear. "Where's the phone? Is he still on the phone?"

Sam jumped out of the bed, grabbed a pair of cut-offs on his way to the door, and struggled to get them pulled up as he made his way downstairs. The phone lay atop the kitchen table, and he picked it up.

"Vic? You there?"

On the other end of the line, Vic was sobbing. "They found Drew, man. Sliced up like . . . I don't know what like. Like that last guy over in Henderson Falls. He's dead, man. Drew is dead . . ."

"Where is he, Vic? Where'd they take him, do you know?"

"No. I don't know."

"Where'd it happen?"

"I don't know, man. All I know is that Drew is dead . . ."

County Memorial Hospital was the most likely place, Sam told Luke when he asked the agent to accompany him. For the second time in only a few days, Sam was on his way back to Henderson Falls.

"I don't think you should be going off the farm," Luke had said at first. "It's one and done now for our killer. He only has to get to you, and then he's finished with whatever twisted thing he's got going on."

"I've known Drew since we were four years old. We did everything together back in school. Played on the same teams, took all the same courses." Sam smiled sadly. "Even went for the same girls. I'm responsible for his death. I have to go."

"I understand why you want to go, and yeah, I'd do the same thing. But as far as being responsible for his death"—Luke shook his head—"that's all on the killer. It's not on you."

Sam drove silently.

"Sam, you know what I'm saying is true."

"What I know is that this guy is killing innocent people because of some grudge he has against me. What I know is that if I hadn't come back here, Drew would still be alive. What I know is that I am mightily pissed off."

"Pissed off is good. Pissed off requires action. Feeling guilty over something that you had no control over just means you've let the guy have control over you that he isn't entitled to. Don't give him that power, Sam. Keep the guilt focused on the killer. Don't let him hand it off to you."

Too frustrated, too angry, too emotional to continue the conversation, Sam turned the radio on softly. He could think of nothing else to say.

When they arrived at the hospital, Sam told Luke, "Get your badge out. They're going to want to see something, and I don't have anything to show them."

"We're looking for the medical examiner's office," Luke said at the information desk in the lobby.

"You mean Dr. Jensen?" the man behind the desk asked.

"Jensen's the pathologist?" Sam asked.

The man nodded. "Downstairs, fourth door from the elevator."

"Why the pathologist?" Luke asked as they waited in the lobby for the next elevator.

"Because he does the autopsies. In Nebraska, the county attorney is the coroner. He can investigate deaths and sign the death certificates."

"Your county attorneys are also doctors?"

"No, but they are coroners, and that's where we get into problems sometimes." Sam looked around for an exit sign and found one. "Let's take the steps. The elevators here have been slow since the day they were installed."

"I feel as if I'm missing something. Go back to the part about the pathologist doing the autopsies?"

"Autopsies are only required in this state in cases of sudden, unexpected deaths involving young children."

"But how do they establish cause of death if no autopsy is performed?"

"Sometimes they don't. Nebraska has traditionally ranked high in number of deaths recorded as 'undetermined' cause."

Luke was still frowning when they reached the stairwell.

"Yeah, I know. Fortunately, some of the doctors who do perform autopsies have taken classes in forensics. Dr. Jensen has the reputation of being one of the best in this part of the state."

An orderly wandering the basement hall directed them to Dr. Jensen's office. His assistant permitted them to wait in one of the autopsy rooms while Dr. Jensen was located.

"Haven't done that one yet," the doctor told them when he came into the room. "Will probably take a look at him later, but I don't see the rush. The cause of death is obvious."

"I think if you take a closer look, you'll find he was strangled," Sam said.

The doctor's eyebrows rose. "He was stabbed, must have been fifteen, twenty times."

"Postmortem wounds."

"How do you know this?"

"We've been studying this killer for a while now."

Dr. Jensen nodded. "All right. Leave your number," he told Luke, "and I'll give you a call as soon as I'm finished."

"May I see him?" Sam asked before the doctor could leave the room.

"Why would you want to do that?"

"He was my friend." Sam didn't trust his voice to say more.

The doctor turned to his assistant and said, "Pat,

take these gentlemen back to room one. But just for a moment. I may start that one a little sooner than I'd planned."

Sam had tried his best to remain objective, to see the crime but not to dwell on the fact that this victim was a man he'd known all his life, one he'd called friend for as long as he could remember. If nothing else, seeing Drew on the table would fuel his anger at this unknown killer. Drew had been a good man, from all accounts a good father, a good husband. Why he had been targeted . . .

Oh, of course Sam knew why. Because the killer couldn't get to Tom and was happy to hurt him in any way he could.

Jensen's assistant opened the drawer and pulled out the shelf upon which Drew's body lay. Sam had to remind himself that his old friend was no longer there, that he'd gone on to someplace beyond this existence, but found it hard to believe when the features were familiar ones.

"Where are the clothes he was wearing when he was found?" Sam asked.

The assistant shrugged. "I didn't see any clothes. He came in just like that."

"The police must have kept them," Luke said. "They're probably processing them right now."

Sam cast a dubious glance in Luke's direction but said nothing. With a heavy heart, he turned from the body and nodded to the young assistant. "Thanks. We can find our way out."

As soon as they passed through the hospital doors, Sam took his phone from his pocket and had just started to dial Chief Dean Worth's number when he saw the patrol car pull into the lot. He returned the phone to his pocket and met the chief halfway.

"Sam." The chief shook his head. "You weren't kidding about this guy, were you?"

Sam shook his head. "No. I wasn't kidding."

"Damned shame about young Novak. Damned shame. I'm on my way in to see him now. Want to make sure he's cleaned up before his folks come over."

"Chief, who found him?"

"The guy who opens up Jackson's over there found him propped up against the back door when he got there this morning."

"Jackson's?"

"Clothing store over there on Prairie Avenue."

"I'm assuming you took his clothes, whatever he had with him at the time, and had it all processed," Sam said. "Could we get copies of your reports once they're ready?"

"I had one of our techs go over the body earlier to see if we could pick up any hair or fibers that we can't otherwise explain, but Drew wasn't wearing any clothes." Worth shook his head. "Nope. Naked as a jaybird when we found him."

It took a second, but Sam got it. Clothe the naked.

Six down, one act left. And that one, he was certain, was being saved for him.

Bury the dead.

The dinner hour at the DelVecchio farm had been a much subdued one. The kids ate earlier, Kitty having cooked hot dogs on the grill for the agents before they took up their evening posts. At eight thirty, Sam was sitting in the kitchen with Kitty and Tom when his phone rang.

"Sam, it's Trula. Are you near a TV?" she asked excitedly. Without waiting for an answer, she said, "You have to put on *Entertainment World Today*. Right now. Hurry."

Sam watched little television and had no idea what *Entertainment World Today* might be, but he asked Kitty if she knew the show.

"Sure."

"Can you put it on right now?" He covered the receiver with his hand. "Someone thinks there's something on that I need to see." He rolled his eyes.

Kitty turned on the TV and found the show.

"There. What's the story?" Kitty leaned closer to the set. "Oh, my," she said. "Isn't that . . . ?"

"Fiona," he said and without thinking, hung up on Trula. He approached the set and leaned in.

". . . Fiona O'Neill, who played Hugh Davenport's daughter, had rushed to the bedside of her TV dad," the male voice-over announced.

Fiona, dark glasses covering her face, her hair pulled back in a bun, was filmed as she left the cemetery holding the arm of a woman who was similarly dressed in black.

"Fiona, how long has it been since you've seen Hugh?" a reporter called out.

Then another: "Fiona, did you make it to the hospital on time?"

"Fiona, are you back in California for good? Is there any truth to the rumor that you're going to be doing a pilot for Fox?"

Without acknowledging any of them, Fiona turned her face and got into a waiting car.

"What the hell . . . ?" Sam said aloud to no one in particular.

"See, Tom?" Kitty punched her husband on the arm. "I told you she looked familiar."

"Who is she?" Tom put his newspaper down.

"She was Fiona O'Neill. Remember? Little Nora on *McGuire, Boston PD*? You used to watch it all the time when it was on."

"Oh, yeah." Tom nodded. "It's still on cable. That was Sam's Fiona . . . ?" He turned to look at his brother, who still appeared dumbstruck. "Sam? You look like you didn't know, either."

Sam shook his head. "Completely blindsided me. I had no idea. She never mentioned it."

He walked from the room and went upstairs, where he called her number.

"You've reached Special Agent Fiona Summers. Please leave a message . . ."

Damn.

"Fiona, it's Sam. I know your secret. I don't give a crap about any of that. Just call me and let me know when you'll be back so I can be there when your plane lands." He paused, then added, "I'm sorry for your loss. I hope you're okay." Another pause while he debated whether or not to tell her about Drew. He decided against it. She looked as if she'd had enough for a few days. There'd be no avoiding it once she returned, but for now, he skipped it. "Anyway, call me when you get this. Please."

TWENTY-FOUR

The call came at seven the following evening, just as they were finishing dinner.

"It's Fiona," she said, as if he wouldn't recognize her voice. "I'm on my way back."

"Where and when?" he asked.

"I'm being dropped off in Brightcliffe. We looked at the map, and that appears to be the closest airport to Blackstone. If it's too far, I can—"

"No, no, it's not a problem. What time does your plane land?"

"A little after two in the morning. I'm sorry, it's such an odd time, but the offer was made and I hated to turn it down and then try to get a commercial flight." She paused. "Did you know there are no direct commercial flights into Nebraska from here? Not even into Omaha."

"It doesn't matter. I'll be there."

"Thank you, Sam. I'll see you soon."

Sam waited to hear her hang up before he did, and then slipped the phone back into his pants pocket. He walked outside and looked around at the vehicles in the yard, then went back into the kitchen where Kitty was feeding the agents in shifts. She was an accomplished cook who wouldn't hear of them driving in to town to eat.

"Luke," Sam motioned to him from the doorway. "Could I speak with you for a minute?"

"Sure." Luke excused himself from the table where he'd just finished eating, and followed Sam out to the back porch. "What's up?"

"I need to use your car," Sam told him.

"Sure. Where are we going?"

"*We* aren't going anywhere. *I'm* going to pick up Fiona."

"No can do, bud." Luke shook his head. "I'm here to keep an eye on you. There's no going off the reservation."

"First of all, I agreed to have you guys here to keep an eye on my family. I can take care of myself, but I can't watch everyone else at the same time. That's why you're here. Look, I won't be leaving until after midnight, and I'm only going to be driving for an hour." Well, it would be closer to two, but what was the difference? "Fiona is on her way back. I told her I'd pick her up at the airport."

"Sam, what if this guy's watching the house? He follows you? Game over."

"Even if he's watching the house—which I doubt, since everyone has to sleep at some point—he won't know it's me driving the car. The windows are tinted. I'll even let you loan me your spiffy jacket with FBI on the back. He won't know who's behind the wheel, so he'd have no reason to follow me."

Sam sensed that Luke was softening, so he added,

"Fiona and I have some things we need to talk about. I'd do it for you, Luke."

"Are you carrying?" Luke asked.

"Not at this moment, but I have my Glock upstairs. It'll make the ride with me."

Luke took the keys from his pocket and handed them over. "If anything happens . . ."

"Nothing will. I'll be back before anyone knows I'm gone."

"If you're not here when I get up tomorrow morning, I'm putting out an APB. And I'm telling Mancini you stole the keys."

"Fair enough." Sam pocketed the keys and slapped Luke on the back. "Thanks, buddy. Let's go back in and see if Kitty is serving dessert yet. She makes one mean peach cobbler . . ."

The drive through the Nebraska countryside was dark but fast. The road ahead was practically a straight line through farm fields that seemed to stretch on forever. The night sky was clear and the stars as bright as he remembered. There was no other place he'd been where they'd shone more brilliantly. A very rare wave of something that was not quite homesickness washed over him. It wasn't that he was sorry he'd left, or that he wanted to stay, he told himself, but it was good to be back, if only for a little while. He hadn't had much of a home these past few years—only a small apartment he moved to after he moved out of the house he and Carly had shared—and he hadn't been aware of how much he missed that feeling of warmth and acceptance and genuine affection he found when he came back to the farm, to his family. It had been comforting, and it had been a while since he'd had much comfort from any quarter.

There were no cars on the road at so late an hour, and with the company of late-night talk radio, Sam breezed along the highway at a fast clip. He remembered how, as a young driver, he'd traveled this empty stretch of road in his dad's pickup, feeling like the only life-form on an alien planet. Somewhere in the dark there were night creatures on the prowl, but from behind the wheel of that old Ford truck on a starry night, a guy might feel as if he'd landed where no man had gone before, as the expression went.

From time to time he looked in his rearview mirror to see if anyone was coming up behind him, but no one did.

Far up ahead he could see faint lights, and he knew he was nearing the airstrip. He was early, so he slowed down, changed the station from the endless chatter about the upcoming Nebraska football season and by how many points they could be expected to best each opponent, and searched for some music. He'd been hoping for some soft rock, but settled for country, and knew he was lucky to find anything at this hour of the night.

He passed the tall cyclone fence that surrounded the small airport and took a left into the parking lot. There was a sprawling one-story concrete-block building between the lot and the runway, and one door that had a light over it, so he went inside, where he found a closed ticket desk and a couple of vending machines. The clock over the door leading to the runway was eight minutes fast, according to his watch, so he searched his pockets for change for the soda machine and dropped the coins in. A can landed with a thud that reverberated through the empty room, attracting the attention of the night watchman, who came out of a side room to see who had invaded his space. He and Sam made small talk until they saw the lights from an approaching plane. Sam stood in the window and watched the small craft land effortlessly. Moments later, the plane's door opened, and steps appeared. Fiona had a bag over her shoulder and another in her hands. She was wearing a white shirt and a black linen skirt that looked as if she'd slept in it.

Sam tossed his soda can into a trash container and went out to meet her halfway across the tarmac. He put out one hand to take her bag.

"I have it," she said. "But thanks."

"How was your flight?"

"Very nice." She seemed to be deliberately keeping about a foot between them. Sam wasn't sure why, but he let her have the space.

She turned back to the plane, and watched the steps retract, the door close, and the plane ready to take off again. She stood in silence till it had taxied down the runway, taken flight, and disappeared into the night sky.

"Whose plane, if I might ask?"

"It was Hugh's. His son, Matt, offered to fly me back here on his way to Chicago. It was the quickest way, so I said yes." She smiled weakly. "Of course, his wife and kids were on the flight as well, and I'd forgotten just how loud a bunch of teenagers could be. Still, it beat hanging out at LAX by a country mile."

The security guard waved and called out, "Night,

folks" as they passed through the building, and Sam returned the wave.

"It's so quiet out here," Fiona whispered, as if afraid to break the silence.

"Nothing around for miles," he noted. "Well, there is Brightcliffe, about a mile and a half through that pasture." He pointed across the road. "But they rolled up the sidewalks hours ago."

He unlocked the car and put her things in the trunk.

"Did you come by yourself?" She frowned. "Why didn't someone come with you?"

"No need. No one followed me, I can guarantee that. The road between here and Blackstone is straight and flat. There's nowhere to hide if you're trying to tail someone. I didn't see but maybe one or two cars on the way out here, and they were both headed in the opposite direction."

"I didn't mean for you to take any risks, Sam."

"I haven't."

Then, to change the subject, he asked, "Are you hungry?"

"Not so much."

"I don't know why I asked that." He rubbed his hand over his face. "There's nothing around for miles except the vending machines inside, but the offerings looked pretty stale to me."

"Really, I'm fine." Fiona buckled her seat belt.

"We'll be back at the farm soon. There's lots of stuff there to dig into."

He started the car and drove out of the lot and onto the highway. Within seconds he was up to what he considered traveling speed. He sat back, trying to think of something to say to her.

Before he could come up with anything that he didn't think sounded lame, Fiona said, "I'm sorry that I left like that. I should have explained, but I was blindsided when I got the call about Hugh."

He looked across the console and met her eyes. "Well, I'm sorry, too. I'm sorry that your friend died."

"He was more than just a friend, Sam. He was the father I needed but didn't have."

"I thought your parents were still alive."

"They are, but they never treated me as if I were their child." She stared out the window for a moment. "I'm guessing you saw some of the coverage of Hugh's funeral, that you saw me there. You were probably a little surprised."

"Everyone saw you there, and yeah, everyone was surprised, to say the least. Me, in particular. A little background right about now might be nice."

"I'm not sure where to start."

"Try where the story begins."

"My parents started me in commercials when I was six months old. They found it could be quite lucrative—I was a pretty baby and apparently quite animated—so my mother quit her job to take me to auditions and shoots. I got an agent and she got me a lot of work. When I got a little older, everyone thought I should be on TV. I got lucky, got picked up for a couple of walk-on scenes, then a couple of small speaking parts. Right about then, my mother decided she'd be a better agent than the one I had—the one who'd gotten me all the work—so she fired her. From then on, my mother, as my agent, and my dad, as my manager, controlled my career. When I was four, I auditioned for the part of the lead's daughter on a new show called *McGuire, Boston PD*. I got the part. Much to everyone's surprise, the show lasted for nine seasons."

"It shouldn't have been too much of a surprise," he said. "It was a damned good show. Drama with the right touch of humor."

"You've seen it, then."

"When it first ran, yeah, I did. I never connected you with little Nora McGuire, though."

"No reason you should have. They thought Nora should be this angelic-looking little girl, so they dyed my dark hair blond. As soon as I could, I went back to my natural color." She was staring out the window again. "Anyway, my parents were the stage parents from hell. They were totally into the Hollywood TV scene. By the time I was nine or ten, I just wanted out. I was going through a very self-conscious stage, and I didn't want to do it anymore. But when I told my mother I wanted to quit, she went nuts. Went on and on about how I had an obligation to my family, that if I quit I'd be taking the roof from over their heads, and how could I do that to my little brother and sister, not to mention to my parents, who had given up their lives so that I could follow my dream of being a TV star."

"Was it?" Sam asked. "Your dream?"

"When I first started, it was fun. I can't deny that. Everyone paid a lot of attention to me, made a big fuss over me. But after a while, it became suffocating. I couldn't go anywhere without people approaching me. I had no friends because I was either studying or on the set most of the day. I became very shy around kids my own age because I didn't know any. I didn't know how to interact with other children. So it all got old very quickly. It didn't take long for me to figure out that it wasn't my dream I was following, it was my mom's. She liked the spotlight, liked being Nora McGuire's mother."

"Sounds like they were getting a lot more out of it than you were."

"You have no idea, Sam," she told him. "I grew to hate the whole thing. The only real friend I had was Hugh Davenport, my TV dad. When I got upset, he was the one who calmed me down. When I was depressed, he talked me through it. When I needed help with my homework, he worked with me between scenes. He was the one who gave me advice, he was the one I turned to when I needed someone to talk to. After a time, our TV roles sort of slipped into our real lives. He was more of a dad to me than my real dad ever was. Sometimes he took me home to be with his kids and do things with them—he had three sons and two daughters. He and his wife were the parents I needed, the parents I'd wished my mom and dad would be. There was so much warmth in their home, and never any in my own."

She smiled in the darkness. "Hugh understood what I was going through because he'd been a child star, too. He saw my parents pushing me into roles I didn't want—I made a movie every year after the TV season ended. He saw how lonely I was, and he even tried to talk to my folks, but they just got pissed off at him. Anyway, by the time I was about seven, I decided I wanted to be just like him. I wanted to be a cop, just like the one he played on TV. I never wanted to be anything else."

"How did your parents take that?"

"How do you think?" She laughed dryly. "I was thirteen when the show went off the air. I did a few other shows—two sitcoms and a medical drama, but none of them lasted beyond a season or two. I did a couple more movies, but I knew that when I turned eighteen, I was outta there. Hugh supported me in that, helped me to look for colleges. He and his wife actually went on a cross-country trip with me and one of their sons to look at schools. My parents never forgave him for supporting my decision to leave the business. I was their meal ticket, their entrance into the Hollywood scene. I was putting an end to life as they knew it."

"Have they forgiven you?"

"Not really. It was my fault that the party invitations stopped coming. My fault that they had to sell the big house and move to a more modest home in a more modest neighborhood. My fault that they couldn't afford private school for my sister and brother. Everything negative that ever happened to anyone in my family was my fault."

"Fiona, I'm so sorry," he said softly. "I wish you'd told me before."

"I never tell anyone. Everyone thinks, oh, poor thing, her parents pushed her into this fabulous career. But you can't imagine what that was like. I was a child who never had a childhood. I had responsibilities that a kid of six or seven should never have to bear. The expectations were just too much for me. I'd made enough to pay my way through college, and I did work a bit over vacations, so I didn't walk away empty-handed. Unfortunately, my parents never invested a dime."

"What are they doing now?"

"Managing my brother's music career." She rolled her eyes.

"When was the last time you spoke with them?"

"It's been a while," she said softly. "I call from time to time and leave messages, but I never get a call back."

"Well, that explains a lot," Sam said. "Why you never went to regular school, why you never went to the prom or played team sports. I'm really sorry you had to go through all that. No kid should ever have their childhood stolen from them, for any reason, especially by their own parents." Sam eased up on the gas pedal. "I can understand why Hugh Davenport meant so much to you that you wanted to follow in his footsteps. Well, his TV footsteps."

"I guess I was young enough that I believed he really was a cop. I idolized him. What a shock when I got old enough to realize he really wasn't a police officer, but by then the idea was planted in my head. I was going to be a cop, just like Hugh. He told me if I was serious about it, though, that I should go all the way and aim for the FBI, so I did."

"Have you ever regretted it?"

"Not for a minute. I really believe this is what I was meant to do. So in a way, I guess it all turned out all right. Maybe I wouldn't have wanted a career in law enforcement if I hadn't been on that show."

"That's what my mom calls making lemonade when life gives you lemons."

"You don't have a choice, really. Hugh used to say, 'Control your life or life will control you.' " Fiona stifled a yawn.

"Had he been ill?"

She shook her head no. "Hugh was the picture of health. You hear about people who are never sick a day in their lives and then one day, bam! Gone? That was Hugh."

"What happened?"

"Heart attack. He just turned sixty-eight last month. His wife, Elisa, said he never complained about anything. The doctors said it happens that way sometimes." She seemed to consider this. "I do think he'd have preferred this way to hanging on with all manner of issues to deal with—he hated anything that threatened to slow him down—but damn, I will miss him so much."

Sam reached across the console and took her hand. She squeezed it and rested her head back against her seat.

"When was the last time you slept?" he asked.

"What day is it now?"

"That long, eh?"

"I slept on the flight out to LA, then a few hours here and a few hours there."

"Why don't you try to get in a few winks now?"

"You wouldn't mind?"

"I'm suggesting it."

"Maybe if I close my eyes, just for a minute . . ."

When Fiona awoke, the car was motionless. For a moment, she thought they'd arrived at the farm and that Sam had let her sleep in the car, rather than wake her. She was okay with that. It had been so good of him to come out in the middle of the night and drive out into the middle of nowhere to get her, and she really hadn't thanked him adequately.

I'm sure I can think of some way to express my gratitude, she thought, smiling.

"I hope that smile's for me," she heard him say.

She opened her eyes and glanced over to the driver's seat, where Sam sat, resting back against the door. She sat up and looked out the window. Through the windshield, she could see a lake surrounded by trees and wrapped in mist, bathed in the palest light imaginable.

"Where are we?" she asked.

"Shelby Lake," he replied. "This was the great make-out place when I was in high school."

Sam turned on the radio and increased the volume.

"Come on." He got out of the car and gestured for her to follow him. She unbuckled her seat belt and pushed open the door.

He'd left his door open and the sweet sound of Dolly Parton's "Heartbreaker" floated out around them. He walked around the car and took her hand in his, then slid his other arm around her waist.

"What are you doing?" she asked.

"Taking you to the prom."

She laughed and they slow danced, their bodies close, then closer. Dolly was followed by a more uptempo "Summer Nights" by Rascal Flatts, then Martina McBride's "Happy Girl."

"I guess country's pretty big at the proms out here," she said, cheek to cheek with Sam for another slow number.

"Sorry. It's the only station you can get until you're a little closer to Henderson Falls."

"I don't mind," she told him. "I always kind of liked Dolly. She always sounds so sincere."

He laughed softly in her ear, then spun her around and dipped her low. "What would a prom be without flowers?" He paused to snap off a stem of black-eyed Susans. "Not exactly roses, but the best I can do in a pinch."

"They're actually one of my favorites, so you're batting a thousand tonight, as far as I'm concerned."

"You mean this morning." Sam pointed across the lake to where the first hint of the new day began to appear.

Suddenly overwhelmed by it all—the grief of losing Hugh, the beauty of the morning, the sheer sweetness of the man who held her—she felt the tears build inside but fought against letting them fall, knowing that once they started, there was no telling when, if ever, they would stop.

When the first sob broke, it was with a strangled cry followed by a surge of weeping that startled even her. She covered her face with her hands, as if to hide from the outpouring of her own pain.

"It's okay, baby, let it out," Sam whispered in her ear as he backed against the car and brought her with him, leaning her against his body and holding her as close as he could. "It's been a bad week for you. Let it go, Fiona. Cry it all out . . ."

As far as she could remember, no one had ever seen her cry for real. On screen, sure, when the part called for it. But not in real life. There'd been few people she trusted enough that she would let them see this much of her. But there was no stopping the rush that had been building inside her since the moment she'd gotten the call about Hugh. Miraculously, she felt no distress, no compulsion to protect herself against Sam. She simply let it go, as he had quietly prompted her to do.

When no tears were left to fall and her legs had weakened and threatened to betray her, Sam's strong hands held her up and rocked her slowly, side to side, as if she were a child.

"The front of your shirt is soaking wet." She sniffed and with her hands smoothed out the fabric, too embarrassed to look him in the eye. "And it's got mascara on it."

"We'll leave the windows down on the way home and it'll air dry. And as for that black stuff"—he looked down at the front of his shirt—"hey, it's only a shirt."

"I'm so sorry. I don't know what came over me."

"You've suffered a great loss, Fiona. You're going to be mourning for a long time." He leaned back and looked down into her eyes. "You don't have to be the iron woman all the time, you know."

"I don't usually lose control like that."

"I promise not to tell anyone." His lips were close to her ear. "Your secret is safe with me."

She nodded, wanted to tell him that she knew that all of her secrets would be safe with him. She turned her head to catch his mouth with hers, and kissed him, silently begging him to kiss her back with everything he had. She sunk her hands into his hair and held on. His hands skimmed her body, slowly at first, gliding over her breasts over her shirt, and her hips

over her skirt in gentle waves. But soon she wanted—
needed—to feel his hands on her skin. She pulled her
shirt from the waistband and started to unbutton it,
her fingers trembling on the buttons, his mouth following the slow exposure of her skin. He lifted her,
turning them both around so that her back was
against the hard metal of the car, pinning her there
with his body while he touched and tasted every bit of
her that was exposed.

It wasn't enough.

She yanked up her skirt and he moved away from
her just enough so that she could pull it up to her
hips. Her legs freed, she wrapped them around his
hips and pulled him as close to her as she could, her
brain filling with a foggy darkness in which there was
only Sam and his hands and his mouth and his body.
Her skin smoldered everywhere he touched and the
heat overwhelmed her.

"Sam," she whispered, needing more. "Sam . . ."

They moved against each other, with each other,
need soon overtaking want.

"Fiona, maybe we should . . ." Sam gasped.

". . . get into the car. Right." She nodded. "Get into
the car . . ."

He carried her, her legs still wrapped around him,
and opened the door to the back seat. He slid her
down his body until she hit the seat, then pushed her
back. She slid along the seat until her head hit the
passenger door, one leg on the floor. Sam eased onto
her, his body moving against hers, his hands and lips
suddenly everywhere, and she could not get enough.
She arched up against his mouth when it covered her
breast, and urged him to take more of her, all of her.

"Make love to me, Sam," she whispered. "I need you to make love to me . . ."

She shuddered when he entered her, soft moans in the back of her throat when he began to move with a slow rhythm, sending tiny ripples spreading throughout her body. Soon the tempo changed, and they moved together, flying together, lost to everything else except each other. She closed her eyes and rode it out, until they crashed together, and slowly came back down to earth.

She lay beneath him, listening to his breathing as it attempted to return to normal.

"So," she said, clearing her throat. "I suppose that was how you do 'after prom' out here in the heartland o' America?"

Sam laughed and buried his face in her hair.

"Is that how you celebrated your first prom?" she asked.

"I'm sure I would have jumped at the chance, but no. I went to my first prom with Phyllis Banks. She had three brothers, all of whom played football at Notre Dame. There was no 'after prom' that year. Besides, I didn't have a car. We went with two other couples in Vic's dad's ten-year-old station wagon."

"Whose car is this, anyway?" she asked.

"Luke's."

"Arrrgghh." She buried her face in his chest.

"What?"

"Luke and I go way back."

"How far back?"

"Like, to the Academy."

"Were you and he, ahhh . . ."

"No. But he's like a brother to me. I can't believe we just had sex in Luke's car."

"Does it help to know it's a rental?"

She laughed and struggled to sit up, wondering where her clothes were. She looked past Sam and frowned.

"Sam, you left the car door open?"

"My legs are too long, I couldn't close the door."

"Didn't you think about what would happen if someone had come along?"

"I wasn't exactly in thought mode at the time." He sat up and looked out the windows and sighed. "Well, that was one hell of a way to greet the dawn, but I'm afraid we're going to have to get back to the farm. Luke threatened to put out an APB if we weren't back by the time he got up."

He glanced at his watch.

"If he's running on schedule, I'd say we have about ten minutes before he rolls down for breakfast."

"How far away are we?" She slipped her shirt over her shoulders and began to button it.

"About twenty minutes." He leaned over and kissed her, then grabbed his clothes and hurried into them. "We're going to have to make tracks if we're going to head off the posse."

TWENTY-FIVE

Drew's funeral is today at three," Kitty told Sam when he and Fiona strolled onto the front porch. Sam knew she was dying to know where he'd been since midnight the night before, and why it had taken him a full eight hours to drive to Brightcliffe and back. And why Fiona had what looked suspiciously like whisker burns on both sides of her neck. But he also knew she'd cut out her tongue before she asked.

"Why so soon?" He frowned.

"The Novaks don't believe in embalming," Tom replied. "Never did, none of 'em. So since the coroner has released the body to the funeral home, there's no reason not to bury him, and a very compelling one why they should."

"That means they've established a cause of death," Sam said. "I'll give Doc Jensen a call."

He excused himself and went inside, Fiona following him. It took him only a minute to find out what he wanted to know.

"No surprise there," Sam told her when he hung up the phone. "Manual strangulation. The stabbing was all postmortem, just like the others."

"Where the hell have you been?" Luke walked into the kitchen as if on a mission.

"Fiona's plane was late," Sam said at the exact moment Fiona told Luke, "We had a flat tire."

Luke's eyes shifted from one to the other then back again. He shook his head and put out his hand. Sam tossed him the car keys and Luke grabbed them in midair.

"We need to have a powwow about you going to the funeral this afternoon," Luke told him.

"There is no way in hell I am not going to Drew's funeral, so don't even bother trying to talk me out of it."

"That's pretty much what we figured you'd say. So let's lay down some rules, okay?" Luke pointed to the table. "Have a seat, and let's talk this out."

Sam sat with his back against the wall, Fiona across the table from him, her cool façade having returned.

"As duly elected spokesperson for the posse," Luke began, "we're thinking that you need to stay in plain sight the entire time. No walking off to have a private word with anyone, no hanging back at the church, no going off alone at the cemetery, understood?"

Sam nodded. "I'm with you so far."

"We're all going to be attending, and will be spread out around the church. It goes without saying that we will all be armed. I think you need to be, too."

"I'm okay with that, too."

"Good. Now, as far as the other mourners are concerned, you are going to need to be hyperobservant. We will be watching the crowd, but we don't know these people. You do. You're going to have to be aware of anyone who's acting out of character. We all know that it is pretty much a given that our guy is going to be in that church."

"I've already thought of that, Luke." Sam nodded. "There's no question in my mind that he'll be there. For one thing, if we are correct in assuming he is a member of this community, he's going to have to be there. Everyone around here knew Drew, the killer included, and most people liked him. And yes"—he addressed Fiona—"I have come to the conclusion that you've been right all along. This guy is someone I know, probably someone I know well. I don't know what set him off, but for the record, I agree with your theory. I want to catch this guy, probably more than anyone else does."

"Then let's all keep our eyes and ears peeled today and see if anyone shows their hand," Fiona said.

"Knowing that someone I've known and probably called friend feels so harmed by me in some way that he's willing to go to such lengths to let me know . . . it's just killing me."

"Well, that's exactly what we're trying to prevent, Sam," Luke reminded him. "Because now, it is all about you . . ."

The air inside the church was close in spite of the fact that air-conditioning had been installed two years prior at the behest of a parishioner who couldn't face one more Nebraska summer Sunday morning without respite from the heat. The overwhelming scent of flowers hung in the air, and as Sam had predicted, the church was packed all the way from the altar back to the front door.

Sam sat shoulder to shoulder with Tom on one side and his nephew Tommy on the other. The pew, the fifth from the altar, was taken up mostly by his family and that of a neighbor. Fiona was somewhere in the crowd, having reminded Sam that she was not there to accompany him to his friend's funeral, but as a federal agent charged with his safety. From time to time he'd glanced around hoping to catch sight of her, but the crowd was too dense, and seated so far up front, he was highly noticeable every time he turned around, so he stopped looking. He reminded himself that she knew where he was, and that was what really mattered.

The other agents, too, were scattered here and there, though none of them in the pews closest to the altar, since those were occupied by the regular church-goers. Sam knew they were all there, all at their most vigilant. He wasn't worried about his back.

The casket stood at the front of the aisle, a grim reminder of why they were there. Sam was lost in memories of Drew and their boyhood escapades when the priest took his place on the altar.

The congregation stood and the service began. Sam's mind wandered from Drew, to his parents, to his two sisters, who were several rows in front of the DelVecchio family, to the last times he'd been in this church. So many of the important events of his life had been spent under this roof. There had been weddings, christenings, and yes, funerals. His parents had been married here, as had his brother and his sister. Tommy, Jody, and Gil, and Andrea's three kids had all been baptized here. Eileen, his sister, had been buried from this church, her coffin once standing exactly where Drew's now stood.

Sam sat back against the hard wooden seat, his eyes straying from the altar where the priest spoke, to the pews across the aisle and the familiar faces of those who sat there. Blake Carter sat with his parents and his wife, his eyes swollen and his expression pained. He and Drew had grown up three houses apart and had been inseparable. A row behind him, Steve Molino sat with his wife. The pew had once been occupied by his entire family, but his parents' divorce a few years following the death of his sister, Tish, had taken Steve from Blackstone to Des Moines. Billy Finnegan was two rows behind Steve, and Sam had noticed Vic when he first arrived at the church, but hadn't had a chance to speak with him. Actually, he hadn't spoken with any of them, the old friends he'd once known so well. One of whom was probably a killer. He glanced at their faces, one by one, but nothing they'd done so far—no expression, no gesture—gave away a thing. Not that Sam would have expected it to be that easy.

It was far from easy, looking at old friends through a different lens to try to determine which of them might have been harboring animosity—justified or unjustified—toward Sam.

One of Drew's cousins was at a podium on the left side of the altar talking about how much Drew had loved fly-fishing in Montana every summer. Sam smiled to himself, recalling the times they'd gone to nearby lakes and fished for bass. Sam had never really enjoyed fishing—even as a kid he'd been bored and restless if he had to stay in one place for too long—

but Drew had mastered the art of standing still in water up to his knees by the time he'd turned ten.

Sam's gaze drifted upward to the stained glass windows above the altar. There were seven of them, all depicting Jesus ministering to his flock. As his eyes made their way from the first to the last, the breath caught in his throat. How many times had he seen these pictures in glass without realizing their meaning?

He forced his eyes back to the first window, where Jesus offered a platter of fruit to a woman; to the second, where He held out a cloak to a man who covered his nakedness with his hands; to the third, where He was giving yet another man a goblet. Sam skipped to the last, where He stood over a prone body, making an open-palmed gesture toward a hole in the ground.

Feed the sick. Clothe the naked. Give drink to the thirsty.

And the last: bury the dead.

He turned to the back of the church, hoping to catch the eye of one of the agents, but couldn't locate anyone in the crowd. Tom elbowed him and he turned back toward the altar, his eyes on the stained glass windows. He turned his head and looked across the aisle. Everyone's eyes were on the podium, where Drew's father spoke. All but one other, whose eyes were lifted to the windows.

Sam studied the once-familiar face as it stared up at the depictions of the Church's corporal acts of mercy. A shock ran through him as it all became crystal clear. Once, long ago, Sam had seen this same face transfixed on those same stained glass windows. That day returned to Sam in vivid detail, and he knew without question who the killer was.

How could it have taken so long to figure out when it should have been so obvious? If he'd used his training as a specialist in criminal behavior, and not permitted himself to be blinded by old friendships, he'd have known.

There was no way for him to alert Fiona or Luke or any of the others. He could only wait until the service was over. All he could do right at that moment was devise the manner in which he'd approach the man after he'd clued in the others. It was all he could do to keep in his seat, all he could do to keep from leaping into the other pew and taking apart the man who had once been one of his best buddies. He closed his eyes and mentally watched it happen in his imagination, since it could not happen in real life. At least, not now, and not here.

Patience, he told himself. There were a lot of people in the church, any one of whom could become yet another victim if Sam moved hastily. He felt certain everyone here would be at the cemetery, and that would be a much better place for a takedown. The agents could come from every side and quietly escort the killer to a waiting car. There would be no shootout, no blaze of glory, just a very quiet and efficient arrest of a serial killer who'd just attended the funeral of his last victim.

Emotionally, Sam would have preferred the leap across the aisle, but intellectually, he knew he had to sit tight and let the rest of the morning play out. Instead, he calmly took note that while the man wore a dark suit—as did almost every other man in the church—he was married to a woman with flaming red hair. If Sam lost the killer in the crowd once the service was over—and there was a good chance that he might—he could keep track of him by following the redhead.

TWENTY-SIX

'm still not sure I understand why we couldn't have tried calling these women first," Kevin complained. "We could have eliminated flying willy-nilly all over the East Coast. And I don't know why you thought it was necessary to involve me in this scheme of yours."

"We thought you'd enjoy this, seeing how much you like to fly, Kevin." Robert sat with his seat back, his eyes closed, and smirked.

"You're a cruel and heartless man, Rob," Kevin told him. "If you're going to make me go with you, the least you could do is buy a bigger plane so that I don't feel quite as claustrophobic."

"Boys, boys. Please." Susanna shook her head. There were times when the two of them reverted to an age somewhere under the established age of reason, which she believed to be twelve. At such times, who would believe that one was an international business mogul and the other a Catholic priest with the weight of his parishioners' souls on his shoulders?

"We already agreed that phone calls were out," she reminded them. "We'd run the risk of giving a heads-up to the woman we're trying to locate. And we need you, Kevin. People will open up to a priest, maybe say things they wouldn't say to a layperson like me or Robert. So, now what we have to establish is what we'll do when we get to . . ." She glanced at the list on the empty seat next to her. "Travesty, West Virginia."

"Now, there's a place where bad things could happen," Kevin said. "Yes sir, if I were to kidnap a child and try to pass him off as my own, I'd head straight for Travesty."

"We haven't talked about what we'll do if we find Ian," Susanna reminded them.

"We call the police. We call the FBI." Kevin sat up and looked directly at Robert, whose eyes were still closed. "We do not force our way into anyone's home, all right? We don't take Ian and run like crazy people. We're going to do this the right way."

He leaned across the aisle and poked his cousin. "I know you heard me. Nod if you're too lazy to speak."

"Kevin's right, Rob. You need to put Ian first in this," Susanna said.

"Of course we're putting Ian first." Robert sat up.

"That means we all keep in mind how terrified he would be if three strangers tried to snatch him and take him away from the only . . ." She was unable to force the word *mother* past her lips. "The only caretaker he knows."

As Susanna expected, Robert prickled. "He's my son."

"He doesn't know that," she said softly.

She could tell by the look of resignation that crossed his face that he knew she was right, but couldn't bring himself to say so. She knew that—

should the gods be with them and they were lucky enough to find Ian—Robert's first inclination was going to be to grab his son and hold him. She couldn't blame him for feeling that way, but at the same time, she didn't want his child's introduction to his father to be tainted with fear.

"We need to do it the right way," Kevin repeated. "We need to go about this in whatever way is least traumatic for Ian."

"It's going to be very hard for you to hold back, Rob," Suse said. "But just remember that there may come a time when he may not even remember what happened. The last thing any of us want is for his return to you to be marked by trauma."

Rob nodded. "You're right. I know you're right . . ."

As the day progressed, Robert had managed to be smart about their attempts to find his son. They'd been to two of the addresses already—one in West Virginia, one in Pittsburgh, but neither door had been answered. A quick canvass of the neighborhood by Kevin had determined that no children lived in either home. Disheartened but encouraged by the fact that only three names remained on the list, they flew to Erie and rented a car. Kevin drove, and navigation directed them to the third house they would visit that day.

They parked down the street from the small Cape Cod to give them time to observe, but even from several houses down, the Big Wheel on the front walk was clearly visible. Robert all but hyperventilated.

"Stay calm," Kevin admonished him. "It doesn't

mean a thing. It could belong to the kid next door. Knock it off, will you?"

In the distance, they saw a woman walking with a stroller. She got as far as the Cape Cod, then stopped and let the occupant out. A curly-haired boy dashed for the Big Wheel and sat, his little legs barely reaching the pedals.

"Dear God in heaven, that's him." Robert's hand was on the door handle.

"It's not going to be that way. We're going to do this right. You agreed," Susanna reminded him. "Kevin, how are you going to handle this one? Do you want me to come with you?"

Kevin's eyes never left the child. He shook his head and told her, "I need to do this alone. I'm not sure what I'll tell her. I'll think of something. But I need to go in alone. Let's just pray that the right words come to me once I get there."

"Prayer isn't much of a plan, Kev."

"Sorry, bro. It's all I've got." Kevin opened the car door and got out. He leaned back in and told Susanna, "Keep him with you."

She nodded and he slammed the door.

"Maybe we should talk to the neighbors," Robert said, clearly unnerved by having to sit by and watch the child he thought could be his, the child he'd been missing for so long—and not be able to go to him.

"What would we say to them?" Suse asked.

"We could ask how long she's lived there. Did she have the child when she moved in? Or did she have him after she moved here? Had she been visibly pregnant?"

"You'd make a good investigator," she told him. "Those are good questions."

"You're humoring me." Robert got out of the back seat, and before Susanna could react, he'd opened the driver's side door and got in. She breathed an audible sigh of relief.

"Yes, I am," she acknowledged without shame. "I'm trying to give Kevin some time to talk to this woman."

They watched as Kevin approached the woman— Carole Woolum—and began to talk to her. He leaned down and said something to Ian, and the boy reached out and touched his hand.

"Jesus, how long do I have to sit and watch this?" Robert held his hands across his abdomen as if he were in pain.

"As long as it takes, Rob. Till Kevin tells us otherwise."

Kevin and the woman talked for a few more minutes, then she picked up the boy and started inside.

"What's she doing? What do you suppose Kevin said to her? Do you think he tipped our hand?" Robert worried aloud.

"Relax, Rob." She wanted to reach out to him, but knew now was not the time. He was fixated on the boy, who had dark curls much like Ian had had. *It must be killing him,* she thought.

She started to say exactly that, when there was a rapping on the driver's side window. Rob and Susanna both turned to look at the same time. A police officer stood next to the car, gesturing to them to roll down the window.

"Hello, officer," Robert greeted him with a friendly smile.

"May I see some identification?" The officer was not smiling.

"Sure." Somewhat confused, Robert pulled his wallet from his pants pocket and handed over his driver's license. The officer looked at it, then leaned closer to the window.

"You too, miss," he told Susanna, who promptly handed over her own license, which he scrutinized as closely as he had Robert's. He walked back to the car and handed them through the window to the officer who sat behind the wheel.

"What do you suppose is going on?" Susanna asked Robert.

"Maybe one of the neighbors called about a strange car being parked on the street here," Robert said. "Or maybe someone was concerned when they saw Kevin go into the house. Maybe there have been burglaries in the neighborhood and people are being overly cautious. In any case, I'm betting the police were called by someone right around here." He looked across the street. "My money's on the woman hiding behind the post on the porch over there. I think we need to think of something fast, unless of course you think we should tell him the truth?"

"We don't know what Kevin is telling Carole Woolum right now."

The officer returned to their car.

"Is there a problem, Officer"—Robert looked at the cop's nametag—"Simpson?"

"May I ask what you're doing here?" Officer Simpson asked.

Robert turned to Susanna, who was as unprepared as he was to answer the question.

"Sir? Your purpose here in this neighborhood?"

When neither answered, the officer waved to his partner, still in the car, presumably checking out their licenses.

"I'm going to have to ask you both to step out of the vehicle," Simpson said.

"Officer, I think I can explain—" Robert started but was cut off.

"You can explain down at the station. Right now, you're going to have to come with me."

TWENTY-SEVEN

While a casual observer might have assumed that his singular focus on the altar during Drew Novak's funeral had been an expression of either devotion or grief—possibly both—Steve Molino's focus had actually been on trying to figure out how to get to Sam DelVecchio in the midst of all these people. It would be a challenge, he knew, but the time had come, and he had to do what he had to do. When the mass ended and the coffin was being wheeled down the center aisle accompanied by incense and six pallbearers— Drew's brothers and cousins—he looked across the way and met Sam's eyes. He saw the cold flash of recognition there, saw the hard resolve in Sam's face, felt the bold challenge, and he knew it would end today for one of them.

He preferred that it be Sam.

Well aware that Sam wasn't going to do anything that could end with someone else getting hurt, Steve took his time easing out of the church. He was halfway to the door when he figured it out. The woman Sam had introduced to him the other day had slipped out the side door, which told Steve several things. One, that she was one of several agents in the church, so the others must be covering different exits; two, that she'd be easier to take than Sam; and three, that Sam would come to find her, thereby eliminating Steve's problem of how to get to Sam. Sam would come to him.

He leaned close to his wife's ear and whispered, "I'll meet you at the cemetery."

"All right," she replied. "I don't know if I'll be able to stay for the entire graveside service, though. The mass lasted longer than I expected. I told work I'd be back before closing."

"Good thing we drove separately." He kissed her on the cheek. "See you later at home."

Steve glanced back to locate Sam in the crowd, and was pleased to see that his ear was being bent by Josie Singletary. He knew from experience that once she latched on to you, she was like a remora. He ducked his head and made his way forward in the crowd, then shot out the side door. The chances were very good that Sam didn't see the move.

"Hi," he called to the agent he thought of as "Sam's woman." "Fiona, was it? I'm Steve Molino. We met at the football field the other day."

"Oh. Right. Steve." She clearly did not wish to be distracted. Good, he thought. Her attention was divided.

"How long will you be staying in town?" he asked as he moved toward her.

"What?" She only half turned. "I'm not really sure."

"Wrong answer," he said as he jammed the barrel of his handgun into the center of her back. "The correct answer is, probably for eternity. Unless, of course, Sam and I work out a little deal. But we can discuss those details later."

She started to turn and he rammed the gun into her right kidney.

"Don't be stupid, Fiona. You're going to toss that Glock onto the ground."

She looked into his eyes, then did as she was told. Without taking his eyes off her, he reached down and grabbed her gun. Sticking it into his belt, he waved his own gun and said, "Turn around. That's good. Now walk as if you and I are chatting in a friendly manner. Smile, damn it. And do not doubt for one second that I would hesitate to blow a hole in you big enough for Father O'Malley to drive a golf cart through."

She walked slightly ahead of him, along the narrow path that ran next to the church, and when they came to a parking lot he told her to turn to the left and head for the gray sedan parked at the opposite end. Beyond the lot was a playground.

"Don't think about making a run for it," he told her. "Because if you think I wouldn't shoot into a crowd of kids you'd be sadly mistaken. I've waited too long for this. Want to know how long?"

"Sure."

He opened the door and shoved her in. "Twenty-six years."

He pointed to her handbag. "Hand that to me. Slowly."

She did as she was told.

"Now strap yourself in."

When she'd done so, he walked around to the

driver's side and opened the door. Setting her bag on his seat, he looked through it, tossing her phone over his shoulder. It bounced off the hood of another car and slid across the macadam. Then he tossed her bag onto the back seat and got behind the wheel.

"I know cell phones can be traced," he told her. "Maybe you were hoping that Sam would be able to track you down, play the hero? Well, believe me, Sam's no hero."

He drove several miles out of town, turning only once, onto a dirt road that led into thick woods.

"I'm trying to decide which would hurt him more," he said after he turned off the engine. "Do I want to bury you alive, then watch Sam frantically try to find you before it's too late? And then when he shows up, kill him? Or maybe I should just ask him if he'd take your place in the box. What do you think, Fiona? Which would be worse?"

"I really don't know," she said, and he laughed out loud.

"Well, we need to keep in mind that today's theme is bury the dead."

He got out of the car and came around to her side, then motioned with the gun for her to get out and stand facing the car. His eyes never leaving her, he reached into the back seat and brought out a length of rope. After tying her hands behind her back, he turned her around.

"Isn't that the way you law enforcement people do it? Secure the suspect's hands behind their back to take away any use of their arms to attack you or to escape?" He drew closer to her and sniffed at her hair. "You smell good, Fiona. Does Sam like that scent?"

He ran the barrel of the gun down the front of her shirt, his eyes staring into hers. "You're good, you know that? You never even blinked. I like that. Shows you've got balls. I'll bet Sam likes that, too. He always admired the spunky girls."

He grabbed her by the arm and turned her toward the trees.

"We're going to take a stroll through the woods."

"Why Sam?" she asked.

"Because he ruined my life," Steve said matter-of-factly, "and now I'm going to ruin his."

Sam stood outside the church, searching for Fiona on the crowded sidewalk. He saw Luke, and waved him over.

"I know who the killer is," he said quietly. "We're going to take him at the cemetery."

"Who is he?"

"His name is Steve Molino. I don't see him right now, but he'll be relatively easy to spot out in the open. His wife is a tall pretty redhead."

"There's a woman with hair like that behind you and off to the right," Luke said. "She's talking to two men. Describe Molino."

"My age and height, brown hair thinning at the front, average build."

"The one guy with her is in his sixties, the other is about five eight. What's he wearing, did you notice?"

"Dark suit, white shirt, like nearly every other guy here."

"Yeah, that narrows it down. Did you notice the tie?"

"It was dark red. Or maroon."

"I don't see a red tie."

"He knows I know, Luke," Sam told him.

"You sure?"

Sam nodded. "But he acted like he knew I wasn't going to move inside the church."

"So he must have bolted as soon as he got outside. Why don't I just follow the wife to the car and see if we can nab him there?" Before Sam could respond, Luke said, "By *we* I mean me and my fellow federal officers. That *we* did not include thee."

"Spoilsport."

"If you're nice to me, maybe I'll give you a few minutes alone with the guy."

The crowd began to thin as the hearse and the cars carrying the family pulled away from the curb. Sam watched as the other mourners got into their cars and fell in line with the procession. He did not find Steve Molino in any of them.

"Luke, do you see Fiona?" Sam asked.

Luke made a 360 degree turn. "No. She's not here."

Sam glanced over the diminished crowd. "Steve's not here either, and I didn't see him get into a car." He took his phone from his pocket and turned it back on, then dialed Fiona's cell. There was no answer. "This is not good."

"There's a lot out back," Sam recalled. "And I think a park. She was seated on that side of the church. Maybe she went out that door and decided to look out back."

They hurried down the walk that separated the church from the rectory, and walked through the cars on the lot.

"This is weird," Sam told Luke as they went toward the playground. "I don't like this."

He speed-dialed her number again. They were almost to the end of the lot when he heard what sounded like her ring tone. Sam stopped and looked around. The sound was coming from behind a Volkswagen Rabbit that was parked next to the fence. He stepped around the car and saw the phone on the ground. He knelt down, picked it up and scanned through the numbers.

"This is her phone. Here, the last call is from me." He looked up at Luke. "I called her right before I went into the church."

Luke glanced around anxiously.

"If he hurts her, I will tear him apart," Sam said.

"No problem, man," Luke told him. "I'll hold him down. But first we have to find him."

Sam fought back the anger and tried to keep his focus on where Steve would have taken Fiona, and how to get her back without getting her killed.

"He's going to make me come to him," Sam said.

"We don't know for certain that he's taken her, though it appears likely. We don't know for sure that he isn't at the cemetery and that Fiona is with one of the other guys."

"She wouldn't have tossed her phone away. Give me your car keys." Sam held out his hand. "Catch up with the others and see if she's with them. Let me know if she is. If not, get to the cemetery and see if you can locate Molino. If he isn't there, get his cell phone number from his wife and have it tracked ASAP."

"What are you going to do?" Luke hesitated, as if reluctant to hand over the keys.

"I think I know where he's taken her."

"What if you're wrong?"

Ignoring the question, Sam took the keys and broke into a run. He couldn't explain to Luke how he knew. It would simply take too long. "Where's your car?"

"It's out front. But Sam, I don't think—"

"Call me from the cemetery, let me know if he's there. I could be wrong . . . but I don't think I am."

Sam trotted off to find the car, and Luke followed.

"Sam, at least tell me where you're going."

They got to the car and Sam unlocked it. "I'll draw you a map from the cemetery. What do you have to write with in here?"

He leaned into the car and came out holding a bag from a fast food restaurant, then searched his pockets for a pen.

Luke handed him one, and Sam quickly sketched a map. "It's easy enough to find."

He handed over the bag and got into the car.

"You think he took her to this lake?"

Sam nodded. "If he isn't at the cemetery, this is where he's most likely to be. This way, we have both places covered. But if he isn't at either, Fiona's a dead woman."

He sped from the lot and took the back roads where he could make up the most time. His heart pounding wildly, he knew that today would be the day when one of them—either he or Steve—would deliver retribution for the sins committed by the other.

A mile from the lake, his cell phone rang.

"We're at the cemetery but Molino isn't here," Luke told him. "The office is already working on tracking his cell, but you know that's going to take a while."

"Follow the map I gave you, but come up to the lake very quietly through the woods. I will try to take him myself, but I'll feel a whole lot better knowing that backup is coming."

"We're on our way now, Sam."

Sam turned onto the dirt road.

"Luke, listen, if when you get here . . . if we're both down . . ." Up ahead, a gray sedan was parked under a tree, but neither Steve nor Fiona was in sight. "If he gets us both . . ."

"If either of you are down, I can promise you that this son of a bitch won't make it out of the woods in one piece."

Through a clearing, the lake lay straight ahead, the afternoon sun sparkling bright on the water.

"It's lovely, isn't it?" Steve noted. "At least, in summer, with the sun shining down, when the water's warm, it's nice. In the winter, when it's frozen over, it's a different story."

Fiona walked in front of him, trying to go as slowly as possible without getting another jab to her kidneys. The last one had hurt. Of course, a sore back was the least of her problems at the moment.

As soon as she saw the lake, she knew who he was, and why he'd brought her to that place. He'd want a showdown with Sam there. She knew, too, that Sam would figure it out, and he'd come for her. She just had to stall for enough time for him to get there.

"You know I was kidding about the coffin, right? I wouldn't bury you alive. At least, I hadn't planned on it. After all, the last act is bury the *dead*, not the living."

"I guess that makes me one lucky girl."

He laughed. "Do you swim, Fiona?"

"Yes."

"I'll bet you're a strong swimmer."

"I get the job done."

"I'll just bet you do."

They reached the edge of the lake and he looked around.

"Perfect. There are no boaters, no one fishing or swimming today. You know why, Fiona?" Without waiting for her response, he said, "Because everyone in the county is mourning Drew Novak. Everyone's at the cemetery to give him a big send-off. Because, you know, Drew was one hell of a guy, everyone loved him, and all that."

"Was Drew here that night?" she asked. "The night your sister drowned?"

"Ah, you know about that, do you? What did Sam tell you?" His face hardened, and for a moment she thought she'd made a mistake in bringing it up. "Did he tell you how he bravely saved his own sister, and let mine die?"

"He told me that your sister was under the ice, that he couldn't get to her. He said that—"

"Bullshit. He pulled out Eileen first, then Cara Novak. But my sister, he let her drown under there. He could have gone in for her, could have saved her."

"Why didn't you?" she asked, and turned to watch his reaction.

"What?" He stopped on the trail and jerked her by one arm. "What did you say?"

"Why didn't you save her? Why didn't *you* try to get her out? Why didn't *you* dive in to try to pull her to safety?"

"Sam was there, he was first in line. He pulled out the other two. He put himself first, it was the job of the first in line—"

"But you could have—" she said, stopping abruptly when Sam stepped out of the woods and walked toward them as calmly as another man might walk to his mailbox to pick up the day's mail. If another man went for his mail with a Glock in his hand.

"No, Fiona, he couldn't have," Sam told her. "Because even back then, Steve was a coward."

Steve spun around, keeping Fiona in front of him, his gun to the side of her neck.

"I see not much has changed over the years, Steve. You're still hiding behind someone else."

"Always the hero, Sam. Here to save the fair damsel." Steve smirked. "I knew you'd come. I thought I'd have to call you but you figured it out all by yourself. I should have known, seeing how you were always the smart one."

"Seeing you staring up at the windows in the church today made me think of your sister's funeral mass, of the way you stared at them that day. You never took your eyes off them."

"I had to look somewhere," Steve said. "I needed to focus on something. Funny that you should remember that."

"But this is where this whole mess really started. The night we took the girls skating." Sam pointed to the lake. "Right out there, remember? You, me, Drew, Vic, Blake—a little pickup hockey game. Who could resist? And the girls were fine, weren't they? They were playing crack the whip with their friends, having fun. Stumbling around on their skates, screaming their heads off, having a great time of it. So they were fine, didn't need us to be hanging over them, right?"

The gun in Steve's hand wobbled slightly, but was still at Fiona's throat.

"All that screaming, yeah, we heard it, but we thought it was just the girls being little girls. Until someone came over and got in my face and told me." It surprised Sam to realize it was almost as hard for him to stand there, in that spot, reliving the story, as it must surely be for Steve. "The girls had fallen through the ice. Eileen, Cara, and Tish. We all sort of froze for a moment, remember, Steve? Like what we were hearing couldn't be real."

Sam kept his eyes locked with Steve's. The other man stared back, as if unable to look away.

"Then we all moved at once, flying across the ice to where the girls had fallen in. The ice was too thin to hold us, remember? Remember hearing it crack?" Sam shook his head slowly. "Or maybe not. Were you with us when the ice cracked, Steve? Now that I think back on it, Drew was the one who suggested we make a chain. I was the tallest, so I was first in the chain. Then it was Drew . . . then Vic . . ." Sam paused. "Where were you, exactly, in the chain, Steve?"

Steve wet his lips nervously.

"I was there. You know I was there," Steve snapped.

"Ummm, yeah." Sam nodded. "About fourth in line, right? Maybe fifth?"

"You guys were taller, like you said. You were stronger, you could have pulled them all out. But you didn't. You saved Eileen, all right. You saved Drew's sister. Why couldn't you have saved mine?"

"Eileen had already gotten herself above the surface of the ice, she was right there when I put my arms out. She was easy to get out. Same with Cara. But Tish was fighting too much, I couldn't get to her." He lowered his voice, hoping that speaking more calmly might serve to calm Steve—and maybe himself—just a little.

"You were right there. You could have jumped in," Steve insisted. "You let her die. You don't understand how it was after that." His voice cracked slightly, and Sam was afraid he'd pushed the man too far. He kept his eyes on the gun and on Fiona. Would she know when to move? "My parents blamed me. Everyone blamed me. Nothing was ever the same after Tish . . ." The words came in a torrent, but he never lowered the gun. "They fought all the time after that. It was as if Tish dying brought out the worst in everyone. My mom and dad divorced, remember? I had to go live in the city with my mom . . . and nothing was ever right in my life after that."

Tears ran down his face, but his expression never changed. "You ruined my life, Sam. You saved your own sister and let mine die. But like the Bible says, an eye for an eye, a tooth for a tooth. A life for a life."

Sam assumed he referred to his recent killing spree, and was about to remind him that he'd taken more than one life in return for Tish's, when Steve added, "A sister for a sister."

Sam cocked his head to one side, not understanding.

"Oh, you didn't get that? You really thought Eileen's death was an accident?" Steve laughed out loud. "Didn't see that one coming, did you, pal?"

Sam stood stock-still, as if he couldn't believe what he'd heard.

"And here's another one you didn't see coming." The tears had stopped and a look of sheer demonic glee spread across Steve's face. "August 15, 2006. You were out of town, as I recall. Your lovely Carly told me so when I rang the doorbell. Of course, she invited me in, since I was an old friend of yours. I was flattered that she remembered me. So many people don't." Steve paused, savoring his moment of triumph. "You'll be proud to know she put up one hell of a fight, Sam."

The blood drained from Sam's face, and his finger twitched on the trigger. But he had no shot. From this angle, Fiona was in the way.

"Now say bye-bye to Fiona." Still smirking, Steve tightened his grip on the gun.

A crack split the air and Steve crumbled, folded at the waist, and went down, the hole in his forehead releasing a torrent of red. He hit the ground face first, the gun still in his hand.

Fiona jumped back as the body fell. "Sam . . . ?"

Sam still held the gun in front of him, still aimed at where Steve had stood.

"Sam?" Fiona went to him, wishing she could put her arms around him.

He met her eyes. "I never suspected, not for a second. My sister . . . my wife . . . ?"

Over his shoulder, she could see Luke and the others running from the woods.

"Fee, are you all right?" Luke called.

"I'd be better if you'd untie my hands."

Luke turned her around and pulled the rope loose, and it fell to the ground.

"You are one fine shot, Luke Parrish."

"Thanks. There was no margin of error. Man, if I'd been off by this much . . ." He held up his hand; less than an eighth of an inch separated his index finger and his thumb. Luke glanced at Sam, who hadn't moved. "Sam?" he asked tentatively.

"Sam, give me the gun." Fiona reached out to him, and he let her take it from his hand. She passed the Glock over to Luke, then put her arms around Sam and just held him.

"What happened?" Luke frowned.

"He did it. Steve killed them both," Sam told him as if still stunned. "My sister. My wife. I never suspected. All this time, I never had a clue . . ."

TWENTY-EIGHT

Look, you can call the FBI," Robert told Officer Gary Duffy, who'd put him in a small conference room. "They'll tell you. They're investigating my son's kidnapping."

"Who's the agent handling the investigation?" the officer asked. "And which office?"

"His name is Luke Parrish. I don't think he's with a particular office. I think he's with some special group."

Robert sighed with relief. Finally, they'd get somewhere. He'd been trying to explain why he and Susanna had been sitting in the car, watching Carole Woolum's house, and why Kevin—Father Kevin Burch—had gone to speak with her, but the police seemed to think the entire story sounded fishy. "I can't believe you don't know about this case. It was all over the news when it happened and for months afterward. Then they found the car with my wife's remains in it a few weeks ago, and—"

"Your wife is deceased?"

"Yes, she died in the car crash. Didn't you hear about it?"

Duffy shrugged.

"Am I under arrest?" Robert asked. He'd tried to be patient, had tried to tell himself that the police were only being cautious. After all, a strange car parked in a quiet neighborhood—he and Suse and Kevin could have been up to no good.

Before he could answer, the door opened and another officer gestured to Duffy to step outside. A few minutes later, he came back in and said, "Your story checked. You're free to go."

"Just like that?"

The officer nodded.

"But what about my son?"

"You're going to have to talk to the chief about that." Duffy walked out of the room and Robert followed.

In the hall, he met Susanna, and Kevin, who'd watched from Carole Woolum's screened porch when the police drove off with the others. He arrived at the station, and discovering that Robert and Susanna had been brought in for questioning, put a call in to Luke Parrish, who'd sounded out of breath when he answered his phone.

"I'm a little tied up right now," Luke had told him, "but give me the name and number of the chief there, and I'll have someone get right back to him."

Ten minutes later, John Mancini called Chief Craig Collier and confirmed that the FBI had an open investigation into the kidnapping of Robert Magellan's son.

"Which still doesn't explain why you were watching Carole Woolum's house." Collier sat on the edge of the desk in his office, facing Robert, Susanna, and Kevin, who sat on folding chairs.

"We believe that Carole Woolum is the person who took Ian Magellan from the car after the accident, and has been passing him off as her own child," Kevin told him.

"What proof do you have?" The chief was obviously skeptical.

"There is a cabin in the woods near the crash site. She was one of several former nuns from a convent in the area who had used it," Kevin began. Robert thought having the priest relate the tale might make it more credible, so he sat back and let his cousin speak for him.

"Have you confirmed that this woman was there at the time of this accident?" the chief asked.

"According to the owner, no one was supposed to have been in the cabin at that time." Kevin knew their theory would sound thin, but he also strongly believed it was sound. "But all indications are that someone had been there with Mr. Magellan's baby. A button—a hand-painted button from a sweater that had been made for Ian—was found in the cabin."

"Which proves only that the child was there, not that Ms. Woolum was with him, or that she had anything to do with taking him there."

"Mother Superior at the convent gave us the names and addresses of the former sisters who had used the cabin. Ms. Woolum was one of them."

"Still proves nothing."

"There were five former nuns on the list. We've been able to rule out two of them already today."

"Again, Father . . ." Collier was losing patience, and interest. "None of this means anything."

"The child is the right age. The right coloring." Kevin paused. "And he has a mark on his right cheek, right below his eye, shaped like a tiny hourglass."

Robert spun around in his chair to stare at Kevin.

"You're sure? Kevin, you're absolutely positive?" Robert grabbed his cousin by the arm.

"There's no mistake, Rob. The mark is there. I saw it very clearly."

"That's it, then." Robert stood, his hands on his hips, and addressed the chief. "So do I call the FBI in, or can you handle this yourself from here?"

"First of all, we have nothing but your say-so that this boy has a mark like the one your boy had—we don't even have any proof that *your* boy had a mark. You're going to need to prove that. Then we're going to have to make a positive ID. We'll want to see the birth certificate," Collier explained.

Robert speed-dialed home. "Trula, I need you to fax"—he paused—"no, email's clearer, isn't it?" he asked the chief.

"Sometimes." The chief nodded.

"Trula, I'm going to need you to fax *and* email a copy of Ian's birth certificate. And pictures that clearly show the birthmark on his cheek." He thought for a moment, then told Trula to hold on. To the chief, he said, "Will fingerprints do it?"

"They'd sure help if they matched. Ms. Woolum would have a lot of explaining to do."

Robert went back to the call. "Okay, Trula, this part might be trickier. I need something with his fingerprints on it. Maybe those plastic keys he used to like to play with . . ." He paused. "What? Seriously? Yes, fax them right now! Then scan them into the computer along with the photos and . . . you don't know how to scan? Ask Mallory to do it, but do it right now. Please."

"You are one determined fellow." Collier handed Robert one of his cards, with both email and fax information.

Robert passed the information on to Trula, then hung up.

"We have his fingerprints," he told the chief. "Trula, God bless her, had Ian printed at one of those health fairs in Conroy when he was two months old. She said she put them in a drawer and pretty much forgot about them. She's sending them over."

"You didn't tell her that we may have found him," Susanna said.

"She's already figured that out. I just want to bring him home, and let her see for herself," Robert told her.

Within minutes, the items Robert had requested arrived. The chief looked over the birth certificate— "You know we'll need to see the original if we go further with this," he'd said—and the photos. He glanced at the fingerprints.

"These aren't going to prove diddly without something to compare them with," he told Robert.

"That's where you come in, chief," Robert replied.

Collier nodded and went into the hall and called for Officer Duffy. "I want you to come with me to Carole Woolum's house. There are some questions I need her to answer."

He turned to Robert and said, "I'll be getting back to you."

"I'd rather come with you."

"Not gonna happen, son."

"Then we'll wait here, if that's okay with you."

"Suit yourself. You can wait in the lobby." Collier tapped Duffy on the shoulder and said, "Let's do this." When he got to the doorway, he turned and said, "There's a coffee shop across the street. You might as well go on over and grab yourself something to eat. This might take a while . . ."

It took two hours for Collier to return to the station. From the coffee shop window, Kevin spotted the cruiser. Chief Collier drove, Duffy sat shotgun, and someone sat in the back seat.

Robert shot out the door, followed by Kevin. Susanna stayed long enough to pay the check before dashing across the street. Collier saw the threesome come through the front door and held up his hand.

"Uh-uh. We're going to go by the book here, folks. Ms. Woolum insists that that boy is her son, Matthew."

"Why'd you bring her in?" Susanna asked.

"She couldn't produce a birth certificate. First she said she'd lost it. Then she said it was in a safe-deposit box at the bank. When I offered to accompany her to get it, she said the bank was in San Diego." Collier shook his head. "It's not sitting right with me."

"We have his prints," Robert reminded him. "Check his prints."

"She won't permit him to be printed."

"Where is he?" Robert asked.

"In the back room, and no, you can't go in. I told her she was welcome to have her lawyer join us, but she said she doesn't have one and doesn't need one." The chief looked like he was about to say something, then decided against it. "Give me a few minutes to talk to her."

When Robert started to protest, Collier turned to him and said, "If you take one more step, I will have you locked up for interfering with an investigation."

Robert backed off.

The chief went to the vending machine and dropped in some change. He made a selection, then grabbed two paper cups from the shelf under the water cooler before making his way to the back of the station. They heard a door open and close.

Robert was in acute pain, and it showed on his face.

"I know how hard this is for you." Susanna stroked his back, her voice soothing. "But it's going to be worth it. We're going to get him back. Just be patient a little longer."

"He's going to need the fingerprints." Robert did not even attempt to hide his anguish. "She isn't going to give them to him."

"Then we'll have Luke Parrish get a subpoena, or a warrant, or whatever it is we need to force her to let him be printed," Kevin said. "A court order, maybe."

"All right, yes." Robert nodded and patted his pockets for his phone. "I'll ask him to get started on that right away."

"He sounded really busy earlier," Kevin reminded them.

"He can get unbusy. What's the number?"

Robert began to dial the number Kevin recited, but the call went straight to voice mail. Robert left a message and hung up.

"I'll call him every hour on the hour if I have to," Robert grumbled.

"Rob, maybe you should call Noah Goodman," Susanna suggested.

"That's not a bad idea. I'm going to need him before this is over anyway." Robert began to dial his lawyer's number. "Do any of us really expect her to admit outright that she took the baby from the car?"

When the attorney picked up, Robert explained the situation. When the conversation ended, he told the others, "Noah thinks we need to file a court order today, to force Carole Woolum to permit us to obtain Ian's fingerprints. He's contacting a friend of his who has a practice up here. He'll know the judges, and he'll know exactly what to file and with whom."

The door to the back room opened and all three of them lunged forward, but it was Collier calling for Officer Duffy to do something. Susanna and Kevin sat down again, but Robert began to pace. He wasn't accustomed to feeling powerless. He didn't understand why he couldn't see his son. And he thought the chief was being overly cautious and taking too long.

Another twenty minutes passed, and Duffy went down the hall and waved the chief out. They conferred for several minutes—"Are you sure? You're positive?" they heard Collier ask, and Duffy nodded emphatically.

"What the hell are they doing down there?" Robert looked like he was close to snapping. "What is taking so damned long?"

Duffy went into the room with Carole Woolum, and the chief went into his office. Several minutes later, he came back out, went across the hall again.

A scream reverberated through the station, bringing everyone to their feet. The door to the room at the back of the hall opened, and Collier walked out, holding the child.

"No, you don't understand!" Carole Woolum fled into the hall, struggling with Duffy and the other officer, who were trying to restrain her. "God gave him to me. He's my gift from God! You can't take him!"

"Mommy!" Ian cried, and the knife twisted in Robert's heart.

"Mr. Magellan, the FBI is on the way," Collier told him. "There's going to be some paperwork, there will be some details to resolve. But there's no question in my mind that this is your son, and I can't see any reason to keep him from you." He handed the frightened child to Robert, who eagerly reached out for him with tears in his eyes. But Ian—Matthew—began to cry.

"Let me try," Susanna said. "Maybe he isn't used to men . . ."

She took the boy from Collier.

"There now. It's all right, little guy." She brushed the dark curls from his face. "You're a little scared right now, aren't you? It's going to be all right soon. I promise."

He rested his head on her shoulder, and she began to sway slightly from side to side. *Just like Beth used to do,* Robert thought. Just like every other mother he'd ever seen.

"What convinced you?" Kevin asked Collier.

"I got his prints off the paper cup, had Duffy compare them electronically. There's no question in my mind who that boy is." He shook his head. "Folks, that is one mixed-up lady back there."

"Chief Collier, perhaps I could have a word with her," Kevin said.

"It may not help, but it probably won't hurt, either. Go on back," the chief told him.

Kevin walked down the hall to the door where Carole Woolum waited to be booked for kidnapping and other charges. He opened the door and went inside.

"What happens now?" Robert asked. "And when can I take my son home?"

"It would sure help if the padre can get Carole Woolum to admit that she found the boy."

"And if she doesn't?"

"Then we'll have another whole mess to deal with. In the meantime, I'm going to have to call in Children's Services. Might as well do that now." Collier headed back to his office.

Robert was aching to hold Ian, but every time he came too close, the child began to cry and clung to Susanna, burying his face in her neck. At least he seemed comfortable with her. It would be a long trip home if Ian continued to cry.

It would be longer still if they had to go home without him.

"Ms. Woolum—Carole," Kevin took her gently by the shoulders and looked into her eyes. "Will you sit and talk with me for a few moments?"

The woman's sobs were huge, wracking cries. "They took my baby away. They took my son . . ."

Officer Duffy met Kevin's eyes, then stepped off to the side.

"Do you remember me, Carole?" He kept his voice soft, and forced a calm he didn't feel. "We met earlier today. I'm Father Burch."

"Yes . . . yes. I remember."

"I told you I'd spoken with Mother Joseph at the convent." He held the woman's hands, and she grasped onto them.

"I remember."

"You were going to tell me about the last time you were at the cabin."

"It's been a while. I . . . I don't remember, exactly."

"Was it summer, winter . . . ?"

"Winter," she said readily. "It was cold. I had to build a little fire there in the fireplace. There was a lot of wood outside, stacked up."

"Why had you gone to the cabin by yourself in the cold of winter?"

"I needed to think." She pulled her hands from his and covered her face with them. "I needed to be alone to think."

"How long ago had you left the convent?"

"Three years. It's been three years. I was Sister Jerome then. Jerome, after my father."

Kevin took a handkerchief from his pocket and pressed it into her hands. She nodded her thanks and began to dry her face.

"I wasn't sure, you see. The first time I went to the cabin, it was to think things through. Did I want to stay in the order, or should I leave? Had I lost my vocation? Was there something else God wanted me to do?" She shook her head. "I didn't know. But I thought if I was questioning it that much, then maybe I didn't have a true calling. So I did leave. I went home. My father was gone, my mother was dying . . . she did die while I was home that time. I stayed in the house for a couple of months afterward, but I started thinking that maybe I should call Reverend Mother, maybe I should go back. I really didn't know where I belonged, do you understand?"

"Yes, I do." Kevin had had his period of doubts, too. He couldn't think of anyone who'd taken Holy Orders who never questioned their decision.

"I remembered that when I was at the cabin the first time, it had been easier to think, it had been so quiet, so peaceful. I believed I would find my answer there. So I went back."

"How did you get inside?" he asked.

"The owner had given me the key when I stayed there the first time. I was so afraid I'd lose it and I wouldn't be able to lock the door, so I had another one made. I just kept it." The crying had stopped completely and she appeared to be thinking things through rationally. "Do you think that was a sin? That I had a key made for a place that wasn't mine? That I trespassed?"

"I think the owner will forgive you."

"I hope so." She appeared to be fixated on this point, so Kevin tried to move the conversation forward.

"Tell me about the day you heard the crash."

"It had been so quiet all morning. There was snow on the ground and it was cold. Then all of a sudden, there was a sort of thunderclap. I went outside to see what it was, but nothing was there. Later that day, though, when I went for a walk, I saw the car in the ravine, and I heard the baby crying. I opened the door, and there he was, my precious boy. My Matthew. My gift from God." She looked up at Kevin, and he could see in her eyes that she was losing her grip on reality. "That's what Matthew means, you know. Gift from God. I had prayed and prayed and prayed for a sign. What should I do? What was my calling? Then God sent me this child, and I knew that he was supposed to be mine. That God wanted me to have him. That was my calling, I could see it then. I was meant to be his mother. I took him back to the cabin and fed him—there was baby food and bottles and diapers and clothes in the diaper bag that I found in the back seat. Everything he needed was there. All I had to do was take him home. See? God had provided everything." She smiled. "That's how I knew he was meant to be my son."

"What about the woman behind the wheel?" Kevin asked.

"What about her?" Carole seemed confused by the question.

"What was she doing when you opened the car door?"

"She wasn't doing anything. She was just lying there."

"Did you check to see if she was breathing?" Kevin asked.

"No," she replied calmly. "She wouldn't have been. God sent her to bring the baby to me, then he let her die because she wasn't needed in this world anymore.

Don't you see? She was an angel, sent to do God's will. When she was done He brought her back to heaven."

Kevin nodded slowly, made eye contact with Officer Duffy, then stood. "Thank you, Carole."

He cleared his throat and walked slowly, as if burdened, down the hall, to the lobby to where Robert and Susanna waited with Ian.

"I think you need to get a lawyer for her," Kevin told Chief Collier.

"What did she tell you?" Collier asked.

Kevin took a tiny recorder from his pocket and handed it over. "It's all on here. We'd like a copy, though."

"Did she admit she took Ian from the car?" Robert asked anxiously.

"Yeah." Kevin sat down next to his cousin. "She believes God put him there for her. That he was meant to be her son."

"Sounds like she got real smart over the past half hour," Collier said. "That sounds like her defense to me. 'Yeah, I took the baby, but God told me to.' Right. Sounds like she just made that up because she knows we can prove he's not her son and she doesn't want to spend the rest of her life in prison."

Kevin shook his head. "I don't think it's an act. I think she really believes it. I think she's believed it since the minute she came across the car in the ravine and heard him crying. She'd been praying that God would guide her, and she believes He guided her right to that car."

"Maybe He did, but I doubt He meant for her to

keep a child that didn't belong to her," Robert snapped.

Kevin turned to Robert. "Remember this: if Carole Woolum hadn't found him and taken him from the car that day, he would have died there. When you are hell-bent to see her behind bars, remember that she did save his life . . ."

think I want to drive back east," Sam told Fiona.
"There are some things I need to think about."

"All right."

"Do you mind?"

"Not at all," she assured him.

So he'd taken Fiona to the airport and watched her
board a plane to DC and felt empty inside the minute
she was gone. But there were things he needed to sort
out that would be much more difficult if she was
there, and things that needed to be done that only he
could do. He rented a car and headed east on I-80
through Council Bluffs and straight across Iowa into
Illinois. At Rock Island, he dropped south and headed
toward Indiana, where he made his way toward Terre
Haute. There was something he had to do there.

He'd called his former boss and asked for a favor,
which John, upon hearing what Sam had to say, immediately agreed to.

Several hours later, Sam DelVecchio sat in the visitor's room and waited for the guards to bring in the
prisoner he'd come to see.

The door opened and an older, thinner Don Holland shuffled in, his shackles restricting his movements. He sat in the chair provided for him, and stared at Sam for a long moment before asking, "What do you want?"

"I want to apologize."

Holland's laughter was as dry as leaves in late November.

"All right," he said. "I'll bite. Why?"

"Because I owe you one. Because you told the truth and I didn't believe you."

Holland's laughter faded, then ceased altogether.

"What brought this about, this change of heart?" Holland asked.

"My wife's killer confessed. He set it up so that I wouldn't suspect . . ." Sam shook his head. "I guess it doesn't matter why he did it. Suffice it to say that I'm sorry for blaming you for something you didn't do."

"I tried to tell you, man. You could have maybe caught him before, instead of letting him run free all this time."

"No," Sam shook his head, "if he hadn't confessed, no one would have ever known."

"Why'd he confess, then, if he'd never be caught?"

"Because he knew it would hurt me to know," Sam told him.

"Like killing your wife didn't hurt?" Holland scoffed. "What was gonna make that worse than it was?"

"He was an old friend," Sam said simply.

Holland studied Sam's face, then asked, "Did you pop him?"

"No. The FBI did."

"I thought you were FBI." Holland frowned.

"I was."

"You *was*? You quit?"

When Sam nodded, Holland laughed. "Why'd you go and do that? You were good at what you did, my man. Brought me down, and I was the best at what I did."

Sam rubbed the back of his neck, not wanting to think about what Holland had laid claim to being the best at.

"You should think about going back." Holland stood, ready to return to his cell. "There are a lot of bad boys outside. A lot of bad, bad boys who need to be caught . . ."

Sam stood and watched Holland shuffle back out of the room. When he reached the door, he turned and said, "Thanks, man. That was decent of you. You didn't have to do that."

"Yeah, actually, I did."

Holland's comment stayed with Sam all the way to the Ohio border, where he had to decide which way to go: through Pennsylvania to Conroy and the Mercy Street Foundation, or through Virginia to Fiona and the FBI.

Once he made his choice, he felt lighter. He called both John and Robert and explained his position. Then he called Chris Coutinho, as he'd promised he'd do once the case had been solved. His last call—and by far, the toughest—was to Lynne Walker, who deserved an explanation of why her husband had to die, and at whose hands. To Sam's everlasting gratitude, she'd not blamed him, but blessed him for bringing peace to her family, and justice to her husband.

The sun had already set when he pulled in the drive at the bungalow. There were no lights on inside and no car in sight, so he turned off the engine and got out and walked to the front steps, where he sat and waited.

It was after ten when she drove up. She slowed when she saw the strange car, but she parked next to it and walked with no apparent concern to the porch. She sat next to him on the step for a while before saying, "Nice night."

"Umm-hmm."

"How are you, Sam?" she asked softly.

"Better than I've been in a long time."

"Good," she said. "That's good."

"I stopped to see Don Holland on my way through Indiana," he told her.

"Oh? How'd that go?"

"It went pretty well, all things considered." He turned to her. "It wasn't as hard as I thought it would be. Apologizing, that is."

"You apologized to him?" Fiona frowned. "Have you lost your mind?"

"He's done a lot of really nasty things, but he didn't kill Carly. He told me that over and over, and I didn't believe him. For that, I owed him."

"You're a better man than I am. I couldn't have done it."

"I wasn't sure I could either, but it worked out all right. One thing he said, though . . ." Sam leaned back, his elbows resting on the steps behind him. "He said I should go back to the Bureau, that there were a lot of bad boys out there who needed to be caught."

"Oh, there's a news flash." Fiona rolled her eyes. "I

picked up a case today—boy howdy, it's a killer. Pun intended."

"There's no end to it, you know?" He exhaled deeply. "I left the Bureau because I had enough of the Don Hollands of this world. I'd seen them all, I'd studied them all. I wanted out so I got out. I used Carly's death as an excuse to walk away."

"Don't you think you're being a little hard on your-self? Sam, your wife was murdered in your home, and at the time you believed she was killed by someone you were tracking. I think you were entitled to take a walk."

When he didn't respond, she said, "Did your travels help to clear your head?"

"Some." He nodded. "It was good to get away, to leave everything behind me. I thought going to all those places, most of them for the first time, would help me to feel again."

"Did it?"

"Mostly I felt responsible. That I'd let Carly down. That's pretty much all I felt," he said. "The best part of the trip was when I got to Italy and spent some time with my parents. They're happy in their lives and with each other, and it was a very good visit. My mom invited a neighbor—a divorcée—to dinner one night to meet me, and I was not very happy with my mother for doing that."

"Why? Was she awful?"

"No, she was lovely, she was a very nice woman. But I felt like I was being unfaithful to Carly. Like I'd be betraying her memory if I let myself be attracted to someone else. After dinner was over, I couldn't wait to drive her home. I dropped her off and came straight back to my parents' place and Mom and I had a few words over the whole thing. I told her I didn't appreciate her trying to set me up, and she told me she didn't appreciate the fact that I was rolling over and playing dead, that I couldn't spend the rest of my life alone, that there was still light and music to be had." Sam smiled. "Her words: light and music." He added, "I was certain she was wrong. I'd just finished traveling through a dozen countries, and there'd been no one I'd felt a connection to. Until now."

He sat up and put an arm around her shoulders. "I hadn't felt the light or heard the music until now."

"So are you saying you're feeling connected, Sam?"

"Yeah. I guess I am."

Fiona smiled. "There now. That wasn't so hard, was it?"

Sam laughed softly.

She leaned against him and rested her forehead against the side of his head, and they sat together on the steps for a while.

Finally, Fiona said, "So what are you going to do, Sam? Are you sticking with the new job, or are you coming back to the Bureau?"

"I like the Mercy Street Foundation. I like the concept. I like and admire Robert Magellan and the fact that he's willing to use his fortune for the greater good. You know, he'd offered a million-dollar reward for information leading to Ian's return. He's splitting it between the Sisters of St. Anthony and Barbara Cooper, the woman who owned the cabin. He's a man of his word, and I respect him for that. The world could use more people like him."

"I hear a but in there somewhere."

"But—I think I belong with the Bureau."

"John will be happy to hear that," she told him. "He'll take you back like that." She snapped her fingers.

"He already has."

"Seriously? You're coming back?"

"After I talk to the others there in Conroy, yeah. I'm coming back."

"Good." She nodded. "That's good."

"So I thought maybe we should do something to celebrate," he told her. "I picked up a bottle of champagne on the way over." He reached behind him on the porch and held up a tall bag.

"That's a good start." She stood and took his hand. She pulled him to his feet and wrapped her arms around him. "Why don't we go inside and break it open, and dance a little to that music your mama was telling you about . . ."

THIRTY

What should I do, Trula? He won't come near me."
Robert's agony was written all over his face.

"It's going to take time, son. The women from Children's Services said we should expect this," she said softly. "He doesn't understand where he is or why he's here, and where . . . where his mother is."

"She isn't his mother. She never was." His eyes darkened.

"He doesn't know that, Rob." He started to protest and she held up a hand. "You may not like it, but that's the truth of it."

Robert sat with his arms resting on the kitchen table. Ian was clearly a very unhappy, lost little boy, and it broke Robert's heart. He'd never imagined his son's homecoming to be like this. Ian cried all the time he hadn't been sleeping on Susanna's lap on their flight back from Erie, and he'd been crying since they set foot in the house. Now, even Susanna wasn't able to comfort him.

"I feel really helpless," Suse told him. "I don't know what he likes to eat." She looked at Trula. "What do two-year-olds eat, anyway?"

"They can eat pretty much what you do, only cut smaller, softer."

"He has to be hungry," Susanna said. "He hasn't had anything to eat all day. I tried to give him soup, I tried pudding, I tried crackers, but he pushed everything away except the milk I gave him, and he was not happy because I didn't let him hold the glass himself."

"We'll have to run out and pick up some supplies," Trula told him. "Sippy cups and toys and so on."

"His old toys are still up in his room," Robert reminded her. "Maybe we should try one of those. I'll run up and get something that he used to like. Maybe he'll remember—"

"He was only three months old when he left," Trula reminded him, "so don't be disappointed if he doesn't seem to recognize anything."

Robert nodded and headed up the back steps to the second floor.

"Shhhh, Ian, shhhh," Susanna tried to comfort him. "It's going to be all right, baby." Ian continued to wail. "I know, I know. It's hard for you right now. But you're back with your daddy who loves you . . ."

The back door opened and Chloe came in, wiggling a long red piece of yarn behind her to lure Foxy inside.

"Why is that baby crying?" She stopped in the doorway.

"His name is Ian, and he's crying because he's in a place that is strange to him," Susanna told her. "He's very unhappy right now and we're not sure what to do to make him happy."

"I know what will make him happy." Chloe

skipped across the kitchen floor. "Foxy will make him smile. She makes me smile."

She went to Susanna and tugged gently on Ian's foot.

"Do you want to play with the kitty, Ian?"

At the sound of her voice, Ian turned his head. She held up the bright red string and dangled it in front of him, and he stopped crying.

"See?" she said. "He wants to play."

Chloe sat on the floor and wiggled the string in front of the kitten. It stood on its hind legs to bat at it, and Ian struggled to get down. He toddled to Chloe and plunked himself down on the floor.

"Here, Ian. Hold the string like this." She held it between two fingers to show him. When he reached for it, she helped him to hold it, then told him, "Hold it up in the air. Yes, like that. See . . . Foxy likes playing with you."

Ian laughed for the first time that day.

Robert came into the room, holding several stuffed animals, a ball, and a pile of books. "I wasn't sure what he might—"

The sound of Ian's laughter stopped him in his tracks.

"What happened?" he whispered to Susanna.

"Chloe." She pointed to the floor where the two children sat playing with Foxy. "Chloe happened."

"Do you think maybe if I sat down there with him . . . ?"

"It wouldn't hurt."

"Chloe," Robert said, "do you think I could play with you and Ian?"

"Sure, but you have to wait your turn for the string.

Right now, Ian has it, then it's my turn again. But then it could be your turn."

"Okay." He sat on the floor next to his son, not close enough to make the child move away, but near enough that he could catch the scent of him. "I don't mind waiting my turn . . ."

"Am I too late for breakfast?" Kevin came into the kitchen from the front of the house.

"You're right on time." Trula pointed to a pile of waffles she'd just plated. "Grab a plate and help yourself."

"Whoa." Kevin stopped in his tracks and pointed out the window to the back patio.

Ian sat in the high chair they'd bought for him long ago, a bright blue sippy cup in one hand, a piece of waffle in the other. Susanna sat on one side, and Robert sat on the other.

"That's quite a different scene from the one I left last night," Kevin said.

"It was touch and go for a while," Trula agreed, "but things have calmed down. There's still a long way to go, but I think it's going to work out okay in the end."

"How'd things go last night? Did he sleep?"

"He slept between Robert and Susanna on Rob's bed. On top of the covers, I should add." She smiled slyly. "Not that I wouldn't like to see that change. Your cousin is blind where Susanna is concerned. Anyone with a pair of eyes could see she's in love with him."

"Even I knew that." Kevin nodded.

"Really? You saw it, too, all this time?"

"All this time." Kevin helped himself to coffee. "Maybe he'll wake up one of these days."

"They make a beautiful family, don't they?" Trula sounded wistful.

"They look like they belong together."

"From your lips to God's ears."

"Exactly." Kevin smiled and sipped his coffee. "Exactly what I was thinking . . ."

The fact that you are holding in your hands a book with my name on the cover is indisputable proof that I am one of the luckiest people *ever*. I have always loved stories, and I love having the opportunity to bring mine to you. I love exploring all those twists and turns a plot or a character's life can take, all those highways and byways that can lead to romance or murder or a new way of looking at my characters' own lives. I love creating places where my characters live and interact with friends and family—I've lived almost all of my life in small towns and know their heartbeat—and I love connecting my books through my characters and my settings.

One of my favorite fictional places is St. Dennis, Maryland, on the Chesapeake Bay, the town that was the setting for another of my romantic suspense novels, *Last Words*. St. Dennis is one of those charming little villages that began in the seventeenth century, with streets of historic homes and beautifully restored inns, fun shops, and great dining. It's a romantic seaside town, the perfect place to fall in love. Who wouldn't want to visit a place like that? It's a town that's so perfect, I've been dying to go back.

I've had a lot of mail from readers who love the characters in the Mercy Street books. The most frequently asked questions? Where is Robert and Susanna's relationship heading? Will he ever see her as anything other than a trusted friend and employee? Or will Susanna spend the rest of her life loving a man who doesn't love her?

So I'm thinking Robert and Susanna should spend a little quality time in St. Dennis, don't you?

So here, on the next few pages—for Walmart readers only—is the epilogue for *Acts of Mercy:* a peek into the future, and a chance to maybe answer a few of those FAQ's.

Enjoy!
Mariah

EPILOGUE

"What's that you've got, Trula?" Robert looked up from his seat at the kitchen table where he, Susanna, and Mallory watched Ian feed himself the lunch that Trula had prepared for him. Since his return to the Magellan home, Ian's every move had been watched by several pairs of eyes: first, because those eyes had been starved for the sight of him, and second, because those eyes were constantly watching for signs that the little boy was becoming more acclimated to his surroundings and was starting to bond with his family.

"A package was delivered this morning," Trula told him, closing the door behind her. "For me."

Trula smiled and placed the box on the kitchen counter. "It's from my friend, Gracie."

She opened a drawer, found the scissors she was looking for, and cut the tape that wound around the box.

"Secure little sucker," she muttered as she pulled the tape from the box. "Must have wrapped it around four times."

"Must be something important," Susanna mused. "I guess Gracie wasn't taking any chances."

Trula opened the box and removed the contents.

"Ah." She lifted a white porcelain coffee mug from the box.

"It's a reminder that I'm overdue for a visit."

"Looks like a coffee mug to me." Mallory looked over her shoulder and grinned. "Because, you know, Trula can always use another."

Trula held up the mug and turned it toward the table so the others could read the side she'd been looking at.

DISCOVER ST. DENNIS! the mug demanded in bold red letters.

"That's Gracie's way of telling me it's time for my annual visit."

"Gracie's a childhood friend, right?" Robert recalled the name.

"Grace Sinclair and I have been friends since we were, oh, I guess five or six," Trula told them. "Her grandparents lived next door to us when I was growing up—she was Grace Abernathy then. She came to visit every summer for several weeks. We used to have one heck of a time, the two of us." Her eyes sparkled with memories. "And your grandmother, too, if she wasn't away at camp the weeks Gracie visited," she told Robert. "The three of us always had such fun."

"Gracie's the one who lives on the Chesapeake Bay, right?" Susanna smiled to herself, wondering what childhood recollections had put that twinkle in Trula's eyes.

"St. Dennis, Maryland. Where the New River meets the Chesapeake Bay. Her late husband's great-great-grandfather settled there back in the early 1800s, built a lovely home facing the water. Sinclair's

Cove, he named it, and it's still called that today. Imagine all the history that old place has seen."

"She still lives there?" Mallory asked.

"She has an apartment in the main house, which her son operates as a B and B, just as she and her husband did in their day." Trula gave the mug a cursory rinse, then filled it with coffee. "Her husband died, oh, it's been at least fifteen years since her Dan passed. Daniel, their son, and his wife took over then. His wife drowned a few years back, and he's been running it alone ever since. Gracie helps out some here and there, but her real love is her newspaper."

"Gracie works for a newspaper?" Mallory asked.

"Owns it. Her grandfather on her dad's side started it up in 1893. She started writing features while she was still in college. Took it over when her dad retired. It was a daily back then. These days, she has her hands full getting it out as a weekly." Trula leaned on the counter and appeared to be deep in thought. "I suppose when Gracie goes, the *St. Dennis Gazette* will fold. No one wants to run a weekly paper anymore, she tells me. Says she has a tough enough time getting ads these days. Mostly she relies on the older businesses around St. Dennis, those that have been advertising with the paper forever." She took a sip of coffee. "Don't know how long that's going to last, though. The town's changed so much over the past few years. Not that that's a bad thing," she hastened to add. "There are lots of lovely shops now right along the main street. New restaurants, art galleries, antique shops, you name it."

"Sounds charming." Susanna leaned over to pick up a slice of apple that Ian had tossed onto the floor.

"Oh, St. Dennis is crazy with charm these days. It's been 'discovered.' It's the new 'in' place to go on the Eastern shore," Trula explained.

"I guess it's overrun with tourists," Mallory remarked.

"There are lots of tourists, but it isn't tacky with them, if you know what I mean. The town's survived a lot over the years—I guess it can survive some shoppers and sightseers. It survived the War of 1812, didn't lose a building even though the British shelled it from the bay. A few of the houses still have cannonballs embedded in the walls, but none of them fell." Trula sipped her coffee. "The son of the Sinclair who built the inn married a British beauty and brought her home. She wasn't real popular with the town's people for the first few years they lived there, it being so close to the end of the war and all that, but she won them over eventually. Gracie could tell you the story. It was very romantic." Trula sipped her coffee. "Yes, that inn is really something. Looks like an old Southern plantation. It's a real popular place, too. Gracie says it's always full. There's so much to do there—it's a real family place. They have boating and swimming, of course. Sailing, for those who enjoy it. Kayaks and canoes for those who like the calmer waters. A children's pool and play area. Beautiful views from most of the guest rooms. A terrific chef. Oh, and there's a wildlife preserve right there on the property."

"Hell, what are we waiting for?" Susanna laughed. "When do we leave?"

"I'm going to go on Tuesday, I think." Trula poked Robert in the ribs. "I think you should come too."

She pointed at Susanna. "And you and Ian. I think it would do you both good to get away for a few days. Take the little guy someplace where he can have fun with you, Rob. Do something together. Remember what the child psychologist told you? Ian needs to experience a whole range of new things with you, he needs to make new memories. I think a few days at Sinclair's Cove would be a lovely start. I imagine there might even be a few kids his own age to play with."

Robert tapped on the tabletop, obviously considering the idea. He looked at Susanna. "Would you go? For Ian? Just for a few days? That is, if you didn't have any other plans. . . ."

"I have no plans," she replied. "Of course, if you think Ian needs me, I'll go."

"Then that's that." Trula drained her mug and stood. "Mallory, you and Emme will be here this week, interviewing to replace Sam, now that he's decided to go back to the FBI. You can hold down the fort for a few days, can't you?"

"Sure." Mallory nodded.

"I'll give Gracie a call, see if she can put a few rooms aside. Since we'll be going in the middle of the week, we'll have a better chance of a vacancy. I can stay with Gracie, but we'll need to reserve a room for you."

"Two rooms," Robert reminded her. "We'll need two rooms."

"Oh. Right. You and Susanna." Trula smiled to herself as she went up the back steps. "Two rooms. Sure. No problem. . . ."

* * *

"Wow, this place is gorgeous. It's everything you said it is, Trula." Susanna stood with her hands on her hips, taking in the glorious façade of the Inn at Sinclair's Cove. Tall white columns rose three stories from the wide front porch that was lined with rocking chairs. A wing grew off each side of the house, and beyond, a wide swath of green led down to the sparkling water of the Chesapeake.

"It really is a pretty place, Trula," Robert agreed. "Thanks for letting us tag along with you."

He unstrapped Ian from his car seat, and set the boy on the drive, which was constructed of crushed shells. Immediately Ian bent over at the waist to pick at a shell that had somehow escaped being crushed.

He studied it carefully, then looked up at Robert. "What is it?"

"That's a shell," his father told him.

"Shell," Ian repeated, holding the bone white shell between pudgy fingers for a moment, before handing it to Robert. "Shell."

"That's right, Ian. Shell." Robert smiled. That Ian had automatically turned to Robert was, in Robert's mind, a victory of sorts, a breakthrough, albeit a very tiny one. But still, Ian had turned to him, not to Susanna or to Trula.

"Let's get ourselves settled, then we can go down to the beach and see if there are other shells to be found. Of course, there's not much beach here, but . . . " Trula's voice faded as she marched toward the porch.

Robert held his hand out to Ian, who took it without hesitation. Robert sighed inwardly with relief. The relationship with his son was still so tenuous. The therapist had reminded him that Ian would come around in time, and Robert understood that. He just wished it wouldn't take so much time. He ached to feel like a dad, like the dad he knew he would have been if his son hadn't been taken from him. A dad who'd play with him and read to him and hold him . . . all the things Ian had refused since they'd brought him back.

He turned to Susanna. "I suppose we should follow Trula, see where our rooms are."

"Good idea." Susanna fell in step with Ian and Robert. "Once we get checked in, we should decide what to do first. Maybe we could go into town and get ice cream. We passed a place right on the main road."

She reached down to take the boy's hand, and he bolted in the direction of the play yard where several other children were joyously using the small slide on their own.

"Oops!" Susanna laughed, watching him run. "I guess he knows what he wants to do."

She and Robert followed Ian to the play park and leaned on the fence with several other parents who obviously felt comfortable enough to allow their toddlers to play on the equipment on their own. Robert tried his best not to appear anxious, but he wasn't sure of Ian's skill levels and didn't know if he should be permitting him to climb that slide or that very low jungle gym. For a moment, Ian stood silently, staring at the other children, just watching, as if taking it all in at once before climbing onto the ladder on the back of the slide.

"First time letting him go on his own, eh?" The man on Robert's left gently nudged him in the ribs.

"It shows?" Robert laughed in spite of himself.

"We were the same way, the first time we brought Drake to one of these little play parks. My wife was scared to death," the man told him. "But he was fine, and he loved being just a little bit independent. It's only three very small steps up to the top of that slide, but the first time he did it on his own, you'd think he'd climbed Everest."

"I guess when you're that small, it would seem like a huge accomplishment." Robert's eyes never left his son. Ian stood on the top step for a moment, uncertain what to do next.

"Step up to the top, Ian, then sit." Susanna called instructions to him, but Ian still appeared unsure. Susanna went to the slide and held her hand out to him. "Hold on to my hand. Now step up . . . that's right. Now hold on to the sides—yes, just like that. Now you want to sit and . . . yes, good, Ian. Go ahead and push . . . yay, there you go!" She applauded and Ian beamed.

The man standing next to Robert leaned over and said, "Looks like your wife has the system down pat."

"Oh, she's not—," Robert began to protest.

"Good job there," the man called to Susanna, giving her a thumbs-up. "We had to give our boy a little assistance on the see-saw yesterday—he was playing with a kid who was much heavier and it didn't work out too well. But he got the hang of it later when we found another child closer to his size. Maybe they'll want to try that together." He pointed to a boy in a red and white striped shirt. "Drake and your boy look to be about the same weight. They'd probably do really well on the see-saw together."

Robert nodded, but wondered how one introduced one toddler to another, how to encourage them to play together. There was so much about being a father, so much about children in general, and Ian in particular, he had to learn.

"Here comes my wife," the man said as a pretty blond in tennis whites approached. "Elisa, see if Drake and . . . what's your boy's name?"

"Ian."

"See if Drake wants to see-saw with Ian, the little guy on the steps there. That's his mom in the white top." He turned to Robert. "I'm Dave, by the way."

"Robert." Robert extended his hand, wondering if he should correct Dave's erroneous assumption about their relationship with Susanna. And if he did, how would he describe what she was to them? He hadn't even been able to define that for himself.

"This your first time here, Robert?" Dave asked.

"Yes."

"It's a great place. You'll love it. Do you sail? They have sunfish you can take out. The river at this point is pretty deep, but the bay is nice." Dave crossed his arms over his chest as he watched his son. "We've been coming here for about six years now. No place I'd rather be in the summer. The kids love it 'cause there's so much to do. We have twins who are seven; they're in an art class back there in one of the cabins." He pointed to Ian. "Your only child?"

"Yes."

"Great place for kids of all ages. Say, do you play tennis?"

"Yes, but—"

"They have a great court here, if you feel like a game later."

"Thanks, but I think—"

"How long are you staying?" Dave asked. "There's going to be a clam bake tomorrow night. The kids love that."

"We'll still be here. I think."

"Hey, I understand." Dave punched Robert's arm playfully. "My wife makes all the arrangements too. I show up when she tells me to, drive where she tells me to go."

Before Robert could correct him, Dave pointed to the see-saw. "See? I was right. The boys are just the right size to ride that thing together."

Robert leaned on the fence and watched his son's face at play. It was the first time he'd observed him playing with a child his own age.

It's all going to be new, every day now, forever, he told himself.

The two boys laughed every time one of them hit the ground, silly laughter Robert had not heard before, and he fought a tinge of something that felt ridiculously like jealousy. He didn't know how to make Ian belly laugh like that.

One more thing he had to learn.

"Daddy!" Drake threw his hands up in the air as his father approached, and jumped off the seat, leaving Ian to bounce onto the ground. Howling with indignation at having been, literally, dumped, Ian ran to Susanna and clung to her legs. She picked him up and soothed his hurt feelings and patted his backside where he'd hit the ground.

"Oh, man, I'm sorry," Dave quickly apologized. "Is he all right?"

"He seems to be."

"They always want Mommy first, don't they?" Dave observed. "The mom always knows what to do."

Robert nodded, his eyes still on Ian, whose wounded spirit—and bottom—had progressed from wailing to mere sniffles after having been comforted by Susanna.

The way she's always comforted me, a little voice inside him whispered. *Susanna knows what to say, how best to soothe, how to bring back the smiles. Hadn't she always?*

"How did you get him to calm down so quickly?" Robert asked.

"I promised him ice cream," Susanna told him. "What do you think?"

"Sure." Robert watched her walk toward him, her gait easy and carefree, her gauzy white skirt billowing around her calves in the breeze, her dark hair twisted up atop her head casually. Her eyes were hidden by her dark glasses, giving her a slightly exotic look.

Had he ever seen her outside of work and looking this relaxed? This happy? This . . . beautiful?

Robert frowned. The answer was a big fat no. He'd never seen her quite like this.

"Here, I'll carry him." Robert held out his arms, but Ian shook his head and struggled to get down.

"Walking," he said, tugging on each of their hands. "Walking for ice cream."

"I guess we're walking." Susanna laughed. "But I think it might be a bit of a distance. You may have to carry him after a while." Before Robert could reply, she laughed and said, "And if it's as far as I think it is, you might have to carry me, as well."

"I think I might be up to the challenge." He smiled at her, and she smiled back, one of those big, happy smiles that made her face glow. From somewhere inside himself, he began to feel the glow too. Deep inside, that little voice told him if he had a brain in his head, he'd nurture that glow, and it occurred to him then that he'd be willing to carry her anywhere.

"Where the devil have you been?" Trula demanded from the top porch step. "I've had people looking all over for you."

"We walked into town for ice cream," Robert explained. "I'm sorry, Trula. I should have let you know."

"Come inside and meet Gracie. We've been waiting damn near half the afternoon for you." Trula's eyes narrowed as she took in the three coming up the stairs together. Susanna, as always, looking cool and fresh, Robert and Ian with ice cream dribbles in exactly the same place on their shirts.

They followed her inside and were introduced to Grace Sinclair, a birdlike woman with white hair tucked into a tidy bun at the base of her neck. She wore a cotton wrap-around skirt, a polo shirt, and a pink tennis cap, and she appeared to be, like Trula, in her mid-seventies. They made small talk until a sleepy Ian began to fuss.

"I'd better take him to my room," Susanna told Trula. "He really needs to take a nap if he's to have any fun at all tonight."

"Good idea," Robert agreed. "You get the key, I'll get your bags and his things."

"Oh. A small glitch." Grace laid a hand on Susanna's arm. "I hope you don't mind, dear, but we had to give you one of the cabins out back. Our new desk clerk made an error, and I'm afraid there is, literally, no room at the inn. Trula said it wouldn't be a problem for you to share, since you both stay with the baby at night anyway. I hope that's all right." She held up a key, glancing anxiously from one to the other. "And there is a separate sitting room with a sofa. . . ."

"We'll be fine." Robert turned to Susanna and hastily added, "Of course, if you'd rather not, we can drive back to—"

"No need to do that," Susanna shook her head. "Trula's right. We do end up staying with him every night anyway. And I can sleep on the sofa, if you think—"

"No, no. If anyone gets the sofa, it will be me," he assured her. He took the key from Grace. "We're grateful you were able to accommodate us at all." To Susanna, he said, "I'll walk you down to the cottage, then I'll get everything from the car."

"I can have someone do that for you, dear," Grace told him.

"It's okay," Robert said. "I don't mind."

"If you're sure, then, we'll see you at dinner. We have seats for you both and a high chair for Ian at our table. Six thirty in the main dining room." Grace added, "Dress is casual."

"Great. Thanks." Robert nodded, one hand holding Ian's, the other at the small of Susanna's back as if to guide her down the steps.

The two women stood on the porch and watched

the man, the woman, and the child disappear around the side of the house.

Gracie sighed. "What a perfectly lovely family."

"Then you do think I'm right?"

"Oh, definitely, Trula. Any fool could see the two of them belong together."

"Yes, well, it's the fool part that has me worried. If ever a man has been a fool, it's Robert Magellan." Trula frowned. "Do you really think we're doing the right thing?"

"Our track record when it comes to matchmaking has been damned impressive," Grace reminded her. "Unparalleled, I might even say."

"True." Trula nodded. "I'd say we've done pretty well over the years."

"Starting with Rob's own grandparents." Grace smiled at the memory. Introducing Grace's brother's best friend to Trula's friend Margarite one summer evening had been nothing less than genius. It had been love at first sight.

"Right on down to your nephew, Carl, and his lovely Rosalie." Trula returned the smile.

"Another match for the ages. We had the loveliest wedding here, right down there on the south lawn," Grace recalled happily. "I just love to see true love win out."

"Well, don't start draping the arbors with tulle and roses just yet." Trula frowned. "I love Rob like a son, but sometimes, that boy is dense as mud. Can't see what's right under his nose."

"That's why he needs us, dear," Grace reminded her.

"And why I called last week. I couldn't sit by and watch him bumble away this chance to be happy with a woman who loves him." Trula watched the three-some as they walked down the path toward the back of the house. "She's always loved him, you know."

"So you said."

They watched as Ian broke away from his father and ran laughing across the grass, Robert in hot pursuit. When Robert caught the toddler and tossed him in the air, Ian screamed with delight. Trula felt a catch in her throat when Robert set his son atop his shoulders and continued across the lawn with Susanna on their way to the cottage.

"They do indeed make a handsome family," Trula murmured.

"Indeed they do." Gracie sighed.

"That was a fun night, don't you think?" Robert busied himself with gathering Ian's toys from the floor of the living area of the cottage.

"It was, yes." Susanna smiled. "Trula did not exaggerate about the chef. The meal was perfect. Everything was . . . well, perfect."

"And Ian seemed to have fun with the other kids."

"He did. The therapist was right, you know. He needs to spend more time with other children."

"Well, in the past, his exposure was minimal, remember. We know now that Carole Woolum kept him to herself most of the time. She admitted to Chief Collier that she was afraid someone was still looking for him and would recognize him."

"They were right about that. We were still looking for him."

"If it hadn't been for you—"

"You've said your thanks, Rob, a hundred times. I

know you're grateful." Susanna's smile was tight. Of course Robert was thankful that she'd devoted so much time to looking for his son. But she was beyond *thankful* and *grateful* now. Neither was enough; neither was what she wanted from him.

"You know," he began tentatively, "all those weekends you left on Friday and didn't come back until Sunday night—"

"How did you know when I left, and when I returned?"

"Sometimes I'd call your house, or stop there, but you were never around."

"You called for work stuff?"

"Mostly," he admitted, "but sometimes I was just lonely and wanted your company."

"Why didn't you say something? Why didn't you tell me?"

"I thought you had a guy somewhere, someone you obviously didn't want me to know about." He seemed to trip over his words, and his awkwardness made her want to smile.

"You thought I was having an affair with someone?" She raised an eyebrow.

"Well . . . yeah, I guess I did. I didn't want to ask you. I figured if you wanted me to know about it, you'd tell me. If you wanted me to meet him, you'd have brought him around."

"The only guy I was looking for was Ian." *Because the only guy I really wanted was you.*

"I know that now." He hesitated for a moment, as if inwardly debating with himself, before saying, "I'm so glad there wasn't someone else. I know I probably shouldn't feel that way—I mean, if you'd been in love with someone who loved you, you'd have been happy, right?"

"Yes. That would have made me happy, Rob," she said quietly.

"So for me to say now that I'm glad you didn't have someone then makes me sound very selfish, doesn't it? I mean, if that's what you wanted. . . ."

"It depends."

"On what?" He frowned.

"On whether or not I'll have what I want now." She crossed her arms over her chest and watched his face. There was a softness there, an expression she hadn't seen before. In that moment, she could almost believe that maybe he'd begun to see her in the same light in which she'd always seen him.

"You're not going to make this easy for me, are you?" he asked.

She shook her head, her smile spreading slowly. "Not a chance."

Robert stared at the floor, then put down the teddy bear he'd been holding. He took the half dozen steps to where she stood and put his hands on her shoulders, his eyes meeting hers.

"You're right. I don't deserve a break. Anyone who's been as . . ." He grimaced. "I hate to call myself stupid, because, you know . . ."

She took his face in her hands and kissed him fully on the mouth, a big, smacking kiss. She'd wanted her first kiss from him to be tender and hot all at the same time, but she'd gotten cold feet, thinking maybe she was misreading the signals he was sending her, and a big, smacking kiss could be explained away as a joke, if she was wrong about the look in his eyes.

Had she been?

She started to pull away, a hot wave of something close to humiliation spreading through her.

"Not so fast," he said, his breath warm and soft on her cheek.

He kissed her then, a way-more-than-adequate first kiss by anyone's standards, she later recalled thinking. Actually, it was a wowzer of a kiss, a kiss designed to make her head spin and her heart beat faster and her pulse race through her veins, the kiss she'd dreamed about for years.

For once, reality surpassed the fantasy.

A soft cry from the other room brought them both back, his lips slowly disengaging with what felt to Suse like the greatest reluctance.

"We should see . . ." Robert nodded toward the bedroom. "Maybe he's frightened, waking up in a strange place. He's probably looking for you. You're always there when he wakes up."

"So are you," she reminded him.

"Maybe between the two of us, we can get him back to sleep quickly." Robert draped an arm around her shoulders, and together they went to his son. "You and I have a lot to catch up on. . . ."